GOING HOME

SHARON MARCHISELLO

Mechanicsburg, Pennsylvania USA

Published by Sunbury Press, Inc.
50 West Main Street, Suite A
Mechanicsburg, Pennsylvania 17055

www.sunburypress.com

For information about special discounts for bulk purchases, please contact Sunbury Press Orders Dept. at (855) 338-8359 or orders@sunburypress.com.

To request one of our authors for speaking engagements or book signings, please contact Sunbury Press Publicity Dept. at publicity@sunburypress.com.

ISBN: 978-1-62006-438-2 (Trade Paperback)
ISBN: 978-1-62006-439-9 (Mobipocket)
ISBN: 978-1-62006-440-5 (ePub)

FIRST SUNBURY PRESS EDITION: August 2014

Product of the United States of America
0 1 1 2 3 5 8 13 21 34 55

Set in Bookman Old Style
Designed by Lawrence Knorr
Cover by Amber Rendon
Edited by Angela Wagner

Continue the Enlightenment!

Let the past be content with itself, for man needs forgetfulness as well as memory.

James Stephens

Dedication

To all whose lives have been ravaged by Alzheimer's. May a cure be found soon for this debilitating disease.

Acknowledgments

First, I would like to thank my husband Michael for his love and support. Thanks also to my friends and family who served as beta readers, the Sassy Sisters Book Club, the Atlanta chapter of Sisters in Crime, and the Peachtree City Writers Group for their feedback and insights while the work was in progress. A special thanks to Molly Samuels, Pat Butler, and Rebecca Watts, who took the time to provide me with detailed line editing. And finally, thank you to the team at Sunbury Press for bringing this novel to market.

Chapter One

My mother never left the front door wide open—no way would she "heat the whole neighborhood."

I jumped out of my rental car and hurried up the walkway. This was my first visit in over a month—since before the awful events of September 11—and although I had spoken to my elderly mother over the phone several times a week, I was not sure what to expect.

"Mom, what—?"

A smile illuminated my mother's face as if someone had twisted a dimmer switch. "Michelle! It's so nice to see you!" She took a step toward me, right through the puddle of blood.

On the tile floor a young woman was sprawled, her blond hair caked with blood. I knelt at her side. No pulse. No breath. Blue-gray pallor. It had been years since I'd been proficient in CPR, and it wasn't coming back to me. How many compressions? "Have you called 9-1-1?" My voice shook as I uttered those numbers.

"What's wrong with Brittany?" My mother squatted beside me as if we were playing a game.

"Mom, what *happened*?" I cried. What if this woman–Brittany–was dead? Ants gathered at a stream of coagulated blood from her nostrils. "Did you call 9-1-1?"

Mom's blank stare confirmed she had not. Unlike most of my friends, I had no cell phone, so I dashed to the black wall phone in the kitchen.

"What is your emergency?" The female voice was pleasant but businesslike, with an East Texas twang.

I gave my name and our address. "My mother's caregiver is unconscious, maybe even dead. I just got here, so I can't say for sure what happened, but it looks like a blow to the head."

"I'll send paramedics right away." She confirmed the address I had given her. "Is the victim breathing?"

"No."

"Is there a pulse?"

"I couldn't find one." My own heart pounded.

"Has anyone started CPR?"

"Not yet. I called you first." Had I made a fatal mistake?

"Is anyone else in danger?"

"In danger? What do you mean?"

"Is the person who did this still there? Is he trying to hurt anyone else?"

"No...I mean, I don't think so. I didn't see what happened."

"Are you alone?"

"My mother's here. But she's 77 years old and..."

"The emergency crew should arrive momentarily. I'll stay on the line until they get there, so leave the phone off the hook. Do you know CPR?"

"I was a flight attendant for ten years. We reviewed CPR every spring in recurrent training, but I never used it for real. And it's been nine years since I left In-Flight..."

The woman politely cut off my blathering with brief instructions to refresh my memory and told me to start CPR.

"Lord!" The voice of Karen Jackson, another of my mother's caregivers, boomed from the entryway.

"Don't do this, Britt!" Karen was bent over Brittany's body when I returned from making the call. Mouth wide open, eyes popping like peeled grapes, Karen looked up as I approached.

I knelt beside her and began chest compressions as Karen tried to blow air into Brittany's lungs.

Good thing about a small town, it doesn't take long for emergency crews to arrive anywhere. And then everybody shows up. Within minutes, our quiet, circa-1950 subdivision was lit like Las Vegas. Three fire trucks, an ambulance, and two police cars arrived with lights blazing and sirens blaring. Radios crackled. Uniformed and non-uniformed personnel from various public service departments swarmed the scene, pushing us aside like pieces of furniture. Cameras clicked.

Two strong paramedics took over CPR and tried to jumpstart Brittany's heart with paddles. After a few valiant attempts, they shook their heads at each other. I turned away, unable to watch the rest. Could I have done more to save her? If I had arrived earlier, might she still be alive?

Neighbors peered out their windows and some even ventured into their yards. I didn't know many of them anymore. For years after I left home my mother had kept me updated about who moved away and who moved in, but lately she had lost interest.

In the past, my mother would have been hovering, offering theories for what had happened, scolding the officers for soiling her carpet. But today during all the commotion, I found her in front of the TV in the family room, staring at a "Golden Girls" rerun. She wouldn't let me turn the set off even when the episode was over.

"Ma'am, mind if I ask you a few questions?" The muscular, plain-clothes detective must have followed me into the family room. His deep baritone sounded familiar, but I couldn't quite place it.

A pair of brown eyes studied me from beneath the brim of a cap. A graying mustache partially covered his full upper lip. He appeared to be around my age—the dark side of forty. Something about his expression and stance seemed familiar as well.

"*Michelle Hanson*? What brings *you* back to Two Wells, Texas?"

We had gone to school together. Usually good with names, I could not recall his, and he wasn't wearing a name badge. "It's Michelle DePalma now." I held out my hand, hoping he would refresh my memory by supplying his name, or perhaps hand me a business card. After all, we were speaking because he was conducting an investigation.

He returned my handshake. "You look great!" As his eyes appraised me from head to toe, my mystery acquaintance continued, "You've barely aged since our ten-year reunion."

The ten-year reunion. I tried to recollect a conversation we might have had. Nothing. "Thanks," I murmured. "What have you been up to?"

"Mary Lynn and I got divorced last year. And our youngest son joined the Army. His unit's headed to Afghanistan."

Afghanistan. I backed up my thoughts, as if replaying a tape. Mary Lynn. Mary Lynn Hodges, head cheerleader, great granddaughter of one of the oilmen who had founded Two Wells. Biggest snob at Robert E. Lee High School. My mother had sent me the newspaper clipping about her fairy-tale wedding to Keith Matthews, football jock, with whom I had my last civil exchange in fourth grade, when we'd made a poster together to advertise the class play.

"I guess it has to be done," Keith was saying. "We have to bring Osama bin Laden to justice. Karl is a brave boy, and I'm proud of him."

"I'm sorry," I said. Sorry about his divorce, more sorry about his son going off to war. It had to bring back memories of Kevin, Keith's older brother, who had been killed in Vietnam when we were in high school. We had not been friends at the time, and I had never told him I was sorry about his brother's death. Now we were having our first polite conversation in over forty years, because of a dead body.

"Hey Man, are you about finished over here?" Keith's burly partner interrupted. "These people are contaminating our crime scene." Greg Dobbins had never said a kind word to me since I had refused to let him copy my history test in fifth grade. I wondered if he still cheated, and if so, what opportunities his chosen profession now afforded him.

Ignoring me, Greg spoke directly to Keith. His upper lip did not quite cover his protruding front teeth, which gave him a slight resemblance to a wharf rat. "I talked to that black lady–Karen Jackson–and she don't know nothing. Got here right before we did. But look what we found in the hedge!" In a gloved hand, he held a 12-inch brass pagoda, the one that usually sat on my mother's mantle. Now it was covered with drying blood, hair, and boxwood leaves. Greg acknowledged my mother and me for the first time. "Either of you ladies recognize this?"

I wondered how I had missed seeing my mother's pagoda in the boxwoods when I arrived; I must have been distracted by the open front door. “A family heirloom,” I replied.

“My pagoda!” my mother cried. She sprang from her chair and drew close to Greg to inspect the object. “What happened? It’s all dirty! Michelle, would you wipe that off and put it back on the mantle? These people! They won’t leave my things alone!”

I patted my mother’s thin shoulder. I could not honor her request; her property was evidence.

“Well, well, well! If it ain’t Michelle Hanson.” Never handsome—even though *he'd* always thought he was—Greg Dobbins had grown uglier over the years. His pockmarked face bobbed on top of his rounded shoulders, covering any trace of a neck. His beer belly hung low over his belt, which circled his hips instead of his waist, barely holding up his baggy pants. He gave them a tug, and then added, “You disappeared on us senior year. Thought you'd left Two Wells for good.”

“I’m just in town for the weekend, to visit my mother.”

Keith snapped into business mode. “Michelle, can you tell us what happened here?”

I shrugged. “When I walked in, Brittany was lying ...”

“You knew the victim?” Keith took a small notebook out of his pocket.

“I’ve seen her a couple times before. She works for the agency that provides home services for my mother. Loving Care, on Front Street.”

“Brittany Landers. Black lady knows her. They work for the same agency. Shift change was at two o’clock.” Greg glanced over Keith's shoulder as he wrote.

“Brittany was lying on the floor, her head bloody.” I shuddered. “She wasn’t breathing, and I couldn’t feel a pulse. I ran into the kitchen and called 9-1-1, then came back and Karen was here.”

“Whose bright idea was it to do CPR on a dead person?” Greg asked. “You tampered with a crime scene.”

“We weren't positive she was dead. I've never seen a freshly dead person before. What if she hadn't been dead, and we'd just let her die? The operator—”

Greg shook his head. "Dumb broad. We're supposed to be one team here. Of course, all she had to go on was what *you* told her."

Keith interrupted. "Did you notice anyone else around? Anyone leaving?"

I thought for a moment. "I passed a car as I was coming up the street."

"What kind of car?" Greg asked.

"It was white," I offered, wishing I had a better memory for details. "And not very clean."

"Two-door or four-door? Sedan or S.U.V?" Greg tugged at his pants again.

Shutting my eyes tightly, willing the image to appear, I shook my head. All I could remember about the drive up my childhood street was the abundance of American flags on display. "I'm not sure how many doors. Sedan, I think. Loud rap music was blaring from the stereo."

"So we'll be on the lookout for a dirty white sedan, playing loud rap music." Greg rolled his eyes.

"What about you, Mrs. Hanson?" Keith turned to my mother, who had been silent since losing her beloved brass pagoda.

"You give me back my pagoda! I saw you take it." My mother shook her finger at the officers. "My father bought that for me on our trip to China, when I was five years old."

Greg's eyes focused on my ranting mother and swept to her bloodstained canvas shoes. He bent closer to inspect them. "Looks like fresh blood on your shoes, Ma'am. Care to explain?"

"She was standing near the body when I got here. There was blood on the floor." After the words left my lips, I was afraid they sounded incriminating.

"Off." Greg snapped his fingers. "We have to get them to the lab."

I coaxed my mother to let me pull her slip-ons off her feet. "Karen," I called, as Mom leaned against me. "Can you please get her some other shoes? The tile is cold."

"Where are you taking my shoes? Why are you taking my things?" wailed my mother. She picked up one of the shoes I had removed from her foot and hurled it at Greg, hitting him in the arm.

He bared those rodent-like teeth. "Watch it, lady!"

"Greg Dobbins, *you* watch how you talk to my mother!" For a second, our eyes locked and we were two stubborn fifth graders again. "Mom." I put my hand on her shoulder. "They'll give your things back. But they have to take them for now." I appealed to Keith, who had so far seemed the more sympathetic of the two. "Can we do this some other time? She needs a nap, and it's time for her medicine."

Greg rolled his eyes again and growled, "Just because she's a little old lady, Michelle, doesn't mean we're going to let her get away with murder! Looks like this Brittany chick was trying to steal her precious pagoda, and your crazy mom whacked her with it."

My jaw dropped like a broken hinge. "You can't be serious!"

Keith held up his hand like a crossing guard. "Michelle, can you bring your mother down to the station tomorrow?"

"Nine a.m. Sharp," Greg muttered. "And make sure she's ready to answer some questions. Now everyone get out of here."

Chapter Two

"We have to leave the house?" I asked. Intellectually, I was not surprised. Emotionally, I felt violated. "For how long?"

Karen had returned with another pair of canvas slip-ons, and we helped my mother into them.

"Until the crime scene investigators are through," Keith explained. He eyed the sliding glass door leading to our back yard. "Can we go out this way? They've got your front entry taped off." With a gloved hand, he slid open the back door.

"Wait! Look." I pointed to the broom handle lying on the floor beside the sliding glass door. "Mom always keeps this in the track for security, even in the daytime."

Keith inspected the broom handle. "We'll try to lift some prints."

Karen took Mom's arm as Keith waved us outside. My teeth chattered, although I was dressed warmly enough for the autumn afternoon.

"These are the wrong color!" my mother blurted, looking at her clean canvas shoes. Karen whispered something in her ear that spurred her to move again.

The overgrown rose bushes were a blur of color and fragrance as we rounded the side of the house and passed through the gate of the chain-link fence. "Of course, we want to cooperate with your investigation," I said to Keith, "but when do you think my mother can get back into her house?"

"Depends… probably a few hours." His eyes were kind. "Before you move back in, you might want to have a professional clean-up crew come. Blood is a biohazard. There's only one company in town doing that kind of thing, and the service should be covered by your homeowner's insurance. I can call them for you if you like. Company's run by a guy we went to school with—Joe Diaz."

"Sure. Thanks." The name sounded familiar, but I couldn't picture Joe's face. Not that it mattered; I would rather have a stranger tasked with cleaning up human blood from my mother's floor. "Where are we supposed to go in the meantime?"

"How about a neighbor?" As Keith spoke, my eyes scanned the crowd of onlookers milling about the front yard. They came to rest on a short strawberry blonde squeezed into orange Capri pants—Shirley O'Keefe. She had babysat my younger brother Mark and me when we were children.

Shirley spotted me at the same time. "Michelle!" We moved toward each other, and she gave me a hug. The physical contact seemed awkward after years of nothing but waving at each other from across the street. However, in the intensity of the moment, a hug felt good. "What went on here?" Shirley asked, stepping away to look at me. "First I thought something had happened to your mother, but people are saying that girl they carried out is dead."

"Shirley, I have a huge favor to ask you." I gestured at my mother and Karen. "Can we stay at your place for a few hours? They have to cordon this area off for the investigators. We're being kicked out of our house!"

Shirley's green eyes panned the three of us; there was a momentary flicker when she came to Karen, but it quickly disappeared. "Of course. Come on, I'll make y'all some tea."

The O'Keefe house was a mirror of my mother's, and just as claustrophobic. After her divorce a couple years ago, Shirley had moved back in to care for her elderly father. When he passed away last year, she had decided to stay in the house. "Easier than cleaning it out," she chattered as she ushered us inside.

The three of us settled on her couch, a classic style with spring down cushions upholstered in a large floral fabric. Potpourri permeated the room. Shirley excused herself to make tea.

I felt a pinprick on my wrist and looked down to find a black ant crawling up my arm. I pinched it off, crumbled its impertinent body into a ball between my thumb and forefinger, and flicked it away.

A wave of nausea hit me. I shook my head to dispel the image of Karen and me trying to breathe life back into Brittany while ants fed on her coagulated blood. I rose and groped my way to Shirley's nearest bathroom. "Michelle?" I heard my mother call after me as I opened the toilet lid by its fluffy cover and vomited the meager contents of my stomach into blue water.

Immediately, I felt back in control. I flushed the evidence, inspected the seat, and then wiped a trace of vomit away with a piece of scented floral-patterned toilet paper. I ran cold water on my face, looked around for an alternative to those perfect rose balls in a shell-shaped dish, and then spotted a matching ceramic pump dispenser filled with liquid soap. I helped myself to one of the perfectly folded guest towels and tried to refold it to mask my intrusion.

Instead of returning to the living room, I ventured into the kitchen to see if I could help Shirley with our tea. "We really appreciate this, Shirley. I hate to impose."

Shirley filled a kettle with water. "Was it awful? Finding the body, I mean?"

I pressed my eyelids together as if that would squeeze away the image. "I'd never seen a dead person before. Except at a funeral, when the body is all made up like a mannequin."

"I found my father. But I guess that was different, though, because he was so ill and we knew it was just a matter of time."

"I wasn't even sure she was dead. We did CPR."

"What happened anyway?"

I glanced out the kitchen window; police cars and a news van were still parked in front of my mother's house. "That's what they're trying to find out."

Shirley set the kettle on a burner and flicked a dial on her new gas range, instantly producing a blue flame, which sizzled droplets of water clinging to the bottom of the kettle. "Gosh, Michelle, I don't think we've talked much since your father's funeral. When was that? 1992?"

"I know," I apologized, with a nod to confirm the year of my dad's death. "When I come to check on Mom, I'm only here a day or two, and I rarely have time to visit anyone else." From the time I graduated from college until my mother's cancer surgery last year, I could have counted the number of visits I'd made to Two Wells on one hand. In the past year, I had come every couple weeks, but the trips were quick—in and out—and I preferred it that way. Two Wells dredged up more failures and regrets than happy memories for me, and at long last, my life was in a pretty good place. Even though I'd grown up here, Two Wells had never been *my town*. I'd always felt like an outcast.

The O'Keefe kitchen was small and cave-like, with crowded countertops like my mother's, but it had a homier feel, like it was an important room in the house. Shirley filled a strainer with loose black tea and placed it in the teapot. At her direction, I took four mugs out of the white-painted cabinet and arranged them on a ceramic tray, trying to ground myself in the present and dispel the image of Karen and me performing CPR on a dead person.

"Your mother has these aides with her all the time now?" Shirley asked.

"We were hoping she could live on her own after her surgery last year, but her progress has been slow. It's like the anesthesia never got purged from her system." I remembered the miserable three months my mother had spent recovering in a nursing home. She had refused to eat or participate in physical therapy sessions, and had constantly begged to go home. I could hardly blame her; I couldn't take more than a few hours there, breathing the stench of ammonia blended with body fluids. "I thought we'd have been able to cut back the help by now, just keep someone around in the daytime, but they say she gets up at night and falls sometimes. And her memory lapses are troubling. One day she's fine, the next she can't recall a conversation you had five minutes ago. So for now, the aides are there 'round the clock."

"Yeah, I see those women come and go all the time. I guess they take good care of her."

"You said you were working in your yard when I drove up today, before all the commotion started." I searched for a sugar bowl and spoon to place on the tray with the mugs. "Had you been out there long?"

"A couple hours."

"Before I got there, did you notice anyone else coming or going?"

"One of the cops asked me that. I didn't pay attention to every car, but I don't remember seeing anyone else stop."

I lifted the lid of the sugar bowl. "This is almost empty."

"I bought a new bag. I'll get it for you."

As Shirley handed me the five-pound bag of sugar, I continued, "Do you pay much attention to the different women who come to my mother's house?"

She grimaced. "A couple of the young ones are loud. They have visitors, and they often take their conversations outside. I wondered if y'all knew, but I didn't want to seem like a nosy neighbor."

"Do you remember any of the visitors? Male? Female?"

"Some guy used to come around a lot. Long stringy hair, probably never washed it. Kind of Indian-looking. You know–" Shirley patted her O-shaped lips—her way of differentiating him from the type of Indian who hailed from India. "It was mostly when *that* girl was working, but sometimes he visited one of the black girls. They'd have shouting matches by the curb, and then he'd drive away, tires squealing. It was dangerous; he could have run over a child or a dog."

"What kind of car did he drive?"

The kettle whistled. Shirley removed it from the stove and poured boiling water into the teapot. "Black Camaro," she replied. "Older model. And I think he'd taken the muffler off. Sure was loud."

So, the dirty white sedan I'd passed had not been Brittany's boyfriend driving away after he'd killed her in a fit of rage. "Have you talked to my mother much lately?"

Shirley peered into the teapot. "I used to see her working in the yard and we'd chat, but that was before her surgery. I stopped by to see her a couple times afterward and brought her a cake once, but those women always told me she was napping." She replaced the teapot lid. "I'm sorry, Michelle, it's been a while. Guess I haven't been a very good neighbor."

"She's not your responsibility. I, on the other hand..." I stopped. Why was I telling her this? Because she had been my babysitter? Because I had once cried on her shoulder after the sneers about my dowdy wardrobe from Mary Lynn Hodges and her gang of cheerleaders? Because I felt guilty that my mother and I had never been able to spend more than a few hours together before we grated each other's nerves? "Sometimes I don't think I've been a very good daughter."

"What do you mean? You're here, aren't you?"

I sighed. "I jet in every few weeks for a day or two. I don't spend much time with her. Strangers are taking care of her. When *your* father was sick..."

"Stop! My life was a mess. I had nowhere else to go. You have an important job, a dreamboat of a husband. Your mom is so proud of you!"

"Really?"

"Oh yeah. Both you and your brother. She'd never expect either of you to come back here and live with her." Shirley checked the status of the tea again, and then signaled me to follow her into the living room with the tray of cups.

"Michelle!" said my mother, when I set a mug on the coffee table in front of her. "What are you doing here?"

"I've been in the kitchen helping Shirley," I replied, as Shirley poured tea into my mother's mug.

"Is that tea?" My mother pursed her face.

"Earl Grey. The best," Shirley replied.

"Don't you have coffee?"

"Mom!" She had never let me get away with bad manners when I was a child.

Shirley handled it calmly. "You want coffee instead, Mrs. Hanson? I'll see if I can find some." She took my mother's full mug away and handed it to Karen. "Is tea okay with you, Ma'am?" Her smile seemed forced and overly polite, as if she'd never entertained a black person and was not sure the rules were the same as for whites.

"Thank you," Karen replied, accepting the mug of tea from Shirley.

Shirley poured my tea and retreated to the kitchen with an empty mug. "Is instant okay?" she called over her shoulder.

"Instant what?" my mother murmured to Karen and me.

"Coffee, Mom," I prompted her.

"Instant coffee?" My mother made another face. "I always brew mine. It's really easy."

"Mom, maybe she doesn't drink coffee."

"Why wouldn't she?"

"Not everyone drinks coffee every day like you do."

My mother smiled and turned to Karen. "I started drinking coffee when I was a little girl, and my daddy told me it would stunt my growth," she explained. "I didn't believe him. But I'm only five foot five, and I'm the shortest person in my family."

I rolled my eyes at Karen. We had both heard this story before. Usually whenever Mom sat down with a cup of coffee.

My mother continued. "Michelle's smaller than she was supposed to be, too. It's because she went on a crash diet when she was a teenager."

"Mom, really…"

"It's true," she insisted. "We measured you when you were two and a half years old." She looked at Karen again, explaining, as if she were telling us this story for the first time, "Double the child's height at age two and a half, and that will tell you how tall she'll be when she grows up. Michelle should have been five foot nine or ten." She looked back at me. "How tall are you, Michelle?"

"Five foot six. And I know—you think I stunted my growth."

"It was all that crash dieting," she agreed. She turned her attention back to Karen. "Do you have children?"

"Yes, Ma'am. Four girls and two boys. You know two of my girls."

My mother sat in silence, as if the last data entry did not compute. She looked around the room and asked, "Where are we?"

"We're at your neighbor's house," I prompted. "Shirley O'Keefe. She lives across the street. You remember her; she used to babysit Mark and me."

As if on cue, Shirley returned from the kitchen with a cup of instant coffee and a plate of cookies. She set the cookies on the coffee table and then carefully handed my mother the cup of coffee.

"What's this?" my mother asked, staring into the black liquid.

"You wanted coffee?" Shirley sat down in a wing chair upholstered in the same floral pattern as the couch.

"I take milk and sugar."

"Here," Karen said. "There's milk and sugar on the table." She stuck a spoon into the sugar bowl and dumped two heaps into my mother's cup.

Once we'd all sipped our beverages, Shirley asked, "So, Mrs. Hanson, let's hear what happened over there?"

My mother scrunched her face. I wasn't sure if it was the instant coffee or the question. "What are you talking about?"

"This afternoon," Shirley prompted. "The crime scene investigators at your house..."

"The what? Someone's at my house?"

Shirley wrinkled her brow.

These memory resets concerned me, too. I tried, "Mom, remember Brittany, the girl they took away? She'd been hit over the head..."

"Hit over the head? Is she going to be okay?"

"I don't think so. Karen and I couldn't revive her. Neither could the paramedics."

"That's terrible."

"Did you see what happened to her?" I continued, willing away the image of Brittany's dead body, of our feeble attempts at CPR.

"Where'd she go?"

"The hospital, I suppose, or maybe the morgue. But Mom, did you see what happened to her? Before Karen and I arrived? Was someone else with her?"

My mother appeared to be concentrating, reassembling the story. But then, as if the TV channel had been switched, she said, "Someone's at my house? Why?"

"Mom, we told you, the crime scene investigators are there, trying to find clues about what happened."

"Shouldn't we be there? I don't want them going through my things!"

"We have no choice, Mom. The police made us leave. Shirley was nice enough to let us wait here at her house until they're done."

My mother set down her cup and started to rise. "Well, I'm going back over there. They can't do this. What if they steal someth—?" An outburst of coughing suppressed her words. Karen pulled her to the couch and gently massaged her back until the coughing fit ended.

Shirley looked sorry she had ever opened the conversation. Trying a new subject, she asked, "So Michelle, how's the airline industry doing? Bet you've seen a lot of changes since September 11."

September 11. As a former New Yorker and an airline employee--married to a pilot who had been in the sky that day--I felt particularly affected by those events. I began telling Shirley about my job as a designer of airport agent training, how new security procedures necessitated rewriting much of our material, how this had been my first opportunity since that tragedy to fly back to Two Wells to check on my mother.

As I spoke, Mom rose again and walked over to Shirley, peered straight into her eyes. "I know you," she said. "You were over at my house this morning, babysitting my kids."

Chapter Three

It was after ten that evening before we were allowed back in my mother's house. The overpowering odor of industrial-strength chemicals evoked memories of the nursing home, but the tile floor shone, and the ant battalions had vanished. I cringed as we tread over the spot where Brittany had fallen, her life now eradicated by cleaning fluids.

The smell dissipated once we reached the sanctuary of the family room. I couldn't tell if anything was missing; the clutter on the coffee table seemed normal. Beside the sliding glass door, the broom handle lay in a sprinkling of black powder.

"Miz Hanson, can I fix you some soup?" Karen asked. She rounded the yellow Formica-covered breakfast bar and entered the kitchen.

With a glance around the room, my mother sank into her favorite chair. Her wizened fingers fumbled for the remote control. She examined it, frowned, and touched various buttons.

"Miz Hanson, how about some warm tomato soup?"

My mother pushed another button and the television crackled to life. She looked at Karen. "Soup?" She made that scrunched face again, like a first grader who'd been shown a worm. "No, thank you."

"Ma'am, what would you like to eat? How about some scrambled eggs?"

Although my mother used to love breakfast foods morning, noon, and night, they rarely tempted her now. Nothing did. Since the cancer surgery, she had been wasting away. Her wrists were like twigs, and her rings would no longer stay on her bony fingers. She and I once wore the same dress size; now we had to shop in the children's department to find clothing to fit her. "I'm not hungry," my mother announced. "Think I'll go to bed."

"You gotta eat something," Karen insisted. "You didn't touch the pizza Miss Michelle ordered for us."

"Mom, what if I make some pasta?" I suggested. "You used to love my Alfredo sauce."

My mother smiled. "That's awfully sweet of you, Michelle. But I'm not hungry. Maybe tomorrow." She rose from her armchair.

"Tomorrow then? Promise?" I'd cook it anyway, and maybe I could persuade her to eat a little.

"Have some Ensure then," Karen said, opening a can of the sweet liquid that had supplied my mother most of her nutrition for the past year. Karen poured it into a cup over ice and stuck a straw in it. "Here you go, Miz Hanson." Gently she took my mother's arm and led her to the master bedroom, holding the cup of Ensure steady as they shuffled across the nylon carpet.

At Shirley's we had sipped tea and danced around the subject of the murder investigation across the street, which had been foremost on our minds. Instead we had compared our parallel experiences growing up on opposite sides of Two Wells during the early days of desegregation and debated our country's response to last month's terror attacks. Now Karen and I were alone, back at the scene of the crime.

"What do *you* think happened?" I asked Karen when she returned from putting my mother to bed. "Did you get the impression the police were starting to suspect *my mother*?"

"Lord!" Karen shook her head, not looking me in the eye. "I don't know what to think! This is like a bad dream!"

"But my mother couldn't possibly have done it! Look at her, for God's sake!"

"Dunno. She sure is strong sometimes. When she don't wanna do something."

"But, assuming she had the strength to wield that pagoda--*why*? Why would my mother kill Brittany?"

Karen kept her eyes focused on a made-for-TV movie on Lifetime. "I ain't saying she did it. But she sure don't like people messing with her things."

Like the police, Karen would not automatically dismiss my mother as a suspect. I went on, "Who could have done it? You knew Brittany better than I did. Did she get along with the other women at the agency?" Most of them were black; Brittany was white. Not that it seemed to make a difference in her generation.

"Far as I know." Karen tore open a giant bag of potato chips and held it out to me.

I declined. "What about boyfriends? Did Brittany ever talk about her love life?"

"Lord! Now there's a suspect!" Karen rolled her big brown eyes. "Them chillern was fighting all the time! I think he hit her, too."

"Do you know his name? Or where we can find him?"

"Thomas? Terrence...something like that. I'll ask my girls. They may know him." Two of Karen's twenty-something daughters, Keisha and Katrina, also worked for the Loving Care agency.

To check my facts against what I had gathered from my kitchen conversation with Shirley, I asked, "What kind of car does he drive?"

"Dunno. White? When he washes it."

The ringing phone interrupted our conversation. Following the sound, I found the portable buried under a magazine on the coffee table. Mark, my younger brother, was on the line. I had promised to call him at his home in Seattle when I arrived.

"I see you got in," he scolded. "How was your trip?"

"The trip was uneventful," I replied. I knew I should have found a moment to call him, but I had completely forgotten. "However, our house is a crime scene!"

"What?" Mark listened to me recount how I had stumbled upon a corpse. "Did you call the Loving Care Agency yet?" he asked. "They'll have to contact Brittany's family."

"I think the police contacted her family. Karen called the agency this afternoon, while we were at Shirley's."

"What about Mom? Was she a witness?"

"She's not talking about it, but she probably was. In fact, I have to take her to the station tomorrow so she can make her statement, because she wouldn't answer any questions while the police were here. Mark, I think she may be a suspect!"

"Let me talk to her. Maybe I can get some information out of her."

Mark was her favorite; I had resigned myself to that fact years ago. Maybe she *would* tell him what she had observed. "She went to bed already; let's see if she's still awake." I stood up and walked the portable phone down the hall to my mother's bedroom.

The television glowed from the darkened room. Mom's tiny frame barely protruded from beneath a thin cotton comforter, dwarfed by the king-sized bed she and my father had once shared. I couldn't tell if she were awake or asleep. "Mom," I whispered. "Mark's on the line."

She reached to take the phone from me, and I stretched out on the bed beside her. "Mark! How are Marie and my grandkids?" She paused a moment. Then, "Is it raining there?" Another pause. "But doesn't it always rain in Seattle?"

My eyes panned the cluttered master bedroom—every surface covered with clothing, linens, personal care items—then focused on my mother as she talked to my brother. When did she get so old? Less than two years ago she was swimming laps, playing bridge with her girlfriends, and traveling the world.

"No," she said. "Did Michelle tell you I was there? She just got here; how would she know? I was at the mall all afternoon, and I didn't see anything."

I rolled my eyes. No one had taken my mother to the mall today, and she certainly didn't drive herself. We had hidden the keys to her Ford Fiesta several months ago, when she got released from the nursing home. Karen used the car occasionally to take her to the doctor or grocery shopping, just to keep it running.

My mother handed back the phone and without a word of explanation turned her attention to the television set. "Mark?" I ventured.

"She didn't tell me anything," he admitted. "I take it she didn't really go to the mall today?"

"Don't think so. Karen arrived right after I did. She's the only one who ever takes Mom anywhere."

"Keep trying, Michelle. Get her story straight before she has to tell it to the police."

Mark and I said our good-byes, and then I leaned my face close to my mother's. "Mom, can I get you anything?"

Her eyelids fluttered; she had been almost asleep. "Who was that on the phone?"

"It was Mark, Mom."

"Mark? How's he doing?"

"Fine. Can I get you anything?"

"No thank you, Dear. Good night."

I kissed her forehead, slid off the bed, and tiptoed out of her room. I started to pull the door closed, but then thought about her occasional falls and left it open. The phone in my hand rang as I started down the hall. It was my husband, Roberto. I had promised to call him, too. "Hi Honey Bear, sorry I didn't call." I turned into my childhood bedroom and launched into my narrative of the day's events.

"My God!" Roberto's voice sounded alarmed. "Look, I can drop my trip and be out there tomorrow."

"Don't do that. We'll be fine." He would come if I asked him to, but I would never ask.

"Is it safe for you and your mother to stay there?"

I had not had time to consider our safety. Murders never happened in our neighborhood—at least not when I was growing up here. But now there was a killer loose, and no one knew his motive. However, there was no need to worry Roberto. "The doors are locked. We won't let any strangers in." As I spoke, I heard a rustle in the rose bushes outside. It had to be the wind. A shadow darted past the window. I pushed aside the dusty Venetian blinds and peered out, but could not see anything. Roberto said something I did not catch. "What was that, Honey Bear?"

"Are you still planning to fly home Sunday?" His voice made me long for our tidy, secure home in Atlanta, my two cats, and our relatively uncomplicated existence.

This was to be the usual quick trip: check on the help, peruse the mail, maybe do a little yard work. But I had the feeling I was stuck in Two Wells for a while, and the thought of that depressed me. "I'm not sure, Honey Bear. It depends on what the police say tomorrow."

I had just drifted off to sleep when the rustle of the rose bushes awakened me. Again, a distinctively human-shaped shadow eclipsed the stream of moonlight through the blinds. I sat up in bed and then went to peer out the window. The rose bushes blocked my view. A car alarm sounded in the distance.

Pulling on one of my mother's robes, I padded into the hallway. The tile floor felt cool through my socks.

In the family room, Karen was dozing on the couch, covered with one of my grandmother's hand-knitted Afghans. I tiptoed past her into the entryway. I felt a chill shimmer down my spine as I recalled finding Brittany's body there. I opened the front door.

The night air was cool and still. The car alarm had been silenced. Had I imagined the intruder?

Something rubbed against my leg and I jumped.

"Meow," said an indignant orange tabby that I recognized as belonging to one of my mother's neighbors.

Relieved, I bent to stroke the cat's head. "Hi there, Tom," I murmured. "You scared me half to death."

The cat's response was a purr and more leg-rubbing, demanding that I continue the petting action. I obliged, thinking about how much I missed Snow and Mickey whenever I left town.

After a few moments, the cat became distracted by a blowing leaf, which allowed me to rise from my crouched position. As I turned to go back inside, I noticed a white business card wedged against the boxwoods in the planter. A piece of trash to be tossed, probably dropped by one of the investigators. When I picked it up, I glanced at the name and then froze: *Mary Lynn Matthews, Realtor.*

Mary Lynn Hodges. The bride of Keith Matthews. How I had let her get to me when we were kids! Like it was yesterday, I recalled our ninth-grade history teacher announcing that the results of the pop quiz he had given would stand.

"How can you do that?" whined Mary Lynn. "You said everyone failed."

"Everyone except Michelle Hanson. She made a 95."

I felt my cheeks flush. I had always been an excellent student, but I hated when teachers called it to everyone's attention.

"Michelle Hanson!" Mary Lynn snorted. "That Yankee doesn't have anything to do but study. No one likes her."

Nobody likes me. Even though I had my share of friends, in Mary Lynn's eyes, they were inconsequential, because they did not run with her crowd—the popular people who mattered. Mary Lynn's words stung, and I sat there mute as a statue, unable to defend myself, unable to shout that her words were lies. I could always think of clever comebacks to Mary Lynn's jibes—only long after the opportunity had passed me by.

Mary Lynn Hodges. Definitely one of my most unpleasant memories of growing up in Two Wells, Texas.

What was Mary Lynn's business card doing here? Had she been to my mother's house? And when?

Chapter Four

My eyes cracked open to sunlight streaming through dusty blinds, creating striped patterns on the butter yellow walls of my childhood bedroom. I pulled the covers over my face, hoping to fall back asleep and wake up somewhere else, without this heaviness inside—the same feeling I always got whenever I visited Two Wells, tugging at me like an undertow. No use. I was in Two Wells, and today I had to take my mother to the police station to try to answer questions about a mysterious death in our home. I dragged myself out of bed.

Mom slept in longer than usual. When Karen and I roused her, she tried to don the same royal blue warm-up suit she had worn the day before. Karen persuaded her to put on one like it, in hot pink, with canvas slip-ons to match. Although my mother owned more clothes than would fit in her bulging closet, she wore the same pieces over and over.

"Where are we going?" Mom asked, inspecting the legs of her hot pink sweat suit as we all walked toward the family room.

"Don't you remember?" I prompted. "We promised we'd go to the police station this morning."

"Police station? Why?"

So much for my hope that a good night's sleep would reset her memory. "Remember yesterday? Brittany?"

"Brittany who? I don't know any Brittany."

"Mom, remember your pagoda? The police found it in the boxwood plants in the front flower bed, covered with blood."

My mother strolled to the shelf where her pagoda had stood for over 40 years. "Did I ever show you the beautiful brass pagoda my father bought me on our trip to China, when I was five years old?"

The phone rang, distracting me from my frustration. I picked up the portable from the coffee table. It was Christina Washington, owner of the Loving Care Agency. "May I please speak to Karen?" Her voice sounded cooler and more businesslike than usual.

I handed Karen the phone and said, "Mom, yesterday somebody picked up that pagoda and hit Brittany over the head so hard she died."

Mom gasped. "That's terrible!"

"Did you see the person who did it?"

She looked at me as if I had landed in a spacecraft. "Where did it happen?"

"Apparently right in our entryway! You saw her lying there when I got here. Don't you remember? The police came..."

Karen set down the phone. She looked from me to my mother. "I'm sorry, Michellc. I hate to do this. But Chris says we can't provide our services here any more. Not until this case is over."

"What? No notice?" Helplessly, I watched Karen pack her things—two romance novels, four magazines, two bags of potato chips. "Karen, you can't think my mother is dangerous!"

She avoided my eyes as she prepared to evacuate. I had hoped Karen would have felt more loyalty to my mother; that she might have tried to reason with Christina. My mother did not react to Karen's exit. She was used to seeing these women come and go.

I picked up the phone and dialed Mark to update him on this latest development. "There has to be something in their contract about giving notice?"

He was silent for a moment. "I don't think it's mentioned. You can check. The papers are in Mom's file cabinet."

Phone cupped to my ear, I pulled out the drawer to the small file cabinet we kept in the family room and fumbled for the folder containing our contract with the Loving Care Agency. My brother, the perfect one who always thought of everything, had been the one to set up the home care arrangements. I opened the folder. Was this it? The contract the agency had provided was basic and vague, like something one would buy at an office-supply store. It discussed payment amount and terms, liability insurance, and what services would be provided—or more precisely, what services would *not* be provided. Termination was not even addressed. The paper shook in my hands. "You still there, Mark? You're right, it doesn't mention anything about giving notice."

Mark sighed. "I'll make some phone calls today. You'd better head over to the police station and get this thing cleared up."

"Mark," I began. "I could take care of her."

He laughed. "You!"

"Why? You don't think I could?" In my family, I had earned the reputation as a free-spirited scatterbrain, perhaps because it had taken me so long to settle down. Taking care of our mother had never been part of my plans, but I resented my brother's implication that I *couldn't* do it.

Mark's mirth subsided. "What about your job? Your husband? Your cats? Your home in Atlanta?"

"They're offering voluntary leaves now. I'm sure I could get one." I didn't have an answer yet to his other questions: Roberto, our home, our cats.

"Well, you might *have* to take care of her for awhile, until we can make other arrangements. Now go to the police station. Call me when you're done."

"You know how to drive my car?" my mother asked as I opened the passenger door for her. "Do you know your way around Two Wells?"

"I can manage." I smiled, fastening her seat belt for her. Her car smelled of mildew, perhaps from sitting idle in the garage so much. It could use a good vacuuming, too.

I walked around the car to inspect the tires, opened the heavy wooden garage door, and then entered on the driver's side. After several cranks, I started the Ford Fiesta's engine and backed onto the concrete driveway. The gas tank was full, and there was a receipt on the dashboard for gasoline purchased last Monday at a station a few blocks away. I surmised the car had not been driven since then. So much for my mother's story about going shopping yesterday.

I slipped the transmission into park, got out, and closed the garage door. My parents had never felt the need for automatic openers; they had read about burglars cracking the code.

"You didn't do the padlock," my mother chided me when I climbed back into the car.

I was about to argue we were not going to be gone long, but then I remembered there was a killer loose, motive unknown. Better to be safe. I hopped out and attached the combination lock that bolted the garage door to its frame.

"Go down Fifth Street," my mother advised me. "That's the fastest way. There shouldn't be much traffic this time of day." As I backed the car down the driveway and into our residential street, she started to hum, then burst into song. "Hark the herald angels sing..."

"Kind of early for Christmas music."

Ignoring my remark, she kept singing.

Police headquarters was located on the town square. While I was growing up, the most prestigious shops were situated here. Now they had all moved to the mall on the south side of town, and no businesses had taken their places—save a few pawnshops and check-cashing services. There had once been two popular movie theaters downtown —one at which I'd worked during a high school summer, selling popcorn tossed in putrid, butter-colored oil. One theater was still there, but instead of mainstream family features, it now showed borderline porno flicks. The other theater building was boarded up. Two of the three banks still had their headquarters on the square, but their Rococo-style buildings had been imploded and replaced with bigger, boxy, modern structures. Much of their business was now conducted at branch offices.

Parking was no longer at a premium downtown. The banks had razed nearby buildings to install parking lots, and the metered spots around the wooded square were seldom occupied. Right in front of the courthouse, we slid into a parking place with time on the meter.

I walked around to unfasten my mother's seat belt and help her out of the car. An aroma of roses wafted from the blooming bushes lining the sidewalk that led to the courthouse steps. Two Wells was almost as famous for its roses as another East Texas town—Tyler, Texas.

"Can you stay for the Rose Parade?" my mother asked, referring to the city's annual October tradition. "We could go to the Queen's Tea together."

To be on the safe side, I dropped a quarter in the meter and twisted the dial. "We'll see."

Every year one of the town's richest families bought their teen-aged daughter the title of Rose Queen. Her duties consisted of hosting the Queen's Tea for the public in the Two Wells Rose Gardens and riding on a flower-covered float in the Rose Parade, surrounded by elegantly gowned ladies-in-waiting aspiring to become future Rose Queens. The year after I left for college, my former classmate Mary Lynn Hodges—oil heiress and the future Mrs. Keith Matthews—served as Rose Queen. The following year, the queen was Sally Jenkins, great granddaughter of the other main founder of Two Wells, and Mary Lynn's most hated rival. My mother had sent me both newspaper clippings.

I glanced at my watch. We were right on time for our appointment with Keith Matthews. I helped my mother up the white marble courthouse steps. How frail she had become!

"Michelle DePalma and Lola Hanson to see Keith Matthews," I told the officer at the front desk. He pointed down the hallway to an open doorway.

I felt like a guest on an episode of *Law and Order* as my mother and I took seats around a polished wooden table in the small, bleak interrogation room with Keith Matthews and Greg Dobbins. "Mrs. Hanson," Keith began. "Can you tell us what you did yesterday afternoon?"

My mother pushed back a wisp of her flyaway white hair. "It's hard for me to remember what happens from one day to the next. Since my husband died...." She batted her eyes at the police officers.

"Try to remember, Mrs. Hanson," Greg prodded. "Concentrate. It's yesterday we're talking about."

My mother's pencil thin eyebrows knitted together. She looked at me. "Michelle arrived yesterday. Didn't you, dear?" She looked at the police with more assurance. "My daughter came to visit me yesterday. She drove all the way from Atlanta."

Actually, I had flown to the Dallas/Fort Worth airport and rented a car, but how I got from Atlanta to Two Wells was immaterial.

"Tell us about your caregiver, Mrs. Hanson," Keith said. Do you remember a woman coming over to take care of you?"

"Those people! They won't get out of my house!"

Greg curled his lip, reminding me again of a large rodent. "Ma'am, do you remember seeing a young woman named Brittany Landers yesterday?"

My mother took a deep breath and leaned forward. "Those people won't get out of my house! They mess up my kitchen, cook smelly food, they spread their things out all over my couch, and they never lift a finger to help me clean the place up. I'm afraid to leave; they might steal something. Will you help me get them out?"

I eyed my mother. She had voiced fear several times that the aides would steal from her. Was it just her suspicious nature? I had never noticed anything missing, but amid all the clutter in the house, who could really tell? Once last spring, I had discovered a series of 900-number calls on her telephone bill, but the aide who had placed them had been fired and the agency had allowed us to deduct the charges from their invoice.

"Michelle, what's she yammering about?" Greg snarled. "I thought you were going to help us get a statement from her today."

Keith tried another tactic. "Mrs. Hanson, what time did Brittany come over yesterday? Do you remember when she arrived?"

My mother looked him in the eye. "I told you, I don't know anyone named Brittany."

"Maybe you didn't know her name," Keith acknowledged. "It sounds like a lot of different aides from this agency pass through, and it's probably hard to remember them all. But can you recall a twenty-year-old white girl who comes over sometimes? Blond, shoulder-length hair? Thin? She was there yesterday."

"Humph," my mother sniffed. "She's sassy and disrespectful. Always having company." She touched her hair again. "Especially that long-haired guy. They fight a lot."

"The long-haired guy. What is his name?" Keith asked.

"How am I supposed to know? She never introduced me. Kids today have no manners."

"But do you hear what she calls him?" Keith pressed.

My mother started to cough. Her bony shoulders shook. I reached to pat her on the back like she used to do to me when I was young, even though I knew it didn't help stop the coughing.

When her coughing fit ended, Keith repeated his question, "Did you ever hear what name she calls him?"

"Who?"

"The long-haired boyfriend."

"Who has a long-haired boyfriend? Michelle is married now. Her husband Roberto is a pilot, and he can't have long hair. They won't even let him have a beard." She turned to me. "Michelle, you don't have a boyfriend, do you?"

I pressed my face into my hands.

"Brittany's boyfriend," Keith said patiently. "You know, the long-haired guy you said used to come visit your caregiver. The white girl."

"Oh, him. He doesn't come around any more. They broke up."

"So he wasn't there yesterday?"

"Who?" My mother coughed again; her fragile frame shook. I made a mental note to stop at the pharmacy on our way home to buy some cough syrup.

When the coughs had subsided, Greg picked up the questioning again. "Mrs. Hanson, did anyone come over yesterday to visit your sitter, Brittany Landers? Does she ever have friends over while she's working?"

My mother fluffed her hair. "How would I know? I wasn't home."

Greg glared at me, then looked back at my mother. "Where were you, Mrs. Hanson?"

"I was doing my laps. I go swimming at the Y every day."

"Mom," I said gently. "You haven't been to the YMCA since before your surgery last December."

My mother's face darkened. "I haven't?" She repeated the words, minus the question mark, "I haven't." Tears welled in her bright hazel eyes and she bit her lip. I caught a glimpse of the pain she must be feeling at the loss of an activity she had once loved.

Greg cleared his throat. "So, Mrs. Hanson, you weren't at the YMCA after all. Did you leave the house at any time?"

"I…I don't think so." She brushed a tear from her cheek with the back of her hand. I touched her shoulder.

"You would have known if someone came over?" Greg continued.

My mother's face went blank, like a TV screen whose signal had been interrupted.

"Mrs. Hanson, did you have a disagreement with Brittany Landers yesterday?" Greg pressed on.

"Who?"

Greg's lip twitched. "Mrs. Hanson, we just told you: Brittany Landers was your caregiver, and she got whacked yesterday in *your* house. And it's beginning to look a lot like you're the one who did it. Now unless you can start giving me some straight answers, there's going to be a nice little jail cell with your name on it."

I jumped to my feet. "Greg Dobbins! She's 77 years old, and she's recovering very slowly from major surgery she had last winter. Look at her! She couldn't possibly have killed anyone." I cast a look at Keith, who seemed the more sensitive of the two. "We're trying to cooperate with your investigation, but this is confusing for her."

As if on cue, my mother started coughing again. Keith reached into his pocket. "I have some cough drops. Want one?"

"Thank you." I took the cough drop from Keith, unwrapped it, and placed it in my mother's mouth as if she were a child.

Greg glanced at his watch and sighed loudly. He turned back to my mother, who was sucking on the cough drop. "Mrs. Hanson, how do you feel about Brittany Landers? Did you want to see her dead?"

"She's terrible! I wish she'd go..." The cough drop slipped down my mother's throat as she spoke. Her face reddened and her eyes widened.

"Mom! Are you choking?" I turned toward her, put my hand on her arm.

Keith bolted up, brushed me aside and, bracing against Mom's fragile frame, gave her a couple thrusts under the diaphragm. The cough drop dislodged and hurled from her mouth. He picked it up and tossed it into a nearby trashcan.

"Thanks," I murmured to Keith, trembling as I smoothed my mother's wispy white hair away from her face.

"By the way, Michelle." Greg turned his attention to me while my mother recovered from her near-choking experience. "What time did you say *you* arrived at the house?"

It took me a second to register that he had plunged back into interrogation mode. "About two o'clock."

"What time did your flight get in?"

"Eleven-thirty. Check with the airline if you need an exact time." I could guess where he was going with this line of questioning.

"Did you stop anywhere along the road? Any purchases? Witnesses who might be able to corroborate your story?"

"I stopped for gas at the Race Trac right off I-20."

"Got a receipt?"

"I probably do." Luckily, I had paid at the pump with a credit card. I reached into my purse and fumbled for the receipt. I came up instead with the business card of Mary Lynn Matthews. "I found this in the front planter last night." I handed the card to Keith. "What was your ex-wife's business card doing in my mother's yard?"

Keith's expression was illegible. Surprise? Discomfort? He examined the card and tucked it into his pocket. "She just got her real estate license, and she's been handing those cards out like crazy. Who knows?"

"That's it?"

Keith averted his eyes, but he must have seen the incredulous look on my face. "I'll check it out."

Greg tapped his fingers on the table. "You were going to show me a gas receipt?"

I retrieved the receipt from my purse and handed it to Greg. "Want to see the credit card I used, too?"

Examining the time stamp on my gasoline receipt, Greg cleared his throat again, a barbaric sound. "So, Michelle, it looks unlikely that you had time to murder Ms. Landers. But Mrs. Hanson had motive and opportunity. Not to mention her fingerprints were all over the murder weapon, along with the victim's."

"Of course her fingerprints were on the pagoda!" I snapped. "She's owned it for over 70 years."

"If she would just tell us what happened, life would be easier for all of us." Greg shook his head. "I'd bring in the police psychologist to talk to her, but he's out of town until Tuesday."

Psychologist? I squeezed my eyes shut, wishing I could open them to a change of scenery.

"We're still interviewing neighbors," Keith said. He had recovered his professional demeanor since seeing the business card with his ex-wife's name printed on it. "So far, we haven't found anyone who admits seeing anything, but we'll keep trying. We're also trying to get a lead on the boyfriend from the victim's family and the women at the agency where Brittany worked. At least one of them should be able to identify the guy." He rose and motioned for us to rise as well. "You'll be around for a while, won't you Michelle? Until we get this matter cleared up?"

I nodded grimly. How would I ever convince them my mother was not a killer?

Chapter Five

My mother shuffled up and down the brightly lit aisles of the drug store and, like a toddler, grabbed items off the shelf, and set them down elsewhere. “Mom!” I cried, as I watched her fumble with a large glass container of bath salts, coming perilously close to dropping it on the shiny tile floor. “Put that back! All we’re getting is cough syrup.”

I located the cough syrup and then we negotiated our way through the minefield to the cash register. The young cashier had a pierced eyebrow threaded with a silver ring; looking at it made my own eyebrow hurt. My mother picked up the bottle just as he scanned it with a flash of laser light. “So expensive! *Five dollars*!”

“Don’t worry about it, Mom, I’m paying for it.” I slid my credit card through the reader and the cashier put the cough syrup in a white plastic bag.

“I can’t let you pay for it, Michelle,” my mother argued. “You’re buying it for *me*.” Her high-pitched voice was loud enough for everyone in the store to hear. “Let me give you some money. Where’s my purse?” She patted her sides. “Where’s my purse? Someone stole my purse!”

“Your purse is in the car.” I took the bag from the cashier and steered my mother outside. “It’s done, Mom. Let’s go home.”

“How about some lunch?” I asked as we walked through the door from the garage into the kitchen. With the aides gone and the television off, only the low hum of the refrigerator broke the silence.

“No, thank you, I’m not hungry. But you go ahead, Michelle.” My mother crossed the kitchen floor and entered the family room, plopped into her favorite armchair and stared at the dark television set.

"Mom, you need to eat something. You didn't have breakfast."

Her eyes started to tear and I recognized the same childish expression I'd glimpsed in the drug store. "I don't want anything!"

I rummaged in the refrigerator and the cupboards. There was not much selection, and I wasn't sure how long some of the food had been around. We should have stopped at the grocery store as well. "How about eggs, Mom?"

"Maybe later." She picked up the TV guide.

I began to prepare scrambled eggs with cheese, runny, the way she used to like them. For myself, I toasted a cheese sandwich. Her old push-button General Electric stove made it a challenge to regulate the heat, unlike the modern six-burner gas stove in my Atlanta home. As I tried to create workspace on her yellow Formica counter, pushing aside appliances, dishes, pots, and pans that had overflowed the cabinets, I longed for my own spacious granite countertops.

I set places for two, first clearing aside stacks of magazines, travel brochures, and mail I would have to sort through later. The table wobbled slightly as I wiped it off. My mother had bought this deluxe card table on sale at K-Mart ten years ago—a reflection of her depression-era frugality—when the breakfast bar had become too cluttered to eat on. We had an antique wooden leaf dining table in the living room—piled high with *things*—but I could count on one hand the number of times we had used it over the years.

My mother had turned on the television to her favorite soap opera. She kept up with the characters as if they were players in her own life. "Amber's not going to tell Rich she's pregnant," she muttered, eyes glued to the screen.

"Lunch is ready, Mom. Want to come to the table?" I set her plate of eggs on a placemat and then helped her out of her armchair. She followed me without protest and eased onto a folding chair at the glorified card table.

"You made this?" She smiled, gazing at the plate of eggs. "Looks delicious! Just the way I like my eggs."

"Take a bite," I prodded, stifling a smile at her compliment.

She lifted her fork and looked over at my plate. "Why aren't you having any?"

"Mom, I don't eat eggs. Remember?"

"Oh...are you allergic?" My mother had never been able to grasp that I cannot stand eggs, her favorite food.

"I just don't like them," I reminded her. I bit into my grilled cheese sandwich. The sharp cheddar cheese failed to cover the taste of freezer-burned bread.

"You don't like eggs? How could anyone not like eggs?"

"Eat yours before they get cold." She was doing a good job of moving them around her plate with her fork, but I hadn't seen any food reach her mouth yet.

"Oh no! Rich is going to find out!" Her eyes strayed to the television, her plate all but forgotten, fork frozen in mid-air.

I set down my sandwich and moved to her side. I loaded a small bite of disgusting undercooked scrambled eggs onto the tines and lifted the fork toward her mouth. "Open up, Mom." Like feeding a baby in a high chair.

She obeyed, let me slip a bite of egg into her mouth. She chewed slowly. "Mmm...delicious." She smiled. "Just the way I like it."

I sat down. "Then eat some more."

She chewed for a long time, then swallowed. A speck of yellow appeared at the corner of her mouth. Her eyes drifted back to the television, which had gone to commercial.

"Ready for another bite?"

"I don't have to eat it all, do I? It's too much."

"Mom, it was one egg!"

She sighed. Fiddling with her fork, she managed to distribute egg around on the plate, like my brother and I used to do when we were children, to make it look like we had consumed more of a food we were being forced to eat.

"Mom, you're going to waste away! Look at how thin you've gotten."

She smiled. "Gotta watch my figure. Don't want to get too fat."

"Well, you're in no danger of that." I returned to her side and loaded another forkful. "Come on, eat some more. You said it was good." I raised the fork level with her mouth, where it hovered like a bee at the entrance to a hive.

But this time, she pressed her lips together tightly, barring the fork's entry. Bits of egg tumbled from the fork and spattered against her mouth. She shook her head.

"Mom, open up. You need to eat more."

She squealed like a fussy two-year-old being forced to take a pill.

"One more bite. Please!"

Grudgingly, she parted her lips and allowed the fork to enter her mouth. Yellow and white particles churned in her mouth, sticking to her teeth and tongue. This time it took her even longer to chew the small bite I had given her.

I sat down and ate the rest of my now-cool sandwich, leaving the tough bread crusts.

Mom finished chewing and stared at the television again. "May I be excused?"

"Whatever happened to cleaning your plate? You never used to let Mark and me leave the table until we'd eaten everything on our plate. Remember that time when I was nine and I wouldn't eat my omelet? You saved it for me all day and wouldn't even let me have spare ribs for dinner that night until I finally ate it." I could still taste the vile, rubbery blob as I choked it down my throat, probably the last egg I ever ate. At the time, I had hoped it had become contaminated with bacteria and that I would die from food poisoning, which would serve my parents right for torturing me, and they would be racked with guilt for the rest of their days.

"I'm sorry." My mother looked at me and then plunged her fork into her scrambled egg, loading another miniscule bite and lifting it to her lips.

The doorbell rang. "Are you expecting anyone?" I asked, rising. Maybe the Loving Care Agency had reconsidered.

The ammonia residue tickled my nostrils as I crossed the entryway to the front door. I peered through the peephole.

On the porch stood a pretty, olive-skinned woman in her late twenties or early thirties, with lustrous ringlets of chestnut hair flowing halfway down her back, accompanied by a lighter-skinned girl who appeared to be about ten years old, her light brown hair neatly braided. They were so nicely dressed, I wondered if they could be Jehovah's witnesses—not something I wanted to deal with at the moment. I cracked the door enough to reveal my face. "May I help you?"

"Michelle Hanson?" the young woman asked. She had emerald eyes framed with long, dark lashes.

"Yes?" I opened the door a little more. Jehovah's Witnesses usually didn't address you by name. Maybe these two were from the Loving Care Agency—although most of those people knew me as Michelle DePalma.

"Wow, you look so young!" she cried. "So pretty!"

I was not sure how to react. Why was she expecting Michelle Hanson to be an old crone?

The young woman recovered and held out a smooth hand. "I'm Isabella Rogers, and this is my daughter, Giovanna." She spoke with a slight accent I could not place.

I smiled and nodded at the child, still wondering why they had come and what they wanted, totally unprepared for the bomb about to explode.

Isabella took a deep breath and looked me straight in the eye. "I'm your daughter-in-law."

Chapter Six

"Daughter-in-law?" I echoed. The words stung like a blast of wind had slapped my face. "I don't have a... You must have the wrong house." I started to close the door, but my hand trembled and would not accept the commands my brain was sending.

"Does March 5, 1971, mean anything to you? The Claudia Crichton Home for Unwed Mothers in Houston?"

I froze. I had only been seventeen at the time; no one was supposed to know except my immediate family—my parents and Mark—and we never *ever* spoke of it. It was the one secret I had kept from Roberto. "What...?" My voice cracked.

For over thirty years, I had willed myself not to dwell on the tiny, perfect baby I had held in my arms only once. I had tickled the soft soles of his miniature feet, and he had responded. For that one ten-minute visit before they took him away forever, we had been mother and son. Besides the chance at a better life, my gift to him had been a pair of red booties I had knitted at the unwed mothers' home during my pregnancy. Every now and then—especially around March 5—I'd fantasize that he'd search for me, produce those booties as proof of our connection, and I'd try to imagine what I'd say to him. But in every imagined scenario, my confrontation was with *him*, not with some woman who claimed to be... "Who *are* you?"

"Jean-Paul was what you named him, wasn't it? I'm his wife. Widow, actually. He was killed in the Gulf War. 1991."

"Killed?" I croaked. It was as if this woman had inflated a balloon with an intricate drawing on it, and then popped the balloon in my face before I'd had a chance to look at the picture. The tiny boy I had held in my arms—whom I had named Jean-Paul, though I'd been told his adoptive parents would most likely change it—had grown up to be a soldier, had given his life for his country, and now he was gone forever. All my fantasies of a reunion would never come true. A tsunami of loss swept over me.

But why was this woman here? And why *now* if my son had died ten years ago? Taking a deep breath to help me digest the news, seek answers before succumbing to emotion, I asked, "What do you want from me?"

"May we come in? It's a little cool out here." Numb, I stepped aside and allowed them to enter. This was not a conversation for the front porch. Isabella continued, "Giovanna is Jean-Paul's daughter, your granddaughter. She's ten."

Giovanna wore a turquoise ring on her pinkie; the stone matched her eyes, which sparkled as she assessed me. For over thirty years, I had been pretending I had no offspring. If Isabella was telling the truth, I was now studying the face of my granddaughter, searching for a resemblance.

"I know you must be in shock, Michelle." *Michelle*, Isabella was calling me. Not *Mrs. DePalma*, not *Ms. Hanson*, certainly not *Mother*. "I know I would be, if I were in your shoes. I'd want proof. I'd have a lot of questions. But I have papers," she assured me. "I can show you pictures. Wouldn't you like to see some photos of your son?"

"Pictures?" I asked. Isabella was empty-handed, except for a small purse strapped over her shoulder and, of course, the girl.

"In the car. I'll go get them. I wasn't sure you'd be home, or if you'd even see us." Before I could protest or offer assistance, Isabella was out the door.

I turned to my alleged granddaughter. "Uh... Giovanna..." Her coloring was similar to mine. Did that prove anything? Did I want it to? "Want something to eat or drink? A glass of milk?"

"Yes, Ma'am."

I still cringed whenever I heard someone address me as "Ma'am." I'd learned that southern tradition the hard way in second grade. "Michelle, have you finished your assignment?" my teacher had asked, hovering over my desk like a cloud blocking the sun.

“Yeah,” I replied, looking up from my doodling to show her my paper.

Her eyes widened as she leaned her plump face toward me. “What did you say?”

“*Yes*,” I corrected myself.

“Yes, *what*?”

“Yes, I’ve finished my assignment,” I added, making my reply into a complete sentence, arranging my pencils neatly on my desk so she could see I was done.

Amid the jeers of Greg Dobbins, Keith Matthews, and their band of tormentors, I was hauled off to the principal’s office, totally baffled about why I was there, until I received a lecture on southern manners. Mr. Dodd, the bespectacled little principal, glowered at me. “I don’t *ever* want to see you in here again, Yankee, or you’ll get the paddling of your life!”

When I got home and told my mother about the incident, she did not believe me. “What do you mean, he called you 'Yankee'? Just because we moved here from New York? No one would say something like that to a child! The Civil War was over almost a hundred years ago. What did you *really* say to get sent to the principal's office?” Because I stuck to my story, which she refused to accept as the truth, she escalated the issue to my father when he got home from work, and he spanked me soundly for being disruptive in class and then lying to my mother about it.

At least Giovanna knew the rules and thus would never have to experience such humiliation.

My mother had moved from the table to her favorite armchair in front of the television, and it appeared she had been dozing. I offered the chair across from her to Giovanna while I went into the kitchen to pour her a glass of milk. Our dirty dishes were still on the card table; on the way, I removed them and set them in the sink. I ran warm water over my mother’s plate to dislodge the drying egg.

As I returned with Giovanna’s milk, my mother stirred. She looked straight into Giovanna’s turquoise-tinged eyes and extended her hand. "Michelle! You're home from school already!"

I glanced at the built-in bookcase, where some of our family photographs were displayed. My eyes rested on one of Mark and me, smiling superficially for the annual Christmas picture, taken when I was about Giovanna's age. There was an uncanny resemblance between Giovanna and me—especially our eyes.

I handed Giovanna the glass of milk, its base wrapped in a paper napkin. "There, be careful; don't spill." Too condescending to say to a ten-year-old? My husband said it to me sometimes, when he brought me coffee in bed.

"Thank you, Ma'am," Giovanna said, taking the milk. If I had offended her, she did not show it.

"Mom," I said, "This is Giovanna Rogers."

A flustered look crossed my mother's face as her eyes moved from Giovanna to me. "Hello." That was it? No third degree, which used to be so typical of her. She picked up a stuffed white rabbit, a gift from one of her bridge group friends when she was in the hospital. The rabbit squealed when you squeezed its rear end, which never failed to elicit giggles from my mother. Grinning at Giovanna, she squeezed the rabbit.

Giovanna's face broke into a smile. She had a thin, white milk mustache above her full lips.

The phone rang. I found the portable on the arm of the couch after the second ring.

"How did it go at the police station?" Mark asked.

The police station. The murder investigation. Discovering I might have a granddaughter had eclipsed the whole mess. "Uh…the police station." This morning's drama seemed like days ago. "Mark, if she remembers anything about what happened, we couldn't get it out of her."

"Were you at least able to convince them she didn't do it?"

"Not really."

He let out a deep breath. "What now?"

"I'm not sure. The officers said they'd be in touch. They're still interviewing the neighbors and Brittany's family and coworkers. And Brittany had a boyfriend she used to fight with a lot, so he might be a suspect. No one has told them his name yet."

"Did she leave anything around the house? Address book, day planner, notes? Anything that would give a clue to his identity?"

"If there were anything important lying around, wouldn't the crime scene investigators have taken it?"

"Not if it didn't mean anything to them."

"I'll check." Phone propped between my shoulder and ear, I sorted through magazines strewn across the coffee table. Titles like *People*, *Cosmopolitan*, and *Ebony* definitely did not belong to my mother, but other than magazines, I didn't notice any personal items that might have belonged to Brittany or any of the other aides. With one eye I watched my mother and Giovanna; they were engaged in intense conversation, although I could not make out what they were saying. Should I tell my brother yet about my surprise visitors?

The doorbell rang. It was probably Isabella. It *had* to be Isabella. What mother in her right mind would abandon her child to a stranger—even if that stranger might be a blood relative? Not ready for a lengthy explanation, I said, "There's someone at the door. Let me call you back tonight. I'll keep looking and let you know if I find anything."

I hung up and moved toward the front door, tiptoeing around the spot in the entryway where Brittany's body had lain.

I opened the door, expecting to admit my newfound possible daughter-in-law. Instead, I found myself face to face with Keith Matthews. Isabella was nowhere in sight. I peered around Keith, searching for another car parked in front of the house. Focused on Isabella's amazing claim, I had not noticed what sort of vehicle she had arrived in.

"Michelle?" Keith followed my gaze. "Were you expecting someone?"

I straightened. "No, sorry." It would be too complicated to explain, and he wouldn't care anyway; it had nothing to do with Brittany's murder and thus the reason for his visit. "Come in. What can I do for you?"

Keith followed me inside. His nostrils flared, like a rabbit sniffing a pile of vegetation. “Smells like my friends from the crime scene cleaning service did a good job.”

“Powerful stuff,” I agreed. “No germ could have survived.” The ants had not returned either.

Still admiring the cleansed entryway, he said, “I was interviewing some of your neighbors about the case, and I thought I'd stop by.”

No use upsetting my mother by bringing the police officer into the family room. I led Keith into the living room and we sat down on the couch. “Did you learn anything interesting from the neighbors?” I asked. “I mean, anything helpful?”

“The woman across the street, at 2809, saw a late model SUV drop Brittany off yesterday morning. She said Brittany was yelling at the male driver, but she couldn't make out what they were arguing about.” He straightened his cap. “Frances Bradshaw, her name is. Said her son mows your mother's lawn sometimes.”

“What else did Frances say? Did she see anyone drive up later, about the time Brittany was killed?”

“No. And she was outside working in her front yard.”

A wave of nausea hit me. Shirley O'Keefe had also been working in her front yard and had not noticed an outsider arrive. “That doesn't mean...”

“Also, we found the boyfriend. His name is Terrence Miller. Brittany's sister had his number.”

“And?”

“Has an alibi. Says he's been working in Dallas all week. We called his employer, who vouched for him.”

“Did you ever ask Mary Lynn how her business card got here?”

Again Keith averted his eyes. “Not yet.”

“There have to be other suspects.”

“There's you.”

“Me?” I could feel the blood rushing from my face.

“I know the timing was really tight. But you could have walked in on Brittany struggling with your mother and taken matters into your own hands.”

“But I...”

"We listened to a recording of your 9-1-1 call, and you do sound genuine. I told Greg it was highly unlikely that you murdered Brittany. Involuntary manslaughter would be the worst we could charge you with."

"I didn't..."

"Michelle, remember that grasshopper that blew into Mrs. Wilson's class?"

"Mrs. Wilson's class? Third grade?" Why was he changing the subject like this when he had just implied I could be a murderer?

"Remember how the guys were all torturing it, and Greg wanted to stomp it? And you picked it up and took it outside, set it free?"

"Vaguely. Why?"

"I knew even back then that you don't have it in you to kill anyone. Not even by accident."

I was surprised he had remembered the grasshopper incident. I had forgotten until he mentioned it. "So I'm not a suspect?" Because of a grasshopper?

"Not at this time."

I shrugged, feeling less burdened now that he'd dismissed me as a suspect. "People change."

"Not that much."

There was a pause.

"But what does that mean?" I almost whispered. "You have no one but..."

Keith's brown eyes were sad. "Michelle, I'm afraid the evidence is pointing to your mother."

Chapter Seven

"My mother? All 90 pounds of her could wield that brass pagoda with enough force to kill a healthy young woman and then chuck it into the bushes?"

Keith's face softened. "I know it's hard to accept. The woman who raised you..."

"Accept? Who said I accept this?" There had to be some other explanation. I could not let them accuse my mother of committing a brutal murder. She had never even received a traffic ticket!

"Listen, Michelle. I'm here unofficially. Like I said, I was in the neighborhood conducting interviews." Keith twisted the cap in his hands. "But next day or so, we'll probably be back with an arrest warrant. I'm telling you this as a friend, to get you prepared, because I trust you not to take your mother and run away."

Run away? Not a bad idea; wish I'd thought of it first. But where would we go?

Keith studied his boots as he spoke. "Under the circumstances, she'll probably have to go before a judge to determine if she's mentally capable to stand trial."

"You think my mother's insane?"

"Not insane." He looked at me. "But from what I've seen, she has some serious memory problems."

"My God, in the last year she's had breast cancer, she's had to rely on strangers to take care of her, and our country's been attacked. She watched those airplanes hitting those buildings on national TV! Over and over again. And now a murder in her own home! Just because she's losing some of her short-term memory doesn't mean —" I stopped. My defense of her mental state sounded too much like my mother's denials of my father's alcoholism back when I was in high school.

Keith's eyes were kind as they looked into mine. He seemed much nicer now than he'd been in school. Or had I ever given him a chance? Did I assume that because he hung out with the popular crowd, he was required to snub the likes of me? Had I snubbed him first? "Michelle, when was the last time you took your mother to the doctor for a complete examination?"

Her aide Karen Jackson took her to the oncologist regularly, but I had no idea what else they checked. Karen usually reported to my brother after the doctor visits, and Mark didn't always discuss them with me. "Her caregivers have been doing it. But now that they've quit..."

"For your own peace of mind, go with her. Talk to the doctor. Find out what's going on." Keith touched my shoulder. "It's hard to watch someone who's been a rock all your life deteriorate like this. I'm not a doctor, so I'm not qualified to make this kind of diagnosis. But I had an aunt with Alzheimer's, and her symptoms were similar to your mother's."

"Alzheimer's!" The dreaded word had been spoken. The dam I'd been trying to plug with my fingers and toes had burst. Tears flooded my eyes before I could stop them.

Keith's arms encircled me. Even though I was embarrassed for him to see me cry, it felt safe to sob against his strong shoulder as I struggled to regain my composure.

"That's worst case scenario. She may not have Alzheimer's at all," Keith tried to console me. "Like you said, look at what she's been through lately. Cancer. September 11! That's enough to change anyone's worldview. Now a murder in her home. The memory loss may be her way of coping with it all." He massaged the back of my neck, which had grown tense.

I bristled. My husband had learned a long time ago that touching my neck was off-limits; it evoked memories of the time my long-time boyfriend, Percy, had tried to strangle me. But Keith had no idea of his *faux-pas*. I sniffled, gradually getting my tears under control, and raised my head from his shoulder. "I hope you're right. What will happen when they arrest her? Surely they won't lock her in jail like Greg was threatening."

Keith shook his head, not even attempting to defend his partner. “It depends on the judge. And the evidence we present. They may put her in a hospital or a nursing home with a guard, or they may release her to you on her own recognizance.” He rose. “If it’s any consolation to you, I’m having a hard time swallowing the scenario of your mother murdering Brittany Landers. I wish we could find some evidence to the contrary, someone else we could place at the scene. If only something could trigger her memory!”

“I’ll keep trying with her.” I felt revived as I escorted Keith to the door. “Look, it apparently happened here in the entryway. Doesn’t that suggest someone came to the door? Maybe someone Brittany knew?”

“Seems logical.”

“The door was wide open when I got here. My mother would never have left it that way.”

He touched my shoulder again as he stepped outside. “Our investigation isn’t over.”

“And I'm sure you're going to examine *every* possible clue.” I hoped he noted my indirect reference to Mary Lynn's business card.

Keith sauntered down the walk, climbed into his police car, and drove away. I was still standing in the doorway when the other car pulled up. A late model brown Grand Prix that resembled many I had driven away from rental car lots.

Isabella Rogers got out. She carried a large photograph album under her arm.

Chapter Eight

I held the front door open for Isabella. "Thought you said you'd left the proof in your car." Had she actually driven away, leaving her ten-year-old daughter with strangers? Was she that trusting? Or was it something else?

Isabella flashed one of those endearing smiles that makes it hard not to like a person. "I'm sorry. I thought I had the album in my car. Then I got outside and realized it was still in our...uh, room. I hope I didn't alarm you."

"I didn't have time to worry," I explained, as we made our way inside. "I had another visitor." I might as well tell her what was going on, if indeed she was family. "Yesterday a young woman—one of my mother's caregivers—was killed here in our entryway. The police are still trying to sort it out. One of the officers stopped by."

"Killed? Right here?" Isabella jumped aside, as if spooked by walking over the spot where a corpse had so recently lain. "An accident?"

I winced. "She was bludgeoned with a brass pagoda that belongs to my mother."

"Are you saying they believe she was murdered?" The olive coloring in her face had faded a shade.

I wondered how Isabella felt now about aligning herself with our family. In truth, there had not been this much drama here since I announced my teen pregnancy. "My mother was apparently home when it happened, but she's having a hard time remembering anything."

"You think she saw something?"

"It's possible. But if she did, no one has had any luck getting her to talk about it."

We entered the family room to find my mother slumped in her favorite armchair, snoring lightly, and Giovanna still seated where I'd left her. Her milk glass was empty. She was reading the aging paperback *Gone With the Wind* that had been wedged in our built-in bookshelf. It was my mother's favorite novel; she had bought me that copy when I was in high school.

"How do you like that book, Giovanna?" I asked.

With a smile, she held up the paperback to show me she had only read a few pages.

"You're welcome to keep it if you like," I offered. "I think you'll enjoy it."

"Thank you! She loves to read." Isabella watched Giovanna finger the yellowed pages of the thick paperback that was now hers. "So did her father. Giovanna, thank your grandmother."

"Thank you, Ma'am." Giovanna reopened the book and continued reading.

"You're very welcome," I said. Grandmother? That word would take some getting used to, and it made me feel as if perhaps I had cheated a bit, skipped some steps in the qualification process, like one of those people who purchases a mail-order degree and then claims to be a college graduate. I bent over my sleeping mother, her head rolling forward unsupported, and nudged her gently. She started. "Mom, want to take a nap? You'll be more comfortable in your bed." She let me help her up and lead her into the bedroom. She seemed not to notice our visitors.

When I returned to the family room, it seemed neither Isabella nor Giovanna had moved, as if the frame of the two of them had been frozen like a photograph, a surreal image of what might have been had I decided to take that other fork in the road, the one which would have required me to keep my baby and raise him to adulthood. Giovanna may have turned a page or two in the book, but her rapt pose had not changed. None of us spoke for an awkward moment, until I broke the silence. "Shall we look at some pictures?"

My heart pounded. For thirty years, I'd wondered what Jean-Paul was like, what had become of him, how he looked. Was I really going to glimpse the son I had given up? The photo album in Isabella's hands promised to hold the key.

Isabella and I sat beside each other on the couch, the album propped on Isabella's lap. Giovanna came over to join us, cuddle against her mother, but she brought her book and continued to read intermittently. She had probably seen these photos before.

Isabella opened the album and the edge of it touched my trembling knee. I couldn't make the shaking stop. A gold bracelet with charms of various animal shapes dangled from her wrist as she turned the first page. To defer the suspense I touched her bracelet and murmured, "Lovely."

"Thanks," Isabella replied with a wistful smile. "It was a gift from my mother."

The first page hit me like a power surge: an eight by ten glossy color photograph of a handsome young man in desert camouflage staring at the camera. His eyes were the same color and shape as Giovanna's. And mine. Hazel flecked with turquoise, framed with long dark lashes. Otherwise, he looked almost exactly like his father.

Percy LaRue had been about that age when I'd first met him, a regular customer at the drive-in restaurant where I worked part time during high school. He was new in town, living with his grandparents while attending Two Wells Junior College. A naïve 16-year-old, I was immediately and completely smitten. Several of my girlfriends and even Mary Lynn Hodges had competed for his attention, but I had won the prize.

Prize indeed. Three years my senior, he soon alienated me from my high school friends, convinced me that we were too cool for juvenile activities like sporting events, dances, and the prom. Instead, we spent a lot of time stargazing in the woods and making out in the back seat of his car. After about six months, I became pregnant.

I was never really sure how he felt about the baby. "You think you can trap me into marriage?" he'd shouted when I first broke the news. "You're an idiot if you think I'm going to settle down and change poopy diapers!"

"No, Percy, of course not. I know, you've told me over and over again, I'll never be good enough to be your wife. Besides, my parents want me to go to college, not be a high school drop-out teenaged mother like my cousin Candy."

So I'd found a home for unwed mothers near the University of Houston, where *Percy* had enrolled in college that fall. With my parents, we wove the lie to cover up my disappearance: that I was off to start college early. Actually, I finished my high school course work by correspondence, behind a swollen belly, surrounded by other teenagers in the same predicament. Percy showed up to see me most visiting days, if he didn't have another date. It was his right to date all the college girls he could, he rationalized; my inconsiderate pregnancy should not stand in the way of his quest to find the perfect woman--one who was truly worthy of him. The day I delivered our baby boy, Percy was nowhere to be found.

But after I signed the adoption papers, Percy raged that I had given away his son without his permission. I lashed out that he had had plenty of opportunities to change his mind, to keep the baby and change poopy diapers if that was what he had wanted.

"You would have made a terrible mother," he stewed. "I didn't have a choice."

After that, the pregnancy was a subject we rarely broached, a part of our past we put behind us as we moved in together and focused on earning our college degrees.

Percy continued to dominate my life all through college and even beyond. His perfect woman never came along, although he kept searching, dating other girls and expecting me to understand, yet exploding with jealousy if I even chatted in the hallways with a male classmate. As I grew older, his charm wore off, his insults stung less, and his threats barely fazed me. I longed to make other friends, participate in activities that did not revolve around him, declare my independence. When I turned 21, I started a full-time job and rented my own apartment, but still could not manage to cut the leash. Today, most people would assign a label to our relationship: abuse. Back then, I endured his verbal assaults as if I deserved them because of my inadequacies.

Six years after winning Percy, I woke up from the fantasy. I didn't love him anymore. I had grown weary of the prize. He did not take it well.

The last time we were together, Percy was straddled on top of me with his hands around my throat, thumbs crushing my windpipe, teeth clenched, a crazed look in his dark brown eyes. I thought my life was over, the price for admitting I had stopped loving him. I did what I had to and managed to survive. The next day, I moved out of my Houston apartment and left no forwarding address. Soon afterwards, I took a position in France as an *au pair.*

I tried to explain to my mother that she must never tell Percy where I'd gone. "Why?" she lamented. "After all these years, after all you've been through together?" My mother had always thought Percy made the sun shine.

"It's over."

"You're sure? What if you never find anyone else? You may never get married!"

No one else will have you had always been one of Percy's threats. "I can live with that."

"But, Michelle, what if he insists? You two should try to patch things up."

"Mom, he tried to kill me! That's why."

"Oh, Michelle." She sighed—her way of accusing me of being overly dramatic. "He must have had a good reason." She had said it jokingly, but I could not help thinking she really believed it.

Despite the resemblance, the photograph of the son Percy and I had created together did not trigger the suffocation I felt every time I thought of Percy now. Here was the beautiful young man, unscathed by Percy, with whom Isabella had fallen in love. I dreaded the inevitable moment Isabella or Giovanna would ask me about Jean-Paul's father.

I fingered the photo through its plastic cover. "When was this taken?" My voice cracked.

Isabella smiled. I watched her emerald eyes, full of love tinged with sadness. "Right before they shipped him off to Kuwait."

"How did he die?"

"His company got ambushed." She flipped to the back of the album and showed me a worn newspaper clipping about three soldiers killed in a skirmish with Iraqis, which, back in 1991, never would have caught my eye. The article did not even mention the soldiers' names—only the unit and base where they were from.

The telephone rang. I shuddered. This was not a good time. But because my mother never bought into the concept of owning an answering machine, after three rings, I went ahead and picked it up.

"Michelle!" sang the voice of Elaine Nelson, my best friend from high school. We had been estranged for decades—since Percy came to control my life—but had renewed our friendship after my mother's cancer diagnosis last year. "I heard you were in town." Her voice lowered an octave. "And I heard about what happened."

I assumed she was talking about the murder in my mother's entryway, which no doubt had been on the local news, not the revelation that I'd borne a child out of wedlock when I disappeared at the beginning of my senior year in high school. "Elaine, I..."

"How's your mom taking it?" During the last decade, Elaine had probably spent more time with my mother than I had, driving her to plays at the Civic Theater, stopping by the nursing home when Mom was recovering from her cancer surgery, running the occasional errand for her.

"Mom's a bit confused about it all. Can't seem to remember what happened." I thrust a longing look at the photograph album in Isabella's hands. "Elaine, I..."

"Well I can imagine! What a shock it must have been for her, after leading such a sheltered life. Listen, Michelle, why don't I come over and talk to her? She and I get along great now—maybe I can get her talking."

Elaine's implication that she had a better relationship with my mother than I did prickled a little. Besides, I wanted to get back to the photos of my son. "Now's not a good time, Elaine. What about tomorrow?"

"Sure. Will you still be in town tomorrow?"

"Yes. See you then." I started to hang up.

"And I want to look at the crime scene. Might be able to feel some psychic vibes."

Psychic vibes? What fad was Elaine into now? "See you tomorrow, Elaine." I cast an apologetic glance at Isabella as I set down the phone.

Settling back to the photograph album, I wondered how I would ever explain all this to Elaine. Even though bearing a child out of wedlock no longer carried the stigma it did when we were in high school, I still wasn't sure I could admit it had actually happened to me. Yet my keeping this secret tethered all these years seemed like a betrayal of our friendship. Maybe it was time to set the secret free.

I turned the page. There were wedding photos of my son in a tuxedo and a young Isabella, radiant in a long white gown. And the rest of the wedding party. "Which ones are his parents?" I asked Isabella.

Isabella pointed out a dignified, graying couple smiling adoringly at Jean-Paul. "They never kept it from him. That he was adopted."

"Where—?" The words died in my mouth as a loud thud came from my mother's bedroom.

Chapter Nine

I jumped up and the photo album slipped from my lap. Had the murderer sneaked in through an open window and attacked my mother?

Isabella followed me down the hallway toward the master bedroom. We found my mother sprawled on the carpet at the entrance to the adjoining bathroom. I rushed to her side. What if she had broken a hip? "Mom!"

She tried to lift herself, but she didn't have the strength to rise from that angle. She gripped my arm for leverage.

Isabella knelt beside us. "Careful. Let's make sure nothing is broken before we try to move her. Mrs. Hanson, does it hurt anywhere?" Her long nimble fingers made a quick scan of my mother's flailing limbs, and then moved to her torso.

"No, I'm fine. Just took a clumsy spill." My mother grabbed one of Isabella's arms and strained to raise herself, as if the two of us were pieces of a jungle gym. She eyed Isabella as she rose. "Nice to see you." Maybe Isabella reminded her of one of the Loving Care aides. I had a hard time keeping them straight myself.

Slowly we lifted my mother to her feet; thank goodness nothing seemed to be broken. I noticed the back of her sweat suit was wet. Her fall had prevented her from reaching the toilet in time. At least that was all the damage done—this time. "Mom, let's get you into some fresh clothes."

We undressed her like the big "three-year-old" doll I had had as a child. The wet pants came off first. Isabella spotted a box of Depends in the corner and showed me how to put the adult diaper on my mother's shriveled body. As a mother, Isabella had more experience than I did; I had never even changed a baby's diaper. And the aides had always been around to handle my mother's episodes of incontinence. I dug a clean sweat suit from the mountain of Mom's clothing piled on Dad's old recliner. It was identical to the soiled sweat suit she had been wearing, except a different color: a bright yellow. "How's this, Mom?"

I took her low moan as an affirmative.

One bony leg at a time, we slid her into the clean sweatpants. Gently we raised her hips and pulled the elastic waistband over the Depends.

She shivered as we peeled off the hot pink top, revealing her scarred, caved-in chest. Because of her age, no attempt had been made to reconstruct her breasts. With perfect teamwork, we slipped her skeletal arms into the sleeves and pulled the clean yellow shirt over her head, concealing again the hideous souvenir of her cancer surgery.

"Want to lie back down? Or come in the family room with us?" I asked when we had finished dressing her. Isabella found a comb and ran it through my mother's wisps of white hair.

Mom burst into another coughing fit like she had had at the police station that morning. Isabella put down the comb and braced my mother's shoulders as she coughed. She gave me a worried look. "That doesn't sound good."

"We bought some cough medicine." I turned around. "It's here on the desk." I pushed aside extra rolls of toilet paper and boxes of adult diapers to retrieve the cough medicine. Before I could open the bottle, the phone rang. I handed the medicine to Isabella and picked up the bedroom extension, an old black dial phone.

Isabella eyed the dial phone with amusement as I cupped the receiver to my ear. "Wow. Retro!" She poured cough medicine into the plastic measuring cap from atop the bottle and directed it toward my mother.

My mother's cough had subsided for a moment, and Isabella administered the medicine. I turned my attention to the caller. "Hello, Hanson residence." It was Bill Martinson, my boss from Atlanta, a voice that seemed to hail from the last century. Had I only been gone a day? Roberto must have called him.

"How are you holding up, Michelle? How's your mom?" To Bill's credit, he didn't say what he was probably thinking: *When can we expect you back at work?*

"We're fine. Did my husband tell you about the apparent homicide here?"

"He did."

"Well, it looks like I'm going to have to stick around until everything gets cleared up. May I take some vacation next week?"

"Of course. Take all the time you need." Bill was an easy-going manager. We chatted for a moment about my current projects. Just when I thought we were finished, he said, "By the way, about the promotion you applied for... I'm sorry..."

"I kind of expected that position to be rescinded." September 11 had changed everything; we both understood.

"Uh..." he was silent for a moment, as if searching for the right words. "We did fill it. And you *know* I was lobbying for you. But in the end, John thought Liza would be the best choice."

"Liza? Liza *Morrison*?" She was the little twenty-something know-it-all I'd been mentoring since she transferred into the department less than six months ago.

"It will be an excellent growth opportunity for her. She has great leadership potential."

"And I don't?"

"Liza said she's really learned a lot from you since she arrived, and she wants you on her team," Bill said.

Nauseated, I tried to keep my professional cool and not say anything negative about my former protégée, soon to be superior. "Thank you for telling me."

"Michelle? There will be other opportunities for you. You're our best designer!"

I was glad he could not see my face. "Listen, Bill. Are they still offering those leaves of absence? The way things are looking here with my mother, that may be the best way for me to go right now."

He was silent for a moment. "I'll check. Since John got promoted in the re-org, we're not sure what our headcount is going to look like."

"John got promoted again? Where's he going?" I resisted the urge to add, "Who did he sleep with this time?"

"Nowhere," Bill replied. "Just a title upgrade, to reflect his increased responsibilities since 9/11. Beverly announced it this morning."

"Please give him my congratulations." Soon, my inbox would contain a rambling e-mail from our Mimbo-boss, riddled with grammatical errors and buzzwords, laying out some new "action plan" and a revised departmental org chart and mission statement.

I was livid.

"Is everything okay, Michelle?" my mother asked, as I hung up the phone.

I sighed. "Corporations! You'd think the idiots would crash and burn once they rise to their level of incompetence, but they don't. They keep rising, lifted up by other idiots!"

Isabella bit her lip, and then burst into laughter anyway. She shook her head, holding up a hand in apology. "Sounds like you need a break from that place."

I took a deep breath. Maybe she was right. My petty whining about office politics must have sounded ridiculous. "Come on Mom, let's fix you something to eat."

"I'm not hungry." My mother allowed us to take her arm and lead her into the family room.

"You have to eat something," I insisted. "You had no breakfast, and you played with your lunch. How about I make fettuccini Alfredo? You love that."

Back in the family room, we eased her into her favorite chair. Giovanna looked up from her book with a shy smile.

"Do you and Giovanna have plans for dinner?" I asked, as Isabella fluffed a cushion and placed it behind my mother. "Maybe having company will disrupt her routine enough to trick her into eating something."

Isabella ruffled Giovanna's long hair. "How about it, kiddo?" Giovanna smiled in agreement, and Isabella replied for them both. "Thanks. We'd love to stay."

I started for the kitchen, and then remembered that Mom would not have most of the ingredients required for fettuccini Alfredo. "I have to go to the grocery store." Would it be a good idea to leave Isabella and Giovanna, basically strangers, alone with my mother? What if I got home to find the house cleaned out, or my mother tied up and tortured? Should we all pile into the car and go? Remembering my earlier trip to the drugstore with my mother, I did not relish the thought of controlling her in the grocery aisles while I tried to shop.

Isabella seemed to read my mind. "Why don't you give me a list of what you need, and I'll go get it?"

She was turning out to be a godsend. "Thank you, Isabella. That will be great." I located my purse, pulled out a twenty-dollar bill, and handed it to her. "Let me make a list. Mom, can you think of anything we need from the grocery store?"

My mother had turned on the television and was staring at some sitcom, giggling when prompted by the laugh track.

When Isabella had gone, Giovanna shut her book and joined me in the kitchen. "May I help you, Ma'am?"

I smiled, wondering if Giovanna was always so well-behaved—or just bored because there was nobody her own age around. There wasn't much to do yet with no ingredients—in fact, I usually didn't like help cooking—but I wanted to take her up on her offer, give us a chance to bond. "Let's see...you could help me set the table."

Giovanna dutifully wiped off the card table with the sponge I gave her and unfolded two more metal chairs to make seating for four. I located four clean plates and handed them to her. "Is that too heavy?"

She shook her head. As she took the plates, she looked into my eyes. "Why do you think people have wars?"

What a question for a novice grandmother, on her first day. Had reading about the Civil War in *Gone With the Wind* sparked her curiosity? Was she thinking about the father she had never known, stolen from her by war? Table topics, I thought, and took a deep breath, remembering my days in Toastmasters, practicing the art of impromptu speaking. *Madame Toastmaster, Fellow Toastmasters, Honored Guests...* "Well, Giovanna, there are lots of reasons people go to war. Boundary disputes, ideological differences, revenge. Sometimes they don't get along..."

The doorbell rang, saved me from finishing. I didn't expect Isabella back from the grocery store so soon, and I certainly hoped my police buddies were not putting in another appearance. "Excuse me, I better see who that is."

Through the peephole I did not recognize the dark-skinned young man in baggy pants and a backwards cap. I engaged the chain lock before cracking open the front door. "Yes?"

He pressed his face close to mine, his eyes so dilated I could not distinguish their color, his breath reeking of whiskey and chewing tobacco. "Where's that crazy old broad that killed my Brittany?" He raised the baseball bat he had been hiding behind his back.

Chapter Ten

I tried to slam the door and lock it, but the intruder rammed it, and the latch would not engage. I shoved hard, wishing I had focused more workouts on building upper body strength. "Call the police!" I yelled. "Mom! Giovanna! Call 9-1-1! Help! He's breaking in!" Adrenalin surging, I leveraged all my weight against the front door as my fingers fumbled for the deadbolt. Thank goodness the chain was holding, giving me a slight advantage in the arm wrestle with this madman.

The door jolted as he struck it with the baseball bat. Wood cracked against wood, like a croquet mallet sending away an opponent's ball. Taking advantage of his strategy shift, I slammed the door shut; the click of the latch sang success. I slipped the dead bolt into place. The house was old, but at least it was sturdy. He wasn't strong enough or clever enough to break the door down. I hoped he wouldn't realize this and go for one of the large-paned living room windows.

Giovanna appeared in the entryway, speaking into the portable phone. "He's still here. He's beating on the front door!" She looked at me. "What's your address? I remembered the street name, but not the house number."

Holding my position, even though the locks were now in place, I took the phone from Giovanna and gave the operator our address.

"There's a unit in the neighborhood, about a block away," the operator assured me. "They should be pulling up any minute."

The baseball bat pounded the door again. "Open up! Let me talk to that crazy old lady!"

My mother shuffled into the entryway. "What's all the commotion?"

Terrified, I motioned her away. "Mom! Go back!"

I thought I heard a siren. Was it real, or the television in the other room? The sound grew closer, and blue light seeped through the transoms, flashing across the ceiling. It was real! Giovanna and I peeked from behind the drapes and watched two policemen jump out of their cruiser. I placed a hand on Giovanna's small shoulder. "Nice job! You got them here in time."

The young man dropped his bat and dashed across the lawn. The officers tackled him, shoved his wrists into handcuffs, and dragged him to the patrol car. Giovanna whooped, "Just like on TV!"

One of the officers stayed with the offender in the cruiser while the other walked to our door. I let go of the drapes, moved away from the window, and went to unlock the chain and deadbolt. "Everyone okay in here?" asked the clean-cut young officer. I was glad he wasn't Greg Dobbins or Keith Matthews. I wasn't up to dealing with them right now. I gave him my statement about what had happened, along with my insight about why the young man might have felt a need to attack my mother. The officer did not seem interested in my interpretation of the perpetrator's motives. "Do you want to press charges, Ma'am?"

"I don't know." Pressing charges seemed cruel considering the man must be grief-stricken, determined to avenge the death of a woman he had loved. However, he had damaged our front door with that baseball bat, and he might have hurt someone had he forced his way inside. "What do I have to do?"

"Sign here."

When he had gone, I relocked the deadbolt and engaged the chain. My mother stood behind me again. "Michelle, why were the police here? You're not in trouble are you?"

I sighed, exhausted from the ordeal. "No, Mom. But Brittany's boyfriend tried to break into our house. The police caught him in the act and took him away."

"Who? Who's Brittany?"

I looked at her sharply. "Don't you remember? We went to the police station this morning and they asked you questions about Brittany and her boyfriend."

My mother scrunched her face. "Really? He was here?"

I touched her arm. "Mom, he seems to think you killed Brittany."

"Me?"

"But you didn't."

"I didn't?"

"Well, I don't think so. You didn't, did you?"

While she pondered her answer, there was a knock at the door. My pulse quickened until I peered through the peephole at Isabella, arms laden with groceries. I had almost forgotten my plans to make dinner.

"There's that Brittany now," Mom said, padding back to the family room.

I unlocked the chain and deadbolt to usher my newfound daughter-in-law inside. "Thanks, Isabella. Can I help?" I reached for a bag.

Isabella pointed to the door with her elbow as she relinquished one of the sacks. "What happened here?"

"Mama!" Giovanna squealed. "You missed all the excitement. There was a man trying to break in and I called the police and..."

Isabella's eyes widened as they met mine. I nodded and let Giovanna, eyes sparkling, recount the story to her mother as we made our way into the kitchen.

"Let me get this straight," Isabella said as she set the groceries on the kitchen counter. "This guy who was trying to break in was the boyfriend of the girl who was killed yesterday?"

Now I was not so sure. I had never met Brittany's boyfriend. "I assume so. He was yelling something, accusing my mother of killing *his* Brittany." As my fear abated, an uneasy feeling replaced it. In my mind, the boyfriend had been the prime suspect. But if he had committed the murder, why would he come here to rail against my mother?

"Judging from the damage to the door, it's a good thing he didn't get inside," Isabella remarked, as she helped me unpack the groceries. "But why was he going after Mrs. Hanson?"

"I guess I didn't mention it. The cops suspect my mother."

"Really?" Isabella folded an empty sack. "Why?"

"No one else was here when it happened. That they can find." My appetite for fettuccini Alfredo had evaporated after my struggle with the intruder, but I was determined to proceed with the plan to entice my mother to eat something.

Giovanna hovered behind me. "May I help you, Ma'am?"

"Want to wash mushrooms?" I held out the package, and Giovanna took it to the sink.

My mother, who had retreated to her favorite chair in front of the television set, burst into a coughing fit. I dropped the brick of Romano cheese I had just opened and started toward her, but Isabella reached her first and motioned me away. "I'll get her cough medicine," she said, as the hacking diminished.

I found a big saucepan and set it on the burner, dropped in a hunk of butter, and then began to chop garlic.

"Do you help your mother in the kitchen a lot?" I asked Giovanna.

"Yes Ma'am," she replied, picking up another mushroom to rinse.

"My mother didn't let me help cook when I was growing up," I said, remembering Mom's meticulous routine to put a bland but nourishing meal on the table at six o'clock sharp every evening. "My father was quite the gourmet, though, and I guess I inherited my love of *cuisine* from him. I'm not sure Mom ever really appreciated his creamy, wine-flavored sauces and delicately spiced marinades like the rest of us did. She was more concerned about the mess he left in thc kitchen." I smiled, remembering my father's culinary talents.

Giovanna brought me the washed mushrooms. "What do you want me to do next?"

"We need to start boiling water for the pasta." I handed her my mother's large spaghetti pot. "Here, fill this up—about three quarters full. Let me know if it's too heavy."

I laid strips of raw bacon on a plate between two paper towels and placed the plate in the microwave. The microwave was another piece of technology my mother had been slow to embrace, but in the last few years, she had done little cooking without it.

As we worked, I watched Isabella in the family room with my mother, giving her the cough syrup, comforting her, talking to her gently. "What does your mother do?" I asked Giovanna. "Does she have a job?"

"She used to work at the hospital in Houston. She's a nurse."

A nurse. I might have guessed, from Isabella's bedside manner with my mother. "What about now?"

Giovanna shrugged. "She didn't say how long we're going to be here."

"What about school?" I asked. Wasn't this a temporary visit? Isabella hadn't mentioned where they were staying. I had assumed the purpose of their trip was to find me, but maybe they were in Two Wells for another reason.

"I'm home-schooled," replied Giovanna.

My eyebrows lifted. I had heard about more and more children being home-schooled by their parents, but so far, had not met any of them. "How do you like that?"

"I liked it better with other kids around."

I tried to imagine that lonely existence. I'd met most of my friends at public school. I used to look forward to getting away from my parents; what if they had been my teachers as well?

I added sliced mushrooms to the pan, and we watched them sauté. Several minutes passed with only the sound of simmering. "So you haven't always been home-schooled?" I ventured.

"No, Ma'am."

I checked the bacon, rotated the plate, and returned it to the microwave. "Do you—"

"The water is boiling," Giovanna announced. "Want me to put in the whole package of fettuccini?"

"Sure. Thanks." I opened the cabinet below the breakfast bar where my father stored his alcohol. Because my mother was not much of a drinker, most of the bottles remained as he had left them nine years ago. I found an open fifth of brandy and doused my sautéing mushrooms and garlic. "How does your mother have time to work and home-school you? Isn't it just the two of you?" I examined the spice rack, seeking herbs that had not passed their expiration date.

"Smells wonderful," Isabella interrupted, as she joined us in the kitchen. "Can I do anything, or do you two have it under control?"

"We're fine," I replied. "Giovanna's been a big help." My mother's kitchen felt especially small with all three of us in it. "Want something to drink? Or something to munch on while you're waiting?"

"No, thanks. I'll keep your mother company. But let me know if you need me to do anything." Isabella retreated to the family room and sat in the chair across from my mother.

I sprinkled oregano and nutmeg over the sautéing mushrooms and turned down the heat on the noodles. Salted water gushed over the sides of the pot, sizzling as it hit the hot burners. "Ooh, I keep forgetting these electric burners don't work like my gas stove!"

Giovanna rushed over with a sponge. "We have one like that now."

I pushed the pot to a temporary new home on another burner and wiped up the hot water spill. Before I could respond to her comment about the stove, Giovanna replied to my earlier question. "I get lots of self-directed study. I guess that's how Mama does it."

I walked to the sink and squeezed the sponge. "I don't mean to sound nosy, but I've never known anyone who actually did home-schooling. Does your mother get official textbooks from somewhere? Lesson plans?"

Giovanna stirred the mushrooms. "I guess so, Ma'am. They look like the books I had last year, at the real school."

After testing the texture of the fettuccini, I slid the pot back to its original burner, which had now cooled to the lower setting. My home-schooling inquiry had reached a dead end. "So, Giovanna, what do you like to do besides read? Do you play any sports?"

"No, Ma'am." She thought for a moment before adding, "I like computers. And I like the beach."

I smiled, my thoughts transporting me to the memory of my honeymoon in Hawaii, with the sound of waves crashing against the shore, the smell of clean, salty air, and the feeling of wet sand between my toes. "So do I." From the refrigerator, I retrieved the whipping cream

Isabella had bought and set it beside the stove. "How are you at grating cheese?" I handed Giovanna the fresh brick of Romano.

I drained the noodles and carried the colander to my pan of simmering mushrooms and garlic. Although I placed a dishtowel underneath the colander to reduce leaking, a few drops of water fell on the floor. In the old days, when my mother was a meticulous housekeeper, she would have been furious; now, she probably would not notice.

I poured the fettuccini noodles into the pan with the mushrooms, stirring to coat them with the buttery mixture. I added whipping cream and a little more brandy, followed by Giovanna's pile of grated Romano cheese. "Want to stir a while?" I asked her. "Careful, this pan is barely big enough."

With Giovanna at the helm, I sprinkled nutmeg over the concoction, and then retrieved the bacon from the microwave, blotted away the grease with another paper towel, and crumbled it into the fettuccini Alfredo. "When your mother is working, who takes care of you?"

"My gran—" Before the words could leave Giovanna's mouth, she let out a squeal. A bubble of steaming sauce had spattered on her hand.

I grabbed a wet rag from the sink and blotted it off, caressing her small hand. "Did that burn you?"

"No." She did not take her hand away until I let go. "But I think it's done."

I poured the fettuccini Alfredo into a serving dish. "*A table*," I called. Two years living in France as an *au pair* and student had caused me to pepper my speech with little French phrases that did not seem to have an adequate English equivalent, and my family had grown accustomed to it.

My mother shuffled to the table set for four. "My," she said. "What a fancy dinner! Are we having company?"

Isabella helped her into a chair. "*Ça sent bon*," she repeated her earlier compliment about the food's aroma. "*Merci*, Michelle."

"*Vous parlez français*," I acknowledged.

"*Oui, un peu.*"

My mother looked from Isabella to me. "My daughter Michelle speaks French. She saved her money and then disappeared for two years to go to school in Europe."

When everyone was seated, I passed the serving dish to my guests and encouraged them to take generous portions. I started to serve my mother.

"No thank you, dear. I'm not hungry. This is too rich for me."

"Mom, it's made with all diet ingredients," I lied, putting a spoonful of fettuccini onto her plate.

A childish grin crept over her face. "Really?"

"No. But have you looked at yourself in the mirror lately? You can afford a few calories."

"It's delicious," Isabella assured her, with a forkful approaching her mouth. She took a bite, with a look at me to confirm her assessment of my *cuisine*. Giovanna nodded in agreement, her mouth full.

When my mother made no move to lift her fork, I loaded a small bite and moved the fork to her lips. "Open up. At least taste it. You used to love my fettuccini Alfredo."

"This is your famous fettuccini Alfredo? Guess I'll have to try some." She took the forkful of cream-coated noodles from me and shoved it into her mouth. "Mmm... good." She set the fork down.

"Have some more," I urged. "There's plenty."

"Honey, it's really not on my diet..."

"Mom, don't worry about your diet. Eat some more, for me." I prepared another small forkful of pasta and lifted it to her mouth. Our eyes locked over the hovering fork; she blinked first and took another bite.

I set down her fork and picked up my own to enjoy my food before it grew cold. My mother kept chewing, very, very slowly.

Turning my attention to Isabella and Giovanna, I asked between bites, "How long are you in town?"

Giovanna looked at her mother, who was still chewing. Isabella covered her mouth with her napkin and blotted her lips before speaking, "We don't know yet."

"But you plan on going back to Houston some time?"

Isabella's head pivoted toward Giovanna. "Maybe—"

A low gurgling rumble, like a volcano threatening to erupt, eclipsed her sentence. My mother's face looked drawn, and her hands grasped her throat.

Chapter Eleven

"She's choking!" Isabella sprang from her chair like a jack-in-the-box and beat me to my mother. Reaching from behind, Isabella pressed her fists into Mom's diaphragm and administered the Heimlich maneuver.

A slice of mushroom flew out my mother's mouth, across the table, and landed on the tile floor behind Giovanna. My appetite was gone. This was the second time today that my mother had almost choked to death in front of my eyes. Both times someone else had jumped in to save the day.

My mother was breathing again. She looked at Isabella. "I'm so glad you were here." She coughed, and Isabella handed her a glass of water. "Did my daughter call you?"

Isabella studied the pasta on my mother's plate. "Do you have a food processor?"

I rose and carried my plate and Giovanna's to the sink. A fork dropped. My hands were still shaking. "Maybe a blender." As I set down the plates and retrieved the fork from the floor, I spotted the old Vita Mix my father had bought at the Texas State Fair in Dallas many years ago, after a hard sales demonstration which promised the machine would pulverize whole pieces of fruit into a nourishing health drink. "We have this old Vita Mix, but I don't know if it still works."

Isabella carried her plate and my mother's into the kitchen. "Even though we consider pasta a soft food, your mother choked on it. We might have better luck feeding her if we chop it up."

"Like baby food?"

"Sort of."

I pulled the Vita Mix from behind a row of jelly-jar glasses, rinsed out the metal vessel, and then unplugged the toaster to free an outlet. Isabella dumped my mother's pasta into the depths of the Vita Mix, secured the top, and turned it on. Metal rattled against metal as the dormant appliance surged to life, churning the strips of pasta and bits of mushroom and garlic and bacon into beige mush.

"Leftovers?" Giovanna brought me the serving bowl filled with the remaining pasta.

I rummaged through the cabinets until I found a warped plastic container, which I handed to Giovanna, and a spatula for Isabella. She scraped the sides of the Vita Mix like an artist spreading her paint, arranging the fettuccini mush into a cereal bowl for my mother.

"Here, Mrs. Hanson, try this. I've chopped up your food so you won't choke on it." Isabella set the bowl in front of my mother and sat beside her.

My mother smiled. "Why how thoughtful of you, dear. What is your name again?"

"Isabella Rogers."

"And my daughter sent you?"

"Here, try the pasta and see how you like it." Isabella stuck a spoon into the mush and raised it to my mother's lips.

Mom complied, smiled again, and then took the spoon from Isabella. She ate about half the concoction without another choking incident and set down the spoon. "May I be excused?" She rose from the table. "I think I'm missing Golden Girls."

Isabella slid her chair aside so my mother wouldn't trip as she padded to her spot in front of the television. The phone rang, but although Mom passed the portable on the coffee table, she paid it no attention.

I picked up the black wall phone in the kitchen. With a glance at the clock, I knew it had to be my brother Mark, because I had promised to call him back and once again had failed to do so. "Has she remembered anything yet?" he asked me.

"I'll let you try talking to her again." I tapped Giovanna's shoulder as she bustled about the kitchen. "Can you get that portable telephone on the coffee table and take it to my mother?" To Mark I added, "So much has happened today. One of the officers came by again and suggested Mom might have Alzheimer's and be declared unfit for trial, some boyfriend of Brittany's tried to break in and attack Mom..."

"What? Slow down..."

"Hello?" Before Mark could finish his response, Mom was on the line.

"Mom, it's Mark," I told her.

"Michelle, is that you? Are you at the airport?"

I waved to her from the kitchen. "No, Mom, I'm on the other line. But it's Mark on the phone. He wants to talk to you." I quietly hung up the kitchen extension as they greeted each other.

Giovanna and Isabella had cleared the table, so I wet a dishrag and wiped it off while watching my mother speak into the phone. "Why yes, there's Giovanna. She's a lovely young girl who looks like Michelle did when she was little. And then there's Isabella—she chopped up my food in the blender so I could eat it." Holding the phone away from her ear, she looked at me. "Michelle, Mark wants to talk to you."

I set my dishrag on the table and walked to my mother's chair to retrieve the portable phone. "Yes?"

"What's she talking about? Are there really some other people over there?" Mark probably remembered my report a few months ago of a long-distance phone conversation I'd had with our mother, when she'd gone on and on about a stray Collie "we" had found and adopted. Later, after speaking with Karen, we'd learned there had been no such incident, no adopted Collie, not even a contact with a dog.

"She's right. Something else happened today," I confirmed, cradling the portable phone to my ear.

"I'm listening."

I walked down the hallway toward the privacy of my childhood bedroom, which my parents had long ago commandeered for storage. I sank onto the ultra-soft mattress; it wobbled like a waterbed under my weight. I thought about my old Barbie doll collection gathering dust under the bed; perhaps Giovanna would like to play with it some time. "Remember my last year in high school? When I had to go away?"

My brother was silent for a moment. I almost thought we had been disconnected. Then he whispered, "The baby?"

"Well, that baby's wife and daughter are paying us a visit."

Another pause ensued. Then a low whistle. "Where's *he*?"

My eyes misted. The shock was still fresh. "K...killed. In the Gulf War." If I had never given him away, could I have kept him safe? Might he still be alive?

Mark was silent for a moment. "Ouch. So you'll never get to meet him."

"No."

"How disappointing for you. You must have wondered about him all your life."

I shifted the phone to the other ear. "Mark, how can you say that? We never talked about it. Not ever!"

"That wouldn't have stopped you from thinking about him."

He was right.

"Michelle, remember when Smokey disappeared?"

"Of course."

"Even ten years later, you were still dreaming up scenarios to explain what might have happened to that cat. Why should I think you wouldn't do that with your own child?"

True. I had scanned the face of every upcoming young movie star, every violent criminal around the correct age, checking the birth date when possible to eliminate him as my possible long-lost son. When I was a flight attendant, I used to fantasize that Jean-Paul would be one of my passengers. Over the years, I'd been extra kind to young men who were around his age. During the Gulf War, I worried—correctly, it now seemed—that he would be called to fight, like so many of his generation. But I never imagined he would die before we could have our reunion.

"Does Roberto know?" My brother's question brought me back to 2001.

"I never saw a reason to tell him." That was a conversation I wished I could delegate to someone else.

"Michelle, how do you know these people are who they say they are? A woman and a child just showed up at the door?"

"She has papers. And photos."

"What papers? Have you looked at them?"

"We started to. But there have been a lot of interruptions."

"Get a good look at those papers, Michelle. What does she have? A birth certificate for him? And one for her daughter, with his name listed as the father? Do you even know what name he was given?"

"I think she has all that. I did see a picture."

"A picture? How would you know what he looked like? Be careful, Michelle."

"But what would they want? Why make up a story like this? We're not wealthy people." It helped to voice the questions I had kept in the back of my mind ever since Isabella and Giovanna appeared at my mother's front door.

"Have you looked at Mom's portfolio lately? It's gone down since September 11, but all those years of frugal living have paid off."

"Still, who would have known about the baby? How would they have found out?"

"What does Mom say about the whole thing?"

"We haven't really explained it to her. You know how she's become used to strange people coming and going; these are just two more. But this afternoon she woke up from a catnap, looked straight at little Giovanna, and called her 'Michelle.' That was eerie!"

"What were you telling me earlier? About the cop thinking she has Alzheimer's?"

"Keith Matthews. Remember him? He was in my class."

"Played football?"

"He's one of the cops working on this case. Stopped by earlier." I told Mark about Keith's aunt who had exhibited similar symptoms and his suggestion that we get Mom a check-up.

"She has a doctor's appointment on Monday. Karen should have marked the calendar on the desk in the bedroom. You'll take her?"

"Of course. I'll be here." My eyes panned my childhood bedroom, its bookshelf buckled under the weight of thirty years of my father's National Geographic magazines, as well as my worn college textbooks.

"I've been in and out of meetings the last couple days, and the kids have been super busy here, so I haven't had a chance to work on getting Mom another caregiver. Are you still okay staying with her a while longer?"

"Sure." My reply sounded more confident than I felt.

"What did Keith Matthews say about the murder investigation? Is Mom still a suspect?"

"Unfortunately, yes. No one admits to seeing anyone else enter or leave the house around that time. They found the boyfriend, Terrence or whatever, but he has an alibi."

"You said something about him trying to attack Mom tonight?"

I switched the phone to the other ear, feeling that young man's weight against the front door, the pounding of the baseball bat on the wood, as I related the story to my brother.

"Wow! How'd you get him to stop?"

"Giovanna called 9-1-1, and the police came. Almost right away, thank goodness. There happened to be a patrol car in the area."

"What was Mom doing all this time?"

Although I had heard my brother's question, my words rushed out to finish my thought. "The guy has definitely proved he's got a temper. And the strength to bash someone's head in. You should see the front door. But if he did it, why would he come here accusing Mom?"

"How did she react?"

"Totally in left field. Wanted to know why the police were here. Couldn't remember anything about Brittany. Every time someone mentions the name 'Brittany,' it's like the first time she's heard it."

"Michelle, do you think Mom's grasp on reality has worsened since September 11?"

I still could not erase the image of those planes crashing into the twin towers, the fear that it could have been Roberto's flight next, that horror footage on every television channel for days afterwards. "Isn't that true for everyone?"

My brother was silent for a moment. Perhaps he was replaying those same images, seeing those billows of smoke, the towers crumbling, remembering what *he* was doing when he first heard the news. "And she grew up in New York. I think that makes it worse."

"I should get back to my guests. By the way, Isabella's a nurse, and she's pretty handy with Mom. Think I should hire her?"

"If you get references. Maybe that's their angle."

"She hasn't asked for a job yet." The idea had just occurred to me.

"Michelle, be careful! Find out what they're up to first. I'll talk to you tomorrow."

I turned off the portable phone and rose from my spongy bed. I thought about calling Roberto, but then remembered he was flying a trip this evening, so I headed back to the family room. Water churned in the dishwasher.

Isabella and Giovanna had finished cleaning up the kitchen. It had not sparkled so much since my mother was a real homemaker. The ladies from the Loving Care Agency did a bare minimum of kitchen chores to maintain *status quo* in a house filled with clutter.

My mother was showing our guests the family photos on the built-in bookcase. Giovanna held one of my mother and Frank, the widower she had dated after my father died. Italy's Amalfi coast filled the background. My mother's face was full and glowing. The trip had been one of the high points in their relationship, and she had talked about it for months after they returned. "I don't know who that woman is," my mother said to Isabella and Giovanna. I froze in my steps, like a knife had pierced my breast. How could she no longer recognize this integral part of herself? Had it vanished completely? Or was it hiding?

"Looks a lot like you, Mrs. Hanson," Giovanna suggested.

Scrunching her face, my mother studied the photograph. "You think so? She's so fat!"

"Who's the man?" asked Isabella. "Is that your husband?"

My mother recoiled. "No! I never saw him before in my life." She took the photo from Giovanna and set it face down. "It probably belongs to one of those people. They're all over my house now. They think they can just put up their photos like they own the place."

Isabella looked at her watch when she saw me. "We should get going. You and your mom are probably tired."

It was late, and she was right, but I didn't want them to go. "But we've barely looked at your album." It still lay open on the coffee table. I also had not inspected the "papers" she had referenced earlier, but it seemed inappropriate to bring that up now.

Isabella shrugged. "I can leave it here if you like. We'll pick it up tomorrow."

Reassured by the thought of seeing them again, I walked my newfound relatives to the front door, where we said our goodnights. It was hard to believe we had just met earlier that day. "You know that was a picture of my mother you were looking at," I told them. "The man with her was Frank, a kind, fun-loving widower she dated after my father died. Frank dropped dead of a heart attack a little over a year ago, right before Mom was diagnosed with cancer. It's been downhill ever since."

Isabella nodded grimly, like she was talking to the family member of one of her terminal patients. She then threw her arms around me and I could smell her light floral cologne and a faint aroma of almond-scented shampoo in her mane of hair. Already, she seemed like a part of my family, and I hoped with all my heart that her claim was true.

After they drove away, I returned to the family room, where my mother had nodded off in front of the television like a hibernating animal. I nudged her gently and her eyes flew open. "Did you come to tell me good-bye?" she asked.

"Want to go to bed, Mom? You're falling asleep."

She allowed me to help her up and escort her to the bedroom. Before I could help her undress, she planted herself on the bed, drew the thin cover around her shoulders, and curled into the fetal position.

"Mom, let's get you changed." I pulled the cover off and tugged at her sweatshirt.

She jerked away from me. "I can do it! You're just like those people!"

Retreating, I held up a hand. "That's great." I opened one of her dresser drawers and pulled out a nightgown. "Here. Want to put this on?"

"As soon as I can get some privacy." Her eyes darted between the bedroom door and me.

I bent and kissed her goodnight. "I'm leaving. Call me if you need any help."

"Have a nice flight," she said, as I walked out of her bedroom.

Alone in the family room, I curled up on the couch with Isabella's photo album, which I hoped would unlock some of the secrets of my son's life.

Chapter Twelve

Telling my mother I was pregnant was one of the hardest things I had ever had to do. But the alien creature growing inside me was stubborn; try as I had—exertion, starvation, prayer—I could not miscarry. Roe vs. Wade was two years away, and only rich people like the families of Mary Lynn Hodges or Sally Jenkins could afford to send their daughters out of the country for an abortion. We had all heard horror stories about desperate teenagers trusting backstreet butchers to terminate their pregnancies, but I did not even have connections for that. I was stuck.

I dreaded telling Mom even more than I had dreaded telling Percy, but that part was over now. The prospect of telling my father still loomed, and I needed all the support I could get.

Mom was folding laundry fresh from the clothesline on the bed in my parents' bedroom. I watched her sort air-dried towels into neat stacks while she hummed a tune from one of her favorite musicals, *South Pacific*. After rehearsing my speech one last time, I picked up one of Dad's T-shirts and started to fold it. "Need some help?"

I never helped fold the laundry, and she never asked me to. She took the T-shirt from my hands, refolded it, and asked, "What's the matter?"

I gulped. The words tasted foreign as I spit them out faster than I'd planned. "I'm pregnant." I winced, waiting for the explosion.

She picked up a stack of my panties and handed them to me. "I was afraid of that."

"You—"

"You haven't had your period all summer."

Gross. Had she actually snooped through my trash can, searching for used sanitary pads?

She sighed. "Is Percy the father?"

I clutched the lacy panties to my breast. "Of course!" The same response I'd had to Percy's question, "*Is it mine?*" What did people think of me?

"Well, he's been in Florida for over a month."

A tear tried to sneak out of my eye, and I brushed it away with the back of my hand. "You know I haven't even been on a date."

Mom carried a stack of Dad's socks to the dresser, opened the drawer, and tucked them neatly inside. "First thing we need to do is get you to a doctor, so they can run a pregnancy test. This could just be a false alarm."

"I already did that."

"You what?"

"I took a pregnancy test on Thursday. It was positive."

"Where did you go? Not to our family doctor?"

"One in the same building. Don't worry, I paid cash and used a fake name."

"Fake name? What fake name? Why?"

"Why?" I couldn't believe I was the one about to speak *her* words, "What are people going to think?"

She made another trip to her dresser to put away more underwear. "People will know as soon as the baby is born and they count back to the date of the wedding."

I cleared my throat. "We're not getting married. We're not keeping it."

She stopped. "Percy won't marry you?"

The way she said, *"He won't marry you"* made me sound pitiful, and that statement was not entirely accurate. Percy probably would have married me, had I insisted. "I don't want to be like Cousin Candy. She dropped out of high school and married Sam when she got pregnant with Terri, and now look at her: an uneducated divorcee with a kid."

"A little late to be thinking about that now." Mom picked up the towels from the bed and headed for the hall linen closet.

I trotted after her. "I found an unwed mothers' home in Houston. If I pay for it myself, I can qualify as low-income, so I'll get room, board, and all medical and adoption costs covered for..."

She stopped in the hallway. "How did you find out about this unwed mothers' home?"

"Mrs. Lawrence at the public library helped me."

"Edna Lawrence? Linda's mother? We *know* her!"

"I told her it was for my cousin. I'm not even sure she recognized me; she hasn't seen me since I was in sixth grade. Anyway, I called the Claudia Crichton home, and they have an opening."

"You called... *long distance*?"

I gave her that exasperated look teenagers reserve for their parents when they are being particularly dense. "It's in *Houston*."

My mother placed the towels in the linen closet and shut the door. "That's where Percy's going to university in the fall, isn't it?"

"That way he can come see me. They allow outings twice a week."

"Percy's going to let you do this? Why doesn't he want to marry you?"

"Percy has to finish college. University of Houston is going to be tougher than Two Wells Junior College. He doesn't need the burden of a wife and baby. If he falls behind and has to drop out or take less than a full load, he'll lose his student deferment." Percy's birthday had drawn number 41 in the draft lottery, so the student deferment was all that stood between him and Vietnam.

"He'll be able to concentrate on his studies with a girlfriend in a home for unwed mothers?" I had followed Mom back into the master bedroom, where she continued to fold laundry. "What are you going to tell people? This could be quite a scandal for our family."

"I could say I'm going to live with Candy in Dallas, and help her with the kid."

"That would be a lie. And besides, what would we tell Candy and her family?"

"Say I'm going to Houston, which is the truth. People know Percy's moving there in the fall. Say I'm going to finish my high school courses by correspondence, which is also true, and then I'm going to start college early. People will believe that."

"What are you going to use for money?"

I swallowed. "I have more than enough saved from my waitress job."

"Your travel fund? For Europe?"

I had always dreamed of a trip to Europe after I finished high school. My parents had been impressed with my determination to save, and they had offered to match my funds when the time came. But since I'd been dating Percy, Europe had grown less important to me; he thought the whole idea was stupid. "Looks like I'm only going as far as Houston now. But if I don't tie myself down with a baby, maybe I'll make it to Europe some day."

Mom sighed. I think my trip to Europe was as much a dream of hers as it was mine. "We'd always planned for you to go to college..."

"I still want to go. And I should still be able to. Fall, a year from now, as planned. I might even be able to attend summer school next June."

"Oh, Michelle! The whole point of your going to college was so you would find a suitable husband, but you already have Percy. If you don't lose him because of this fiasco."

Percy had been in my life less than a year, but already, he was my world. I had learned to tread softly around my own needs to keep him pleased. "I'm sure to lose him if I force him to marry me and raise a baby he doesn't want."

"I hope you know what you're doing. No one else is going to want you after this."

I felt my breakfast rising to my throat. With a hand covering my mouth, I dashed to the bathroom and threw up. When I looked up from the toilet bowl, my mother was standing over me, offering a damp washcloth.

She shook her head. "Your father is going to be furious. He'll say it's my fault, because I've always been too permissive."

She gave me that line a lot. Permissive? Her? Compared to what? I had the earliest curfew of all my friends. "Will you help me tell him?"

Percy was invited for dinner that night. Mom cooked potatoes and rotisserie chicken. My brother Mark was away at Boy Scout camp, for which I was grateful.

We had decided it would be best to break the news to my father before he started drinking. But Percy was late, a habit of his. We were supposed to do this together.

When I saw Dad take the bottle of gin out of the liquor cabinet, it was time to plunge off the high dive. "Dad? Can I talk to you a second?"

He looked at me without stopping his cocktail preparations.

"I messed up. I didn't listen to you and Mom."

He set down the bottle and gave me his full attention.

"Percy and I..."

My father's glacial blue eyes bored into me as I spoke.

I gulped. "We didn't mean for this to happen, I know you gave me a lecture when it happened to Candy, but... I'm pregnant." I paused to assess his reaction, but his eyes registered no emotion. I continued, "Once I start showing, I'm moving to an unwed mothers' home in Houston, where I'll give up the baby for adoption. And don't worry about the cost: I'll pay for it."

He broke his laser-like gaze and looked up at the ceiling. "Well, I should hope so. Thank God for that."

"The name of the place is—"

"What about your education?" His voice was like a thunder clap.

"They have teachers there, but I only need three more credits to graduate high school, so I'm going to take them by correspondence. I've already ordered the materials. I might even finish before I have to leave for the home."

The doorbell rang, announcing Percy's arrival. My mother, who had been silent and neutral, slipped away to open the door. She returned a moment later followed by Percy, looking handsome and sophisticated as ever. My heart tingled and I flashed him a shy smile.

My father finished making his cocktail. He gestured toward the martini shaker as Percy entered the family room. "Want one? You're a man now."

Sometime during my confinement at the unwed mothers' home, I stopped hating my baby. The pronoun changed from "it" to "her," and even though it was not possible to learn the sex of the child in advance, I felt it would be a girl, and I named her Monique—because it sounded French, and I'd always wanted to go to France.

My closest friend at the home was Janet M. Her smile lit up the room and she made us laugh until we forgot where we were. She was about a year older than I, and three weeks more "senior" so hearing about the changes her body went through helped prepare me for what was happening to mine.

Most of the other girls were no longer dating the fathers of their babies, and few of them even took advantage of the twice-a-week visiting afternoons. I felt like a celebrity when Percy came to pick me up and four or five girls would peer out the window to catch a glimpse of him as we left.

"He's *so* handsome," Susan W. told me one night when we were on dishwasher duty together. Susan was a short, plump redhead who reminded me of my friend Elaine. "Are you going to marry him when you're older?"

I rinsed a plate and handed it to her. "I hope so." We both giggled as we loaded the dishwasher.

My seventeenth birthday arrived while I was at the home. My mother sent me a card with a note giving news about Two Wells, and the girls surprised me with a cake. I thought Percy would take me out, because my birthday fell on a visiting day, but he said he couldn't make it. Big test coming up, and a girl in his sociology class had offered to coach him.

Janet M. went into false labor twice. Going into false labor and then coming back from the hospital still pregnant was humiliating. It was like crying wolf, angling for undeserved attention. I was so afraid it would happen to me and I would have to endure the snickers of the other girls. I was one of the only people who talked to Janet after that. When real labor finally came, she barely made it to the hospital in time.

Janet M. was different when she came back to the home and moved into the "mothers' room," the special area where girls who had recently given birth stayed for their final week. Her baby gone, she was ready to leave the rest of us behind, as if she'd never known us. I was thankful when I had a moment alone with her and, with the familiar smile I had come to love, she pressed into my hand a slip of paper with her address and real last name. I wrote to her after I left the home, but I never heard from her again.

My baby came a week early. That surprised me, because my mother had warned that both Mark and I had been late, thus, my baby would also be late. I had never felt labor pains but I knew right away when they hit. The night nurse did not want to take any chances after the close call with Janet, so I prayed all the way to the hospital that this was the real thing. Before I left, I begged Susan W. to call Percy for me.

Labor and delivery were a blur. They say a woman doesn't remember the pain, because if she did, she would never have more children. All I remember was being surprised, and a tad disappointed, when they told me my baby was a boy, not Monique. I struggled to come up with another French name, and settled on Jean-Paul. I was told it didn't much matter, because the adoptive parents would change it.

I shared a hospital room with Cathy C., another teenage girl from the Claudia Crichton home. Her parents came to visit that afternoon and brought her a big bouquet of spring flowers. Cathy's side of the room was decorated with cards, flowers, and stuffed animals; my side was bare.

Cathy's father asked me when *my* parents were coming, and I said they didn't even know yet that I'd had the baby. At any rate, they lived in Two Wells and would not be coming anyway. I found out later from Cathy that her family had driven down from San Antonio.

When Cathy's father returned that evening, he brought a bouquet of daffodils for Cathy and another for me.

I felt tears cloud my eyes as I sniffed the daffodils, which I discovered did not have much scent. "Thank you! How sweet of you!"

Cathy beamed. "That's just the way my dad is."

Percy had gotten the message from Susan W., and he called me that night after visiting hours were over. He sounded a little put-out; as if I could have controlled the timing of our baby's birth. He said he would visit me the following day.

Unwed mothers were allowed one optional ten-minute session with their babies, and it had to be done before they left the hospital. I made arrangements to meet my baby during Percy's visit. Cathy C. was going to be holding her baby at the same time. But Percy never showed up. A nurse brought me the baby anyway.

I knew Percy would be angry, but because I had to check out of the hospital the next day, I could not forfeit this only opportunity. When the nurse placed the tiny bundle into my arms, I stroked his soft skin and gazed into his dark blue eyes, marveling at how I could have had a hand in creating this perfect miniature human being. I had not expected to feel such a strong connection with Jean-Paul. Too soon, time was up.

Back at the home, a celebrity in the "mother's room," I began to understand why Janet M. had become distant. The girls all wanted to talk, to hear about my experience, and I wanted to be polite, but I couldn't stand to look at their swollen bellies anymore. I, too, was different.

Not signing the adoption papers had never occurred to me, but I hadn't expected it to be so hard—so final. Before I left the office, I brought out the pair of red booties I had knitted for "Monique" during my stay at the home. "I made these. Can you give them to Jean-Paul?"

The woman set down her pen and examined my handicraft. "Nice work. But we can't guarantee which child will get them. Do you still want...?" She looked up and stopped speaking for a moment when she met my eyes. "I'll try to see that they go to him." She stacked the papers neatly on her desk and rose, signaling that our interview was over.

As I opened the door, ready to walk into the next chapter of my life, she said, "You're doing a good thing, Michelle. There are so many couples who want children desperately and are ready to take care of them. You'll have another one when the time is right."

I gazed back at the photograph album in my lap, full of pictures of a young man growing up, milestone moments I had missed. A young man I had created, but never got to know. And it had been my choice.

Chapter Thirteen

The dream was back. Underwater, I fought for breath, an anchor tied to my ankle. I kicked and thrashed. Through bubbles, I saw Percy's evil grin as he pulled my leg toward him, deeper into the mire, his coal eyes mocking me. I struggled with every bit of strength I could muster, expended my last bit of air, and broke free, propelled my body to the surface with a gasp.

My eyes flew open. The top sheet had become twisted around one of my legs. It was 2001. Percy was ancient history. Breathing normally again, I rearranged the bedding and tried to fall back asleep on the spongy mattress.

I tossed and turned, reliving the events of the day: Giovanna's timid smile, Keith's amateur diagnosis of my mother's Alzheimer's disease, the thud of the baseball bat against the front door as I tried to hold it closed. I heard my mother cough a few times, but the spells dissipated quickly. I feared she would try to get out of bed and fall, and I would not be able to help her.

The coughing started again, and then... sobbing? Barely audible at first, the sobs amplified into bawls.

I slid out of bed and hurried into my mother's room. She was lying on her back in bed, shaking, tears streaming down her cheeks, her eyes closed tightly. I touched her shoulder. "Mom, wake up!"

She jerked, blinked away moisture.

"Mom, what's wrong? Why were you crying?"

"Charles... he was taking me for a ride in a little airplane. We were flying over the island of Capri."

"Well, that doesn't sound like anything to cry about!" Although my father had been a pilot in the Air Force during World War II, he had never flown a plane afterwards, as far as I knew. Frank, on the other hand, had been a private pilot, and had taken my mother up in his Cessna several times.

"And then we started flying between the skyscrapers."

"Skyscrapers? On Capri?"

She bit her lip. "I said, 'Charles, what are you doing?' but he couldn't hear me. We started to fly straight into the building!"

I leaned down and embraced her. "It was a bad dream."

"No, it was real." She continued to sob. "There were big billows of black smoke, and flames lashing out like dragon tongues."

"Mom, you're remembering September 11. It was a horrible day for our whole country. But that was a month ago. You're home in your bed. You're safe. You and Dad didn't fly into any building." I smoothed her thin hair.

"Oh." She propped herself on an elbow and looked around the darkened bedroom. "Where's Charles?"

"Mom, Dad died ninc years ago. You remember, don't you?" Surely that memory would return when she surfaced from slumber.

She looked at me, her face flickering like an aging TV screen. "Did you know Charles was an alcoholic? I think he drank himself to death."

I rearranged the covers around her. She had not changed into the nightgown I had laid on her bed. "Yes, I remember he was an alcoholic."

"Sorry."

"It wasn't your fault."

"He could have lived longer if he hadn't been."

"Maybe." I glanced at the digital clock on her headboard, not wanting another conversation about my father's drinking. For years I had tried to tell her, and she had threatened to wash my mouth out with soap. "He's just a social drinker," she'd argue. To which I would reply, "Sure, that's why he drinks himself into oblivion every night in front of the TV—alone."

After I left home she joined Al-Anon. Once, when I returned for a visit, she took me to a support meeting and introduced me to her sponsor. I shook the woman's hand and thanked her for helping my mother.

"You're damaged, too," her sponsor had told me. "You need to join Al-Anon. Alcoholism destroys a family."

"You don't have to let it," I replied. "My father was there for me. He wasn't always sober, but he was there." The sponsor didn't talk to me any more after that.

My mother stared around her darkened bedroom. "Try to get back to sleep," I told her.

Her eyes fluttered. "There were people in those buildings. I could see them working at their desks, then running for their lives."

"Don't think about it any more. It was a bad dream. You're remembering what we saw on TV every day for weeks." I shivered, replaying the scene of commercial airplanes crashing into the World Trade Center towers that awful day. If only that had been a bad dream. My husband had been flying that morning, and I could still feel the fear like a rodent gnawing my insides, all those hours awaiting news that *his* plane had landed safely, somewhere in Canada, where he had to wait for days until the U.S. Air traffic system opened again.

My mother's breathing had become more rhythmic, though I could hear her congestion. She was drifting back to slumber. I sat on the edge of the bed for a few moments, watching her sleep, wondering when I had become the adult in this relationship.

Unable to sleep, I padded into the family room. I started to open the photograph album, but then I was afraid looking at it would make me dream about Percy again. Maybe reading would summon drowsiness. The day's mail lay on one of the end tables where I had hurriedly tossed it earlier. Might as well go through that first.

A brochure advertising a European vacation. An "official" notice of a million-dollar prize Mom may have won; just send a check for $19.95 to cover processing costs. I flung both into the trash. Electric bill, water bill—both within normal range. While our mother was in the nursing home, we had arranged for the utilities to be automatically debited from her bank account. This confused my mother when she first came home; she would open a statement and stare at the remark, "Do not pay."

She would wave her checkbook around in frustration, "Why would they send me a bill if they don't want me to pay it?" Now she didn't bother to open them.

The next envelope resembled one of those credit card solicitations I promptly shredded. But this one looked more personalized, and I recognized the return address as my mother's bank. I sliced the envelope with the letter opener and pulled out what appeared to be a loan application. A loan application? For what? Mom had everything she needed, and it was all paid for. I skimmed the fine print; they were returning the forms because some of the necessary data was missing. Several blanks had been highlighted with yellow magic marker. It was an application for a fifty-thousand-dollar home equity line of credit.

I studied the signatures at the bottom of the application: there was my mother's shaky handwriting. Over the blank for co-borrower, rolling cursive letters spelled "Brittany Landers." Brittany Landers and my mother applying for a loan together? No way!

I wanted to shred the papers. My brother and I had feared someone would take advantage of our mother's confused state and bilk her out of her life's savings. Obviously, the salary from the Loving Care Agency was not enough to satisfy Brittany Landers. Lucky for us, Brittany had been careless filling out the loan application. And now Brittany Landers was dead. We no longer had to worry about her stealing from our mother.

I eyed the incomplete loan application in my hands, the words in the terms and conditions swimming in a blur. The police would want to see this document, and I could imagine what conclusions they might draw. Evidence of a motive for murder.

Chapter Fourteen

Morning came, despite my inability to sleep. I had almost gathered the courage to phone Keith Matthews about my late-night discovery when my old friend Elaine Nelson showed up at the front door. I had forgotten she'd said she was coming over.

A flaming redhead, Elaine stood barely five feet and was about half as round; Roberto had once referred to her as "a fire plug." But she carried herself like a runway fashion model, miraculously managing to find clothes that flattered a small, stocky frame.

"Michelle!" she cried, giving me a hug. "What happened to your front door?"

"It's a long story." I bent to return her embrace and peck her cheek. I had missed my friendship with Elaine.

"You're looking good, Girl, as always. I hate you; you're still so slim!" she squealed. "And I love your hair short like that. Perky and corporate. The blond highlights look so natural." Elaine stepped back from our embrace to admire me and wait for my return compliment.

"Thanks, you look terrific, too," I assured her. "Can you believe we're pushing the big Five-O?"

"So how's your fancy job in Atlanta? What are you, Vice President by now?"

"Yeah, right." Elaine's hyperbole reminded me of the promotion I'd just lost to Liza Morrison. "Come on in."

"How's your mom?"

"Confused. She can't recall anything about what happened here the other day."

Elaine shuddered. "Is this where it happened?"

"Still gives me the creeps." As we left the entryway, I stepped around the spot where Brittany had fallen.

"Your poor mom must have been traumatized. Maybe I can talk to her." Elaine followed me into the family room. "Where is she?"

"She'll be out in a minute. Want some coffee?"

My mother waddled from the hallway as I made my way toward the kitchen to pour coffee. She had not changed her outfit from last night. "Coffee, Mom?" I asked her. "You remember Elaine, don't you?"

"Elaine! So nice to see you." My mother held out a wizened hand to my girlhood friend. "I'm so glad you and Michelle made up."

With a slight roll of her eyes, Elaine grinned at me as she shook my mother's hand.

"Boyfriends may come and go, but a girlfriend is forever," my mother continued. Her platitude dredged up the memory of how Elaine and I had competed underhandedly for Percy. I had won Percy but lost Elaine. And by getting pregnant senior year and leaving town, I had lost out on a high school social life. So much for winning.

"So, Mrs. Hanson, what's been going on here?" Elaine raised her voice although my mother was not hard of hearing.

My mother gestured around herself. "Can't you tell?"

"You've lost weight?" Elaine guessed.

My mother giggled like a schoolgirl, but shook her head, although she probably *had* lost weight since the last time Elaine had seen her. She leaned forward and said in a stage whisper, "They're gone."

"Who?" asked Elaine.

"Those people!"

Elaine looked at me as I approached, balancing three mugs of coffee: black for Elaine, cream for me, heavy on the milk and sugar for my mother. "What's she talking about? The police?" she mouthed, relieving me of the mug of black coffee.

"Michelle made them go away," my mother continued. She smiled serenely as I handed her a mug of coffee, the milk and sugar containing probably half her daily caloric intake.

"I think she means the aides from the Loving Care Agency," I explained to Elaine, taking a sip of my own coffee. "She didn't like having different strangers coming and going all the time, but what else could we do?" Elaine's nod validated my dilemma. "After Brittany Landers was killed, they cut off their services."

Elaine gasped. "What are you going to do?"

"I hope it's temporary, and just until the police find out who killed her caregiver. Mark is making some calls in case Loving Care won't come back."

"Mark. How is he? I don't think I've seen him since high school!"

"Still perfect. Got his PhD and a great job as an engineer for Bill Gates."

"Who?" Elaine's brow furrowed.

"Bill Gates. You know, Microsoft." Elaine's brow unfurrowed so I continued, "Anyway, Mark has a dream job in Seattle and his wife stays home taking care of their precocious kids, a boy and a girl."

"Is Mark coming to see me?" My mother's face brightened as she overheard us discussing my brother.

"Not today, Mom." I took another sip of coffee.

"Lola, I hear you had some excitement here the other day," Elaine said.

"Excitement? Here?" My mother laughed, holding the coffee mug with both hands, and burst into a rendition of "Oh Come All Ye Faithful."

Elaine clasped a hand over her mouth to keep from sputtering coffee. Her freckled face reddened as she stifled a giggle, peering at me to gauge my reaction.

"Mom," I interrupted. "I don't think Elaine wants to hear Christmas carols right now."

My mother stopped singing abruptly and looked at me as if I had imagined the whole outburst.

"Nothing out of the ordinary happened, Lola?" Elaine prompted. "I heard the police were here."

My mother scrunched her face as she sipped her coffee. "The police? What happened?"

"Michelle says to me, she says, a girl you knew was murdered here."

"Murdered? Someone *I* know?" Her pitch increased. "Who?"

Elaine looked at me for help. "What was her name again?"

"Brittany Landers."

"Brittany Landers," Elaine repeated to my mother. "She worked for you. Don't you remember Brittany?"

"Who?"

I murmured to Elaine, "Imagine sitting with her at the police station."

"Yeah, Keith says to me, he says, she started coughing and acting like she couldn't understand anything, and they couldn't get much information out of her."

"You talked to Keith Matthews? When?"

Elaine blushed a shade of pink that almost clashed with her orange-red hair. She was never much good at keeping secrets. "He is divorced, you know."

It took a minute to sink in; I recognized the glow on Elaine's face. "You and *Keith*?" Elaine had been married three times and had dated men from all different social and income levels, but somehow, one of *us* going out with one of *them* felt strange. Like we were back in high school and she had crossed some invisible barrier.

She nodded, grinning. "The sex is out of this world!"

"Spare us the details, please!" I motioned toward my mother.

With a faraway look, Mom began to sing again. "*Que sera, sera*! Whatever will be, will be."

Elaine and I looked at each other and giggled like schoolgirls.

"Mom!"

"The future's not ours to see. *Que sera, sera*!" Mom smiled like a proud performer.

A few bars of music from a popular song I could not place emanated from Elaine's bag on the couch beside her. "Yeah?" she murmured, cupping the cell phone between her mouth and ear.

"What's that?" My mother leaned forward, eyeing the silver box that had upstaged her.

"Her cell phone," I whispered.

"A phone? But why does it play music?"

"No, I don't care," Elaine said. "Go ahead and get it. Again? Okay. Bye." Shaking her head, she snapped the phone closed and muttered, "Kids. They think I'm made of money."

"A cell phone," my mother marveled at the instrument Elaine put back into her bag. "Isn't that how we knew so much about the terrorists? People on the planes had cell phones."

I winced. "That's right."

We observed a quick moment of silence for all those who had lost their lives that terrible day. More than a month had passed, but the horror was still fresh.

Elaine broke the spell. "Lola, try to concentrate. I know you can do it. You just remembered 9/11, something that happened over a month ago. Do you remember Thursday, when a girl who worked for you got hit on the head?"

My mother set down her mug. "My pagoda! My beautiful brass pagoda! She took my pagoda."

Elaine and I looked at each other. "What did you do then?" Elaine prompted.

"It's gone!" My mother shook her head sadly. "Over seventy years I had that pagoda. Did you ever see it, Elaine? Michelle? My father bought it for me in China when I was five years old. Now it's gone." She spread her hands, showing us they were empty.

"Was Brittany trying to steal it?" Elaine asked. I resented her following the same theory and line of questioning the police had used. But after today's revelation about the latest man in her life, I wasn't surprised.

"I don't know." My mother's eyes glazed over as if someone had pulled down the shades. She picked up her mug again and sipped.

"Did you *think* she was trying to steal it?" Elaine pressed. "Did it make you *mad*?"

"Elaine! We don't know that's what happened." If enough people painted the same picture, my mother might start to believe it, true or not. "Why don't you ask Keith about...?"

My mother launched into a coughing spasm and splattered coffee all over her sweat suit. I rushed to her side. Prying the mug from her hands, I steadied the sloshing and moved it to the end table so she couldn't spill any more. Luckily none of the hot liquid had touched her skin.

The coughing subsided after a moment. "Sorry," my mother croaked.

I patted her shoulder. "Come on, let's get you more of that cough medicine." I helped her to her feet. "Elaine, would you excuse us a minute? Mom needs to change her outfit."

My mother gave Elaine a little wave as we moved down the hall to the master bedroom.

After administering the cough syrup, I helped my mother pick out another sweat suit from her mountain of clothing. We removed the coffee-stained one and tossed it into the clothes hamper. She was determined to put on the fresh outfit herself, but when she tried to push her head through one of the sleeves, I stepped in and adjusted it for her. I noticed her sweatpants were backwards as she pulled them up over the fresh diaper I had managed to get on her, but she refused to let me turn them around for her. After a couple tries and a subtle suggestion, I gave up. It didn't make much difference; she wasn't going anywhere.

When she was dressed, my mother reclined on the bed.

"Tired?" I asked her.

She nodded, shutting her eyes.

"Elaine is still here," I reminded her. "Want me to tell her good-bye for you?"

"Tell her I'm sorry," my mother replied, nodding.

The phonc rang. The extension in Mom's bedroom was closest, so I answered in there.

"Michelle? Doll? How are you holding up? Roberto told me about your mama." I recognized the veil of a New York accent masking the old-world Italian: my mother-in-law, Suzanna DePalma.

"Suzanna!" I greeted her. "How are you?" My mother-in-law and I had become close when Roberto and I first got engaged, right after I'd been bumped out of our Los Angeles flight attendant base because of downsizing. The only way I could hold a schedule was to transfer to New

York, and Suzanna had invited me to stay with her whenever I had to overnight there.

"Doll, I'm doing great. Did they catch the guy yet?"

"Not yet." I told her how the police suspected my mother, how the Loving Care Agency had withdrawn its services, how my mother's memory seemed obstructed. I said nothing about Isabella and Giovanna; Roberto deserved to find out first.

"Want me to come out there and help, Sweetie?" Even in her late seventies, Suzanna had no qualms about jumping on an airplane at a moment's notice.

"Suzanna, that's nice of you to offer, but it isn't necessary." Ordinarily, I enjoyed chatting with my mother-in-law, but today I cut the conversation short. "Listen, you take care of yourself, and we'll see you at Thanksgiving."

"Looking forward to it, Doll. Sure you don't mind cooking?"

"Not at all. You've seen my kitchen—best toy I ever had."

"I'll be there. Don't be afraid to put me to work. And Michelle, take care of your mama. I love you, Sweetie."

"Love you, too, Suzanna." As I hung up the phone, I marveled at how the L-word, rarely uttered in the Hanson family, rolled so easily off the tongues of the DePalmas. The adversarial relationship I'd had with my parents during my teen years had morphed into civility, but never the closeness that bound other families.

I checked on my mother. She had drifted into a light sleep, whinnying rhythmically. I started into the family room where I'd left Elaine.

My heart stopped as I spotted Elaine curled up on the couch, shoes off as if she were in her own living room, perusing the photograph album Isabella had left. Since we were children, Elaine could never keep her hands off my things, never thought to ask permission before snooping into something that was supposed to be private.

I took a deep breath. There was nothing in that album to tie those people to me, no one she would recognize; for all she knew, it could belong to one of the Loving Care aides. Of course, if Isabella and Giovanna were going to become a part of my life, everyone would know the truth sooner or later, and this might provide the opening for me to tell Elaine, once my best friend, my long-held secret. With her newfound law enforcement connections, she might even be able to help me determine whether Isabella's claims were legitimate.

Elaine looked up and smiled as I entered the family room. With that same cat-that-swallowed-a-canary expression I remembered from our childhood, she pointed at the album. "This is a good picture of Isabella."

Chapter Fifteen

I felt the color drain from my face. When I caught my breath, I managed to squeak, "How do you know Isabella?"

"Percy introduced us," Elaine said, as if all this should fit together for me.

"Percy?" I groped for the nearest chair and sank into it. The thought of Percy froze my insides. Was that lecher now pursuing a woman young enough to be his daughter? "When did you see Percy?"

"He's been in town for a few months. Moved into his grandfather's old place. You know, about three blocks from here."

"Percy? In town?" New revelations were coming at me like snowballs, and I could only process them one at a time.

"That's what I said. He lost his tropical fish business down in Houston, practically had a nervous breakdown, then hung it up and came back here. The house is paid for, so he doesn't have to worry about foreclosure."

Percy had started the tropical fish wholesale business the last year we were together. Even after I had moved into my own apartment, I had handled his books as a favor until the day he tried to strangle me. I wasn't surprised he had lost the business; just that it took him so many years to lose it. "When did you start speaking to Percy?"

Elaine shrugged. "We went out a few times after he moved here."

"You and Percy?" That had to say something about the supply of eligible partners in our age group in Two Wells, Texas.

She wrinkled her dainty freckled nose. "He's not my type. Glad I let you have him, way back when." Her blue eyes sparkled. "We still talk, though."

Right now I was more interested in how Percy knew my alleged daughter-in-law than in any attraction he might have felt for Elaine. "What did Percy tell you about Isabella?"

"He says to me, he says, she was married to *your son.* You two have a granddaughter now: Giovanna."

I felt my face flush. I had been about to unlock the vault to unleash the secret, only to find the vault empty, the secret long since escaped. "Who else knows?"

"What do you mean?"

"Who have you told?"

"Who would I tell?"

"Keith?"

"Why would I tell Keith?"

Of course not. I was nothing to Keith. I was nothing to most of the residents of Two Wells, Texas. No one cared now what Michelle Hanson had done in high school. "Look Elaine, I'm sorry I couldn't be the one to tell you."

"I know. Scandal." Elaine laughed.

"It was hard back then."

"And having a child out of wedlock wouldn't do for perfect little Michelle Hanson."

"Elaine, we weren't even good friends any more by then."

"Yeah, Percy took care of that, didn't he?" Her blue eyes misted. "He cut you off from all your friends."

"I was seventeen, not even out of high school. I couldn't be a mother."

"If I'd known back then. If only my mother had known!" Elaine pushed a tendril of red hair off her forehead. In her effort to cover the gray, she had chosen a shade even brighter than it had been when we were in high school. "You don't know how she nagged me. She said to me, she said, 'Why can't you be more like Michelle?' Every time she ran into *your* mother, Lola would crow about your accomplishments. Lola said to my mother, 'Michelle went off to study in Europe! Michelle got her master's degree! Michelle got a glamorous job as a flight attendant, and she travels all over the world! Michelle married a rich airline pilot!' Momma says to me, 'Michelle Hanson can do no wrong!' Blah, blah, blah!"

"My pregnancy wasn't the kind of news that would fit into those Norman Rockwell family Christmas letters Mom used to mass-mail every year."

"Up until last year," Elaine reminded me. "Can't believe I'm saying this, but I actually missed Lola's Christmas letter." She gripped Isabella's photo album and pointed it at me. "I wish I'd had this ammunition when my mother swallowed all that rah-rah stuff. Whenever your name came up in conversation, Momma made me feel about this tall." Elaine gestured with her index finger and thumb.

Summarized and censored for the Hanson family Christmas letter, my life must have sounded pretty successful. "I admit it. Michelle Hanson was not the saint she pretended to be. How long have you known?"

"A few months. Since I hooked up with Percy."

"And you never thought to mention it to me? You knew I had a granddaughter?"

"I figured you weren't ready to talk about that time."

I never would have been ready, if Isabella had not showed up on my mother's doorstep. "But how did Percy and Isabella find each other?" I had been anticipating questions about Jean-Paul's father from Isabella as our relationship progressed.

"You mean, because you gave the boy up for adoption? And the records are supposed to be sealed?"

"They didn't even let me put Percy's name on the birth certificate, because we weren't married."

"You'll have to ask Percy how Isabella found him; I never did get the story."

"Like I'm really going to talk to Percy." The thought of him made me cringe.

"He told me you're afraid of him! I says to him, 'What happened between you and Michelle? Y'all were close for so long. So close that no one else mattered.' And he says to me, 'I don't know what I ever did to Michelle, but she won't come near me.'" Elaine laughed as if my fears were totally unfounded.

"He tried to kill me," I told her. "That's plenty reason to stay away from someone, don't you think?"

"Tried to kill you? For real? How?"

I pantomimed choking. I was in no mood to recount the whole sordid story.

"Oh Michelle! Gosh, I had no idea. I'm so sorry."

"It was a long time ago. I've put it behind me. But now you know why I have no desire to see Percy."

Elaine shifted in her chair. "Well, Percy couldn't hurt a fly right now."

"And why is that?" When I thought of Percy, I pictured a poisonous spider, poised to snare a victim into its web. I took a sip of my cold coffee as if it could wash away the bad taste memories of him left in my mouth.

"He's dying. Prostate cancer."

I gulped. How many bombs was she going to drop on me today? "Percy has cancer?"

"It was diagnosed a few months ago, but he's going down fast. Isabella took him to the hospital on Thursday. Maybe for the last time."

Although part of me wanted to gloat that Percy was getting what he deserved, I mostly felt sad—as I would for anyone suffering from cancer. "Poor Percy," I murmured.

"You should go see him."

The breath that escaped my nose sounded like a snort. "Why?"

"Last chance."

"Which hospital?" Not that I really had any intentions of going to see him.

"Medical Center. I have the room number if you like." Elaine reached for her oversized purse on the couch beside her.

"You can give it to me, but I'm not planning to visit him. I have my hands full right now."

Elaine handed me a scrap of paper with Percy's hospital room number scribbled on it. "What are you going to do about your mom?"

I glanced at the room number, and then shoved the paper into my back pocket. "I don't know. First thing is to get her cleared from suspicion in this murder investigation. Then we have to do something about her living arrangements. She wants to live on her own, but we're not sure she can."

"Have you thought about assisted living? My mother's in a facility by Lake Palestine, and she loves it."

"Mark and I have talked about that. Sounds better than the nursing home she was in after her surgery."

"Oh yeah! Momma has all kinds of friends, plays cards all day. Doesn't have to worry about cooking and cleaning. She says to me, she says, 'Elaine, I should have done this years ago.'"

I sighed. "My mother has lived in this house since we moved to Two Wells, back in 1958. She doesn't want to leave."

"Momma didn't either, when my sister first suggested it. But then a couple of her friends died, and one went to the assisted living facility, and pretty soon, she was okay with the idea. We just have to help them handle the change. Kind of like they did for us when we were growing up."

Her suggestion reminded me of how our roles had changed, how youth had somehow marched by us, leaving middle age and all the responsibilities that came with it while our parents drifted out to the sea of old age.

Elaine looked at her watch, a fake two-tone Rolex, one of several bangles on her wrist. "I should get going. Timmy has a soccer game." She gathered her purse and stood to leave. "Sounds like you'll be in town for a while this time."

"Until this murder investigation gets wrapped up." I rose to escort her out. "Did you ever meet Brittany Landers?"

"I don't think so. But my daughter Stacy used to waitress with her at the Golden Corral, if that's the same Brittany Landers. The only aide I really remember is Karen." Elaine retrieved her car keys and tossed the bag over her shoulder. "She's nice."

"Someone had to have a motive," I said as we started toward the front door.

"Keith will find out," Elaine assured me. "And he'll go easy on your mom."

"She didn't do it." We were standing in the entryway where the faint residue of cleaning fluids again triggered my memory of finding Brittany's body. "Ask Keith how his ex-wife's business card got into our planter."

"Mary Lynn?" Elaine winced.

I pointed to the boxwoods. "Right there. A business card. For real estate services. Mary Lynn Matthews."

Elaine shook her head. "That doesn't prove anything. Anyone could have dropped it any time."

"Keith didn't seem very interested in finding out."

Elaine touched my shoulder. "He will. He doesn't have any reason to protect Mary Lynn, especially now that they're divorced. He'll look at every clue. And even if it turns out Lola killed Brittany, it was probably an accident."

I followed Elaine outside into the sunshine. The warm air felt good. "She didn't do it," I insisted. My mother could never kill anyone, no matter how confused or frustrated she had become.

"Let's do lunch later in the week, since you're in town for a while," Elaine suggested, as she started down the walk.

"Call me," I agreed.

Before going back inside, I spent about ten minutes freeing some of the boxwood plants in the front bed from the chokehold of invading grasses.

Finding the loan application crumpled underneath Isabella's photo album, I remembered my plans to call my mother's bank. Fortunately, they offered full service until noon on Saturdays.

"Oh, yes," said the young loan officer. "There were a few more things we needed on the application, so I mailed it back to her. As soon as we get it completed, I'll go ahead and cut the check."

"Why is my mother applying for a loan?" Wrong question, I realized as the words escaped my lips.

There was silence on the other end of the line. "Are you authorized to transact business on behalf of your mother?"

My brother had power of attorney, not I. My mother had drawn up the paperwork shortly after my father's death. "Uh, I'm listed on all her accounts...payable on death." Another preparation she had made in the months following my father's passing, despite our protests at the time that it seemed morbid.

"One moment, please." Before I could protest, I heard the on-hold music from a local rock station whose repertoire had not changed much since I was a teenager. They called themselves an "Oldies" station now.

I was humming along to a song I hadn't heard in ages, the name I could not remember, when a different voice returned to the line. "Are you Brittany Landers?"

"Brittany Landers?" Anger mixed with fear rose inside me as I clutched the incomplete loan application, a symbol of my mother's vulnerability. "Brittany Landers is dead."

"One moment, please." The song I liked had ended, replaced by a tire commercial. I skimmed the loan papers and studied the cutesy cursive signature next to my mother's shaky scrawl. How had Brittany been able to get my mother to sign her name to this? The only debt my parents had ever incurred was their mortgage, and that had been paid off for over fifteen years. They even paid cash for their cars. At least Brittany had applied for a loan, instead of making an outright withdrawal from my mother's bank account.

Another voice came on the line. I'd lost track of whether it was a new one or someone to whom I'd spoken before. "Can you put Mrs. Hanson on?"

"She's napping. This is her daughter Michelle."

"I understand that, Ma'am, but we need to speak with Mrs. Hanson."

"Look, please cancel this loan application. My mother has changed her mind."

"I'm sorry, but we'll need to speak with Mrs. Hanson or Ms. Landers."

"Mrs. Hanson and Ms. Landers won't be returning the papers you sent." I slammed down the phone and started ripping the loan papers before I remembered I was destroying evidence.

As if someone had intercepted my thoughts, the doorbell rang. I went to answer it with the partially torn loan application still in hand. Peering through the peephole, I saw Keith Matthews.

Chapter Sixteen

"You were reading my mind," I told Keith as I opened the front door to admit him. His aftershave buffered the waning smell of cleaning fluids. "Did you talk to Mary Lynn yet about her business card?"

Keith grinned, shaking his head. "I left her a message." He paused to examine the damaged front door and then he looked at me as he entered. "Where's your mother?" He glanced at a paper in his hand.

"Napping." I studied his face in a new light, trying to picture him and Elaine together. Thirty years ago, who would have believed it? "What can we do for you?"

"I'd like to talk to her." He showed me the paper. "I want to see if she knows this man."

I eyed the mug shot and then escorted him into the living room. "That's the guy who tried to beat down our front door the other night. Guess you noticed his handiwork. Terrence Miller? Mom has already said he used to come around here to visit Brittany."

Keith sighed. "It *is* the guy who was here the other night. But his name is not Terrence Miller. It's Steven Graham."

I scrunched my face before I realized I had inherited one of my mother's annoying mannerisms. "So Brittany *did* have more than one boyfriend?"

"It appears so. That's what I'm trying to find out."

More suspects. That should take the focus off my mother. "You told us Terrence Miller had an alibi. What about this guy?"

"Nothing we can verify."

No one had placed him at the scene, either, so I didn't want to raise my hopes. "I'll wake her. But first I have something to show you." Would revealing the loan application be a betrayal of my mother, shifting the spotlight of suspicion back to her? I took a deep breath and yielded to my curiosity for information that perhaps only the police could find out. "This came in the mail yesterday. I didn't open it until this morning." I handed him the partially ripped papers. To his raised eyebrows I explained, "They weren't ripped like that when they arrived. I tried to salvage them when I realized they might be important."

Keith thumbed through the tattered pages and examined the signatures at the end.

"An application for a home equity line of credit. From a woman who never borrowed a cent in her life—except for the mortgage, which was paid off years ago." I looked over his shoulder. "Look who the co-borrower is."

He whistled. "Have you talked to your mother about this?"

"Not yet." A tear slipped out the corner of one eye and I turned my face so he wouldn't see. Not again. "I tried to call the bank, but they wouldn't tell me much." My voice shook, "Because I wasn't Br...Brittany Landers."

"Hey." Keith slid a protective arm around me. "We'll get to the bottom of it." He folded the loan application with his other hand and stuffed it into his pocket, along with Steven Graham's mug shot. He then produced a handkerchief and gently wiped my cheek.

"Sorry." I sniffed, composing myself. In another decade, I might have fanned the embers of attraction between us, with disregard for the fact that I was happily married to Roberto and Keith was dating Elaine. But now, I would ensure that our connection stopped at friendship. Pulling back, I took his handkerchief, finished wiping my face, and returned it to him.

"It's a rough time." He retracted his arm from my shoulders, stuffed the handkerchief back in his pocket. "Shall we see if your mother will talk to us?"

"I'll go check on her."

Keith remained in the living room while I headed down the hallway to the master bedroom. The closed blinds concealed the sunny day. The whole house was dark and musty, such a contrast to the airy home Roberto and I owned in Atlanta, full of windows and skylights and high ceilings.

My eyes focused on the king-sized bed, searching for the small bumps that made up my mother's shape. As I grew closer, I realized she was not there. "Mom!" She must be in the bathroom. My heart skipped a beat as I rounded the bed, remembering her fall yesterday. Fortunately, she wasn't on the floor. I peered into the adjoining bathroom, opened the shower door.

"Mom!" Had she somehow slipped out to the family room? The hall wasn't wide enough for us to pass each other without noticing. The makeshift bookshelf bowing under a full set of Encyclopedia Britannica made it even narrower. I stuck my head into my own bedroom. No sign of her. I checked the guest bathroom across the hall, flung back the shower curtain to expose the bathtub. I peered into Mark's old bedroom, which my father had converted to a study, complete with a desktop computer my mother had never learned to operate.

I passed through the family room, half expecting to see my mother settled in her favorite chair, watching whatever was on television and calling it "Golden Girls." Her chair was empty. I could see she was not in the kitchen, but I walked in there anyway, searched the adjoining laundry room. The washing machine was almost obscured by a pile of soiled linens and garments.

The door to the garage remained locked; that slowed the racing of my heart as I peered through the window. Thankfully, her car was still parked in its usual spot. I opened the door anyway, in case she could be rummaging in there, perhaps searching for some of the clothes Mark and Marie had boxed during their last visit.

"Mom!" I called again, my voice echoing in the stuffy stillness. Where could she be?

Keith had ventured into the family room by the time I returned. I looked at him in alarm. "I can't find her."

"You're kidding! When did you see her last?"

"I had a friend over—uh, Elaine." No use pretending it was just "some friend" as Keith was intimately acquainted with this one. "Mom lay down shortly after that. But I haven't left the house! I'd have seen her go out!"

At the same instant, our two pairs of eyes strayed to the sliding glass door leading to the back patio. The latch was in the unlocked position. I reached the door first and slid the glass open. Shielding my eyes from the bright sunlight, I glanced around the back yard. Keith followed me outside, slid the door closed. We looked in my father's shed, which smelled ten times as musty as the house. Several inch-long cockroaches scattered when we opened the warped wooden door, their brown legs scratching against the concrete floor. Nothing inside but old, rusty tools cloaked in spider webs.

We walked the perimeter of the back yard, more weeds than lawn. I picked up some stray branches from the towering elms my father had planted as saplings when we first moved in.

In the back corner of the yard, Keith and I crossed the patch where my father used to plant his garden; it was overgrown now, and the weeds here were particularly green. My foot sank into a low spot, probably the remains of one of the rotating compost holes.

I made my way to the chain link fence, scanning the empty field behind us—one of the few areas of our subdivision that had remained undeveloped. Someone had recently mowed it; the smell of cut grasses tickled my nostrils.

"Mom!" Calling seemed futile; there was no sign of her. Traffic whizzed by on the Loop, punctuated by the mournful wail of an ambulance. Surely, she had not gone that way?

I turned to Keith. "How could she have just vanished?" I hoped he did not think I had staged her disappearance.

"Where does she like to go? Does she take walks? Does she have a favorite place?"

"I can't remember the last time she went anywhere on foot. And her car is still in the garage."

"What about your rental car?"

My heart pounded like it was going to bounce into my throat and choke me, although I couldn't imagine my mother fishing the keys out of my purse without my knowledge and then driving an unfamiliar rental car when her own beloved Ford Fiesta was available. But I ran toward the side of the house, past the rusty poles that once held up a clothesline, past the neglected rosebushes. Fragrant blooms drooped from the branches, and petals scattered on the ground.

The gate was slightly ajar, with the latch up. Keith and I hurried through and dashed around the side of the house. My rental car was still parked where I'd left it. I took a deep breath to push my thumping heart back into my chest where it belonged. She couldn't be far; she had not left in a vehicle. But where was she? My eyes scanned the street. I tried to remember what color sweat suit she had last put on.

"Are you absolutely sure she's not in the house?" Keith asked, fingering the cell phone on his belt.

"I'll check again." I still expected my mother to magically reappear and wonder what all the fuss was about.

We went back inside, but a second, more thorough search of every room, including the closets and underneath the beds, did not produce my mother. A wave of nausea lashed at me. My mother had gone missing right under my nose. What kind of caregiver was I? What if the killer had come back for her?

"You're white as a sheet, Michelle. Sit down a minute." Keith opened his cell phone and called police headquarters to put out an all-points bulletin about a missing "little old lady with Alzheimer's." I winced, but at the same time, I was grateful others would be helping me look for my mother. As we walked outside again, he phoned Elaine. "Michelle and I are going to take a ride in the cruiser. Can you come over and wait here in case Mrs. Hanson shows up?"

He held the car door open for me. I had never been inside a police vehicle before and would have been fascinated by all the gadgets and controls, had I not been so preoccupied with finding my mother. Keith spoke to another unit on the radio; apparently reinforcements were nearby. He instructed them to go door-to-door, soliciting information from neighbors.

As we pulled away, we passed another police car. Keith paused and spoke to the driver. I couldn't concentrate on what they were saying to each other; it was like they were speaking a foreign language over the added cacophony of two radios.

Moving again, we slowly combed the block, each scanning a side of the street, peering between houses, behind trees. We turned onto Pine Crest and then took a right on a street parallel to ours, creeping along, searching methodically.

"How long did you say she's been gone?" Keith asked again.

"I tucked her in not more than two hours ago. She spilled coffee on her clothes, and I helped her change her sweat suit. Green! It's a bright Kelly green. After she changed, she lay down on the bed. I still can't figure out how she got past me. I was in the family room most of the time, with a view of both exits. Except when I walked Elaine out the front door..." A chill crept over me, although it was warm outside.

On the next parallel street, we spotted three pre-teen boys riding bicycles. Keith pulled alongside them. "Have you seen an elderly woman in a green sweat suit walking around here?"

Balancing their bicycles, they looked at each other as if to confer, and then shook their heads in unison.

"If you do, please call 9-1-1," Keith instructed. "Any of you got cell phones?"

One of the boys held up a pocket-size silver box.

"Use it if you see her." With a one-finger wave, Keith put his hands back on the steering wheel and drove off.

The street continued past Pine Crest. Keith hesitated, looking at me. I shrugged. Who knew which way she might have gone? We moved straight ahead, crossing Pine Crest.

We slowed behind two middle-aged women with tight perms who were power walking, clasping small weights in both hands, their over-sized derrieres jiggling under their sweatpants with each step. *It's a long road to fitness for them,* I thought, *but I admire people their age who at least get out and try.*

When parallel with them, Keith called out, "Excuse me, Ma'am...Sandra Tuttle?"

The woman squinted as she peered into the car window.

"Keith Matthews," he introduced himself. "Weren't you in my sister Kimberly's class?"

She's younger than I am, I thought. Kimberly Matthews had been three years behind Keith and me.

"Yeah! Why, I saw Kim at the mall the other day, with that new gran'baby. I didn't recognize you at first, Keith," she drawled. "You sure are handsome in that uniform."

Keith turned to include me. "Do you remember Michelle Hanson? She was in my grade. She was the one who wrote that 'Armchair Traveler' column in the school newspaper." I had almost forgotten my brush with high school journalism; it surprised me that others remembered.

Sandra smiled, revealing several thousand dollars worth of shining crowns. "You were gone by the time I got to Robert E. Lee, but my brother Gary used to bring your columns home. They were so funny! He loved them." She turned to her power-walking partner. "This is Janis Goodson. Remember Janis Smith? She was a grade behind me and Kimberly." Young Janis Goodson nodded while jogging in place.

Keith reined the conversation back to the business at hand. "Michelle's mother wandered off. She's a little confused, so we're trying to find her." I was grateful he did not utter the awful word "Alzheimer's" again.

"She's a tiny woman, with sort of flyaway gray hair, and she was wearing a Kelly green sweat suit," I offered.

Both Sandra and Janis puckered their faces with concern. "We haven't seen anyone since we've been out, but we'll sure keep an eye out for her," Sandra promised.

"Hope you find her," Janis called as we drove away, leaving them to resume their power walk.

Three blocks later, we spotted a pre-teen girl on a bicycle that seemed too big and unmanageable for her. Her light brown hair was tied back in a ponytail and she wore no helmet, no fancy spandex outfit. The scene brought back memories of the times I used to explore these neighborhoods by bicycle, daydreaming that it was the pony I asked for every Christmas and never received. As

Keith slowed the cruiser beside the girl, I sensed something familiar about her size and shape, the way she moved.

At the sound of Keith rolling down his electric window, she turned to face us.

"Giovanna?" I gasped.

Chapter Seventeen

"Miss Michelle!" Giovanna almost slipped off the bicycle as she raised a hand to shield her eyes from the sun and peer into my window. She was polite enough not to ask what I had done to land myself inside a police car.

I wondered how I would explain her to Keith, or if it even mattered. I settled for a generic introduction, names without relationships. "Keith Matthews, Giovanna Rogers. Giovanna, my mother has taken off, and Keith is helping me look for her. Have you seen her?"

Giovanna had climbed down from the bicycle. She brushed away a strand of brown hair that had escaped from her ponytail. "No, Ma'am. But I saw an ambulance over on Pine Crest, near your street." Her words were muffled by a transmission from Keith's radio.

"Following a dog.... Pine Crest...smelling some roses..." the male voice crackled.

Keith leaned over me to make eye contact with Giovanna. "What time did you see the ambulance?"

"Half an hour ago? I'm not sure, Sir." She looked at me. "Miss Michelle, I hope your mother is okay."

"Giovanna, can you show us where you saw the ambulance?" Keith asked. Turning to me, he continued, "My colleagues radioed that your next-door neighbor's son was walking his dog, and she started following him, asking to pet the dog. She dropped behind them near a house up on Pine Crest, where she stopped to smell roses; he didn't see her after that."

My pulse raced. "How did she look to him?"

"Apparently he wasn't concerned that there might be anything wrong."

At least my mother had not been abducted.

Giovanna looked from the car to the bicycle. "Do you want to follow me over there?"

"It'll be faster if you get in. Can you leave the bike somewhere?"

Giovanna's little face looked worried. "Will it be safe? I borrowed it."

"Sure." Keith hopped out and helped Giovanna tie the bicycle to a nearby tree, and then he opened the back door of the squad car for her.

I turned sideways in my seat so I could see Giovanna behind the Plexiglas panel. She gazed around the police car; it was probably her first time in one as well. A new experience we were sharing together, grandmother and granddaughter. "Where's your mother?" I asked.

"She went to the hospital to visit my grandfather." Grandfather. I pictured some old white-haired guy with a walker, and then it registered. *I* was her grandmother. Isabella and Giovanna must be staying with Percy—or rather, in Percy's home, because he was in the hospital with prostate cancer; hence the reason Giovanna was out riding a bicycle in our neighborhood.

I tested my theory. "This grandfather. Is his name Percy?"

"Mr. Percy. Yes, Ma'am." She leaned toward Keith. "Turn left on that main street. Pine Crest, I think it's called."

Keith's colleagues had beaten us to the house where my mother had last been seen, where Giovanna had observed someone being loaded into an ambulance. They were questioning the residents on the lawn, a thirty-something couple whom I had never met. As we pulled up, one of the policemen approached.

"They say an elderly woman tripped off the curb here. When they saw she couldn't get up, they called for an ambulance. Gotta be her, don't you think?"

My heart felt like it was expanding into my airway. I leaned toward Keith and ducked my head so I could see his colleague at the window. "Which hospital?" I squeaked.

"Medical Center is where we take all emergency cases, or any victims we can't identify," Keith answered for him.

My mother was a Jane Doe! Would they even treat her without knowing if she had medical insurance?

The radio squawked again; it sounded as if some other disturbance was going on. "Roger," Keith replied. Putting the car in gear, he said, "Let's have Elaine take you to the hospital, Michelle. I have to answer this call, and you're too upset to drive yourself." He punched a number into his cell phone, although Elaine was not more than two hundred yards away.

Elaine came outside, closing her cell phone as we pulled in front of my mother's house.

I bolted out of the police car, forgetting Keith and Giovanna. "Did you lock the door?" I asked Elaine.

She gave me a look that said locking the house was the least of my worries.

"I need my mother's insurance information," I explained as I passed her and pushed open the front door.

Elaine had left the television on, which I switched off with the remote as I entered, sinking the family room into an eerie silence. My eyes did a quick search for my mother's purse. I hurried into the master bedroom, still hoping to glimpse her tiny shape undulating from under the bedcovers. Let that woman in the ambulance be someone else's mother. On the floor beside the bed, I located her Mexican leather handbag. I pulled out her fat wallet, a Gucci knockoff I had bought for her in Korea. Medicare card, driver's license; it looked like everything we needed was here—and more; I didn't have time to purge. I grabbed my mother's wallet as well as my own purse and keys, and then rushed back outside, locking the front door behind me.

The police car was gone and Elaine sat in the driver's seat of her Dodge Durango, listening to the radio and applying bright coral lipstick in the visor mirror, her mouth open in a tight oval. I climbed in the passenger door, pushed aside her overflowing purse, a child's baseball cap, and a wadded-up Burger King sack before I could sit down. She relaxed her mouth and recapped her lipstick tube. "Ready?"

"How are they even going to treat her without proof of insurance?" I explained, waving my mother's wallet. I stuffed it into my purse and pulled the car door closed.

I tilted back the electric seat as we pulled away from the curb. Elaine's seat was all the way forward; her child-sized feet still dangled over the pedals. Tilting gave me a better view of the back seat, piled high with dry-cleaning, textbooks, empty soda cans, and forgotten shopping bags. Elaine's car was as messy as her bedroom had been when we were kids.

"You're pretty sure it's her then?" Elaine asked as we sped down my childhood street, the familiar houses a blur.

"Where else could she have gone?"

Elaine turned right onto the Loop, not bothering to turn on her blinker. "How'd she get out?"

It sounded like we were talking about a runaway dog. "She must have gone out the back while you and I were talking in the front yard. I didn't check on her when I went inside; I assumed she was still sleeping."

"Does she do this often?"

"Karen never mentioned it, if she does."

We caught the left-turn arrow at the intersection with Fifth Street. Elaine's turn was wide, and she spilled into the right-hand lane without signaling. She punched the accelerator until we were almost ramming the bumper of the car in front of us, at which point she jabbed her foot on the brake pedal and whipped into the other lane, again without looking or signaling. A honk from behind announced that she had cut the maneuver a little too close.

"Careful. We don't want to end up as hospital patients, too." The critical words escaped before I could stop them, words my mother might have said to me when I was learning to drive.

"Ah, you sound like Keith." Giggling, she looked at me instead of the road as she continued to weave through traffic. Another honk caused her to swerve at the last second, preventing us from broadsiding a pick-up truck.

I fixed my eyes straight ahead as my foot involuntarily reached for a brake pedal. Luckily, Medical Center was a ten-minute drive from my mother's house—make that five by ambulance or with Elaine driving—although it seemed like eons.

Miraculously, we managed to avoid an accident en route to the hospital. Elaine performed her version of parallel parking, her front tires jammed against the curb and the rear of the SUV jutting into the street. As we got out, she examined her parking job, shrugged, and locked the car with her remote key.

I was already walking toward the entrance. I stepped onto the grass to bypass an elderly couple ambling down the sidewalk entirely too slowly.

"Hey, wait up," called Elaine, her shorter legs straining to catch up with my rapid strides. As she rounded the elderly couple, a catchy musical bar reverberated from inside her purse. She decelerated, digging for her cell phone. "Yeah?" Elaine replied. "Y'all are done already? Can't you get a ride?"

I entered the building ahead of Elaine and approached the reception desk, where two young women were shuffling papers. I cleared my throat to get their attention. "Excuse me, did they just bring in an elderly woman with no identification?"

Shifting a wad of chewing gum from one side of her cheek to the other, one of them looked up.

I fished my mother's wallet from my purse and pulled out her driver's license. Not a bad picture, but it was taken a few years ago, when her face was much fuller, bathed in a smile. "My mother disappeared from her home this morning, and we were told that an elderly woman fell off a curb and was taken to this hospital a little while ago. It happened near our house, so I have a feeling it might be her. She didn't have any identification or insurance information with her when she left."

The receptionist smacked her gum as she studied my mother's driver's license. "Can I take this for a sec, Ma'am?" She picked it up and left the reception area. My heart pounded. Part of me wanted Mom to be here, cared for, so the mystery of her disappearance would be solved, but the other part did not want the poor injured woman to be my mother. That part hoped Mom would return from a pleasant walk, find the spare key hidden under the air conditioner, let herself inside, and be sitting in her chair watching television or reading a magazine by the time I returned from my fruitless trip to the hospital.

Elaine had finished her call and joined me inside. I paced. The other woman at the receptionist desk ignored us.

I started to say something to Elaine, but she had dialed her cell phone again. "Yeah Stacy." Stacy was Elaine's twenty-seven-year-old daughter by her first husband, whom she had divorced right after Stacy was born. Although she had her own apartment and a part-time waitress job, Stacy spent most of her time at Elaine's. "Can't you go pick up Timmy? He says to me... he needs to get home and do some schoolwork... Thanks, Hon."

I opened my mouth, but Elaine made another call. "Timmy, Love, your sister's coming to pick you up."

As Elaine hung up, the first receptionist returned. She handed back my mother's driver's license. "Ma'am, I think it may be her in ICU. I can let you in for five minutes, so you can give us a positive ID."

"Is she okay?" As the words tumbled out of my mouth, I knew I sounded like a character on the soap operas my mother liked to watch. *"Of course she's not okay,"* I often wanted to scream at the TV. *"That's why she's in the hospital!"*

The receptionist beckoned me to follow her down a glistening tile corridor. Elaine trailed at my heels. "You'll have to turn that cell phone off, Ma'am," the receptionist said.

Hospitals haunted me. Clinical smells, patients hooked by tubes to humming machines measuring their tenuous claim on life, ghost white coats of staff whisking from room to room. The intensive care unit contained an even greater density of machinery, awash in bright fluorescent lights. Thin translucent curtains separated the immobilized patients surrounded by mechanical and human monitors.

Thin wisps of white hair and my mother's ashen face provided little contrast with the bed sheets. A clear plastic oxygen mask covered her nose and mouth. "Mom!" I cried, rushing to her side. I turned to a nearby critical care nurse. "What's wrong with her?"

"She fractured her left hip when she fell off the curb, Ma'am." How could the nurse be so matter of fact? Broken bones at my mother's age could be a death sentence.

"Also, she's dehydrated, and she has pneumonia," the nurse continued.

Dehydrated? That had to be my fault. When was the last time I had offered water or Ensure to my mother? Last night? And pneumonia? I'd suspected her cough was bad news, and had planned to take her to the doctor on Monday. Not soon enough.

"Mom, I'm sorry," I murmured. A tear slipped from my eye.

There was no response except labored breathing through the oxygen dispenser. My mother's eyes were closed, shutting out the garish light. I reached for her small, gnarled hand beneath the IV attached to her wrist. "Mom, it's me, Michelle. Squeeze my hand if you can hear me," I begged.

Her cold fingers tightened unmistakably around mine. Elaine caught my eye and smiled.

The nurse touched my shoulder. "Who's her doctor, Ma'am?"

I could still see the note Karen had jotted on the calendar, for the appointment on Monday, but I could not read the name of the doctor. Mark would know; he had mentioned him in some of our conversations. The information was stored in the hard drive of my mind; it was just taking time to retrieve. Dr. Wilson, our family doctor, had retired several years ago, and this young doctor had taken over his practice. His name sounded like a fruit. "Uh, Dr. Plum," I supplied.

"Dr. Lawrence Plum, Ma'am?"

"I guess." I'd never heard his first name.

"He's on duty tonight; he'll be in later." The nurse made a note on the chart.

The receptionist who had led us into ICU spoke up. "Ma'am, we need you to fill out some admission papers." She motioned us to follow her.

Reluctantly, I released my mother's cold hand. "I'll be back," I assured her.

Chapter Eighteen

Back in the lobby, I filled out admission forms while Elaine talked on her cell phone, orchestrating her children's journey home like Mission Control. My hand trembled as I wrote. I didn't have all the answers to my mother's medical history; I hoped the information was on file with her doctor.

I watched Elaine cradle her cell phone. My brother Mark really needed to know what was going on with our mother, and there was not a public phone in sight. "Hey, do you think I could borrow that thing?"

"Sure. I have unlimited minutes on weekends, anywhere in the country."

"You don't mind if I call Mark in Seattle?"

"Go ahead. Tell him I said 'hi'."

I stared at the tiny metal device, wondering which button to push first. The lime green screen glowed expectantly.

Elaine grinned and showed me how to dial. "You've never used one of these?"

A faint ringing was followed by the sound of my brother's voice. "Hello? Mark? Can you hear me? I'm on a cell phone."

Elaine covered her reddening face as she peeked around the waiting room. Stifling a giggle, she then showed me how to hold the phone so I could hear and talk at the same time.

"Mom's in the hospital," I continued. The cell phone felt unnatural to me–too small–although the connection was quite clear. I tried to relate the day's events without making myself sound negligent.

"I'm coming down there," I heard Mark say. "I'll call you back when I know what flight I can get on."

He had hung up before I realized it. I held the phone out to Elaine. "What do I do now?" She showed me how to disconnect the call. I started to hand the phone back to her. "Can I call Roberto, too?"

"Sure." Her grin mocked me. The only kid on the block who didn't own a cell phone, *and* I didn't even know how to *use* one. "Remember what to do?"

I punched in my home telephone number, watched the digits appear on the screen, and located the transmit key. With a defiant look at Elaine, I listened to the ring, and then Roberto's deep voice on our answering machine. "Hi Honey Bear, it's me," I began. It felt awkward leaving a message from a cell phone in the middle of a public area, like a crazed homeless person talking to myself. I turned away from Elaine as I spoke. Once I had summarized the day's details, I found the disconnect key and pressed it. "Thanks, Elaine," I said, handing the phone back to her.

"I can't believe you and Roberto travel as much as y'all do, but y'all don't own a cell phone." She closed the case and put the phone back in her purse.

"We've talked about it," I conceded. "Especially for emergencies. Roberto is shopping for the best deal."

"How long does that take? You go into the cell phone store and pick the one you like."

"Oh no. He has to research it in *Consumer Reports* and on the Internet. Once he figures out what brand and features he wants, he compares prices so he doesn't pay one penny more than he has to. But with technology, sometimes a model becomes obsolete in the meantime, and then the whole process starts over."

"Poor baby!"

After I returned the completed forms to the receptionist, Elaine asked me, "What now?"

I looked at the receptionist. "When can I see my mother again? What are your visiting hours?"

The receptionist thumbed through some papers. "Once she's stabilized and out of intensive care, they'll move her to a room. Then you can visit her any time you like."

Elaine touched my arm and asked, "Want me to take you home?"

"That's probably best, because I don't have a car here." I should straighten the house for Mark, do laundry, buy groceries.

The sun waned as we stepped outside, although it was not yet five o'clock. The fading of summer's light always made me a little sad.

We reached Elaine's SUV, undisturbed and unticketed despite its lousy parking job. I buckled my seat belt and braced for the roller coaster.

"Guess your mom won't get arrested for now," Elaine said as she started the engine.

"What do you mean?"

"You know, for that girl's murder." Elaine backed up and whipped the car around in a U-turn.

What a time to bring up Brittany Landers. "There's no proof that Mom did it."

"They don't have any other suspects." Elaine paused at the stop sign as if it were a mere suggestion, and then pulled into traffic with a jolt.

"Elaine! You've known her most of your life. Seriously, do you really think she could kill someone?" Cars whizzed by. "Besides, Keith said..."

Elaine looked at me instead of the road. "She didn't mean to do it. She probably didn't even realize she killed someone. Look at her, Michelle. She's sick."

"She's not too sick to know right from wrong!" My mother's whole illness had been a nightmare, but I'd been able to wake up periodically and go back to my orderly life in Atlanta after my brief trips to Two Wells to check on her. Now I was being forced to live in the nightmare. "Please watch the road. You almost hit that guy!"

Elaine swerved to avoid another collision. Her cell phone rang, and she scrambled in her purse to find it, again taking her eyes off the road. "Yeah, Tim. Good. Go do your homework. I'll be home in a few minutes." She glanced at the road and sailed through an intersection as the traffic light changed from amber to red. "Well, why didn't y'all stop at the store? Okay. I'll get some." She hung up as she made a left turn onto my mother's street, cutting across two lanes of Loop traffic and causing one car to slam on its brakes.

I sighed, relieved to have cheated death again. A big fluffy-tailed squirrel dashed in front of us. "Look out!" I cried. Elaine swerved and almost hit a parked car, but managed to miss the squirrel. I took a deep breath and concentrated on slowing my pounding heart.

Elaine dropped me in front of my mother's house. "Thanks for staying at the hospital with me," I told her as I shut the passenger door, thankful to feel solid pavement beneath my feet.

"What are friends for?" She blew me a kiss with one hand while controlling the SUV with the other.

I unlocked the front door as Elaine drove away. Sidestepping the spot where Brittany Landers' body had lain, I proceeded into the family room. I surveyed the bookshelves stuffed with photo albums and knickknacks, the coffee table and end tables piled high with magazines, newspapers, and catalogs. Despite the clutter, my childhood home seemed empty without my mother in it.

I sank onto the couch, feeling the rough nylon upholstery against my palms. I reviewed the events that had unfolded since I'd left my office on Thursday morning. A dead body. My mother a suspect. Finding only someone else's memories of the son I'd never known, could never know. The surprise of a granddaughter. And now Mom in the hospital...

Tears gushed and I let them fall.

Chapter Nineteen

Our contract with the women of the Loving Care Agency had specified "light housekeeping" and their interpretation of this clause was mostly reactive cleaning: mopping up spills, changing the bedding, running the dishwasher. I spent a couple hours doing laundry and cleaning house, but the results were probably not up to my sister-in-law Marie's standards. If she came with Mark, she was going to have to live with it, or else start scrubbing—which she had been known to do.

After tidying the house, I went to the grocery store and loaded up the cart with basic provisions. I was probably leaving out something Marie would consider a staple for her vegetarian cuisine, but at least I remembered the Tamari, the tofu, and the alfalfa sprouts.

"Michelle!" The feminine drawl behind me sounded vaguely familiar. "Did y'all ever find your mom?"

I turned around to face Sandra Tuttle, one of the women walkers Keith and I had passed earlier. Her kind face wrinkled with the appropriate amount of concern.

"Oh hi, Sandra," I greeted her with a polite smile and glanced at her basket brimming with frozen pizzas, cookies, and ice cream. Tastier fare than mine.

"Your mom's okay then?" she persisted.

"Yes. Thanks for asking." I didn't have the energy to discuss my trip to the hospital and my mother's situation with someone who was practically a stranger.

As the grocery store clerk scanned my items, Sandra asked, in a softer, more conspiratorial tone, "Do they still think she killed that girl?"

I winced. So, Sandra Tuttle had heard about Brittany Landers, and that my mother was a suspect. I shouldn't have been surprised. Two Wells was a relatively small city, where murders were rare. The local news had probably given the story full coverage; I just hadn't been listening.

The clerk announced my total and I slid my credit card through the reader. I gave Sandra a tight-lipped smile as I waited for the charge slip. "Of course not." The machine spun mercifully into action, returning my approval code.

As the clerk handed me my receipt, I collected my groceries and started out. "Nice seeing you again, Sandra. Have a good evening."

The house was completely dark when I returned. I'd forgotten to leave the porch light on, which my mother always did whenever someone in the family was out for the evening. As I negotiated the key in the lock, I heard the phone ringing. It stopped before I could reach it.

I put away the perishables and as I closed the refrigerator, the doorbell chimed. I cut through the living room, drawing the drapes on my way to the front door.

Through the peephole I spotted a twenty-something young woman who strongly favored Brittany Landers, which sent a shiver up my spine. Disheveled, dishwater-blond hair hung halfway down her torso, partially covering the slogan on her baggy black T-shirt.

I turned on the porch light and cracked the door. "Yes?"

"Are you... uh...is this where...uh...who are you?" Squinting, she shifted her weight between feet.

"Who are you looking for?" I wasn't in the mood to cut her any slack.

"Uh, I'm Tiffany, uh, my sister used to work here. She, uh..." With a loud sniff, Tiffany pushed her hair away from her face, revealing tear-swollen eyes. A tiny rose tattoo adorned her neck.

I opened the door a little further. "And your sister was...?"

She sobbed, still not looking me in the eye. "Br... Brittany. My sister was k...k... killed here." Tiffany appeared close to Brittany's age; it was not obvious which one was older.

My heart thumped. "Listen, I'm very sorry about your sister. But why are you here?"

"Wh...where did it h...happen?" She craned her neck to see inside my mother's house.

I stepped aside slightly, without allowing her entry. "There's really nothing to see." Maybe Tiffany wanted closure to her sister's death, but I didn't have time to let her in and help her reminisce. And after finding that loan application this morning, I wasn't feeling too charitable toward Brittany.

Tiffany blinked, releasing fresh tears. "W...were you here? Did you see what... happened?"

My thoughts flashed to the image of my mother standing over Brittany's inert body, with black ants filing into her facial cavities. Not a sight for someone who loved her. I shook my head. "I didn't see what happened. But I did... see her."

Tiffany wiped some tears away with the back of her hand and took a deep breath. When she turned her hand over again, a fleck of gold caught my eye. Closer inspection revealed an intricately chiseled gold dome ring. The only one like it I'd ever seen belonged to my mother. Pointing at Tiffany's hand I remarked, "Interesting ring. Where'd you get it?"

"It was a gift." Not meeting my gaze, she wiped fresh tears from her eyes. "The old woman. Is she... is she home?"

I should be at the hospital instead of helping Brittany's sister come to terms with the murder. "No, my mother isn't here."

"My boyfriend Steven, he said she...she did it. Did they put her in j...jail?"

Losing sympathy, I continued to cling to the front door, guarding my mother's fortress. "Your boyfriend Steven said she did it. Was he here when it happened?" *Steven.* Steven Graham? The man who had tried to beat down Mom's door the other night? Tiffany's boyfriend? Or Brittany's?

My question brought another sputter of tears. Tiffany covered her face and dashed down the walkway. Shielding my eyes from the porch light, I glimpsed the silver outline of a sedan parked at the curb. I wasn't sorry she was leaving, but at the same time, I thought of more questions I should have asked her, mostly about Brittany's relationships. But surely the police had already gathered that information. Should I mention Tiffany's visit to Keith? And where was my mother's gold ring?

Hearing the engine start, I locked the front door and chained it. I packed an overnight bag with a few things for my mother. I searched her jewelry box, but did not see the ring that resembled the one on Tiffany's finger. Of course, that did not mean it was not stashed away somewhere, and I did not have time to weed through drawers and boxes to locate it. Before setting out for the hospital, I ensured that all doors and windows were locked, including the sliding door through which my mother had most likely left.

Different receptionists were on duty. One gave me directions to the private room where my mother had been moved. She also handed me a large brown envelope of personal items found on my mother. I peered inside: her watch and two rings, but neither was the gold one like Tiffany's. Dr. Plum was making his rounds, the receptionist said, so I should be able to catch him.

I made my way to the room number the receptionist had given me. I tried not to look inside the other patients' rooms, tried not to breathe the smells of medicine, Lysol, and bedpans—the sensory reminders of sickness and impending death. Stopping where I thought my mother's room was located, I was surprised to see a uniformed policeman standing guard at the door. I double-checked the room number. Most of the other patients had their names typed on a card in a holder above the room number, but there was not one for my mother.

"Is this Lola Hanson's room?"

The young policeman straightened with military precision. "Who are you, Ma'am?"

"I'm her daughter, Michelle."

"Do you have some identification, Ma'am?" He spoke like someone who dreamed of serving in the Marine Corps.

I opened my purse and produced my driver's license. "My married name is DePalma," I explained.

He studied my documentation, shifting his eyes from my driver's license picture, with shoulder length brown hair, to my face, framed in a short blondish bob. His eyes became a tape measure as he compared my height and weight with the numbers claimed on my license. Satisfied, he stepped aside. "Go on in, Ma'am."

I hesitated. "May I ask what *you're* doing here?"

He looked at his feet, and I noticed his lips moving as if he were having a silent dialogue with some invisible entity. He then met my eyes and replied, "It's part of the murder investigation, Ma'am."

"Murder investigation!" Were they afraid their prime suspect, a 77-year-old invalid lying in a hospital bed with a fractured hip and pneumonia, would try to escape? "She needs an armed guard? In a hospital? And she hasn't even been charged with a crime?"

"Yes Ma'am, there have been some threats against her."

Chapter Twenty

"Threats! What kind of threats?" I pushed some hair off my forehead to air-dry beads of perspiration.

"Leave him alone, Michelle." The bulky shape of Greg Dobbins emerged from my mother's room.

I spun sideways to face him. "Why do you feel the need to have an armed guard in front of my mother's hospital room? And by the way, what are *you* doing here?"

"Your mother still has some explaining to do." With a flash of his protruding front teeth, Greg switched a wad of something from one cheek to the other like a cow chewing its cud.

"You were in there *interrogating* her?" I wanted to slap his face; the knowledge that it would probably land me in jail restrained me. Threats! Really.

Heaving an ursine sigh, he gave me a condescending look like I'd seen on the face of John, our incompetent department head. "That same punk kid who tried to beat your door down the other night is out on bond. He was making noises about going to finish what he started."

I flashed back to my battle at the front door as I had struggled to protect my family from a madman. The police had let him out on bail, even though he had made threats against my mother? Where was justice? "He was here?" I croaked.

"Naw. But we're ready for him." Greg patted his holster.

"Keith told me you have another suspect. Is he the one? I heard he doesn't have an alibi."

"Tsk...Keith shouldn't be discussing suspects with you."

"Speaking of suspects, I just had a visit from Brittany's sister." I paused, waiting to see if my revelation would interest Greg.

"Brittany Landers' sister? Which one?"

"How many sisters does she have? This one was named Tiffany."

"She ain't no suspect." Greg snorted. "But what was she doing visiting you?"

"I don't know. But she did bring up something puzzling. Said her boyfriend Steven *knew* my mother did it. How would he know? Maybe he was there that day." I thought about Tiffany's ring but decided not to mention it; I had no proof that it had once belonged to my mother.

Greg placed a fist on his hip. "Why didn't you report this to the police?"

"I'm telling you now."

He shook his head. "Duh!"

"It just happened. She stopped by as I was leaving to come here."

"And you didn't think to call us?"

"Like I said, I'm telling you now. Do you think it's important?"

"Let us decide what's important. Now why did the sister visit you?"

"I have no idea." I sighed. "May I see my mother now?"

"Just one minute." Greg fumbled in his breast pocket for paper and pencil. "Which sister did you say this was?"

"Said her name was Tiffany. Did Brittany have more than one sister?"

Greg waved his pencil at me. "What did she say to you?"

I shifted my weight from one foot to another. "She wanted to see where Brittany was killed. She was crying."

Greg puffed his cheeks. "I mean, what did she say about the boyfriend? He was there?"

"No, she didn't say that. She said he *knew* my mother did it. She burst into tears and left when I asked her what she meant."

Rolling his eyes, Greg shoved the pad and pencil back into his pocket. "Thanks a lot, Michelle. You're such a *big* help."

"You're welcome," I replied, as if he'd been sincere. "Why don't you go talk to Tiffany yourself? Then *you* can decide what's important. I'm going in to see my mother now."

Despite the ruckus outside her room, my mother seemed to be resting peacefully, her tiny frame barely a bump in the white bed sheets. Tubes connected her wrist to a bag suspended from a chrome pole beside her metal headboard. An oxygen mask covered most of her face.

"Mom," I whispered over the soft hum of the oxygen machine.

"Michelle," she murmured through the mask as I moved into her field of vision. She added something unintelligible.

"Did they tell you to keep that thing on all the time?" I asked, indicating her oxygen mask.

Her little hand grasped at it as more words tumbled out of her mouth, garbled as if she were underwater.

"Wait!" I deflected her attempts to thrust away the device. "Let's check with a nurse first."

She stared at me, but then ceased trying to pull off her mask. "Don't need it," she muttered.

"Have you seen Dr. Plum yet?" I asked, placing a finger over my lips to indicate that she needn't try to speak.

Mom shook her head and pointed at the television mounted on a wall across from her bed.

"Want me to turn it on?"

A crisp-uniformed nurse swished into the room, her soft-soled shoes barely making a sound as she strode across the tile floor. "Good evening," she said. In one sweeping movement, she nudged me out of the way and took my mother's pulse.

"Excuse me," I addressed her. "Does my mother have to keep that oxygen mask on all the time? She can't talk with it on. Can't you replace it with one of those tubes to her nose?"

"She can take it off to talk." The nurse glanced at her watch, wrote in my mother's chart, and inspected the monitors and tubes. "But don't leave it off too long."

"She wants to watch television. Can she?"

"Sure." The nurse showed me the remote attached to my mother's bed, which included a buzzer for assistance. She pressed a button and the screen illuminated into a crime drama in progress, sound blaring. After showing us how to adjust the volume, she left.

Another worker entered with a tray. This young woman seemed cheerier than the higher-ranking nurse, her full pink cheeks matching her uniform. “Chow time,” she said with a smile, setting the tray on a moveable table with an extension to fit over my mother’s bed. She cranked the bed until my mother reached a sitting position.

“How’s she supposed to eat?” I asked, pointing to the oxygen mask.

The woman looked at my mother as if it were the first time she’d noticed the plastic face cover. She shrugged, and then examined how it was connected to the tubing. “Here,” she replied, pulling off the mask.

“You’re sure?” I pressed.

“Put it back if she needs it,” she suggested. “Need any help feeding her?”

I shook my head and she shuffled out of the room.

The cellophane wrapper from the tray was labeled “soft” but some of the foods required chewing: canned green beans, whipped potatoes, macaroni and cheese, pudding. My stomach rumbled. Although I had only eaten a few cheese samples at the grocery store all day, my mother’s tray of bland carbohydrates on parade did not tempt me.

“Come on,” I said, trying to muster her enthusiasm for the hospital food. “Have some dinner.”

My mother looked from me to the tray, and then back at me again. “You expect me to eat that?”

My sentiments exactly, but I couldn’t let her know. “You have to eat something. You need to get your strength back.”

“I’m not hungry. You eat it.” Her voice sounded hoarse, and her words came out slowly.

“No, Mom. It’s your dinner.”

“Why didn’t they bring you a tray? You’re my guest!” She strained to sit higher in her bed and craned her neck to look around. “I’ll have them bring you something.” Heavy breathing punctuated each word.

“No, I just ate,” I lied. I dipped the fork into the whipped potatoes and propelled it toward her mouth. “Here, take a bite.”

She pressed her lips closed and glared at me, so I set the fork down. I pushed the tray table aside and took her hand in mine. Tube ends taped to her wrist tethered her to the machines beside her bed, like a dog leashed to a backyard tree.

She smiled. "Nice of you to come."

"Where else would I be?" I smiled too, glad she was not bringing up all the times in the past that I was not there.

"Mark is coming?" she croaked.

"He'll be here tomorrow."

She looked at me, her hazel eyes sad. "Why am I here?"

I squeezed her hand. "You fell. Do you remember falling down on the street?"

Again she studied my face. "I fell down?"

"Yes."

"Where?"

"Near the end of our block. They say you tripped off the curb."

Her brow knitted together. "What was I doing there?"

"I don't know. You took off and I didn't know where you were. A neighbor said you were following a dog."

"A dog? I used to have a dog when I was a little girl."

"Topsy. You told us all about her."

"I did? I told you about my dog?"

"About the time she ate your steak. But you loved her anyway."

Mom smiled, as if remembering Topsy. "All kids should grow up with a dog. But Charles didn't like dogs. You kids never got to have a dog. I'm sorry."

"No reason to be sorry. Dad let us have cats. We loved our cats. I still have cats."

She looked at her shriveled hands, bare of rings. "Look what they've done to me. Someone stole my rings."

I pointed to the envelope sticking out of my purse. "No, Mom. I have your rings right here."

She eyed the envelope. "Really? My rings are in there? Thank you, Michelle. How did you get them back?" Her eyes took on a faraway glaze. She muttered, "What is this place?"

"It's a hospital, Mom. Medical Center. You've been here before, last year when you had your surgery."

She nodded, thoughtful. "Why am I here?"

"I told you, you fell."

"I fell?" She looked at me sadly. "Is Mark here yet?"

"No, I told you, he's coming tomorrow."

"Tomorrow? You told me that?" As I nodded, a tear sneaked out the corner of her eye. "It's terrible when you lose your mind."

A kinder person might have protested, tried to cheer her up by assuring her that her mind was fine, perhaps the trauma was interfering with her memory, but my mother would not have been fooled. I realized that on some level, she understood what was happening to her, even though she couldn't stop it. And she knew her family knew, and that made her ashamed. I squeezed her hand and glanced back at her tray. "Sure you don't want something to eat? It might make you think better." Letting go of her hand, I pulled the table toward her.

She eyed the tray of food. "Where did that come from?"

I loaded some mashed potato onto the fork and started moving it toward her mouth. "They brought it a few minutes ago."

Her eyes strayed to the television mounted on the wall, where a police chase was in progress. "While I was gone."

I didn't contradict her. "Open up." The forkful of mashed potato almost touched her lips.

She ignored the food in her face and gazed at her bare hands. "I wish I could click my heels together and turn back the clock, and my rings would magically appear on my fingers."

"Mom, your rings are safe." I pointed to the envelope.

"You have my rings?"

"The ones you were wearing when you fell. But remember that gold one with the carvings that came from the Philippines? I haven't seen that in a while."

"My Moray ring? My mother gave me that for my sixteenth birthday. I wear it all the time."

I opened the envelope and showed her the contents. "I don't see it in here."

Mom peered into the envelope. "I guess it's at home then."

I wanted to ask her when she had last seen it, but did not want to worry her. "I'll take your rings back to the house so you won't lose them. Will you try a bite of mashed potato before your dinner gets cold?"

Distracted by cars careening across the television screen, she parted her lips enough for me to slip the fork into her mouth, like a letter into a mail slot. As soon as her tongue made contact with the substance, she started retching and gasping for air.

I dropped the fork, still white with mashed potatoes, and grabbed the buzzer to summon a nurse. "Mom, I'm sorry!" I pushed the tray table away from her bed and fumbled for her oxygen mask.

The nurse entered and pushed me aside. "What happened?"

"They brought her food and I tried to give her just one bite." My heart thumped almost as loudly as the oxygen machine beside my mother's bed. "She started gagging and now she can hardly breathe."

The nurse wiped my mother's mouth and reaffixed her oxygen mask. "Has she had any incidents of choking before?"

"Once or twice, but with more solid food. The other night, we pulverized her pasta and she was able to swallow it. I didn't think these mashed potatoes would be a problem."

The nurse clutched my mother's wrist, made a note in her chart. Breathing steadied almost as soon as the oxygen mask returned. "She's got an IV pumping glucose into her. She doesn't need the food tray."

After lowering my mother to her former reclining position, the nurse left us alone with the television. The crime drama had ended, replaced by a silly sitcom with an obnoxious laugh track. I groped for the channel changer. My mother ignored the screen, lost in her faraway world again. "Want me to turn this off?" I asked her.

She looked at me, eyes widening. Muffled through the clear plastic mask, over the sound of the television, I made out, "Don't tell him!"

"Don't tell whom what?"

"Don't! Just don't!" Her words grew urgent. She struggled to sit up.

"Mom, what are you talking about?"

More muffled sounds from beneath the oxygen mask. I lowered my head, straining to make out the words, but she may as well have been speaking a foreign language.

Her outburst ended almost as soon as it had started, and she drifted off to sleep. I pressed the TV power button, snuffing the laugh track, and then waited for a reaction from my mother. There was none.

Another worker entered to take the dinner tray. "Ma'am?" she addressed me.

"Yes?"

"I need you to leave for a few minutes, while I change the patient's bedpan and get her cleaned up." As I stepped aside, she pulled some curtains around my mother's bed, like translucent mosquito netting.

I retreated to the hallway. The policeman was still there, eyes glazed. He nodded at me in recognition, but with no invitation to chat.

Pacing the hallway, I fumbled in my pocket for a Kleenex to combat an onslaught of the sniffles. I had almost killed my mother by forcing her to eat! Along with the tissue, I pulled out the tiny slip of paper on which Elaine had scribbled Percy's room number. He was in this hospital.

Chapter Twenty-One

Percy's floor had the same cold gray tiles and ice white walls, the same hum of life-monitoring machines as on my mother's floor. I passed a nurse but did not make eye contact. I was probably not on Percy's visitation list. I half expected to find a policeman outside *his* room; Percy was a more likely killer than my mother.

When I reached his unguarded room, I hesitated. What was I thinking? The last time I saw Percy, he had tried to choke the life out of me. We had spoken on the phone a few times afterwards, when he had managed to get through the switchboard at my office—before the days of caller I.D. —but I had never again agreed to meet him. He had tried to glean clues from our brief conversations about where I had moved, but fear kept me from revealing any information that would help him find me. Once or twice I thought someone was following me after I left work, and one night my upstairs neighbor's German shepherd caused a ruckus, but Percy never managed to track me down. A few months later, I escaped to a new life in Europe.

Deep breath. As Elaine had assured me, Percy was sick, unable to hurt anyone any more. I took a step through the open doorway. I needed to find out what he knew about our son, how Isabella had located him, and whether he believed her story was genuine.

It was a double room, but the roommate's bed was empty. For an instant, I thought Percy must have checked out and I was looking at his roommate, a stranger. Percy had been six feet tall with a healthy build; the emaciated man in this bed looked like a refugee from Darfur. I remembered Percy with a full head of dark brown hair; this man was completely bald. Sensing my presence, his eyes popped open. No mistake: those hypnotic brown eyes belonged to Percy—eyes that used to cast a spell on me.

"M…Michelle?" His hoarse voice could have belonged to an old man.

I nodded, unable to speak. Any response would have been judged stupid by Percy.

His head fell back against the pillow. "Wow!"

"Been a long time," I said tritely, wondering again why I had come. To see for myself that he had been disarmed? To gloat? Had I been hoping for a final showdown? This invalid could hardly defend himself. *Damn you, Percy.*

His eyes studied me from head to toe. "You don't look so bad."

Was that supposed to be a compliment? I dared not risk a "thank you" and leave myself open for a jeer.

"You married?" he asked.

"Yes." *And you thought no other man would have me,* I refrained from adding. I had been in my mid-thirties when I met Roberto, but he had definitely been worth the wait.

"Happy?" Percy asked.

"Very," I replied. "We love each other," I could not resist inserting.

"Kids?" He ignored my editorializing.

I shook my head no. "Cats."

He closed his eyes. "Of course." When we lived together, I was always taking in stray cats. The only one he ever liked was Bowser, a gray and brown tiger-striped kitten with orange patches whose mother had been run over by a car. Bowser had broken her leg when Percy threw her onto the pavement after she accidentally scratched him. As we nursed her back to health, he fell in love with her. My biggest regret about leaving Percy was that he kept Bowser, and I never got to see her again.

"What brings you here?" His next question interrupted my reverie.

"My mother. She's here in the hospital," I explained, in case his ego was inflating with the thought that I had made a special trip to see him.

"Ah. How is the old dingbat?" Although my mother had adored Percy, he always made cruel fun of her behind her back, saying he could see where I inherited my infinite stupidity.

"Hanging in there." I certainly did not want to delve into my mother's recent woes with an unsympathetic Percy. He would probably tell me that of course my mother murdered Brittany Landers, and I was an idiot for defending her.

"And your father?"

"He died in 1992."

"Ah. The booze got him. I heard that."

I glared at Percy. "And clean living has helped you reach a ripe old age?"

He squeezed his eyes shut, a grim smile on his parched lips. I almost felt sorry for him. He wasn't going to pout; he seemed to realize it would no longer work with me. "I never meant to hurt you, Michelle." His voice had grown huskier.

"Hmph. You had a funny way of showing it." The words rushed out before I realized they sounded exactly like something my mother would say.

He snorted. "You still think I was trying to *kill* you?"

I glared at him again. His memory must be as cloudy as my mother's. "I blacked out for at least a full minute."

He shook his head. "If I'd wanted to kill you, I would have."

Sometimes when I told people the story about how Percy had tried to strangle me, less sympathetic listeners—usually male—had brought up that point. A few had forced me to finish the story, the part I had tried to blot out. Roberto never had, for which I was grateful. He had never pressed for any details about my past.

I winced, remembering how I had struggled and begged, as Percy's strong, slender fingers opened and closed around my throat, cutting off my breath until I saw stars, and then releasing his grip. "Do you promise to have sex with me whenever I want?"

I hesitated and got the vise on my throat again. Panicking, I nodded.

He eased the pressure. "*Wherever* I want?"

Fear made my head nod again.

"No matter who you're involved with? Even if you get married?"

Tears streamed down my cheeks and he squeezed my throat again. “Liar! You're just telling me what I want to hear.”

Lightheaded, unable to breathe, I squirmed and pounded his shoulder.

He eased the pressure and cocked his ear to my mouth. “You have something to say?”

“I'm telling the truth,” I panted. “I promise.”

That creepy grin again. “Tell me.” His grip had relaxed, but his hands were still around my throat.

“You're the best lover I've ever had. You'll always be the only lover I'll ever have.”

He nodded. “That's better. Was that so hard?”

I shook my head and touched his hands, trying to remove them from the vicinity of my throat under the guise of a tender gesture. With one hand still on my throat, he stroked my breast with the other, and then slowly worked his way downward.

Only after it was over did he release his grip on my throat. He cooed and stroked my hair tenderly, as if our intercourse had been consensual. I thought he would never leave. Fortunately, he had to pick up a shipment of tropical fish for his store that night. I declined to accompany him as I had to go to work early the next morning, and he accepted my excuse.

“See you tomorrow,” he said, and gave me a kiss good-bye.

As soon as he had gone, I locked the doors, took a long hot shower, and started packing up my apartment.

Looking at Percy now, I still saw a monster. Even after all these years, I couldn't get past it.

“I thought I was giving you what you wanted.” Percy's high forehead wrinkled, as if he had just discovered his revision of history might be a fantasy.

“What I wanted!” Was his mind really that twisted?

His eyes searched my face. “It never occurred to me that you had stopped loving me. That you wanted to date other guys. Even after you moved out. I thought we still had something.”

"So when I told you, you decided to come over and force yourself on me? Take me, dead or alive?"

He was silent for a long moment. Was he going to express remorse, like a normal person? "It was the only way you would cooperate. I didn't mean to hurt you."

I felt sick to my stomach. Twenty-five years had not erased the horror. I couldn't look at Percy any more, couldn't bear those beady brown eyes. The questions I had about our son, and Isabella, and Giovanna, remained unasked. I had cut through the scar and reopened the wound. "Good-bye, Percy," was all I could mutter.

As I hurried out of his hospital room, I ran smack into Isabella.

Chapter Twenty-Two

Isabella's face showed as much surprise as I felt. "Michelle!" She glanced at her watch. Visiting hours were over.

I wanted to ask about her connection with Percy, but instead I found myself doing the explaining. "Did Giovanna tell you my mother is here?"

"She did, and I'm so sorry, Michelle. Is your mother on this floor?"

"No, she's down on four."

Isabella smoothed her long, chestnut mane and waited.

I felt too drained from my confrontation with the past to talk about Percy now. I didn't have the energy to ask her how she had happened to find Percy instead of me and how, after finding him, she could have anything to do with such a despicable human being. "I need to get back."

"Give her my love," Isabella called, as my feet propelled me down the hallway, like a fish trying to escape the range of Percy's net.

The dozing guard jerked to attention when I returned to my mother's room. He nodded at me in recognition. A doctor, stethoscope draped over his white coat like an ascot, was on his way out.

"Dr. Plum?" I had never met the man, but Mark had described him: tall, sandy-haired, thirty-something.

He extended a hand. "You must be Lola Hanson's daughter."

I returned his handshake. "How is she doing?"

"Stable," he replied into his clipboard. "It won't be much longer."

"Much longer? Until she can go home?"

With a glance at my mother's bed he said, "I'll be surprised if she lasts through the weekend."

My pulse raced. *If she lasts...* "Doctor, what are you saying?"

His clear blue eyes were not unkind, but he did not inspire reassurance like an older doctor might. "The pneumonia has caused her lungs to fill with fluid, and her body doesn't have the strength to clear it out. It's already becoming infected."

"Well...can't they... pump it out or something?"

He opened her chart and showed me an X-Ray, the skeletal image ghostlike against the black background. "She has a broken hip. At her age, in her condition, it's not going to heal. She'll never walk again." He pointed to a thin fissure along her pelvis, like a tributary on a map.

"But..." It was like talking to a veterinarian recommending that my aging cat be put to sleep.

"With her dementia and now the hip—believe me, this pneumonia is a blessing. For her as well as her loved ones."

"A blessing?" When I was a child, my mother had always warned me to bundle up before heading out into the cold. "You're going to catch pneumonia and die," she would admonish, as if pneumonia were her greatest fear.

The doctor's voice brought me back to the present. "Ma'am, are you aware your mother has a living will on file with us? She instructs us not to resuscitate her if her heart stops. Not to use extraordinary methods to prolong her life."

"Extraordinary methods to keep her alive in a vegetative state, no," I agreed. "But that doesn't mean you can't try to cure what's wrong!"

He studied my face. "Ma'am, what do you know about Alzheimer's disease?"

I winced. There was that word again. "Tell me."

With a glance at my mother, Dr. Plum began, "Of course, it's a mysterious disease and we don't yet know everything about it. But I'll tell you how I've seen it work in the patients I've treated and... in my own family." His last few words trailed off in a whisper, and then he continued at full volume. "First it steals your memories. Short-term, then eventually long-term. With the memories, you also lose cognitive skills you need to survive: to protect yourself from cold, from heat, from pain, from fear. You lose the ability to make sensible decisions: to distinguish truth from lies, right from wrong..."

"My mother can distinguish right from wrong!" My heart pounded.

"I didn't say she couldn't." His tone sounded slightly peeved. "The disease affects each person in different ways, at a different pace." He looked away from my mother, stared at his clipboard. "As the disease progresses, the body loses its ability to perform involuntary functions: swallowing, elimination, and finally, circulation and breathing. Believe me, you don't want to see her in that last stage. And *she* doesn't want to experience it."

"No." I studied the tile-patterned floor. "She doesn't."

"Believe me, Ma'am, we're doing everything we can to keep your mother comfortable," he assured me. "Do you have any more questions?"

"What about that oxygen mask? Can't you put on something less intrusive, so she can talk? My brother will be here tomorrow." I gazed past him at my mother, draped in white sheets, breathing rhythmically through clear plastic.

"The mask is the most efficient way for her to get enough oxygen." Dr. Plum looked back at his clipboard and opened the chart of another patient.

Bitter words formed, but I bit my tongue. "Dr. Plum, this is my mother we're talking about. And you don't know for sure that she has Alzheimer's."

He sighed, and I detected the hint of an eye roll.

"I'm going to find her another doctor."

His brow lifted slightly, as if he were not accustomed to being challenged. "That's certainly your prerogative, Ma'am. But we're short-staffed on weekends as it is." With body language indicating he had to finish his rounds, tend to his more important patients, the ones worth saving, Dr. Plum escaped into the hallway, leaving me alone with my mother.

Dr. Plum was right. I had no success at the reception desk. The woman on duty, who had no authority to change anything, tried to convince me that Dr. Plum was a talented physician, perfectly capable of handling my mother's case.

Crushed by defeat, I retreated to my mother's room and picked up her latest *Reader's Digest*, which I had brought to the hospital in hope that she would feel up to reading, yet knowing full well she no longer comprehended words on a page. I was pretending to read, trying to escape into someone else's story, when Isabella came in.

"Michelle," she greeted me.

I looked up from the circle of light shining on my magazine. Her leonine hair defined her silhouette in the doorway. "Hello Isabella." I shut the magazine and set it in the chair beside me.

Isabella swept to my mother's side and peered over the bed rails. "How is she?"

"Giovanna says you're a nurse." I shielded my eyes from my reading light.

"I could read her chart if it were around here." She brushed a wisp of grayish white hair off my mother's oxygen mask.

"Do you know Dr. Plum?" I rose from the chair to stand beside Isabella. For the first time, I noticed she was several inches taller than I.

"Doctor... Who?"

"My mother's doctor. He's given up on her. He thinks she has Alzheimer's."

Isabella turned to me, her green eyes full of compassion. "Some of these doctors have no tact. I'm sorry he made you feel that way. Shame on him!"

"But is it true? Is there really no hope of a recovery?"

"There's always hope. Sometimes that's all you can do." She looked at my mother's hands, examined the tubes leading from her wrists. My mother did not stir, but I could hear and see her cadenced breathing with the aid of the oxygen. It sounded like she was snorkeling through a coral reef.

"Isabella, do you work here now?"

"In this hospital? No, but I'm on leave from Memorial Hospital in Houston."

Memorial Hospital. Where my Jean-Paul was born. "Are you in Two Wells because of Percy?"

She swallowed. “How did you know Percy was here in the hospital?”

“My friend Elaine Nelson told me. I think you know Elaine as well.”

“Elaine who?”

After her three marriages, I had lost track of what surname Elaine went by. Each of her children had a different one. “Nelson was her maiden name. Short red hair? My age? I’m not sure what her last husband’s name was. He’s a well-known criminal lawyer. Tillman? Or maybe she’s using Edwards?”

“Elaine Edwards?”

Phillip Edwards was the name of Elaine’s second husband, Timmy’s father. He had been a highway construction worker, killed on the job by a careless truck driver, leaving Elaine with a life insurance check big enough to put aside a nest egg for Timmy’s college education, as well as buy herself a brand new sports car, dress better, and start attracting a higher class of suitors. She must have resumed that surname after divorcing her third husband, on account of Timmy. “Yes, Elaine told me Percy was here.”

“You know about the prostate cancer?”

Although I could conjure no real sympathy for Percy, it was not hard to put on a grave look. If Isabella had feelings for this man, her daughter's grandfather, I wanted to be supportive.

“It’s not looking good.” A cloud of sadness enveloped her, like early morning fog hugging the trees.

“How long have you known Percy?”

Isabella wiped away a tear. “He was at my wedding.”

“To Jean-Paul?” Percy had actually *known* our son? I felt a prick of jealousy, like I’d been stung by a gnat. “But… how…how did you find him?” And what I really wanted to ask was, “Why? Why did you, or Jean-Paul, go looking for *Percy* all those years ago and not *me*?” Wouldn’t it have been easier to find the birth mother? The hospital had not even allowed me to put Percy’s name on the baby’s birth certificate.

She answered before I could reach the obvious conclusion. “He found us.”

Chapter Twenty-Three

Even though I had heard Isabella perfectly, I repeated her statement to allow my brain to catch up. "*He* found *you*? How?"

Isabella sighed. "I'm not sure how he connected all the dots. He surfaced right after our engagement picture appeared in the *Houston Chronicle*, so there must have been some key information in the article."

Turning away from Isabella, I returned to the chair and sank into the faux leather. My mind flashed back more than thirty years to another hospital room, the one I had shared with Cathy C. The one where I had looked into Jean-Paul's dark blue eyes, tickled his tiny toes, and cooed to him as if I was really going to be his mother.

After I signed the adoption papers, I thought how I would never again look into those dark blue eyes, never see them look back at me with recognition, never find out whether they would stay blue or turn hazel like mine, or brown like Percy's. Swallowing hard, fighting back tears I had not expected, I had presented the social worker with the red booties I'd knitted during my pregnancy: my baby's only tangible proof that his seventeen-year-old birth mother had loved him.

Percy had flown into a rage when he learned I had signed the papers. He wouldn't speak to me for two days. I had expected his usual irritation about how I could never do anything right. I knew he was hurt that I had held the baby without him, even though it was his own fault for not showing up at the hospital when he said he would. But the intensity of his anger I had not expected. I reminded him that the whole purpose of my going to the unwed mothers' home was to give the baby up for adoption. He had had months to change his mind. Was it harder for him because "Monique" had turned out to be a boy?

After Percy's anger subsided, after I left the unwed mothers' home and tried to return to my teenage life, tried to get back on course for a college career, Percy and I almost never spoke of our child. Every now and then, in the heat of an argument, when he was searching for a particularly wounding insult, he would trot out the accusation, "You gave away *my son*!"

"Michelle?" Isabella's voice brought me back to 2001. "You should go home and rest. I'm about to do that myself."

"So Percy got to know Jean-Paul?" His ultimate revenge.

"A little. Paul didn't quite trust him. And his adoptive parents were very disturbed when Percy showed up on their doorstep."

"But he invited Percy to the wedding?"

"Actually, that was my idea. I felt sorry for Percy, reaching out and not getting much of a welcome. I had the impression it took him years to gather the courage to make contact. I don't think he was prepared for rejection."

"Was Jean-Paul curious about his birth parents?" *About me*?

"He knew he was adopted, and like all adopted children, I think he wondered what his birth parents were like, and why they gave him up. But he had invented a Cinderella image of you guys, and I think he was afraid of shattering that image if he started looking for the truth."

"What did Percy tell him about me?"

"I…" Isabella did not meet my eyes.

"Surely Jean-Paul must have mentioned something." I steeled myself for the wicked witch picture Percy had surely painted of me.

Her breath was barely audible. "He said you were very young. That you had moved on."

"That I didn't care," I supplied.

"I never thought that."

"Did Jean-Paul want to find me?"

"This all happened so fast. As I told you, he was shipped to Kuwait not long after our wedding. He didn't have much time to think about it."

"And you kept in touch with Percy?"

"When Paul was killed, I felt obligated to tell him. And Giovanna had just been born." If Isabella noticed my sour expression, she did not acknowledge it. "I needed all the support I could get, and Percy was there for me and Giovanna."

"What about Paul's adoptive parents?" I held my breath; my Jean-Paul was not the only one who had conjured a Cinderella story.

"They were great, too. Not crazy about having Percy in our lives, but they respected my decision to include him."

"*Were*?"

Tears flooded Isabella's eyes. With a brave sniff and a flick of her hand, she wiped them away. "September 11. Gone."

I stared at her in disbelief.

Isabella nodded.

"Where were they? In the Twin Towers? On an airplane?"

"No, visiting friends in Indiana. When all the flights were grounded, they rented a car to get home. Witnesses say they swerved to avoid a drunk driver and ran off the road." She winced. "The car rolled down an embankment."

"Isabella, I'm so sorry!" I opened my arms and she collapsed into them, sobbing.

"So you see," she sniffled. "I *had* to find you, Michelle. For Giovanna's sake. There's no one else left."

I didn't know yet if I was glad she'd confronted me. Things were happening too fast. I stroked Isabella's hair, afraid to broach the subject of *her* side of the family, afraid it would unleash more tales of tragedy.

Isabella pulled away, composing herself. "I should go. Giovanna is with a neighbor, and I don't want to leave her there all night." She turned to my mother, still fast asleep, breathing steadily with the help of the oxygen infusion. "Good night, Mrs. Hanson." Stroking my mother's tube-laden arm, she slipped into her nurse role. "Don't stay too long, Michelle. You're more help to your mother if you keep your strength up. I'm sure the hospital will call if there's any change."

Alone again, I leaned close to my mother, brushed my lips to her cheek. "I have to go now, Mom. But I'll be back tomorrow. And Mark will be here."

Maybe it was my imagination, but her eyes fluttered when she heard my brother's name.

Although I was exhausted when I got home, I couldn't fall asleep right away. I opened my father's liquor cabinet and selected a bottle of Amaretto. There was a time when I thought I might become an alcoholic like my father had been. Once in my twenties, after a particularly embarrassing night of over-indulgence and blathering to casual acquaintances, I had attended an A.A. Meeting, stood up and said, "My name is Michelle Hanson, and I'm an alcoholic."

I poured myself a snifter of the dark, sweet liquid and deemed it potable. I no longer believed I was an alcoholic. The tendency was there; it would have been easy to slip into despair and blame it on genetics. The key to keeping the beast at bay was moderation, control. One, maybe two drinks, I could handle. Roberto helped, because he could be content with one beer, or one glass of wine with dinner. Like my father, I loved the taste of alcohol, loved the warm feeling it gave me as it ran through my veins, but unlike him, I was not going to ruin that soothing sensation by letting alcohol control me. I settled into my mother's favorite armchair with my Amaretto, picked up Isabella's photo album, and perused the wedding pictures for Percy.

My eyes came to rest on a photo of Isabella and Jean-Paul with his parents. At the time, they were probably in their mid-forties, younger than my present age, but they looked much more mature. Maybe that's what raising a child does for you; someone has to be the grown-up.

Even though I'd never met Jean-Paul's adoptive parents, a wave of sadness washed over me when I thought about the car accident that took their lives. A fantasy had been forming where Isabella would introduce me to her in-laws, and they would share with me all the milestones of Jean-Paul's childhood that I had missed. They would thank me for the wonderful gift I had given them, thus validating my decision to give my baby up for adoption. Now I knew this could never happen. More doors were closing. When I was younger, I felt I could go in any direction, open any door. But as I grew older, one by one, doors were closing. Reunion with my son: closed, bolted shut. Having a child I could actually raise: most likely closed, too.

Revenge on Percy? Peace with Percy? That door was one click away from being locked. I examined more photos of crowd shots. Would I even recognize him?

It looked like a happy wedding. Elegant guests toasting with champagne flutes, laughing, having fun. It also looked expensive. As a bride pushing forty and self-supporting, I had paid for my own wedding ceremony. Roberto and I had kept the guest list to twenty-five. When you work for an airline, you can fly to Hawaii to get married, but there are few people who can afford the airfare to join you for the ceremony in a tropical garden overlooking the Pacific Ocean. The witnesses included our closest family members and some airline friends—mostly people who also had free travel privileges.

The wedding of Jean-Paul and Isabella seemed more traditional, with an abundance of middle-aged guests that suggested parental funding. Was Isabella's family well off? Did they incur huge debt to make their daughter's dream come true? She had never mentioned her relatives, and I could not detect them from the pictures. There was something slightly foreign—even exotic—about Isabella; perhaps seeing her parents would provide a clue to her origin.

Then I saw it. Jean-Paul shaking hands in the receiving line with an older version of himself, handsome in a dark suit, a full head of salt-and-pepper hair: Percy. Father and son. My heart pounded as if it would bounce up my throat and out of my body.

I shut the photograph album and drained the last of my Amaretto. I stared at the bottle, still sitting out on the counter, taunting me. No, I was not an alcoholic. I would not become my father. I rose, put away the bottle, took my glass to the sink, and rinsed it out. I had to pull myself together before my brother arrived.

Chapter Twenty-Four

The next morning, as I prepared to return to the hospital, the doorbell chimed. I walked to the peephole while inserting earrings into my lobes. On the doorstep, a twenty-something black man in baggy clothes swayed to an inaudible beat. Padded headphones covered his ears and uneven dreadlocks dangled almost to his shoulders.

I cracked the door without removing the chain. "May I help you?"

He squinted, pressing his face closer to the door. Beads of perspiration clung to the sides of his nose. "Who are *you*?" His voice boomed over muffled rap music.

"Who are you looking for?"

He bobbed his head as if he had come to a favorite part of a song. "Where Brittany?"

"Brittany?" I felt a chill.

"Yeah man. Don't she stay here no more?"

"Not any more." Was I supposed to break the news to this kid?

He squinted at me again. "Yeah? Okay then." Spinning to the beat, he danced down the walkway, not bothering to ask where Brittany was staying now.

I watched Brittany's visitor bounce down our driveway and slide into an unwashed white sedan. The same vehicle I had passed on my way up the street the day I arrived, the day Brittany had died! Fumbling to fling off the chain, I called, "Hey! Wait! What's your name?" I ran onto the porch. "Sir!"

If he heard me, he ignored my sudden interest in his identity, and my transformation from fearful white woman peering over the chain. The car—a Ford Taurus, I noted—cranked and pulled away, loud rap music blaring. At least I had the presence of mind to look at the license plate this time.

Repeating the combination of numbers and letters to myself, I rushed inside to write them down before they slipped from my memory. I searched the coffee table for Keith's business card, stashed away somewhere in my straightening frenzy to prepare for my brother's arrival.

I located the card by the kitchen wall phone and dialed Keith's number. Voice-mail. I left a detailed message recounting my latest visitor, a description of the car, the license number, and a reminder of when I had last seen that car. Maybe I would redeem myself, make up for my original sketchy account.

When I walked into my mother's hospital room and touched her hand, a smile crept over her lips. Her eyes fluttered, but she said nothing. I watched her for a few moments, wondering whether to talk. She could probably hear.

"Another one of Brittany's boyfriends stopped by this morning," I began. "How many did she have? No wonder you were upset about all the *people* coming and going! This one didn't seem to know she's dead, though."

Talk of Brittany did not rouse my mother. I changed the subject. "Mark is flying in later today. He got a connecting flight into Jenkins Field; I'll have to leave in a little while to pick him up. Marie may be coming, too. I cleaned house for her, but I'm sure she'll find a lot more to do."

"Mark," my mother murmured.

"He's not here yet. It'll be a couple more hours."

She drifted off without acknowledging my response. After a few minutes, I picked up the *Reader's Digest*. The words danced on the page and I found myself rereading the same paragraph over and over again.

When a nurse chased me out so she could change my mother's bedpan and clean her, I strolled the corridors. I ended up back at Percy's room.

Percy's beady brown eyes watched me enter. When we were together, I had never thought of his eyes as beady—although they could shine like glowing coals when he was angry—but back then they were framed with thick, dark lashes. The cancer and chemotherapy had changed that.

"I want to hear how you found Jean-Paul," I demanded. "Isabella told me you tracked him down right before they got married."

Percy chuckled, stroking his hairless chin. For a couple years in his early twenties, he had sported a full beard, and he would stroke it when toying with me. "So you've met Isabella?"

"And Giovanna."

His eyes brightened at the mention of Giovanna, our lovely grandchild. "Nice girl, Giovanna. Quiet. Spends lots of time on the computer, though. I think that's where kids have most of their conversations these days."

"Tell me how you found them. And why."

Percy leaned against his pillow. If there were a nurse around, she would probably tell me to leave, to stop needling the poor sick man. "Didn't you ever wonder about our son? Or did you put it all behind you when you signed those adoption papers?"

"Of course I wondered about him." I shifted my weight to the other foot, not daring to approach close enough to lean on the rails of his bed.

"But of course, you got to hold him."

"You could have held him, too, if you hadn't been out with Donna Simpson."

"Donna Simpson? Oh yeah, that was her name. You were always jealous of her."

I wasn't going to play his game. "You had the opportunity to hold your son, and you chose to do something else."

"I went by the nursery the next day to see him, and all I could do was look at him through the glass! They wouldn't let me hold my own son."

"We did what was best for him. We agreed. I was seventeen years old, for God's sake."

"That was one of our biggest problems. You were too young."

"You never said *you* were ready to be a father back then. At twenty."

"I had a *son,* and you gave him away to strangers."

I had navigated the rapids of this conversation thirty years ago; I was not going down this part of the river again.

"You never stopped wondering about your son and you decided to track him down. How did you do it?"

Percy straightened in bed and focused his eyes on me. "I never found my son."

"What do you mean?"

"Isabella is just a friend. Giovanna is a lovely girl, but she's not our grandchild." He leaned back to enjoy my reaction. "Ooh...you'd like her to be, wouldn't you?"

"*What?*" I felt my knees go weak.

"We just wanted to see how you'd react." Percy coughed. "If you'd even care."

I wanted to take a towel and wipe the self-satisfied smirk off his ashen face, maybe cut off his breathing supply in the process. "How could you play such a sick trick? And involve a child? Tell her I'm her grandmother, when I'm a total stranger?"

Percy grinned, that sick smile I'd glimpsed when he was strangling me. "It worked, didn't it?"

I spun toward the door. "Good-bye, Percy!"

"Michelle?" His voice had softened.

"What?"

"Do you really think I'd make all that up? Involve a young lady and her child in a scam?"

I stopped, glared at him.

Percy shook his head, his face covered in mirth. "You're still so gullible!"

No! He was playing me like a yo-yo. Disgust overwhelmed my curiosity to learn more about my son and how Percy had found him. "And *you're* still a jerk!" I retorted, hurrying out of the room before he could stop me again.

Back in the sterile hallway, I tried to calm down. Percy could press buttons I had forgotten had wiring.

When I reached the stairwell, I bolted up two flights and then down again, panting, shaking my head wildly to free the rage I felt. I did it again. And again. After a deep, slow breath, I walked the two flights down to my mother's floor, running my fingers through my hair to coax it into place.

Keith Matthews stood outside my mother's room, chatting with the guard. Keith grinned as he saw me approach. He had a toothy smile that lit up his handsome face. I smiled back.

"Got your message," Keith said. "Thanks. They're bringing the guy in for questioning."

"That was quick." I stopped beside him, hoping I did not smell of sweat from my brief jog in the stairwell.

"With the license plate number, we found him right away."

"Sorry I didn't get it before."

Keith shrugged. "You had no reason to."

Of course not. Unlike Percy and Greg, Keith made me feel better about myself. I nodded, grateful.

"Sorry about your mother," Keith offered.

I locked my eyes with his. "Help me prove she didn't kill anyone."

My mother was sleeping. Her breathing seemed more labored, even with the steady flow of oxygen. I touched her hand, withered and cool. "Get some rest, Mom," I murmured. "Mark will be here soon."

"Miss Michelle?"

I looked up to see Karen Jackson's large black shape filling the doorway. "Karen! How are you?"

"Ooh, Girlfriend! I heard about your mama!" Karen swept across the room and stood next to me at my mother's bedside. I hugged her broad shoulders, willing myself not to start crying.

"She was supposed to be taking a nap!" I disengaged to look into Karen's big brown eyes. "Next thing I knew, she had been rushed to the hospital."

"Mm, mm," Karen shook her head.

"Did she ever wander off like that when you were watching her?"

Karen pressed her big lips together and shook her head again.

"The doctor says she has pneumonia," I continued. "Pneumonia! That doesn't develop overnight. I noticed her cough when I first got here. How long has she had it?" Some of the blame for my mother's predicament surely belonged with her caregivers.

Karen shrugged. "I noticed it on Tuesday. I was off on Wednesday. Told them other girls to keep an eye on it." She picked up my mother's hand and studied her I.V. As Isabella had done. "Has she talked to you much?"

"Yesterday. Not today."

She nodded. She pulled back my mother's covers and tilted her tiny frail body.

"Did you deal much with Dr. Plum when you were taking care of my mother?" I stepped aside to get out of her way.

"Sure. He was usually the one we went to see."

"What did you think of him? I mean, he doesn't seem too concerned about helping my mother get well. He thinks she has Alzheimer's."

"What that man say?"

"That pneumonia is a blessing, and they aren't trying too hard to get it under control."

"Mmm, mmm, mmm," Karen clucked, rolling her big brown eyes in sympathy. "Doctors!"

"Can you recommend another doctor? I know about the living will—no extraordinary procedures to save her life—but if she has a chance, I don't want this Dr. Plum to let her die because she's old and a little confused."

"I'll stay with her," Karen offered. "A lot of families hire someone to sit with their loved ones in the hospital, to make sure they gets the care they needs."

"You'd do that? What about your agency? I thought they didn't want you to have anything to do with us any more."

Karen plopped herself into the chair beside my mother's bed. "Girlfriend, I know your mama didn't kill no one. And even if she did, she ain't going to do it again, not in the state she's in."

Although Karen's offer eased my mind about my mother's condition, it reminded me of the unsolved murder that may have precipitated it. "Who do you think killed Brittany Landers? The police still suspect my mother."

"Lordy. I been talking to my daughters about her. That Brittany had all kinds of enemies. Owed people money. Played the mens for fools. Stole other girls' boyfriends. My

Keisha saw her arguing with another white woman the other day, when she showed up for her shift."

Arguing and murder were not the same, I knew. "Was it her sister?"

"She has a couple sisters. Coulda been. But I don't think so."

"This white woman, did Keisha say what she looked like?"

Karen shrugged. "Twenties. Long bushy hair."

Not much of a description to give the cops. I could hear Greg Dobbins jeering now. "Did Keisha tell the police yet?"

"She talked to the police, but I don' know what she said."

"People keep coming to the house, asking for Brittany," I said. "It's weird. Some young black guy was there this morning. Didn't even know she's dead."

"Where he been? It's all over the news."

Probably doesn't watch the news, I thought. I hadn't watched it lately, either. "And Brittany's sister Tiffany came over the other day. Was she around much, when Brittany was working?"

"No telling."

"A couple nights ago, some guy almost beat our front door down, saying he wanted to talk to the old woman who killed 'his' Brittany! That's why they have a guard outside the room here; he threatened to come after her again."

Karen's eyes widened. "Well, I'll be!"

I glanced at my watch. "Look, Karen, I have to pick up my brother at the airport now. Let me discuss your proposal with him. We'll get back to you?"

"That'd be fine, Honey. I ain't going nowhere."

Chapter Twenty-Five

Jenkins Field was a small regional airport, but not nearly as small as I remembered it, when my uncle used to fly his Piper Cherokee in for visits. Back then, there were no metal detectors and no chain link fence surrounding the runway. Our whole family would walk onto the tarmac to greet my uncle planeside. Today, I had to stay in the waiting room, watching through the plate glass window for my brother to deplane the commuter flight.

Would Marie really be with him? Part of me wished she would stay home, leave Mark and me to deal with this family crisis on our own. She was sure to criticize the way I'd handled things, and would likely imply that if she and Mark had been here instead, our mother would never have been accused of murder, and she certainly never would have wandered off and injured herself. On the other hand, if Marie didn't come, who would eat all that tofu I had purchased?

The commuter plane taxied to a stop in front of the concrete walkway to the terminal. Its whirring propellers blew the tall grasses that hugged the chain link fence. A uniformed airline agent waited on the tarmac for the pilot to cut the engines before the stairs came down.

Mark was the third passenger off the plane. Tall and broad shouldered, with a full head of sandy hair ruffling in the wind, my younger brother strode down the steps, shielding his eyes from the sun as they scanned his surroundings. Was he flashing back to our childhood here as well? Marie followed. Her long, dark hair was tied sensibly in a braided ponytail, almost unaffected by the wind, and her coordinated pantsuit did not even appear wrinkled after the long flight from Seattle and plane change at Dallas/Fort Worth. She still looked like a runway model, even after two children. I waved.

In a moment, they were inside the terminal and my brother scooped me into a bear hug. He had grown a beard since I'd last seen him, and the fur felt soft against my cheek. After he released me, Marie and I exchanged a reserved embrace. She smelled of unscented soap; I'd forgotten she was allergic to all kinds of perfume and, by habit, had applied my Chanel Number Five this morning. At least I had not refreshed it for hours.

Over Marie's shoulder I glimpsed for the first time their traveling companion, who had stepped back to allow a family of five to deplane ahead of him. A smile lit my face as my eyes met Roberto's. Even though he was almost five years younger than I, his well-chiseled features framed by neat salt-and-pepper sideburns gave him that distinguished look which caused people to assume he was older. Marie and I disengaged and I rushed toward him, arms extended.

"You didn't tell me you were coming, too," I murmured, as we embraced.

"Better cancel your date," he teased, ruffling my short hair and tilting me so we could look into each other's eyes. His were filled with an adoration that never ceased to amaze me, like he was looking upon a goddess instead of a middle-aged, mediocre mortal.

"Damn," I said, playing along. "You should have seen the party we were planning! Hope I can catch him in time."

We smiled at each other and kissed. "Missed you," he whispered, caressing my lips with his mouth. His lips were soft but responsive, his cheeks smooth, and he smelled faintly of the Lagerfeld aftershave I'd given him for Christmas last year. When we came up for air, Mark and Marie were already on their way to Baggage Claim.

"Did you bring Mom's car?" my brother asked when we caught up with them.

"No, the rental," I replied.

"Did you call the rental company and extend the contract?" Roberto asked me.

I slapped my hand to my forehead. "I meant to." It was due back today at the Dallas/Ft. Worth airport.

"Are the papers in the glove box?" Roberto asked, with a glance at the moving carousel.

"Yes."

He picked up his small, black roll-aboard, verifying the nametag and the Italian flag decal on the side. "I'll go call them now. Give me the keys."

I handed them over. "It's in the short-term lot out front. Red Grand Am. You'll leave it unlocked for us, won't you?"

"Of course." He was already wheeling toward the exit.

Marie gazed after Roberto as Mark dragged their large suitcase from the carousel. "Your husband is sure full of energy, isn't he?"

The carousel stopped as Mark retrieved a duffel and a make-up case. "Is that it?" I asked.

"Isn't that enough?" Mark grinned, strapped the duffel to his shoulder, and pulled out the handle of the large suitcase so he could wheel it to the car. I carried Marie's make-up case.

"Where are the kids?" I asked as we headed outside. "They're not old enough to stay home by themselves yet, are they?"

"They're with Mommy and Daddy," Marie answered. Marie's parents lived in the same subdivision as Mark and Marie; her father worked for Boeing. Marie's family ties had influenced their choice to settle in Seattle. "We didn't want to take them out of school right now."

I was neither thrilled nor disappointed to miss my niece and nephew this trip. They changed so much each time I saw them, both in appearance and behavior, that I never knew from one visit to the next whether I would like them or not.

Mark and I arranged the luggage in the trunk while Marie settled into the car. Claiming to suffer from carsickness, Marie usually commandeered the front seat. I climbed in back with my brother.

Roberto returned and slid into the driver's seat. He would need me to navigate the unfamiliar town, but he always insisted on driving. It did not offend me; I preferred to be chauffeured.

"You're all set, *Carina*." He stuck the key in the ignition, turned to the passenger side, and did a double take when he saw Marie there. Not missing a beat, Roberto craned his neck to address me in the back seat. “We have it until the end of the week. Same airline rate.”

“Thanks, Honey Bear.” I patted his shoulder and stroked the edge of his neatly trimmed black hair, which, like his sideburns, also contained flecks of gray. “Turn right on the highway when you pull out of here.” I turned to my brother. “When did you all plot to meet up with each other?”

Mark shrugged. “Roberto called me last night, because he hadn’t been able to reach you at Mom’s house. You were probably over at the hospital.”

When it came to our personal travel, Roberto had always put me in charge: researching the flight schedule and availability, listing us as standbys, making all the arrangements at the destination. Now he had planned and executed an entire journey without my knowledge or assistance. “Any trouble finding each other?”

“Roberto was waiting for us at the gate in Dallas,” Marie supplied. “His flight got in first.”

I leaned forward to pat Roberto’s shoulder in approval. He took one hand off the steering wheel for a moment and caught mine, clasping it briefly before returning his attention to the road. “Are we going straight to the hospital?” he asked.

“I think we'd better.” I turned to my brother. “Mom’s been asking about you.”

When we parked in front of the hospital, Roberto jumped out and opened the back door for me. He circled to the passenger side to open the door for Marie before my brother had extricated his six-foot frame from the back seat. Not that Mark would have rushed to open the car door for his wife anyway. A feminist at heart, Marie usually shunned such “nonsense” on the part of well-meaning men, but she seemed to enjoy Roberto’s bursts of chivalry.

I led them into the hospital, straight to my mother’s floor. It felt grim, parading through the corridors with an entourage of relatives. Like Mom was on her deathbed or something, and I refused to believe she was. The sterile, medicinal smells tickled my nose. Being confined in a place that smelled like this would give me all the incentive I would need to get well.

The guard nodded at me, not bothering to check the identification of the new visitors. Either security had become lax, or else he trusted me by now and had decided not to harass me. My brother nudged me as we passed. "What's with the police guard? They afraid she's going to escape?"

"It's a long story."

Roberto took my hand as we entered my mother's room. I squeezed his, grateful for the support.

My mother's eyes fluttered open as we assembled around her bed. Gently, I pulled aside her oxygen mask so she could speak to us. The television on the wall across from her was blaring a football game in its final quarter. Marie found the remote control and shut it off. Mark leaned over my mother and touched her hand. "Charles!" she murmured. "You've finally come."

"It's Mark, Mom," I corrected her. "You were asking about him earlier, and now, here he is. Marie and Roberto are here, too."

Mom's eyes darted from my brother's face to Marie, and then to Roberto, without a flicker of recognition. "Nice to meet you."

Marie stepped beside her and took one of her hands, ignoring the fact that my mother had not acknowledged her. "How are you, Lola? You gave us all a scare! Travis and Tina couldn't miss school to be here, but they send their love."

My mother had no reaction to the mention of her grandchildren's names.

"In fact," Marie continued. "They made you a get-well card." Out of her purse she took a plain greeting card that her children had decorated with colorful drawings of hospital patients smiling. Inside, the children had each taped an autographed school photo, along with their scribbled get-well wishes. Marie opened the card and brought it close to my mother's face. "See? There's Tina; she's wearing her hair long now. And look how big Travis is getting! He's on the soccer team this year."

My mother closed her eyes. Marie stood the card on the nightstand. She flashed Mark a weak smile and then retreated.

We waited a few minutes, but my mother had drifted into slumber. Roberto looked at his watch. "What do you think, Michelle? Let her rest, and come back later?"

"Excuse me." From the doorway, Isabella caught my eye. The late afternoon sun highlighted flecks of gold in her mane of chestnut hair.

My heart raced. How would I explain her? I had not rehearsed my confession to Roberto. And what did Marie know? After twenty years of marriage, surely my brother had confided my secret to her. But if so, she had never brought it up. "Uh," I began. "Isabella, this is my husband, Roberto." I paused; Roberto identified himself with a salute. "My brother Mark, and my sister-in-law, Marie. Guys, this is Isabella Rogers."

My brother's eyebrows raised as a glint of understanding lit his face, but he played my game, keeping my secret. The others did not seem suspicious that I had not elaborated on Isabella's credentials for being in my mother's hospital room.

"So nice to meet you all." Isabella smiled warmly, still hovering in the doorway. "Can I borrow Michelle for a minute?"

I broke away from the group, giving Isabella a questioning look.

She led me outside the room, past the guard, into the hallway. "It's Percy," she whispered. "He's asking for you."

Chapter Twenty-Six

"Percy!" His name left a bitter taste in my mouth. "What does he want with *me*?"

Isabella continued to lead me down the hallway, her chunky heeled shoes striking the tiles. "He wants to clear some things up. He said you had questions. About Giovanna and me."

I stopped. Touching her arm, I forced her to stop as well, silencing the echo of her shoes. "Tell me, Isabella. Who *are* you, really?"

"What do you mean?" Her face reflected fear of the monster Percy had described.

"Were you really married to the son I gave up for adoption? Is Giovanna his daughter? Or are you just some impostor friend of Percy's, messing with my head?"

"I..." Isabella stepped back.

"Because I have a husband in that hospital room who doesn't know a thing about this situation, and I'm trying to figure out a way I can explain a couple of long-lost relatives, while my mother is fighting for her life—and a murder charge to boot. If this is all a joke..."

"Is *that* what Percy told you?"

"Why do you think he would tell me that?"

We had come to a part of the corridor with big picture windows overlooking the parking lot. Dusk was overtaking the bright autumn afternoon; red streaks of sunlight electrified the darkening blue sky, pierced by pinpricks of city lights coming on. Isabella gazed out. "I always took him at his word. That he was Paul's natural father. That he had managed to get hold of the adoption records." Her voice trembled. "You're saying it's not true?"

"I don't know what to believe." I watched Isabella gaze outside, her chest heaving. It dawned on me that I was not the only one in turmoil. "Come here." I held out my arms and she flung herself into them. We stood propped together in the corridor for a moment, silently shifting the burden of family illness, murder and imminent death, and deep dark secrets until we felt refreshed enough to each pick up her own load and carry on.

"You don't know what he wants to tell me?" I asked, when we resumed our march toward Percy's room.

"You've got *me* curious now."

Percy was dozing when we tiptoed into his room. Isabella strode to his bedside, fluffed his pillow and wiped his lined face like a devoted daughter. His eyes popped open at her touch, and a smile illuminated his face. I hovered near the door, observing their cozy rapport like a voyeur. Briefly I wondered if their relationship had ever crossed into the romantic realm, but I quelled those thoughts as soon as they formed.

"I brought Michelle," Isabella told him.

Percy's eyes shifted in my direction. I couldn't read the expression on his face; it could have been remorse, guilt, or sadistic amusement. "Hello, Michelle."

"Isabella said you have something important to tell me." My voice remained even and businesslike.

"Oh, yes." Percy stretched like a cat waking from a delicious nap, with all the time in the world.

"So, what is it?" The impatience in my tone caused Isabella to flinch.

"Come in. I don't bite." His voice rasped. Reluctantly, I moved closer to the bed so he wouldn't have to strain his vocal chords to talk to me across the room.

"Michelle doesn't have much time," Isabella explained. "Her husband and brother are here, visiting her mother."

"Husband, huh?" Percy chuckled, stroking his bare chin. "How come you didn't bring Mr. Wonderful with you?"

I made a point of looking at my watch, although I would not have been able to recite the time had anyone asked. "You had something you wanted to tell me?"

"Forgive me for disrupting your busy schedule. Time is inconsequential to a dying man confined to a hospital bed." Percy did his best to look pitiful.

Isabella shot me a pleading smile. I wondered what Percy was like with her. Was he a normal father-in-law and grandfather? Whatever that was, as I had experienced neither. But the petulant, domineering Percy I remembered would not fit my image.

"Last time you were here—forgive me, I can't recall when that was. Yesterday? Today? Last week?" Percy cleared his throat. "I said some things that were not true. I played with your head. I wanted you to feel guilty about giving away my son."

"You can't make me feel guilty." I shook my head, looking away from him. "I did the right thing. What kind of screwed-up life would our son have had, being raised by a couple of immature kids like us? No money, no education." I looked at Isabella. "He certainly would not have been able to find a nice wife like Isabella here."

Isabella brightened at the compliment, but her eyes remained concerned as they darted between the two of us.

"I found my son, though." Percy continued as if I had not spoken. "You couldn't keep him away from me forever." His dark eyes scanned my face for a reaction.

"How?" I was genuinely curious how one might obtain supposedly sealed adoption records.

"It's not something you'd be bright enough to pull off."

"Then tell me how you did it. Step by step, so my pea brain can comprehend."

Percy paused as if waiting for a drum roll. "After you left me, I dated some of the ladies at Faith Home." Faith Home was the adoption agency that had placed my son; they had an agreement with the Claudia Crichton Home for Unwed Mothers.

I rolled my eyes. "You're right. I guess that would not have worked for me."

He shot me the same look my father did when I'd interrupted adult conversation with an impertinent remark. "The first one was not cooperative. The little goody-two-shoes clung to her business ethics like a stupid bulldog."

"So you dumped her," I guessed. For the six years that Percy and I had been in a supposedly committed relationship, he had been unwilling to stay faithful to me.

Memories of the rationale he gave for beginning and ending each of his many affairs flooded back.

"Her best friend was better, but she didn't have access to the archives. By then my son had been with strangers for five years." He stroked his chin. "You can't imagine the drivel I had to listen to from those idiots!"

I glanced at Isabella to assess her reaction to Percy's diatribe. She was studying the subtle pattern in the tile floor. "So you found one who gave you the information you were after?" I prompted Percy, not wishing to hear him belittle the poor women at Faith Home who had committed the sin of finding him attractive and believing he felt likewise about them, never guessing his agenda.

"Her supervisor. Butt ugly!" He emitted a feeble whistle. "Afterwards, she kept calling me, wanting to get together again." His face contorted like my mother's when she refused a meal.

Again I glanced at Isabella, wondering if she had seen this side of Percy. "How many women did you have to sleep with? Total?"

He glared at me with those beady brown eyes, glowing like hot coals in his pasty face. "It was what *they* wanted." If he'd had a wife or a steady girlfriend at the time, he would have rationalized that his actions did not constitute cheating; he was performing a service to obtain a commodity; if anyone was the victim here, *he* was.

That old, sick feeling crept from the pit of my stomach. I willed myself to concentrate on reaching the end of the story, blocking thoughts about Percy's penchant for philandering and twisting the truth. "When you found out where our son was, what did you do?"

"All I could get was his new name–Paul Rogers–and the name of the couple who adopted him. The bitch wouldn't give me their address. She claimed she didn't have it. And Paul Rogers is not a unique name." He licked his lips and swallowed to lubricate his throat. Isabella picked up a plastic pitcher of water from Percy's nightstand and poured him a glass. With a tender glance at her, he took the water and drank deeply. "I made a lot of phone calls." He cleared his throat. "Got cursed out by a lot of people.

Including the couple who adopted him. They *lied* to me when I called them."

"So how did you find him?"

"Years went by; I'd reached a dead end. I missed seeing my son grow up." He studied my face, as if looking for guilt I refused to exhibit. I had missed seeing my son grow up, too—a trade-off I had accepted for giving him a supposedly better life. "Then I saw the engagement photo of my son with the lovely Isabella." Percy looked at Isabella fondly. "I noticed the resemblance immediately, along with the name 'Paul Rogers.' His parents' names matched, and of course, he was exactly the right age."

"So, that was how you found him?"

"It wasn't quite that easy. The paper didn't print their address, and the witch at the society desk refused to give it to me. His parents' phone number was unlisted. But the article mentioned that his fiancée, Isabella Marchisio, was a nursing student at the University of Houston." He took another swallow of water from the glass at his bedside.

"You got to *him* by stalking *her*?" I glanced at Isabella for confirmation.

"Stalking!" He sputtered. "You always did have a filthy mind!"

Again, Isabella looked at us in alarm. Was her high opinion of Percy starting to deteriorate? Or was she looking at me through his eyes, perhaps deciding I was an unfit grandmother for Giovanna?

I turned to Isabella as a mediator. "I agree *stalking* is a strong word. But Isabella, how did it make you feel, as a young college student, to be followed by an older man, a stranger, with no legitimate reason to be on campus? I'd have freaked out."

Isabella shot me a tight-lipped smile. "I was nervous when I first noticed him watching me. But when he approached me, he was kind, and he got to the point right away." She stared at the off-white wall, as if remembering those carefree days on campus, before she married and quickly became a mother and a widow. "He *looked* so much like Paul, it wasn't hard for me to believe him."

"And you agreed to introduce Percy to Paul?"

Isabella nodded, taking over the story while Percy drank more water. “I knew Paul was adopted, but he’d never mentioned his birth parents, never seemed curious about them. His adoptive parents hadn’t provided any information, other than the fact that he was adopted, that he was chosen, that it was God’s will. They’d never encouraged him to find out more.”

“What did he say when you told him about Percy?”

She flashed a glance at Percy. “He was suspicious. Thought Percy was after something more sinister. Paul's parents were well off.”

“He also thought it a bit strange that his birth *father* was the one looking for him, when his birth *mother* couldn’t care less,” Percy chimed in.

“We met at a Mexican restaurant. Just the three of us; we didn’t tell Paul’s parents,” Isabella continued, tuning out Percy as she might do with Giovanna if she tried to interject her own spin on a story. She smiled, her eyes focused on a distant screen with memories playing. “Paul kept staring at Percy, like he was looking in a mirror. And he listened.”

“Did he feel like his birth parents had abandoned him?” I had read that many adopted kids harbor that fear, and meeting the birth parent can sometimes clear up latent insecurities. I addressed Isabella, but was not surprised when Percy answered.

“I explained that it was his *mother’s* idea to give him up.”

“He told us you were younger, that you were only seventeen when Paul was born,” Isabella added. “That your parents were very strict and expected you to go to college, and that’s what you did.”

“It was a very hard decision,” I said, as if Isabella could channel my words to Jean-Paul. “I never stopped thinking about him, wondering what had become of him.” What I really wanted to ask was, did he wonder about me? Upon finding his birth father, did he also want to meet his birth mother? But after the image Percy had painted of me, I was afraid to hear the answer.

“I think he wondered about you, too,” Isabella continued, as if she had been reading my mind. “I know I did. We talked about it, and we agreed that after he got home from Kuwait, we'd try to find you."

I flashed back to 1991, when my son and his new wife had entertained the idea of searching for me. I was still flying, a newlywed camping out with my mother-in-law Suzanna in New York City, trying to figure out a way to live and work in the same city as my husband, commuting between bases and layover cities, trying to carve out more time together, never feeling like I could settle down and rest. How would I have reacted? More importantly, how would Roberto have reacted?

"Then Giovanna was born, and Paul was killed." Isabella blinked, her long lashes moist.

"He never got to see her?" My chest felt heavy.

"I had the first baby pictures developed and sealed in an envelope ready to send to him."

"I'm so sorry." Even though it had all happened more than ten years ago, the words felt right as I observed fresh pain flash in her eyes.

"I gave Isabella your parents' address," Percy interjected. "Thought you might want to know what had become of your son."

"You did?" I would not have been hard to find at all. My parents had lived in the same house since I was six years old, when we moved to Two Wells from upstate New York.

"Tell her about your visit to them, Isabella."

Isabella looked down. "They wouldn't tell me where you were. They said you had married, but they wouldn't give me your new name. They told me not to try to contact you."

"Your drunken father told her never to darken their doorway again," Percy added.

My father could be quite intimidating, especially when he was drinking. Many of my high school suitors never called again after the first date, but Percy had stood up to him, eventually gaining his respect. At that terrible moment when we had broken the news that I was pregnant, both my parents had stayed surprisingly calm, treating Percy and me as adults with an important decision to make. But my parents never spoke of their first grandchild after it was all over, and I'd had no idea how deeply the episode had affected them. "I'm sorry," I told Isabella. "It was probably a shock for them."

"I'm not sure I was ready to meet you," said Isabella.

"I'm glad you gave it another try." Would I still be glad after I broke the news to my husband that I was a grandmother? I looked at my watch; nearly an hour had elapsed since I'd left my family. What excuse could I possibly give for my absence? "I have to get back now. Percy, thanks for clearing this up for me. I hope you can beat this cancer thing and get out of the hospital soon." Almost meeting his eyes, I patted his stiff foot through the bed sheet.

"This is it? You won't be back to visit me again?" he croaked.

I looked over my shoulder as I left the room.

Chapter Twenty-Seven

The television was blaring the evening news when I returned to my mother's room. Karen tended to my mother, wiping her face and smoothing the wisps of pale gray hair against the clinical white pillow. She looked up. "Miz Hanson, Michelle's back."

I detected a slight movement of my mother's eyes. "Where is everyone?" I asked Karen.

"Your brother'll be back directly. He ran them others to the house so they could get unpacked."

An empty feeling swept over me, like being late for a party, and finding it over already. "Did you talk to Mark about hiring you to look after Mom?"

She nodded, indicating a small overnight case in the corner. "I'm here for ya'll."

I wasn't convinced there was much Karen could do for my mother that the hospital could not, but she cared about Mom, after all the time they had spent together. I'd read articles about the decline in hospital care—overworked staff, unhygienic conditions, inattention to medical charts —so maybe this was how other families guarded against their loved ones falling victim to neglect. What could it hurt? Financially, for now at least, we could afford the extra vigilance. My conversation with Dr. Plum had given me the uneasy feeling that he was waiting for Mom to expire and free up another bed. A representative with a little medical knowledge stationed at her bedside might prevent him from hastening the inevitable. I looked at Karen. "Do you think she'll get better?"

Karen stepped away from my mother's bed to make room for me. "That's between her and the good Lord."

Though I'd hoped for a better prognosis, I knew Karen was being honest. I looked at my mother, so frail and shriveled, lying unresponsive in that unfamiliar bed. Like the winter wind whipping around the house, trying to sneak into the cracks, the fear of losing her had been hovering, trying to seep in. A tear slid from the corner of my eye and I wiped it away with the back of my hand. I bent to address my mother and clasped her small, cold hand. “Mom, I went to see Percy. You know he’s in this hospital, too?”

My mother made a sound between a groan and hum. Did she remember Percy?

“Dying of prostate cancer,” I continued. “Who would have thought?” I watched for a sign that she was listening. I’d read stories about people in comas hearing everything going on around them. She wasn’t even in a coma. “Sometimes people get what they deserve.” As soon as the words left my mouth I felt tarnished, and I wished I could recall them. “I shouldn’t have said that,” I apologized. “No one deserves to get cancer.” My mother had had cancer! Did she even remember? Her face looked slightly more peaceful; maybe it was my imagination. “You never wanted to hear the whole story about how I cut my ties with Percy,” I explained, caressing her shriveled fingers. “You didn’t believe he really tried to strangle me.” I looked at Karen, her bulky frame spread in the chair like parcels without a storage place. Though she had one eye on the television, I could tell she was eavesdropping. I didn’t care. I’d gone to let the secret of my teen pregnancy out of the vault and found the door wide open.

“Percy and I discussed that this weekend; he claimed he didn’t really intend to kill me. But at the time, he had me convinced. I blacked out for a few minutes, you know.” I took a deep breath. “That’s not normal. A woman shouldn’t have to put up with abuse like that, even if he says he didn’t mean it.” Years of suppressed feelings pushed to get out, like a stampeding crowd. “Even back then, blinded as I was by infatuation with Percy, convinced that he was my destiny, I figured out something was off.”

“I know you thought I should have stayed with Percy, after all our history together, that otherwise I’d grow to be an old maid. But that episode scared me. I had put up with Percy's verbal abuse for years, just like we all did with Dad when he was drinking, but this was the first time

Percy had turned violent. What would he do next to control me?"

"For the first time, I decided being an old maid was better than putting up with Percy! I should have left him after..." I glanced at Karen. "When I was still a teenager." I lowered my voice, "When I got out of the home. But Percy pursued me, charmed me, made me feel safe and loved. He was the only one who was there for me at one of the lowest points in my life." I flashed back to that crossroads of my life; my friends had forgotten me, and even my family had turned cold. I could not have endured the aftermath of giving up my child had it not been for Percy.

"But I'm a slow learner. Six years of my life it took. Like you, I thought Percy and I belonged together. Maybe I wanted to prove that I could hold onto him after... you know. Pride! That's what it was. He was so good-looking, so charming when he wanted to be. I loved the way other girls looked at us with envy whenever we went somewhere as a couple. I was so proud I had won the Percy prize, that I was able to hang on, and I wouldn't let go, even when I didn't want it any more. Face it, he made me miserable all through college. I got the college degree, but not the college experience." I took a deep breath.

"It took me until I was thirty-five to find Roberto, but he was definitely worth the wait. I'm happier than I ever would have been with Percy." I knew I should get beyond the psychoanalysis of the past and move on to the more important present: Isabella and Giovanna. Although my mother had met them, had dinner with them, I had never really explained to her who they were. Not that she would have been able to remember from one minute to the next. Eying my quiescent mother, I took another deep breath, lowering my voice so Karen would have to strain to hear me over the television. And if she heard, so be it. "Percy was always angry because I gave up our...uh...our b... baby." The words tasted foreign; I felt like a soap opera character delivering a soliloquy. "But the whole time I was p..pregnant, he never hinted that keeping the child might be an option. Even when I was in the hospital, he never said he'd changed his mind." When I'd first told Percy I was pregnant, he had accused me of doing it on purpose, violating his trust, trying to trap him into marriage. Even now, that conversation hurt too much for me to paraphrase it out loud to my mother.

"After we broke up, Percy tracked down our son." Was it my imagination, or had my mother twitched? "He pulled some strings, hit a few dead ends, but he got a chance to meet our boy when he was all grown up and engaged to be married. Can you believe it? Percy actually went to Jean-Paul's wedding! I've seen pictures! Pictures of your first grandchild. Remind me to bring them tomorrow. There's one of Percy standing next to Jean-Paul, and they look so much like father and son!"

Mom's face wrinkled, as if I had lost her. "Jean-Paul. I never told you what I named him. I know you said not to name him, like you didn't want me naming kittens from a litter we had to give away." When I returned from the unwed mothers' home, she had not wanted to hear a word about my experience; she wanted me to erase it from my mind, wipe that chapter from our family's history. One of the hardest parts about the whole ordeal was that I'd yearned to talk about it with *someone*, and there was no one to listen. I'd tried to reach out to Janet M., got some relief from writing it down, but she had never responded to my letters. Percy was the only rock I could cling to. "Unfortunately, Jean-Paul—actually 'Paul' was what his adoptive parents named him: Paul Rogers—joined the army and went off to fight in the Gulf War."

Was my mother still awake? Had she heard a word I'd said? Now that I had started unloading, I had to continue as if my ramblings were processing. "Isabella—the girl he married—became pregnant before he left, but he never got to meet their daughter." I felt tears filling my cranial cavities, trying to block my next words. "My son was k... killed. Now *we'll* never meet him, either, Mom." I took a deep breath, squeezed my mother's hand, willed myself not to sputter.

A few moments of silence gave me better control of my emotions, allowed me to steady my breathing and halt the flow of tears. My mother still showed little reaction. Karen seemed absorbed in a sitcom with a raucous laugh track, but maybe she was politely pretending not to listen.

"Anyway, Isabella named their daughter Giovanna, and now she's ten years old. By blood, she's my *granddaughter*, your great-granddaughter." Even after I'd had a couple days to get used to the idea, it sounded strange: *I was a grandmother.* "You met them the other day. Remember, they had dinner with us? Isabella put your pasta in the food processor so it would be easier for you to eat."

I smiled at the thought of how caring and responsive Isabella had been to my mother's needs, an angel sent from heaven, how I had entertained the idea of hiring her as a caregiver. Would my mother have grown to trust her more than the women of the Loving Care Agency? I sighed. Would home care for my mother ever be a concern again? "But now I have to figure out how to explain Isabella and Giovanna to Roberto." As I spoke, my mother flinched.

"Good luck with that." I heard Mark's voice behind me.

"Mark." I still clung to Mom's hand as I made room for him beside her bed. "Are Roberto and Marie settling in?"

"Yeah, Marie's blood sugar was low, and we didn't know how long you'd be."

"Did she find the tofu and veggies in the refrigerator?"

Mark smiled. "You did good."

"Want to stop at Burger King on the way home?"

"Can we?"

"Whenever you're ready." I could not remember my last meal. My stomach had passed from the growling, deprived state into the numbness of fasting, but the mention of food awakened it.

Mark turned toward our mother. "Any change? Has she said anything?" He took her hand from my grasp and caressed it.

"No. When she first got here, she was talking. But today..." She had not yet acknowledged my brother's presence and that had to hurt. I added, "Yesterday I told her you were coming, and it seemed to make her happy."

Mark set down my mother's wizened hand. "I'm going to speak to Dr. Plum. Seen him lately?"

As if on cue, Dr. Plum walked in, the stethoscope draped around his neck like a towel around the shoulders of a tennis star.

Mark moved forward, hand extended. "Dr. Plum."

"Mr. Hanson." Technically, my brother was "Dr. Hanson," having earned a PhD in physics, but my mother was the only one who insisted on addressing him that way. Mark took no offense at the salutation as he shook hands with Dr. Plum. Standing side by side, both over six feet tall, they resembled twin towers.

"What can you tell us about her condition?" Mark asked.

Dr. Plum bent over our mother and listened to her chest. He shook his head. "Her lungs are still clogged with fluid, and she doesn't have the strength to expel it. It won't be long now."

We both winced. Mark eyed Dr. Plum. "Are you doing everything you can?"

"Of course we are." Dr. Plum sighed. "But her body is shutting down. I'd suggest moving her to a hospice facility, but I think the move would be too stressful for her. By the time you made the arrangements, she'd be gone."

I covered my face with my hands, as if I could shut out his harsh words and thus nullify them. At least he did not mention "Alzheimer's" again. "Surely you're not the only doctor on duty at this hospital this weekend. Can we get someone else to give us a second opinion?"

Dr. Plum bristled. "I understand how you feel, Ma'am. But let me assure you, I *have* been conferring with other doctors about her condition."

Mark swallowed; I could see the lump sliding down his throat. "What can *we* do?" I'd thought my brother, the rock, would be more forceful, able to convince this uncaring doctor that our mother's life was worth saving, but he seemed as meek and powerless as I.

Dr. Plum glanced at her chart and made a notation. "You're doing it. Talk to her. Say good-bye."

I uncovered my face and looked Dr. Plum in the eye. "But there's still a chance she could recover, isn't there? If she can expel that fluid from her lungs."

He looked at me with something akin to pity, making me forget I was an adult almost old enough to be his mother. "You can always hope for a miracle. But she doesn't have the strength, or the will."

My mother did not have the will to live. That was what this was really about. I remembered Dr. Plum's description of the progression of Alzheimer's disease; no doubt my mother had pondered that fate in moments of lucidity. The thought echoed in my head as Dr. Plum excused himself to continue his rounds. I flashed back to last December, when my mother had been diagnosed with breast cancer. Although she had been told they could operate, and there was a good chance the tumor could successfully be removed, she had calmly accepted the fact that her life was coming to an end. She had even written a farewell letter to her friends and family in lieu of her usual Christmas newsletter.

After the surgery, my mother had been transferred to a nursing home for three months to recover. She had seemed so miserable then, like a prisoner chained to her bed, and she had often wailed to me that she was dying. Her own mother had died quietly in her sleep, of an aneurysm, at age sixty. Mom had often told me that was the way *she* wanted to go as well, and that she had never expected to live past sixty-five. This slow death, she told me, was hell. "Mom, you don't have to die. You can get better," I kept telling her. But she would cry and moan, "Why me? Why am I being tortured this way? Why can't I just die in my sleep like my mother did?"

I looked at my mother lying in the hospital bed, with a machine helping her breathe. Had she really given up? Were Mark and I and her grandchildren not worth living for? And what about the murder she had most likely witnessed? Did she secretly hope she would be blamed and perhaps executed for the murder? Or had Alzheimer's disease stolen her survival instinct?

I turned to my brother. His face remained stoic, but I could tell Dr. Plum's words had convinced him our mother's condition was worse than we had thought. "We can't let her die an accused murderer!" I declared.

Mark's reddened eyes betrayed a man who had not slept much during the past few days. "No," he said, "but what can we do?"

Indeed, I thought. What can we do? The police seemed content with my mother as their prime suspect, despite my efforts to steer them in other directions. They had no sense of urgency about finding the real killer. Once she died, they would probably close their case, mark it solved. No way was this the legacy my mother should leave. Time was running out, and we had to step it up a notch. "Mark," I said. "The police need more help." My brother gave me a questioning look as I turned to Karen. "Do you have Brittany's family's address?"

Chapter Twenty-Eight

Karen had to phone one of her daughters, but in a few moments, we had obtained the address for Brittany's family. Their home was located near the railroad tracks in the poorer section on the north side of Two Wells, which had been all black when I was growing up.

Mark and I stopped first at a Burger King on Front Street to fortify ourselves for our mission. I devoured a Whopper Jr. with cheese, and my brother tackled the full-size Whopper. Fast food is rarely part of my diet, but it had been so long since I'd eaten that the infusion of fats and carbohydrates tasted wonderful.

Mark licked his lips and wadded the empty wrapper. "Marie is going to be disappointed."

"How will she know?"

"She'll know." With a paper napkin, he brushed evidence off his mustache and beard.

"She can't turn you into a vegetarian if you don't want to be one." My brother and I had been down this road before.

"She says the toxins from eating meat pollute the air, and she won't have it in our home." His exasperated look said he didn't believe it, but had given up fighting.

I rose, piled our trash onto a plastic tray, and dumped it into the receptacle by the doorway. "Roberto will pollute the house enough for all of us. He'll probably ask for spaghetti and meatballs tomorrow." While I was staying with her, Roberto's mother Suzanna had taught me her secret meatball recipe, and Roberto could never get enough of them. When he came home from a four-day trip, nothing made him happier than smelling meatballs and chunks of Italian sausage simmering in a rich, spicy tomato sauce.

Mark and I climbed into our mother's Ford Fiesta. He had left my rental car at the house so our mother's vehicle would get some use. "Piece of junk," I murmured, slamming the door on the passenger side.

"Our parents never did have good taste in cars," Mark agreed, starting the engine. "Cramped my style in high school."

I grinned. "Probably the way they wanted it."

Indoor and outdoor lights burned at the Landers household, a small, ranch-style wood-frame with peeling paint, crooked shutters, and a broken bicycle in the mostly-dirt front yard. Part of me had been hoping no one would be home. A large mongrel dog barked furiously as we got out of the car.

Heavy metal seventies music blared from inside. We rang the doorbell, but doubted anyone could hear it over the stereo. Voices argued over who should answer. The music stopped. Footsteps shuffled across wood floors as shadows darted behind the curtained windows. More footsteps pounded as they neared the front door, and then retreated. I looked at Mark. He rang the doorbell again.

In a moment, the door opened. A haggard, stringy-haired woman from our generation stared at us through glazed eyes. The aroma of marijuana smoke drifted outside. "Yeah?" she asked, looking at the space around us rather than at our faces. When she opened her mouth to greet us, I noticed she was missing two of her incisors.

"Mrs. Landers?" I asked. "Brittany's mother?"

Her affirmative answer was a groan.

I continued, "I'm Michelle, Mrs. Hanson's daughter, and this is my brother Mark. Brittany was at my mother's house when she was....uh...when she died. We want to let you know how sorry we are about your loss."

Fresh tears filled the glazed eyes and she stepped aside, beckoning us indoors. "Y'all coming to the funeral Tuesday?"

Mark started to shake his head, but I nudged him. *The funeral. A good place to observe the cast of potential suspects*. "Where is it?" I asked.

Bedroom slippers shuffling over the scuffed wood floors, she led us to a worn upholstered couch covered in crumbs and dog hair, and invited us to sit down. A newspaper folded open to the obituary page covered the rickety wooden coffee table. She pointed to an announcement about Brittany Landers, which contained the details of the funeral service.

She sat in an adjacent bent cane rocker, took a tightly rolled joint from her bathrobe pocket and lit it, puffed to get it going, and then inhaled deeply. She held it toward me. I declined, as did Mark.

A cloud of sweet marijuana smoke enveloped us as Brittany's mother toked alone. Her eyes focused on a faraway point. "My baby shouldn't have pissed off that woman. That girl could sure get people riled up!"

That woman, I thought, was my mother. Had Mrs. Landers not comprehended that she was talking to the children of the woman who had allegedly clobbered her daughter to death? I cleared my throat. "What people?"

"Huh?" Brittany's mother squinted at me, joint poised at her lips.

"Who else did she rile up?" Mark prompted. Mrs. Landers' attention span was about as long as my mother's.

"Men. Lots of men. Played 'em for fools. And other women, too. Even her own sister! Stole her man right out from under her nose."

"So you think there might have been a lot of people who wanted to see Brittany dead?" I summarized. I doubted the police would buy the idea of Brittany's sister killing her over a spat about a boyfriend, but then again, homicides are most often the result of domestic discord.

"Heaven knows what she said to that old woman, to push her over the edge. Lord knows, I wanted to smack her smart mouth many a time."

"Mrs. Landers," I said. "Our mother is 77 years old, recovering from cancer surgery, and she weighs less than a hundred pounds. Do you really think she had the strength to hit a healthy young woman like Brittany with such force that it would kill her?"

Mrs. Landers let a cloud of smoke escape from her mouth. In a throaty voice she replied, "That's what them cops told me. If you can trust a cop."

"That's the only explanation they could come up with. Mom was supposedly alone with Brittany, and she couldn't tell the police what happened. Her memory fades in and out, and if she witnessed anything, she can't remember it well enough to talk about."

Mrs. Landers frowned. "Then what did happen?"

"That's what *we're* trying to find out. I think someone else was there. Maybe Brittany was quarreling with a friend, or a boyfriend, and things got out of hand."

"Yeah?"

"Do you think that's what could have happened?"

"Well, yeah. It would make more sense than what the cops are trying to make me believe."

"Did Brittany ever talk about arguments with my mother? Did she say she was violent or abusive?"

"Well, no. That old woman was always giving her nice things."

I felt a jolt. "Giving her nice things? Like what?"

"Jewelry. Clothes. Knick-knacks, pretty stuff." The joint had grown too small for Mrs. Landers to keep holding without burning her fingers, and she fumbled for a clip.

Mark and I exchanged alarmed looks. "Yeah, right," Mark muttered. While not stingy, our mother was not the type who gave presents to strangers, especially not high-value items. I thought of the ring I had seen on Tiffany's finger. Had that been something my mother had "given" to Brittany?

I cleared my throat. The smoke was affecting me. Roberto and Marie would smell it and wonder where Mark and I had been. Marie would speculate that we had paid a visit to one of Mark's old high school buddies. I willed myself to put aside thoughts about my mother's possessions, and how Brittany had come to acquire them. "So, you don't think my mother would have turned on Brittany, tried to kill her?"

Mrs. Landers sucked in the last of the smoke from her roach and set it down, still attached to the clip, in the ashtray. "Beats me what happened. But I wouldn't be surprised if them pigs was lying to me."

It had been a while since I had heard the term "pigs" in reference to the police. Like some of Mark's old cronies, Mrs. Landers seemed stuck in the early seventies. Did living in a small Texas town allow people to remain in a bubble? Did we step into a time machine whenever we went back to visit? I tried to focus Mrs. Landers on the murder investigation. "Think about that last day, before Brittany went to work. Did she have any visitors, phone conversations? Did anything happen out of the ordinary?"

Tiffany emerged from one of the back rooms, doused in sweet perfume and made up heavily, sporting a mini-skirt and thigh-high boots, ready for a night on the town. It surprised me to see her; I had pegged her as too old to live at home. It sounded as if Brittany had lived at home as well. Was that the trend these days? Under-educated, under-employed, twenty-something children sponging off their parents, like Elaine's daughter Stacy? Tiffany eyed us with suspicion.

"Tiffie, who was that Izzy dude Britt was talking to on the phone the other day?"

"Don't know him, Ma. Can I take your car?"

Mrs. Landers tossed a set of keys; they jingled as they flew into Tiffany's cupped hands. I could not see if she was still wearing my mother's gold ring. "Be careful, hear?" her mother said. "And put some gas in it this time." She looked at us with a shrug. "Before Brittie left for work that morning, she was arguing over the phone with some guy she called Izzy. That's all I know." She sighed, focusing on a point on the wall. "She argued with all her boyfriends. Girlfriends, too. Angry all the time. I didn't think nothing of it." Her eyelids drooped from the effects of the pot.

"This Izzy," I prompted. "Did you ever meet him? Talk to him on the phone?"

She yawned, reached for a dish on the coffee table, and grabbed a handful of peanuts. She offered the rest to Mark and me, and when we declined, popped several into her mouth. "Honestly, I couldn't keep up with her friends. She never kept any of them very long."

Mark and I looked at each other; we had run out of questions. I scanned the room; maybe there was a photo or some other clue we were missing to complete the puzzle. My eyes came to rest on a fairly recent portrait of Brittany, Tiffany, and another young woman, with a plumper, older face and long, frizzy brown hair. "Do you have another daughter besides Brittany and Tiffany?" I asked Mrs. Landers.

Mrs. Landers turned toward the photo I had been viewing. “Stephanie is my oldest. She's on leave from the Army.”

Mark pointed to his watch, a reminder that we both had spouses at my mother’s house who would not be thrilled about our detour to play detective.

I rose. “Thank you very much for your time, Mrs. Landers.” Mark followed my lead and moved toward the front door. “Maybe we’ll see you at the funeral,” I said over my shoulder.

The dog howled again as we stepped into the fresh night air, careful not to trip on the buckled concrete driveway. I pulled my cardigan around my torso to ward off the autumn chill.

Before we reached the street, headlights blinded us and a speeding pick-up truck turned up the driveway, nearly mowing us down as it screeched to a halt. Mark yanked my sleeve and we jumped to the lawn for safety.

A heavyset woman emerged from the truck, hands on her hips. Stephanie Landers? She resembled the third sister in the photo I had just observed but seemed larger and tougher in person. “What do you think you're doing?”

I opened my mouth to explain, but then realized she was not asking a question.

“Get out! My mother has been through enough.” Stephanie stepped toward us menacingly.

I sprinted like a gazelle toward my mother’s car, Mark right on my heels.

I was shaking as we climbed in. I locked the doors and looked at Mark. “Whew! We got out of there just in time.”

Mark cranked the engine a couple times before it started. “Piece of junk,” he muttered. Luckily, Stephanie had already gone inside. “What do you think we accomplished?” he asked.

“I’m not sure,” I answered, wishing I’d gone in with more of a plan. I’d had no experience as a detective and no need for it until now. As we drove away I murmured, “But I don’t think Mrs. Landers is convinced that Mom killed Brittany.”

Chapter Twenty-Nine

Marie was curled up on my mother's couch, engrossed in a paperback mystery novel, with a large box of Kleenex perched on the arm and a tissue crumpled in her hand. She looked over her reading glasses as we entered. "There's stir fry left over if you want some." She blotted her nose.

Mark bent to give her a peck on the forehead. "Thanks, but we stopped for a bite." He did not mention where. "Allergies acting up?"

Marie sniffled. "It's the dust." Before my brother could pull back from his greeting kiss, she wrinkled her nose like a bunny in a garden. "You smell like smoke."

"Where's Roberto?" I interrupted. When we drove up, I had noticed my rental car was gone.

"Out to get ice cream. Your mother's has freezer burn." Marie closed her paperback, marking her place with a monogrammed leather bookmark. "How's your Mom?"

"Same," Mark replied, sinking into my mother's favorite armchair. "We made a stop on the way home."

I cringed. Was he really going to tell Marie about our visit to Mrs. Landers? Did he have to tell her everything?

"Where'd you go?" She gave him a sly look. "Besides Burger King?"

He smiled like a little boy caught misbehaving. "Michelle and I went to visit Mrs. Landers. Brittany's mother."

Marie scrunched her face. "You did what?"

"Something isn't right about that girl and her family," I said. I set down my purse, took a seat on the opposite end of the couch, and turned to face my brother. "The older sister seems like a psycho. And you didn't get a good look Tiffany's hands, did you?"

"What do you mean?"

"The other day she was here, and I noticed a ring on her finger that looked exactly like Mom's. You know the thick gold one with the olive leaf etching?"

Mark gave me a blank look but Marie said, "I always loved that ring! The design is unusual. I've never seen one like it." She tapped the arm of the couch. "I'll look for it tomorrow. Maybe it's stashed here somewhere, and this Tiffany's ring just reminds you of your mom's ring."

"I asked her where she got it, and she said it was a 'gift.' Mark, remember how Mrs. Landers said Mom was always 'giving Brittany nice things'? That doesn't sound like Mom. Especially because she talks about those aides like she can hardly stand having them around."

"Her personality has changed a lot since she's been sick," Mark said. "You never know."

"Also..." I fumbled through papers on the coffee table, looking for the loan application, but then remembered I had given it to Keith Matthews. "We got an application in the mail the other day for a $50,000 home equity line of credit! Cosigned by Mom and *Brittany Landers*!"

"What?" Mark and Marie gasped in unison.

"I didn't have a chance to tell you, with everything that's happened. Looks like that girl was stealing us blind. She didn't get away with the loan because she was too stupid to fill out the application completely, and they mailed it back to us."

Mark's jaw dropped open, but no sound came out.

"What does this mean?" asked Marie, with a hand on her husband's shoulder.

"I don't know yet," I muttered to the coffee table. "Unfortunately, the police probably see it as a motive for Mom to murder Brittany Landers."

"Did you tell them?" Mark asked.

"Keith Matthews is checking it out. I wonder what else Brittany stole."

We exchanged concerned looks, none of us courageous enough to verbalize doubts about our mother's innocence. As if not saying it would change anything.

The silence was broken by the sound of the front door opening and Roberto's whistling. In a moment, he appeared in the family room, clutching a grocery bag. "Ice cream, anyone? I got Rocky Road and Butter Pecan."

The four of us moved to the card table, where I had dined with Isabella, Giovanna, and my mother the other night. Roberto and Mark took heaping helpings of Rocky Road; I opted for a small serving of Butter Pecan. Marie claimed she didn't want any ice cream, but she picked up a spoon and whittled tiny bites off Mark's mound of Rocky Road. I wasn't sure whether she thought she was doing him a favor by sparing him from too much fat and sugar, or if she subscribed to the dieter's rationale that calories obtained from another person's plate do not count.

The sound of spoons clinking against ceramic bowls eventually gave way to conversation. Marie was the first to break the rhythm. "Michelle, who was that young woman?"

I knew I had been naïve to hope that Isabella's appearance in my mother's room had not sparked questions, but I played innocent. "What young woman?"

"The one at the hospital, who called you away right after we got there."

"Oh, her," I pretended to search my memory for an insignificant piece of trivia. "Her name is Isabella Rogers."

Like a stray cat who smells food, Marie refused to let it go. "Who is she? How do you know her?"

"She's a friend." I rose, collected the empty ice cream dishes, and walked them to the kitchen sink, careful not to make eye contact with my brother, who was probably putting it together, if he had not already. I rinsed the dishes, hoping the sound of water running would suspend conversation momentarily, and then placed them in the dishwasher; the spoons jingled as they tumbled into the silverware basket. Yawning, I announced, "Think I'm ready to turn in for the night. It's been a long day." I strolled by the table where the others were still seated. Looping my arms around Roberto's neck, I kissed his head of salt-and-pepper hair and murmured, "What about you, Honey Bear?"

Marie and Mark had commandeered my mother's king-sized bed, leaving Roberto and me to my spongy double bed. It made sense, they pointed out, so we didn't have to change sheets on two beds. "You have seniority," Roberto grumbled as we undressed. "Why didn't you say something?" At Roberto's insistence, we had slept in my mother's bed once, while she was in the nursing home, and its firm mattress had been quite comfortable, but usually when I went home I automatically settled into my childhood bedroom.

"Sorry," I replied. "That's the way it worked out."

He sat on the bed, bouncing the springs slightly, watching it ripple like a partially-filled waterbed. "My back will be screaming in the morning."

I leaned over and kissed him. "Thanks for coming."

He returned my kiss with passion. Our arms encircled each other and we fell back as one against the worn foam rubber pillows. "Where else would I be?" he murmured against my neck. "I love you." When we stretched out, our feet reached the edge of the small bed.

"I love you, too," I whispered. As I held my husband tightly, I thought about how timing had shaped so many lives. Percy, like Keith Matthews' brother, Kevin, had lived in the shadow of the draft and the dreaded Vietnam war, unable to concentrate on studies but bitterly aware of the consequences of dropping out and losing that student deferment. By the time Roberto reached eighteen, the draft was over. Because military service was a great way for a young man without much money to start a career, Roberto had joined the Air Force and served his four years in peace time. He had not seen a day of combat, had lived in reasonable comfort on U.S. And European bases, and learned to fly big jets at government expense, which had opened the door to a free college education and a lucrative job as a pilot for a major airline.

My son had not been so lucky. And now the son of Keith Matthews faced that fate as well. Both had joined the service to train for a career and ended up getting sent to fight terrorists in uninhabitable desert terrain. Their military experience meant watching friends and enemies die violently, always haunted by the fear of coming home maimed or, as in Jean-Paul's case, not at all.

As Roberto covered my face and neck and chest with tender kisses, I planted some of my own on his fine nose and strong shoulders, stroking his neatly trimmed hair and running my hands down his bare back, breathing in the residue of his aftershave mixed with sweat. The nightgown I had just donned slipped off. His warm hands caressed my flesh, awakening my desire like no other lover ever could. Images of Isabella and Giovanna and Percy and the photo album and my mother began to fade, replaced by involuntary spasms and moans of pleasure. Would it ever be the same once he knew? I willed myself to banish that thought, not to think of anything but the moment, the warmth and security I felt in my husband's arms, our bodies fitting together like building blocks.

Entwined, we drifted off to sleep. At some point, I extricated a numb limb and changed positions, my back against his furry chest, his arms encircling me like protective armor, his even breaths tickling my ear. If we could only stay like that forever and not have to deal with my intruding past and the fear for my mother's future.

I felt the feathery touch of Roberto's finger grazing my cheek to push a strand of hair behind my ear. Squinting into the incandescent light emanating from the bulb of the bedside lamp, I focused on my husband sitting up in bed, thin foam pillow between his back and the wall to serve as a headboard, reading an Ann Rule true crime book. "What time is it?" I muttered.

"It's almost noon in Frankfurt," Roberto replied cheerfully.

"We're in Texas." I snatched the travel alarm off my nightstand and stared at the numbers. "And it's four fifteen." I pulled the sheet and blanket over my head. "Go back to sleep."

"Can I make coffee?"

"At least wait until it really *is* noon in Frankfurt," I conceded, peering at him from under the covers, knowing he was probably up for the day. Changing time zones so frequently in his job wreaked havoc with his body clock. "Mark and Marie are asleep in the next room." I ducked back into my dark cocoon of bedcovers and shut my eyes, willing sleep to wash over me again.

"Why does Marie call her parents 'Mommy' and 'Daddy'?" Roberto said, as I was about to recapture my dream. "It sounds so childish."

"What?" In my twilight daze, it took a moment for his words to register.

"Why does Marie...?"

"I don't know." I pulled the covers off my head, giving up on a few extra hours of sleep. "That's what she has always called them. Does it bother you?"

"What does your brother call them?"

"George and Betty. So do I." George and Betty were fun-loving, beer-drinking, meat-eating Irish Americans, a decade my senior, which would have made them teenagers when their oldest daughter Marie had been born. Somewhere along the line, Marie had become the designated adult in that family.

"I'm glad you're not like Marie. She's kind of a pain in the ass. I feel sorry for your brother."

I sighed, flipping onto my back. "Don't. They're happily married."

He leaned over and kissed me tenderly, seeming gleeful that he had succeeded in waking me up. "Like us," he murmured. He closed his book, place marked, and slid under the covers so our faces lined up. I touched his cheek, now bristly, and looked into his deep green eyes, framed with long dark lashes. "I love you," he whispered.

"I love you, too," I murmured. As our lips met and our tongues danced, I felt his hand reaching under my nightgown, pressing buttons that wiped away all thoughts except those of making love.

The second time we awakened, it was really morning, and I could hear Mark and Marie stirring. Roberto looked at me and smiled. "What time is it?"

I glanced at the bedside alarm clock. "In Two Wells, or in Frankfurt?"

He chuckled. "You gave me a tranquilizer."

I kissed him. "You needed your rest."

He pulled back the covers and climbed out of bed, exposing a glimpse of his lean, fuzzy body before he could slip on a pair of shorts and a T-shirt. The physical attraction I had felt when we first met, working inside an airplane on the way from Los Angeles to Honolulu, had never diminished in the ten years we had been married. "I'm going to go make coffee."

"Honey Bear." I sat up in bed. Marie would soon ask more questions about Isabella. "There's something important I need to tell you."

He had almost reached the bedroom door. "Wait until I've had my coffee."

I busied myself straightening the room, making the bed, anything to avoid putting in an appearance in the family room. Roberto had to know the story first. I could hear male voices too low for me to decipher; perhaps Marie had not yet surfaced, and my brother was preparing her daily dose of herbal tea. As the rich aroma of coffee wafted through the air, I heard her shrill voice over the gurgling of the coffee maker; she announced plans to spend the day boxing up clothes that no longer fit my mother. She had probably lain awake last night, haunted by the mountains of identical sweat suits and bargain outfits with tags still attached, anxious to begin cleaning and organizing.

Moments later, Roberto pushed through my bedroom door, carrying two steaming cups of coffee. Mine was heavy on the milk, the way I liked it.

"*Café au lait au lit,*" I squealed. "*Merci monsieur.*"

"*Au lit?*" He looked around, eyes resting on the newly made bed. "Did the maid come while I was out getting our coffee?"

I patted the spongy mattress, already covered with the yellow floral bedspread. "Sit down, Honey Bear. We have to talk."

He looked at me sharply. "Talk? You don't want a divorce, do you?"

"Of course not, Silly." I squeezed his leg. He said that whenever I initiated a "serious" discussion; it was his way of eliminating the worst-case scenario up front.

"The coffee's no good?" he asked, sitting beside me and taking a swig. "It's the best I could do with what I had to work with." At home, we drank dark French roast, and Roberto ground the beans. The coffee my mother stocked came pre-ground in a can.

I took a sip to show my appreciation. "The coffee is fine." I took another sip and set the cup on the bedside table. "I have to tell you something about my past, Roberto, before you hear it from someone else."

"You're having an affair?" His tone was less joking than before.

"Of course not." I glanced at his face, which had tensed at my mention of *past*. "You never wanted to know anything about Percy and me, or any other boyfriends I had before I met you," I reminded him. I could still remember the exact moment, shortly after we had become engaged, when I had tried to unload my confession. He had stopped me cold. *"I'd be naïve if I thought you'd never been with another man,"* he had said. *"You know I've been with other women. But we're together now. Forever, I hope, and that's all that matters. Don't destroy that illusion. Don't make me think about you with anyone else. Don't tell me about your high school sweetheart, or your French lover, or your Italian lover, or some guy you picked up on a layover, because I don't want to carry around that picture in my mind. Whatever happened in the past doesn't change who you are, the person I fell in love with."* Percy's name had surfaced briefly in conversation from time to time, and Roberto had always seemed anxious to change the subject. I could feel his muscles tightening now. I took a deep breath and plunged in, like a diver off the high board into a cold swimming pool, depth unknown. "When I was seventeen years old, I gave birth to a baby out of wedlock. Percy was the father."

I could hear Roberto's breath catch. His face had hardened like a finished sculpture.

I rushed on. "I went away to an unwed mothers' home in Houston. I gave the baby up for adoption and thought that was the end of it. You never wanted to know about my past, and I saw no reason to tell you."

Roberto stared at me. I couldn't read his expression, but his green eyes no longer twinkled.

I reached for his leg again.

He jerked it away as if I had touched him with a hot poker. "Then why are you telling me this now?"

"Remember the woman who came to Mom's room right after we arrived? Isabella Rogers?"

"She's your daughter?" His voice was harsh.

"No, I had a son. I found out Friday that he was killed in 1991, during the Gulf War."

"Then why..."

"But before he left for Kuwait, he married Isabella and they had a daughter, Giovanna." My lips curled into a smile as I spoke Giovanna's name. "I have a ten-year-old grandchild."

Roberto looked away, as if my smile made the pain worse. "Son, granddaughter," he muttered. He turned to face me, his eyes burning. "Don't you think this was something you should have told me?"

"I didn't know..."

"You just found out about your granddaughter. But you always knew you had a son."

I faced his gaze, attempting to make my voice sound braver than I felt. It still cracked. "Yes. I tried."

"You *tried*? Not very hard!"

"I'm sorry."

"'Sorry' doesn't fix anything."

"Like I said, when I gave that baby up for adoption, I thought the story was over. No one had to know. My family never talked about it, like it never happened. My son was never a part of my life. He had nothing to do with *us*. It doesn't change who I am." I tried to give Roberto a kiss, but his face was stiff and again he rebuffed my touch.

"It changes everything. Doesn't it?"

"But you said those exact words: 'Whatever happened in the past doesn't change who you are, the person I fell in love with'."

He just stared at me, and I couldn't read his expression.

"Isabella found *me*."

"And now they're going to be part of our life," he added coldly.

"I think so," I replied, wishing he could get past this initial shock and not project his anger at my omission onto innocent strangers. "I'd like to get to know my granddaughter; I never got to know my son. And Isabella has been a big help with Mom."

I could feel the bedsprings rise as he got up, his voice oozing with sarcasm. "One big happy family. I suppose that means you'll have to include what's-his-name—Percy."

I touched his leg. "I'm sorry, Honey Bear. I love you. If I could turn back the clock I would."

"Yeah." He started for the door.

"Does this mean you want a divorce?" Those were playful words we always tossed at each other whenever a disagreement became too intense. Usually, it brought the situation back into perspective. Today, my attempt at lightening the mood fell flat. I bit my lip to punish it for letting those words out.

"I need some air." He banged the bedroom door behind him, and the wire hanger hook jingled with the force. One of my mother's jackets slipped to the floor.

I knew better than to follow him. Roberto and I never had arguments, never worked things out with shouting matches. When he was angry, I left him alone until the storm passed. Sipping my lukewarm coffee, I listened for any interchange he might have with Mark or Marie, wondering if one of them might unwittingly diffuse him. I heard the front door open and slam; a few moments later, the engine of my rental car revved. Through the Venetian blinds of my bedroom window, I watched my husband drive away.

I could only imagine what was going through Roberto's mind. When would I see him again? Would life ever return to normal? Checking the hallway to ensure the coast was clear, I crossed to the guest bathroom, where I turned on the shower as hot as it would go, steaming up the mirrors and the window. I stripped off my robe and stepped in, adjusting the temperature so as not to scald my skin. Lathering with shampoo, I replayed my conversation with Roberto. How could I have handled it better? Unlike the written word, there was no opportunity to edit what had been spoken. Even when I prepared what I wanted to say before hand, the conversation never unfolded as planned, because the other person never followed the script. I rinsed, relishing the warm water cascading around my body.

Knowing the limits of my mother's hot water heater, I reluctantly emerged from the shower. I dried off and combed my hair, glimpsed my reflection through patches of fog on the bathroom mirror. To my chagrin, I was beginning to look more and more like my mother. Would my life end like hers?

I dressed and bravely headed into the family room. My brother stood in the kitchen, peeling a banana. Marie sat on the couch sipping her tea and sorting through a pile of my mother's clothing, chucking most of it into a large cardboard box. "These outfits are way too big for her now, don't you think?"

"Probably," I answered, even though she was most likely talking to Mark.

"Morning, Michelle," Mark said. "Want a banana?"

Marie had artfully arranged my fruit purchases in a bowl on the breakfast bar. I grabbed a banana, thinking my brother and I must look like a pair of monkeys, standing side by side in the kitchen, stuffing bananas into our faces.

"Where'd Roberto head off in such a hurry?" Marie asked, inspecting a pair of slacks with the tag still on it. My mother could never resist a bargain, even on something that didn't fit. "Did you send him out for donuts?"

I finished chewing before replying. "I doubt he'll be back any time soon."

Marie looked up from her sorting with feigned surprise.

"He's trying to process the idea that he's married to a grandmother." I opened the cabinet door under the sink and dropped my banana peel in the trashcan.

"What...what are you talking about?" Marie asked.

I took Mark's banana peel from his hands, disposed of it, and then shut the cabinet door. "Marie, don't pretend you don't know." I glanced at Mark, who had guilt plastered all over his face. "Mark, I don't mind that you told her. The secret is out. Even Elaine Nelson knows I was a teenaged unwed mother."

"Your old friend Elaine?" Mark asked, walking from the kitchen into the family room to sit on the couch beside his wife.

I poured myself the last of the coffee and placed the mug in the microwave. "Percy moved back to Two Wells a few years ago, and he and Elaine hooked up for a while."

"Percy?" Mark echoed.

"I didn't get a chance to tell you. Percy is the one who tracked down our son. He and Isabella have been in contact all these years, after Paul was killed in the Gulf War."

Mark whistled.

A ding from the microwave signaled that my coffee was hot. I added a generous dose of milk and put the mug back in the microwave. "Percy's in the hospital, dying of prostate cancer, two floors up from Mom." I looked at Marie. "You asked where Isabella wanted to take me yesterday: Percy's room. Even on his deathbed, he's trying to mess with my head." Another ding and I retrieved my coffee, warming my hands on the ceramic mug as I took a sip.

"Percy has cancer?" Marie spoke his name as if she knew him, when in fact they had never met. But she had heard my brother and me mention him often enough, especially my tale about his attempt to strangle me.

"Couldn't have happened to a nicer guy," I muttered.

"A lot of people recover from prostate cancer these days," Mark said.

"I think his is too far along; it has already metastasized into other organs," I replied. "From the looks of him, and from what Isabella has told me, I doubt he'll ever leave the hospital."

"That's a shame." Mark's comment lacked sincerity. Undoubtedly, he had not forgotten Percy's dismissal of him as a "pesky little brat" and some of the cruel practical jokes Percy and I had played on him when we were dating.

"Michelle, how did it feel to see Percy again?" Marie asked.

I sat at the table, turned my chair to face them, and then took a long sip of coffee. "Toward me, he's the same asshole. But Isabella cares for him, so there must be another side of him that's halfway decent."

The doorbell rang. Leaving my coffee cup on the card table, I leapt to answer it.

As if they had overheard our conversation, Isabella and Giovanna stood on the front porch.

Chapter Thirty

"Michelle." Tears streaked Isabella's face. "I hope this isn't a bad time..."

"Come in." I flung open the front door. The fresh air tinged with Isabella's perfume masked the residue of cleaning fluids in the entryway. "Roberto took off when he heard our news, but my brother and his wife are here."

Isabella did not ask what I meant by *news*. "Percy has taken a turn for the worse, and I have to get back to the hospital." She hesitated in the entryway, which I would forever remember as the scene of a violent crime. "The neighbor who's been watching Giovanna had to go out of town, and Giovanna's too young to stay in Percy's room. I know you're busy with your mother..."

"Come into the family room." I touched Isabella's shoulder to propel her through the entryway and took Giovanna's hand. It felt soft and warm and tiny. Looking into her eyes was like staring into a mirror and plunging back forty years in time.

As I entered the family room with my daughter-in-law and granddaughter, my brother rose and lumbered into the kitchen. I ushered my guests into his vacated spot on the couch beside Marie. She scooted closer to the end table, picked up a Kleenex, and blew her nose.

I sat in my mother's armchair. "Marie, Mark," I raised my voice so my brother could hear me from the kitchen over the sound of cornflakes pouring into a ceramic bowl. "You met Isabella in the hospital yesterday. And this is her daughter, Giovanna. My granddaughter."

Marie smiled. Warm, motherly. "Jo... Jovanna? You favor your grandmother. Especially the eyes." She glanced at me for confirmation, and then turned her attention back to my granddaughter. "What grade are you in?"

"Fifth grade," Isabella answered.

"I'm home schooled," Giovanna added.

"Home schooled." Marie nodded, with a look I knew well. A look that could never be accused of mockery or disrespect, yet conveyed unmistakable disapproval.

"In fact, she has lessons to do, so she won't be in your way," Isabella said.

To Marie's raised eyebrows I explained, "Isabella has to get to the hospital, and I said we'd look after Giovanna. We can take turns visiting Mom; she doesn't need all of us hanging around her room all day."

Mark started to protest, but Marie held up her hand. "I was going to suggest that you two go by yourselves today anyway. There's plenty for me to do here, and Lola doesn't need me there." Had Marie's feelings been hurt yesterday when my mother failed to recognize her? Or did she just relish the opportunity to tackle the clutter with no one around to stop her from tossing useless items with dubious sentimental value? She flashed her motherly smile at Giovanna. "Giovanna and I will be fine, won't we, Giovanna? I can even help you with your lessons."

The doorbell rang again. Roberto? After his abrupt departure, would he feel the need to be invited back in? I sprang like a jack-in-the-box to answer it, leaving the two branches of my family tree alone to get acquainted.

Tiffany Landers stood on our porch, clad in faded jeans with symmetric holes in the knees, looking at a cardboard liquor box clasped in her thin arms.

When I opened the door she thrust the box toward me. Still averting her eyes, she murmured, "Ma and Stephanie said to give you this."

"What...?" I peered inside the box, recognizing a Chinese vase I had not seen in ages, with a long, velvet-covered jewelry box propped against it.

"They think my sister Brittany stole this stuff from your mama." Tiffany transferred the box from her arms to mine, hesitated a second, pushed a stringy strand of blond hair behind her ear, and pulled the gold ring I had noticed the other day off her finger. "She probably stole this, too."

I studied the ring Tiffany had just handed me, admiring its carvings, remembering my mother wearing it, when it still fit her finger. Should I let Tiffany keep it? She had lost her sister in this house; maybe the ring would serve as a remembrance. On the other hand, maybe the ring would conjure the image of Brittany as a thief, not how her family wanted to remember her. Besides, it might cheer up my mother when I told her about the property recovered from "those people." Her paranoid ramblings about the help stealing from her had proved true. "Thank you, Tiffany." I put the ring in my pocket.

I had not detected the approach of Isabella behind me. "Michelle, I have to get going. Thanks so much for helping with Giovanna." We brushed hands, and I stepped aside so she could slip out the front door.

Isabella's eyes locked briefly with Tiffany's. "Hey," said Tiffany, as Isabella started down the walkway. "You worked with my sister, didn't you?"

"No," replied Isabella, continuing toward her car.

Tiffany shook her head and glanced at me. "I thought she looked familiar."

"Really?" I watched Isabella get into her car and start the engine.

"But I guess I'm wrong." Tiffany looked uncomfortable. "She reminds me of someone."

"Thank you for bringing my mother's things back," I told her again. "And I'm very sorry about your sister."

Tiffany hurried down the walkway and climbed into the passenger side of a waiting pick-up truck, probably the same one that had almost run me down the night before. I closed the front door and, balancing the cardboard box between my body and the wood panel, re-locked it with one hand. Back in the family room, I set the box on top of the paper-strewn coffee table.

"What's all this?" Mark asked, strolling over from the kitchen.

"Yeah, I thought we were trying to get rid of stuff from this house, not accumulate more," Marie said.

"Looks like our visit to Mrs. Landers last night provoked an attack of conscience." I removed from my pocket the gold ring Tiffany had relinquished. "Remember I told you the ring Brittany's sister was wearing looked familiar?"

"Wow," said Marie, taking it from me to get a closer look. "I remember when Lola used to wear that ring all the time."

"Let's take it to the hospital today and show her." I picked up the long jewelry box covered in worn black velvet. "Oh my." I pulled out a string of perfectly round, gold-tinged opera-length pearls. "I didn't remember Mom had real pearls."

"Yes, they were your Aunt Catherine's," Marie said. "Lola showed them to me once." Aunt Catherine was actually my great aunt, my mother's aunt, a sweet woman who loved children but never had any of her own, who had died of breast cancer when I was in elementary school. My mother had probably owned the necklace at least that long. Marie inspected the pearls. "It's a shame Lola never wore them. They're beautiful."

I spied a flat square cardboard box and pulled it out of the jumble. "My Hermès scarf!" I cried. A present I'd received from my married French lover; I had re-gifted it to my mother, not because I couldn't stand the reminder after we broke up, but because, in those days, I had no idea how to tie a scarf. Apparently my mother had had no idea what to do with it either; the scarf still held its original creases. I unfolded it gently, holding it to my chest. "I have half a dozen outfits that would look great with this!" I murmured, admiring the bold colors and intricate pattern. Since learning the art of scarf tying from my mother-in-law, Suzanna, I now wore them to work all the time.

"Then take it home," Mark said.

"Please. Go put it in your suitcase right now, so you don't forget," Marie agreed. She lifted the vase out of the box. "The Ming! I'd wondered what happened to that."

"Brittany sure was able to zero in on what was valuable," Mark commented. "There wasn't much in this house worth anything."

"Maybe that's why she tried to get Mom to take out a loan for her," I muttered. "She ran out of good stuff to steal."

Marie shot me a warning look and gestured toward Giovanna, who fingered the pearls, oblivious to our ill words about the dead. I pictured Giovanna some day putting on a prom dress, or a wedding dress, complemented by those pearls. Or would Mark and Marie insist the pearls go to their daughter Tina instead? I shook my head, filing those petty thoughts for another time. "Giovanna, how hard do you have to study?"

She looked up. "My mother told me to study my Texas history so I wouldn't bother you. But I've already read the book twice."

"Come on." Rising, I motioned her off the couch. "I have something you might like. More fun than studying. Even though Texas history is pretty colorful."

I escorted her out of the family room and down the hallway to my bedroom. My breath caught as I glimpsed Roberto's suitcase, open on the carpeted floor. At least he hadn't taken it with him. The scent of our commingled sweat still hung in the air, a reminder of how good things had been between us a few hours ago.

Glad I had made the bed, I motioned Giovanna to sit. My nightgown draped the desk chair, occupied by my open bag.

"Was this your bedroom, Grandma Michelle?" Giovanna asked, surveying her surroundings, unperturbed at the mess.

Grandma Michelle. Me? It didn't sound right, but what would? It was more personalized than "Ma'am," which she had called me when I first met her, two days ago.

"It was," I replied. I knelt on the carpet, reached under the bed, and pulled out a couple of dusty vinyl cases: my Barbie collection, one of the few personal items that remained in my childhood bedroom. Most of our toys had been sold in garage sales or given away to charity over the years, to make room for the growing mountain of my mother's clothing. But the Barbie collection had managed to survive; whenever my mother approached me about selling it, I assured her I was saving it for my own daughter. A daughter I never got around to having. I looked at Giovanna, still trying to digest the fact that she was my granddaughter. "Do you have a Barbie doll?"

"No," she said. "But some of my friends in Houston do."

"Well then, meet Barbie and Ken and their friends." I opened the first case to revive the plastic characters who had once animated my summer afternoons.

"Awesome," Giovanna murmured as I unsheathed doll after doll. "Vintage Barbie!" She picked up Skipper,

Barbie's little sister, and smoothed her long blond hair, slightly wrinkled from the box, like she had awakened to a bad-hair day.

I held up one of her tiny, home-sewn, now out-of-style dresses. "Think you'd enjoy playing with Vintage Barbie and her friends?"

Giovanna's eyes sparkled, her smile brighter than I had ever seen it. "Will you play with me?"

I had intended to occupy Giovanna in self-directed play with the world of Barbie while Mark, Marie, and I sorted through the items Brittany had stolen and tried to piece together what had happened. I was shutting her in my bedroom the way I put my cats in the basement with big bowls of food and water, a litter box, and toy mice when Roberto and I left town for a weekend. I didn't have time to play Barbie. I had a murder to solve, and I had to get to the hospital. Like Isabella. A single mother with many attentions, she probably had to leave Giovanna to her own devices more often than she wanted.

I looked at Giovanna sadly, a child juggled by adults. "For a little while. Want to be Barbie or Midge?"

"I want to be Skipper," said Giovanna, still stroking the smaller doll's long hair. "You be Barbie."

"You look like Skipper," I agreed, which earned a beam from my granddaughter. "Let's set up their houses. These cases make great apartments."

So absorbed was I in our game of make-believe that I did not notice Mark standing in the bedroom doorway. He cleared his throat. "Are you coming to the hospital with me, Michelle?"

I looked apologetically at Giovanna. "I have to go visit my mother in the hospital. You remember her from the other day, don't you? When we all had dinner here? She's very sick now."

Giovanna's eyes showed more understanding than I would have expected from a ten-year-old. "Okay."

"But please play with the dolls as long as you like. Maybe Marie can join you later." I rose, stepping over Barbie paraphernalia to grab my purse off the desk.

The doorbell rang as I followed my brother down the hallway.

Chapter Thirty-One

Mark reached the front door first. Not having been present to see Brittany's body crumpled in the entryway, he trod over the sacrosanct spot as if nothing had happened there. The door opened to daylight, and my heartbeat quickened as I anticipated seeing my husband again, ringing the doorbell because he had not taken a key, ready to kiss and make up and accept my newfound family members.

"You must be Mark Hanson," said a pleasant, familiar voice. "Keith Matthews from the Two Wells Police Department. Is Michelle here? I have information about a lead she gave us."

"I'm here, Keith," I spoke from behind my brother. "Come in."

Mark stepped aside to admit Keith, and I led the procession around the brick planter divider into the living room. "About the loan application?" I asked, fearful that any new information might strengthen the motive for my mother to bash Brittany's skull.

"Not yet," Keith replied. "I have an appointment this afternoon with the loan officer at the bank." Seating himself beside me on the couch, he looked into my eyes. I was warmed by how un-cop-like his manner with me had become, even though I tried not to forget he still regarded my mother as a suspect. "Your friend in the dirty white car: Jamal Johnson. We've matched some prints we found at the scene to him."

"Really?" Mark and I exchanged glances. I was encouraged that evidence was being uncovered to allow the police to focus on another suspect. However, the thought of that guy inside our house, pawing my mother's possessions, gave me the creeps. No wonder my mother had become so upset about "those people" trampling through her home while she watched helplessly.

"He admits stopping by the house the day of the murder, about the time Michelle saw him driving down the street."

"So much for the eyewitness testimony of two neighbors, who claimed they didn't notice anyone," I muttered.

"I'm going to talk to those neighbors again, see if I can jog their memories. Jamal claims he knocked on the front door, heard female voices arguing, then a crash, so he hightailed it back down the walkway and drove away, thinking it wasn't a good time for a visit. Claims he went to the drive-thru at the Dairy Queen on Fifth Street for a coke. Then he started thinking something might be wrong, so he cruised by the house again about twenty minutes later. He was trying to make up his mind about whether to stop, when he saw a car drive up the street—must have been you, Michelle. When that car pulled into the driveway, he figured someone else would take care of whatever had happened."

"But his fingerprints at the scene...how does he explain that?" Mark asked. "He's not admitting to going inside the day of the murder?"

"Claims he visited Brittany at work the day before."

"Can't you tell the age of a fingerprint?" I asked, a little disappointed in forensic science.

"Unfortunately, not that precisely. We can try to press charges, but I don't know if a grand jury will indict him."

"I don't understand." Mark shook his head. "His fingerprints were found at the scene, he was spotted driving down our street moments after the murder took place, but a grand jury wouldn't indict him? My *mother* is a more likely candidate?"

"He had no motive that we can determine, and his only prior arrest was for shoplifting a couple years ago," Keith explained.

"Shoplifting?" I perked up. "Then he's a proven thief. His motive could have been robbery. Maybe Brittany was trying to stop him!"

"Yeah, he was honing in on her territory," muttered Mark.

Keith raised his eyebrows. Mark and I must have looked like my two cats when I surprised them sneaking into the forbidden living room.

"Brittany's sister Tiffany was here again this morning," I explained. "She returned a box of valuables Brittany had stolen from my mother over the course of her employment."

Keith scratched his chin. "Your mother did seem awfully worried about the aides stealing from her."

Wincing, I saw the pendulum of suspicion once again swing toward my mother. "Do you need to see the items? Jewelry, heirlooms, a Hermès scarf I brought her from France." I hoped my newfound souvenir would not be taken into evidence; I already had plans for wearing it.

"Looks like there was good reason for her paranoia." Keith studied my face. I had had no plans to tell him about the treasure trove Tiffany had delivered, because I had convinced myself it had nothing to do with the case. Again, it now appeared we had something to hide.

"Where is the stolen property now?" Keith asked.

I led him into the family room. Marie had gone into the garage with a box of my mother's clothing. The box of valuables Tiffany had returned sat where I had left it. Keith bent to inspect the items, but made no move to confiscate anything. He straightened. "I can see why your mother would be upset."

"If she even knew Brittany took these things," I added.

"She caught Brittany stealing the pagoda." Keith moved away from the box, as if he'd lost interest.

"Not necessarily," I argued. "She got upset when she saw *Greg* with the pagoda."

"Where does that leave us?" Mark asked.

"Reasonable doubt," I said. "A good lawyer could get Mom off based on reasonable doubt."

Mark eyed Keith. "Should we be hiring a lawyer?"

Keith sighed. "I don't like to recommend that citizens hire lawyers, but it is her right. She hasn't been arrested yet, though."

"She's still in the hospital," I reminded him. "In fact, we were just leaving to go see her."

Keith started for the door. "I hope she's better soon. We're praying for her."

Who was "we"? He and Elaine? Mary Lynn? He and Greg Dobbins, who would as soon throw my mother in jail, hospital bed and all? "Thank you," I said, escorting him out. Whoever "we" meant, my mother could use all the prayers she could get, so I was not about to question Keith's sincerity in offering them.

It was one of those sparkling fall days when the sunlight makes colors especially vivid and the humidity of summer has evaporated. The air held a faint smell of wood smoke, and birds sang as they prepared for winter. This kind of day normally made me want to be outside, carefree as a cat, soaking in the clean, fresh air before the sunlight faded, but today, the brilliant autumn sunlight mocked the emotional turmoil brewing inside me.

Mark drove us to the hospital in our mother's Ford Fiesta. "Think I made a mistake mentioning the stuff Brittany stole?" he asked, his eyes focused on the Fifth Street traffic.

I sighed. "We don't want to be accused of withholding evidence. Better Keith find out from us than some other way."

"You two seem kind of chummy."

"Keith and me?" I took my eyes off the familiar landscape floating past. "Did I tell you he and Elaine are dating?"

"That's the reason?"

"If that's the way it seems."

We were silent for a moment while he made a left turn.

"Seems like the evidence keeps pointing at Mom." Mark looked over his shoulder as he switched into the right lane and signaled. "I don't like it."

"You're not starting to believe she could have done it?"

"Of course not. The police are dealing with flawed assumptions." Jaw set firmly, Mark stared at the road as if it were one of his children about to sass him.

The guard nodded at us as we entered our mother's room, and then returned his gaze to whatever he was contemplating on the ceiling. I wondered if he were permitted to read a book or magazine to alleviate the boredom of his job.

Motionless underneath the oxygen mask, attached by tubes to complex machinery, my mother breathed like she was underwater with scuba equipment. The TV blared a game show, and a bleary-eyed Keisha Jackson slumped in the chair beside the bed. She looked like a younger, slightly smaller version of her mother.

"Morning, Keisha," Mark addressed Karen's daughter. "Any change in Mom's condition?"

Keisha smiled, flashing a set of big white teeth. "I don't think so, Mr. Mark. Nurse came by a few minutes ago checking her vitals, but she didn't tell me nothing."

I walked over to my mother and picked up her cold hand. "We're here, Mom. Mark and I." I felt her grasp my fingers.

Mark joined me at her bedside. "Hey, Mom."

"We're all waiting for you to wake up and come home," I told her. "Marie's here, too, and she's doing your fall cleaning. She'll stop by later." There was an almost imperceptible groan. "Don't worry, we won't let her throw away anything important."

Mark grinned at me, not saying a word to defend or incriminate his wife.

"I have some great news," I continued. "Brittany's sister Tiffany—I don't know if you ever met her—she brought back a whole box of your things that Brittany had taken. Your opera-length pearls, that brass vase you used to put silk flowers in, that Hermès scarf I gave you. And your gold ring with the hand carvings." I reached into my pocket and retrieved the ring that had adorned Tiffany's finger. "Look, Mom. You used to wear this all the time." I pressed the ring against her hand.

Her fingers caressed its outline, and her eyes opened into slits. Mark smiled, stroking her other hand. "We'll put everything away for safe-keeping, so it will be there when you get home." He looked at me. "Maybe the jewelry should go into the safe deposit box?"

"Good idea." I glanced at Keisha, wondering if she resented our implication that, because Brittany had been a thief, none of the Loving Care aides could be trusted. Her red-rimmed brown eyes were glued to the television screen. Like her mother, she could put on the alligator front.

A nurse breezed into the room, making a beeline for my mother's bed, followed by a trainee. "Please step aside. Excuse us, but we need to check the outputs and get the patient cleaned up." She muscled her way past Mark and me, and then drew flimsy translucent curtains around my mother's bed.

I looked at Keisha. "Want to go get some coffee with us?"

"I don't drink the stuff, but I could use a break, if that's what you mean."

Not far from my mother's quarters was a sitting area set apart from the corridor by a rectangle of institutional brown carpeting spattered with flecks of gray the same color as the surrounding tile. Except for vending machines against the gray walls, the area resembled a living room. The wall-mounted television was turned to a news program with the sound muted.

"When does your mother come back?" I asked Keisha as we sat down on the couch.

She glanced at her watch. "She'll be here around noon."

"Has anyone else come to see our mother?" I asked. "Besides family?"

Keisha's broad black forehead wrinkled. "What do you mean?"

"They have those police guards stationed outside her door. Have you heard anyone trying to get past them?"

"No, Ma'am. I don't think so."

"Want something to drink?" Mark strolled toward the vending machine and examined the choices.

"No, thanks," I told him. I glanced at the selection of magazines displayed on the coffee table in front of us, but nothing caught my interest.

"Can you get me a Diet Coke?" asked Keisha. "I don't have any change, though."

Mark put coins in the machine and made a selection. The can fell with a thud.

He returned with a Diet Coke for Keisha and a regular Coke for himself.

"Thanks," said Keisha, taking a swig.

I reclined against the faux leather. The couch looked more comfortable than it actually was. "So, Keisha," I ventured. "How well did you know Brittany Landers?"

Keisha looked down. "What about her?"

"I mean, were you friends, did you..."

"No, Ma'am." Her big lips pressed tightly together.

I looked at Mark, who was sipping his cola. "You didn't like her?"

"Humph," Keisha snorted. "Nothing there to like."

"Know anyone who might want to see her dead?"

Keisha sipped her Diet Coke. "Can't say anyone's too sorry about it."

"Not being sorry is one thing. But can you think of anyone who might have wanted to kill her?"

She looked me in the eye. "Beside your mama?"

I looked at my shoes, and then back into her eyes. "You don't really think our mother did it, do you?"

Keisha took another swig of Diet Coke. "I suppose it coulda been someone else. Don't know who, though. I tried to stay as far away from that girl as possible." Seeing me still watching her, she offered, "One of them men, maybe. She was always pissing off the men."

"Did you ever meet any of these men?"

"No, Ma'am. Just heard about 'em."

"If Brittany had so many personal problems, how could she take care of Mom?" Mark interjected.

"Humph," said Keisha. "I think Chris Washington might have been getting ready to fire her ass."

"What about women?" I asked. "Did Brittany argue with women?" I remembered an earlier conversation with Karen. "Your mother told me you saw her arguing with a young white woman the other day. Do you remember what she looked like?"

Keisha sniffed. "I try not to pay them white trash no mind."

"Your mom thought she was twenty-something, with bushy hair."

"Oh, her. Yeah, I'd only seen her once before. Hollering at Brittany."

"Can you remember anything more about that woman? Her name? What they were fighting about?"

"She had brown hair. Long and bushy." She held her hand below her shoulder to indicate the length. Keisha stared into space as if trying to capture a thought, and then it was gone like the flicker of a firefly. "Maybe her sister."

"Sister?" I did not think the "bushy hair" description fit Tiffany. Stephanie, maybe?

"Yeah, she has a sister or two. Didn't get along from what I hear."

"Did Brittany make friends with any of the other girls who worked at Loving Care?" I pressed.

"My sister Katrina hung out with her sometimes. Don't know why."

"Then Katrina should know more about Brittany's friends and enemies? And sisters?" I felt hopeful at the thought of another lead.

"I think she's said all she's going to, to them cops." Keisha took another gulp of Diet Coke, draining the can.

I looked at my watch, wondering if enough time had elapsed for us to return to Mom's room. "Is Katrina helping with my mother at the hospital, too?"

"If Mama ask her to." Keisha reached for the remote control on the coffee table.

"I think we can go back now," Mark said, crumpling his Coke can. After tossing it into a trash receptacle, he held out his hand for Keisha's empty can, which she had set on one of the end tables.

When Mark and Keisha returned to my mother's room, I remained to chat with the Marine wannabe guarding the door. "Has anyone tried to get into my mother's room who didn't belong?"

He reminded me of one of those mute, Busby-headed guards stationed at Buckingham Palace who refuse to smile or speak, no matter how much taunting they receive.

"It's a simple 'yes' or 'no' question."

"No, Ma'am."

"Do you know how much longer you'll be here then?"

"No, Ma'am."

"Don't you get bored sitting here, staring into space, waiting for something to happen?"

I thought I detected the hint of a smile before he replied, "It's my job, Ma'am."

Before I could decide whether to continue my one-sided conversation with the guard, Dr. Plum strolled up, clipboard in hand as if it were another appendage.

"Good day, Ma'am," he said with an efficiently pleasant smile. So much for my request to the hospital that he be replaced.

I followed him into Mom's room, where we joined Mark and Keisha. Mark stepped away from our mother's bedside to make room for Dr. Plum.

Moving aside the sheet, the doctor pressed his stethoscope against my mother's chest and listened intently. He studied her fluid level and IV, and the oxygen monitor, writing on his clipboard after each observation.

"What's her prognosis?" I asked.

"As I said before, her systems are shutting down. I didn't think she'd last through the weekend; she has more fight in her than I thought. But it won't be long now."

"Isn't there anything we can do?" I felt like a child begging for a reprieve from bedtime even though I knew it was hopeless.

He gave me a refined version of the Greg Dobbins expression. "You're doing it now. You're saying good-bye."

"That's it?" Mark pressed.

Dr. Plum softened a tad. "I'm sorry."

Mark and I exchanged helpless glances. Keisha looked away. My eyes followed Dr. Plum as he slipped back into the hallway, past the guard; I wondered if he could see the irony. The police had planted someone round the clock to protect my mother from a potential killer, while her own doctor was content to stand back and watch her die.

My mother's countenance was serene, as if her mind were far away from the sterile tubes and monitors. Was she dreaming of days gone by—a carefree childhood, falling in love, raising a family—editing out the bad parts, purging regrets, and remembering the good? Was she looking down that tunnel of light, searching for familiar faces, preparing to cross over to the next world?

Mark and I each held one of her hands. We did not speak, did not interrupt whatever thoughts she might be pondering, whatever film was showing on the screen inside her closed eyelids. Was this all there was? Had I run out of chances to be a model daughter, to impress her, make her proud? There were so many dramatic last words I should utter: apologies for our many fights, from childhood to adulthood; explanations for regrettable actions; answers to unasked questions; and above all, thanks for doing the best mothering job she knew how and for loving me as much as she could. Yet I could think of nothing at all to say.

Muffled commotion outside the door broke our concentration. A shrill voice demanded, “Young man, do you know who I am?”

Chapter Thirty-Two

I peered outside my mother's room to find Elaine, hands on her hips, nose to nose with the seated guard. "Michelle!" she cried when she spotted me.

"She's okay," I assured the guard, with a pang of guilt. Had our earlier chat about unwanted visitors prompted his added scrutiny of Elaine?

Ushering Elaine into my mother's room, I hoped she would sense our solemn mood. How did my mother feel about so many people invading her space, seeing her in this compromised position, hooked up to an oxygen tank and an IV, skin graying as life slipped away? Dying should be a private matter, like sleeping or taking a shower.

"Mark," cried Elaine, rushing to hug my towering brother like they were meeting at a class reunion. "How long has it been?"

Mark gave her a reserved grin as he bent to hug her. "High school?"

"Michelle says to me, you're a big shot in Seattle, working for some famous software company?"

"I wouldn't call myself a big shot."

"How's Lola?" Elaine stopped short of my mother's bed, as if assessing her condition for the first time. "Oh my!" Her face registered alarm as she turned back to Mark and me.

"I know, she's not cooperating with your cop friends," I snapped, as if Elaine's relationship with Keith made her culpable.

Elaine winced and then swallowed. "Look, I wanted to tell you, I talked to Jerry, my ex-husband. Jerry Tillman—he's a damn good lawyer, one of the best in the state. If anyone can get her off, guilty or not, it's Jerry." She looked at me with pleading eyes, like when we were kids and she had somehow incurred my wrath. "He's coming from

Austin tomorrow, and he agreed to defend Lola, *pro bono.* He says to me, 'I remember Lola Hanson from when we used to take her to the Civic Theater, and that woman wouldn't hurt a fly.'"

"I'm glad *someone* thinks she could be innocent." I was sorry I had lashed out at Elaine, especially when she was trying to help. Wishing I could wipe away the pain on my friend's face, I added, "Thanks, Elaine. That's so kind of you."

"Yes, thank you," Mark said. "We spoke to Keith Matthews today about whether we should hire a lawyer."

"Have you told Keith you asked Jerry to defend her?" I did not want to cause strife between Elaine and her newfound love interest.

Elaine wrinkled her freckled nose; I sensed she probably had not. "Aw, Keith knows Jerry and me are history." She walked to my mother's bed again. "I have to get going. But let me tell your mama good-bye." Leaning over my mother, grasping her hand, Elaine murmured, "You hang in there, Lola. You remember Jerry? The one who gave me that sable fur coat you liked so much? He'll be here tomorrow to get you out of this mess with the cops. Okay?"

My mother remained unresponsive. Elaine squeezed her hand for a few seconds and then broke the trance to move away. She held out her hand to Mark. "Great seeing you again, Little Brother."

After their handshake, Elaine and I hugged, her jasmine cologne tickling my nostrils. "Thanks again, Elaine. I'm glad you came."

"Hey," Elaine said as we pulled apart. "Did you ever go see Percy? I told you he was in this hospital, didn't I?"

"You did." It was hard to admit to Elaine that I had been to see Percy.

"Might be too late now. I stopped by earlier, and they were working on him, wouldn't let me in. Isabella says to me, she says, he's been drifting in and out of consciousness."

"Getting pretty bad, then?" I led her out of the room, not wanting to discuss Percy in front of my brother, mother, and Keisha.

We passed the guard and then stopped in the hallway a few paces from the doorway to my mother's room. "You'll always regret it if you don't go see him," Elaine continued, her blue eyes meeting my hazel ones. "Hard to believe he's almost gone. The end of an era."

"I did see him, and I regret that," I confided. "Nothing has changed between us."

Elaine raised her finely penciled eyebrows; for once, words escaped her.

"I should have let you have him," I continued.

"I never wanted him!" Elaine lied. Though she had never articulated it to me, she must have thought at one time or another that I'd gotten what I deserved. I had gained Percy's trust by painting Elaine as the conniving one, when in fact, I had been just as conniving in my efforts to win his affections. Turning, Elaine almost collided with Karen Jackson, who had come to relieve Keisha. "Hey, Karen," Elaine greeted my mother's caregiver.

"Hey there, Miss Elaine," Karen replied. She nodded at me. "Miss Michelle. How's your mama this morning?"

Elaine took Karen's arrival as her cue to leave, and slipped quickly down the hall. I could hear bars of the now-familiar tune emanating from her shoulder bag as she reached inside for her cell phone. "Hello? No, I'm just leaving." Her shrill voice faded as she approached the elevators.

"Mom's about the same," I answered Karen. "Not so good."

With a nod to the guard, I followed Karen into my mother's room.

"Did Elaine leave?" Mark asked me, as Karen and Keisha greeted each other and chatted quietly about topics not concerning my mother.

"Yeah," I replied. Unlike his wife, Mark did not press me to disclose any details of our conversation, nor probe the subject of Percy that had been broached before Elaine and I had adjourned for the hall.

Keisha left, and then Karen approached my mother. Mark and I yielded our positions at her bedside as Karen checked her tubes, felt her pulse, and adjusted the oxygen mask. I was afraid to ask Karen for a prognosis; the frown on her dark face already told me it would not differ from that of Dr. Plum.

Retreating from my mother's bedside, Karen plopped into the black chair where Keisha had camped out. I decided to divert the conversation from my mother's failing health. "Karen, is Katrina going to be coming around? There are some things I'd like to ask her."

"Hmm... She went to Dallas for the weekend with a girlfriend; won't be back until late tonight. She'll be at the funeral tomorrow though."

"That's over at Lonnie James, isn't it?" I remarked. Several blocks from the hospital, Lonnie James was the same funeral home where we had held my father's memorial service nine years ago. I remembered their cozy viewing rooms with fine furnishings and soft lighting, and the sensitive staff attempting to comfort the bereaved.

Karen gave me a sharp look. "Y'all going?"

Mark sighed loudly, casting a warning glance my way, but I ignored him. "We thought it might be a nice gesture."

"Hmm, mm, mm." Karen shook her head. "Lordy."

"We went to see Brittany's mother last night," I said. "She invited us to the funeral."

"For real?" Karen probably wondered how I had the gall to go near Brittany's family, but she would never say it.

"Yes," I continued. "She doesn't really think my mother could have killed her daughter."

"Well, I'll be!"

"In fact, she thought my mother was some generous old dowager who was always giving Brittany her finest jewelry and most prized possessions."

"Say what?"

I proceeded to tell her about Tiffany's visit and the loan application I had found. Karen's eyes popped further with each revelation. Before I could finish, or offer any theory besides the obvious motive for murder, the telephone on my mother's bedside table began ringing. I had not even realized she had a phone in her room.

The three of us looked at each other; my mother was obviously in no condition to answer it.

Mark took a step sideways and picked up the receiver. “Hello? Lola Hanson’s room.” He listened for a few moments. “Okay. I’ll tell her. Bye.” Hanging up, he announced, “That was Marie. She said to tell you Roberto is back.”

Chapter Thirty-Three

"Go on, take the car." Mark tossed me the keys. "Marie will pick me up later, or you and Roberto can."

My heart pounded like I was preparing for a first date. Was Roberto ready to forgive me, or had he just returned for his suitcase? "Want me to bring you anything to eat?" I asked Mark.

My stoic brother shook his head. "I'll be fine. I can always grab something at the cafeteria if I feel peckish."

I waved with keys jingling in my hands and started down the corridor, the now-familiar hospital scene a blur. The elevator doors parted and transported me to the lobby with a ding. Where had we parked the car? All of my arrivals at this hospital over the past few days had jumbled together. My feet engaged the autopilot and propelled me to my mother's Ford Fiesta without any navigation efforts from my brain.

The car's interior still smelled of mildew. I pulled the seat forward, cranked the engine, and rolled down the driver's window to admit some fresh air before leaving the parking space. I turned the radio to the local oldies station. It crackled to life, as if it could hardly believe it was being called to service. My mother had always considered the radio an unnecessary distraction to the business of driving.

As I turned onto our street, I held my breath, hoping Roberto had not already left. A glint of sunshine reflected off the rental car parked in Mom's driveway. Good, he was probably still here. Although tempted to block him in, I pulled alongside the rental car and hurried to the front door.

"Michelle? Is that you?" Marie's voice called from the family room. A moment later, Marie materialized, hair wound around the top of her head, clad in comfortable clothes for the deep cleaning task she had tackled. She spoke into the portable phone in her hand, "She just walked in."

"Roberto?" I mouthed.

Marie shook her head firmly and replied in a stage whisper. "Liza Something. From your office."

I was glad there was not a mirror close by, so I could not see the sour look I felt creeping onto my face. Marie had already gone back into the family room to resume her cleaning mission. I detoured into the living room. I took a deep breath as I settled onto the couch, half tempted to push the button and claim an accidental disconnection. "Yes, Liza?" Was she really my boss now? Already?

"Oh, Michelle," she gushed. "I'm so glad I caught you. The facilitators are in a rage about your international ticketing class! There's no answer sheet to the review questions."

"Did you look on the common drive? It's right there with the rest of the documents for the international ticketing class. I told Bill about it on Friday."

"Oh." I could hear the clicking of her keyboard as she smacked her gum. Was she still in her cubicle adjacent to mine, or had they moved her into the vacant corner office yet? "'Answer Sheet.' Okay, never mind. When are you coming back, anyway?"

I sighed. "I'm not sure. Bill told me Friday I could take this week as vacation."

"What? You didn't give us much notice!"

Wincing, I kept my voice calm. "My mother is dying. Those things are hard to plan for."

Liza was silent for a moment. "I thought he said she just had some kind of legal problem. I'm sorry." I could hear her typing. "I don't understand. How am I supposed to show this on the schedule? Death in the family, or vacation?"

I inhaled slowly, letting the air fill my lungs, something my mother could no longer do. "Liza, my mother was admitted to the hospital over the weekend with a fractured hip and pneumonia. I'm taking a week of my *earned* vacation to be with her, so don't expect me back before next week." *Earned* vacation, of which I had plenty, I was tempted to point out, unlike Liza, whose company seniority entitled her to the minimum two weeks per year.

The ding of an incoming e-mail punctuated my last sentence, and I could hear Liza typing again, probably responding to a message that had nothing to do with our conversation. Multi-tasking, showing that she could be a productive manager. Just when I thought she had forgotten I was on the line, she replied, “Well, do you think you’ll have everything wrapped up by next week? The funeral and all that?”

I could picture her filling out the staffing spreadsheet, trying to cover projects, needing to know what names could be inserted, hence the reason for her awkwardly-worded question. Although seething inside, I kept my voice calm. I tried to muster the patience I had practiced when I’d guided Liza through her first train-the-trainer session. “Liza, my mother’s not dead yet, and I’m still hoping she’ll recover. Why don’t I give you an update at the end of the week?”

“So it’s not that serious then? I mean, I thought you said she was *dying*.” When I did not reply, Liza added, “Of course, we all hope she gets better.”

“Thank you, Liza.”

She smacked her gum again. “Can I call you again if I need you?”

“Certainly.” I couldn’t resist adding, “If it’s important.”

“Is this the only phone number? You got a cell or anything?”

“No.”

“For real?”

“For real.” I supposed I should be telling her congratulations on her promotion, but I could not make the words form on my lips.

“Well, can I e-mail you some stuff to proofread? You should have time to do that, shouldn’t you? I mean, aren’t you just sitting around the hospital a lot anyway?”

“No, Liza. My mother doesn’t have a computer hooked to the Internet.”

“Well…”

“Good-bye, Liza. Talk to you next week. And congratulations on your promotion.” With great fervor, I punched the button to disconnect her. Career-limiting move? Perhaps. But I did not have time to think about it now. Where was Roberto?

As I moved into the family room, portable phone still in hand, I could see Marie in the kitchen, scrubbing the inside of one of the cabinets, its contents squeezed onto the already crowded counter, awaiting a refurbished home. A brimming trash basket stood in the middle of the kitchen floor; not all the cabinet's contents would make it back.

Down the hallway I continued, turning right into my bedroom. There sat Roberto and Giovanna, side by side on the carpeted floor, backs propped against the foot of my double bed, surrounded by my Barbie collection, intently poring over the pocket atlas Roberto always carried. "Italy's here. Croatia's here. See how it winds along the coastline? All that area used to be called Yugoslavia."

I stood in the doorway watching for a moment, not about to interrupt the amiable interaction between my semi-estranged husband and my newfound granddaughter. "Mama's going to take me there some day," Giovanna said, leaning closer to the pages where Roberto was pointing. "Then I'll get to meet my grandparents, and my cousins, and..."

Roberto detected my presence and looked up. "Oh, hello." His face appeared kind, shed of the anger that had covered it when he stormed out of the house that morning. "Giovanna told me her mother's family comes from a little town in Croatia. And I showed her where my relatives came from in Italy."

I sank to the floor beside them, leaning close to Roberto's face. "I missed you." Our lips met in a warm peck. Hoping that his earlier wrath had really vanished, I began, "I see you've met Giovanna."

Giovanna smiled on cue. She was such a good-natured, attractive child; who could begrudge her existence for long? Certainly she must have her bratty spells, and the rebellious, know-it-all teen years remained ahead; she probably knew how to pout, how to whine until she got her way, but I had not witnessed any of that thus far. The spell of the idyllic granddaughter had not yet been broken for me, and I was pleased my husband had been able to see this image. "How is your mother, Miss Michelle?" Giovanna asked, like a polite little adult.

"Any change?" Roberto chimed in. "I'm surprised to see you home this early." He must not have known Marie had called me.

I smiled to myself. "Taking a break. She's still unresponsive." Glancing around at my forgotten Barbie collection, I asked, "Giovanna, did you have enough of Barbie? Or, uh, Skipper?"

Roberto chuckled, a sound like music to my ears. "Oh, she sucked me into that." In a falsetto, he continued, "I was Ricky." Picking up the nearby doll, he started walking it toward Giovanna playfully. "Come on, Skipper, let's take the sports car! Ken taught me how to drive."

Giovanna giggled and asked, "Have you ever been to Croatia, Mr. Roberto?" She was obviously more interested in Roberto's atlas than my ancient Barbie collection.

Roberto set down the Ricky doll. "No, I haven't. But Michelle has."

I nodded. "In the early eighties when I was a flight attendant, some girlfriends and I traveled to Dubrovnik. It was still Yugoslavia then. Beautiful place. So your mother is from Croatia?" I had detected an accent from Isabella but had been unable to identify it. The Balkan war had been raging around the time Isabella married my son and Giovanna was born; had she been a refugee, or just a foreign student? What had become of her family?

"Yes," Giovanna replied, reaching for Roberto's atlas to show me the town. "Here." She pointed at a name I could not pronounce.

"Does she ever get back there?"

Giovanna shook her head, her angelic face wistful.

"Has anyone from there come to visit?"

"Not that I remember. We have some old pictures of our relatives, though." Giovanna kept staring at the point on the map that represented her family heritage.

I smiled, wishing I could erase the sadness from my granddaughter's face. "Will you show the pictures to me some time?"

"Mama has them," Giovanna replied.

Roberto looked up, and I followed his gaze to the doorway where Marie had appeared. "Is anyone hungry for supper? I made a nice salad."

My rumbling stomach reminded me that I had not eaten lunch. Marie made wonderful salads. "Sounds good to me," I answered, rising, holding out a hand for Giovanna.

Roberto followed. "Girl food," he muttered. "Got anything else in the refrigerator that I can eat after the appetizer?"

"I made fettuccini Alfredo the other night," I whispered to him. "We have leftovers."

"It was really good," Giovanna assured him as we made our way to the kitchen.

The kitchen remained in a state of disarray: the contents of some of the cabinets still sat on the counters waiting for triage; the trash can in the middle of the floor brimmed with expired food products, chipped plates, cracked glasses, used aluminum pie plates; another box beside it was packed with excess dishes, pots, pans, and utensils in good condition destined for charity. The chaos before the transformation.

"You've been busy," I remarked to Marie. The card table was set with matching placemats and napkins I didn't know we possessed, no doubt trolled from the bottom of one of the kitchen drawers.

She smiled proudly. "Should be easier to work in this kitchen when I'm finished."

Roberto inspected the box of giveaways and picked up a stainless steel garlic press. "You're throwing this away?"

Marie shrugged. "I found three of them. How many does Lola need? I suspect none, since she doesn't cook any more. But I left the nicest one anyway."

"Can we have this?" Roberto asked, still fondling the barely-used stainless steel garlic press. He showed it to me. "Looks like one of your dad's."

"By all means. Put it in your suitcase right now. Get it out of here." Marie set a big bowl of brightly colored salad on the card table. It featured the romaine lettuce and many of the vegetables I had purchased the day before.

Roberto stuck the rescued garlic press in his shirt pocket and sat down.

Marie dished some salad for Giovanna first, a maternal gesture that had never occurred to me. "Honey, do you like cucumbers? Avocado? Tomatoes? Green peppers?" She waited for Giovanna's agreement before including each on her plate.

"Do you have any ranch dressing?" Roberto asked.

"It already has dressing on it," Marie replied, as she continued to serve our plates. "It's made with sesame oil and rice vinegar, with a hint of tamari and fresh garlic."

"It's delicious," I assured her, taking a bite.

Roberto dug his fork into the mound of salad Marie had given him, chewed tentatively, and then gave her the thumbs-up.

"This is good, Miss Marie," Giovanna proclaimed.

"Thank you, dear." Marie smiled at her. I felt proud that my granddaughter was so polite, although I really had had nothing to do with her upbringing.

"Did anybody else stop by today?" I asked, between mouthfuls. To Marie's puzzled look I clarified, "This place has been Grand Central Station since I got here. You saw it this morning. Strangers looking for Brittany Landers, the police..." I trailed off before "long-lost daughters-in-law" could slip out.

"No," she began, as the doorbell rang.

Chapter Thirty-Four

Shirley O'Keefe stood on the front porch, a homemade sheet cake in her arms. "Sorry to bother y'all, but I heard your mama was in the hospital." She thrust the cake toward me.

"My favorite neighbor! Come on in," I beckoned, breathing the aroma of rich chocolate frosting. "The cake looks delicious."

"I don't want to disturb y'all's dinner," she murmured as we entered the family room. Everyone was still seated around the card table.

"We were just finishing," I assured her.

I made quick introductions before taking the cake into the kitchen. Marie stood to shake hands with Shirley. "I remember you came by when my father-in-law died."

Roberto, also standing, shook Shirley's hand as well. "Weren't you the one who made that wonderful chicken spaghetti dish, with all the cheddar cheese? I asked Michelle to get the recipe."

Shirley beamed. "I just had time to make a cake today. Hope y'all like it."

"And this is Giovanna," I continued, not sure how to introduce my granddaughter. Shirley knew I had no children.

"Your niece?" Shirley peered into Giovanna's face. "My, she really favors *you*, Michelle."

With a furtive glance at me, Marie offered, "Shirley, won't you join us for cake?"

"No, thanks; I have to run. Y'all enjoy." Shirley turned to leave.

"I'll walk you out," I said, following her.

As we reached the front door, I asked, "Shirley, the other day, when you were working in your yard, do you remember a dingy white Taurus stopping in front of our house? Just before you saw me arrive?"

Shirley glanced at her watch. "I'm sorry. Maybe I went inside for a minute. I don't remember." She bit her lip.

"The guy claims to have stopped by before when Brittany was working. Ever seen a car like that here?"

Shirley shook her head, a tight-lipped half-smile on her face. "Sorry." She stepped onto the porch and kept walking across our lawn.

"Thanks again for the cake," I called after her.

When I returned to the family room, the others were clearing the table and loading the dishwasher. Again I marveled at how helpful Giovanna appeared to be, unprompted.

"We should pick up Mark before we cut the cake," Marie announced. "Poor guy probably hasn't had anything to eat."

"He said he'd get something at the hospital cafeteria," I said.

Marie sniffed. "Nothing good for him."

"I'll go pick him up now," I offered. "Anyone want to come along?" I looked from Roberto to Marie. "We could all go."

Marie shook her head firmly, rinsing another plate. Before placing it in the dishwasher, she rearranged some other dishes that had already been loaded. "I'll go tomorrow. Lola doesn't know I'm there anyway." A hint of self-pity tinged her voice, but not enough that she would dare acknowledge if accused.

"We don't know that," I reminded her.

"Giovanna and I will stay here and finish cleaning up." Marie glanced at Giovanna for confirmation. "Honey, do you know what time your mother will be back to pick you up?"

"Isabella's probably still at the hospital," I said. "I'll see if I can find her." That might mean another trip to Percy's room, the prospect of which I did not relish. I turned to Roberto, busily wiping off the cleared card table. "Come with me, Honey Bear?"

He straightened and walked the sponge into the kitchen, maneuvering past Marie to rinse it off and set it beside the sink. He reached into his pocket and produced the keys to my rental car. "Let's go."

As we made our way through the shadows of our front yard to the car, I imagined the trees morphing into strangers lurking in search of Brittany, bent on revenge for my mother and anyone related to her. I felt somewhat safe with Roberto by my side, but the memory of the young man beating on our front door with a bat the other night had shaken my sense of security in my old neighborhood.

I was glad I had not blocked the driveway with my mother's car. Although the storm of Roberto's wrath had apparently passed, I still felt like I was tiptoeing through a minefield. My husband did not fly into ranting rages like Percy used to, but his stony silences could evoke a different agony.

Neither of us spoke as we drove down the tranquil street. I helped scan for oncoming traffic before we turned right onto the Loop. Not sure if his silence meant he was still angry or just pensive, I decided to test the waters. "So...what do think of Giovanna?"

He glanced at me sideways, one eye on the road. "Cute kid. Just how I pictured you at that age."

Encouraged that in a way he was acknowledging she could be a part of me, I mused, "I'm still processing the whole thing. I skipped the motherhood stage, you know." Lowering my voice, I asked, "How do you feel about being married to a grandmother?"

His lips curled into an almost-grin. "You sure don't look like *my* grandmother!"

I leaned across the console and gave him a peck on the cheek. "Thanks. I sure don't *feel* like a grandmother." Straightening, I continued, "But, Roberto, please understand, shock that this is for all of us, now that I know about Giovanna, there's no way I can shut her out of my life."

Taking advantage of the green arrow at the intersection of the Loop and Fifth Street, Roberto concentrated on making a left turn.

When it was apparent he had no reply, I continued, "I never got a chance to know my son." I started to tear up; I wasn't sure if it was because of that loss, or the hovering fear of losing Roberto because of it.

Roberto looked directly ahead, focused on driving. The familiar sights of my childhood hometown passed in a blur, distorted like they were part of some surrealistic painting. Just when I thought he had checked out of the conversation, he muttered, "But that was your choice."

I took a deep breath. "Yes, it was." How different my life would have been had I saddled myself with a baby at age seventeen! I looked out the window as we passed Two Wells Junior College's majestic Hodges Hall, named for Mary Lynn's grandfather, oil baron like his father and one of the benefactors of the school. My parents had always hoped I would attend Two Wells junior college for my first two years, living at home and saving them money. But my pregnancy drove me out of Two Wells, and I ended up completing all the coursework for my bachelors degree at the University of Houston. Would I have managed to graduate from college had I chosen teen motherhood? "I know this isn't what you signed up for, Roberto," I went on, "But I hope you'll come to accept the situation. You think Giovanna's a nice kid."

"Does this mean I have to put up with that jerk...Percy? A man who tried to kill you?" Roberto's green eyes flashed, a warning bolt of the anger I had seen in them this morning. "Is he part of the package?"

"No." Roberto did not know Percy lay dying in the same hospital as my mother, where we were headed now, but this was probably not the best time to bring up that detail.

With a grimace, Roberto turned to me, his voice a whisper, "I don't want to share you with him. He doesn't deserve you."

"Never," I promised, touching his arm. "You'll always have me all to yourself."

We had stopped at a red light. Roberto turned his face toward mine and our lips drew together like magnets. In a moment, a beep from the car behind us announced the light had changed to green, and we quickly pulled apart so Roberto could move the car through the intersection.

"I don't know," he said, as we approached the hospital. "Things are different when children are involved. And ex-spouses. That's what I've always liked about *us*. No baggage: no kids, no exes."

I could not promise him nothing would change. With a grandchild in our lives, how could everything stay the same? "We'll be fine," I assured him. "You'll see."

"I'm not convinced yet," he said. "But you have a lot more to worry about right now. You need me on your side."

After we parked, he came around the car to open my door. He extended a hand to help me out, and our hands stayed clasped as we entered the hospital.

The guard stirred from his reverie as we approached my mother's room. He nodded to grant us entrance.

Mark and Karen were watching a news program; my mother lay supine against the white sheets, her breaths magnified by the oxygen tank.

"We didn't forget about you," I assured Mark.

Roberto and Mark shook hands. "How's she doing?" Roberto asked.

"Still hanging in there."

"Have you seen Isabella?" I asked. "Giovanna is still at the house."

"She hasn't come by."

I dreaded the thought of going to Percy's room again. And it was almost like deceiving my husband, because I had assured him Percy would not become part of our lives. Roberto's attention had shifted to the news program Karen was watching and they had just shared a comment. I was glad to see Roberto behaving civilly to Karen; in the past, he had harbored suspicion toward the women of the Loving Care Agency, considering them an unnecessary drain on my mother's assets with little return on the investment. Roberto would not have been the least bit surprised to discover Brittany's thievery.

Mark's eyes met mine. "Want to check on Isabella before we leave? You know where she is?"

"I should. We might need to find Giovanna a place to sleep tonight."

"My old bedroom would work." After my brother and I left home, my father had turned Mark's room into an office, with the single bed doubling as a couch. Although the closet was now stuffed with my mother's clothing, the room could still serve as sleeping quarters.

I gave Roberto a kiss as I moved toward the door. "Be right back, Honey Bear." I slipped out of the room before his lips could form a question I did not care to answer.

My heart pounded as I approached Percy's room. Maybe he would be too weak to spar with me; Elaine had mentioned earlier that she had not been able to see him. I fought pangs of guilt that my husband would not approve of my visit. Too soon after our delicate reconciliation, I was daring the wounds to reopen.

The room was empty. No tubes, no machines, no medical staff, no Percy. Isabella sat crumpled on his stripped bed, sobbing.

I rushed to her side, making room for myself beside her on the bed, breathing the antiseptic smells of wounded life and clinical death. "Isabella."

She tumbled into my arms, sobbing harder. Had they taken him off to an operating room? Or...?

"Percy's g...gone," she sputtered. "Oh, Michelle! I don't know what I'll do."

"I'm sorry," I told her, stroking her thick mane of hair. "I'm *so* sorry." My words were sincere; I did actually feel some sorrow, for her anguish, maybe even a little for Percy, for his abbreviated life and the physical pain he must have suffered at the end.

"He...he was so good to us," she sobbed. "All these years after Paul died."

"I know." She had told me. Saint Percy.

"You were the love of his life," she went on.

That caught me off guard. "Yeah, right." The sorrow I had felt a moment ago melted into anger, the smoldering anger at Percy for the torment he had caused me years ago, and fresh anger at him for dying now, after Isabella and Giovanna had become dependent on him. "Love means wanting the best for someone, not wanting to control that person. Percy never figured that out."

Isabella wiped away a tear. "I think he did. He was asking about you at the end. Wondering whether you were coming back to see him. He was sorry things always..." Her voice trailed off and she threw up her hands, as if she couldn't find a word in the English language to fit her meaning. "You were always hurting each other."

I shook my head, not wanting to dig up the past again. Put the dirt back in the hole and cover it up, stomp it in place. Memories of happy times with Percy must linger somewhere, but I had not been able to retrieve them for many years. Maybe they had been erased when he tried to strangle me.

Isabella looked at me through red-rimmed eyes. "You were together for six years. Surely there must have been something you loved about him."

I strained to think, to come up with some kind words to comfort her, to validate her high opinion of Percy. I'd loved his eyes. I'd loved his smile. I'd loved his hair. I'd loved his body. Percy was one of the best-looking men I had ever seen, and I had loved the envious attention we attracted from other women wherever we went. Especially Mary Lynn Hodges. For the first time, I had something Mary Lynn wanted that she couldn't have. After I started dating Percy steadily, she looked at me differently, with something akin to respect. "You two make a lovely couple," she'd said to me one day after class.

But loving someone based solely on physical attraction and the ability to make others jealous seemed ridiculously shallow. Was that really all there was? I looked at Isabella. "He was great with the tropical fish. Especially the African cichlids. He'd found a business where he could make a contribution. And for someone who claimed to hate cats, he sure loved Bowser." I felt a wet spot on my cheek. As I wiped it away, I realized more tears were falling. Tears for Percy?

Isabella and I embraced, and I let myself join her in sobs. I cried for the dream that never came true, the happiness we could never find, and for the family Percy and I could have made together.

"Isabella," I said after a moment, as our sobs subsided. "Why don't you come home with us?"

She closed her lips and eyes tightly, shook her head. "I can't right now."

"You shouldn't be alone."

"I need to be." She opened her tear-filled eyes again and looked directly at me, as if that would strengthen her case. I didn't know her well enough to argue.

"What about Giovanna? Want us to keep her overnight?"

"Would you?"

"Of course. Sure you'll be okay? Are you going to drive anywhere?"

"I'll be fine. I just need to be alone for a while."

I sensed my cue to leave. I was surprised no hospital staff had come in yet to shoo us out, to sterilize the room and prepare it for the next patient. "We're going home now. Call if you need me." After another supportive hug, I left her alone to grieve over Percy.

"*Carina*! Finally," Roberto said as I returned to my mother's room. "Can we go now? Your brother's had a long day."

We brushed lips and fingertips, and then I made my way to my mother's side. I felt like we'd been ignoring her, even though we were dutifully gathered in her room. "Sleep well, Mom. We'll be back tomorrow." I took one of her cold, limp hands and cupped it in mine to warm it, grateful that I could still touch her, fighting away the image of Isabella sobbing in Percy's empty room. I detected a faint squeeze.

Mark and Roberto were on their way out the door. "Bye, Karen," I said, picking up my purse to follow. I would tell them about Percy soon; I just had to find the right moment.

Chapter Thirty-Five

Giovanna had slept in the study, wearing one of my mother's nightgowns, and the night had passed uneventfully. Now Marie gathered candidates for a load of laundry, primarily so Giovanna could have clean clothes.

As the washing machine churned, I perused my suitcase for something suitable to wear to a funeral. I settled on my all-purpose long, black knit skirt and a black turtleneck. I draped the Hermès scarf around my neck and inspected my image in the mirror, for a moment recalling the naïve *Américaine* who had thought she could conquer Paris, now wearing the fine silk scarf like a Purple Heart.

Dressed, I wandered into the family room, where my brother and husband sprawled on the couch, reading the Two Wells newspaper. "Who's coming to the funeral with me?"

Roberto looked up. "What funeral?"

"Brittany Landers. Her funeral is this morning."

He turned a page. "I didn't think you knew her very well."

"Not well. But it would be a gesture of respect to her family." I plucked a white cat hair from my black skirt. "Besides, I'd like to get another look at some of the suspects."

Mark set down his part of the paper and gave me a pleading look. "I don't think this is a good idea."

"Come on, go with me. Mrs. Landers invited us." My brother had chosen a fine time to stop playing detective.

He shook his head and returned to the comics. "I'm not going."

"Honey Bear?" I batted my eyes at Roberto.

Roberto rose, setting down the meager *Two Wells Times*. "Why should I go to a funeral for someone I never met? I want to take a look at that front door, see if I can fix it.

And the lawn needs mowing." He gestured toward the sliding glass window. "Does that old mower still work?"

I sighed. I had not really expected Roberto to accompany me to Brittany's funeral, but I had thought Mark would. Marie and Giovanna, now clad in clean clothes, emerged from the hallway that led to the bedrooms. "Marie," I began, as my sister-in-law buzzed toward the kitchen. "Want to go to the funeral with me? Your husband won't go."

Marie looked at me like I had proposed a trip to the moon. "Your mother is in the hospital and you're going to a funeral for someone you barely knew?"

"Brittany worked for us. She was killed here. Mom would go to the funeral if she were able."

Marie shook her head. "I still have cleaning to do. And your brother and I are going to the hospital in a little while."

"Guess I'm going by myself." I glanced at my watch, not wanting to arrive too early.

Giovanna looked at me, her small face timid. "Can I go with you, Grandma Michelle?"

I swallowed. My first outing alone with my granddaughter? A funeral for someone I hardly knew and didn't even like.

"Giovanna, have you ever been to a funeral before? Would your mother approve?" Marie asked.

"She took me to one last month."

Paul's adoptive parents, I remembered. Killed on September 11. The day our country had lost its innocence. The day that changed all of our lives in ways we were just beginning to fathom. I had been about Giovanna's age when President Kennedy was assassinated, and I can still picture my teacher delivering the shocking news, just after our class returned from the cafeteria. But even that event now seemed trivial compared to 9/11. I looked at Marie; Giovanna should be able to handle attending a funeral.

"This funeral may be different, though." Marie placed her hands on her hips.

"Giovanna, I'd be honored to have you come with me, if that's what you want to do." I avoided looking at Marie, not caring to gauge her reaction.

It was another bright fall day without a cloud in the azure sky to threaten the flow of sunshine, one of those days you feel you are wasting if you stay inside. I took my rental car, leaving my mother's Ford Fiesta for Mark and Marie.

Giovanna settled into the front seat, fastening her seat belt like a small adult. She smiled at me as I adjusted the driver's seat and started the engine. "Is this funeral for my grandfather?"

My hands almost slipped off the wheel as I backed down the driveway. "Your grandfather?" Was this why she had been so eager to join me?

Giovanna blinked, her dark lashes framing moist hazel eyes. "I know he's old and sick."

"Old? Like me?" Elaine and I had once sworn we'd kill ourselves before we hit the decrepit age of forty; to someone Giovanna's age, Percy and I must seem ancient.

Despite the teary eyes, Giovanna smiled. "No, Miss Michelle. You're not old! You're young, like my mama."

"Well, I'm not quite *that* young." I moved the gearshift from reverse to drive and we headed down the street.

"Mama said he was going to die."

It was not my place to break the news to her that Percy *was* dead. I opted to dodge the truth without actually lying, buying time for Isabella so she could tell her daughter in her own way, with the sensitivity of one who had loved him. "No, Giovanna, didn't you hear us talking about it? This funeral is for a young woman who used to work for my mother. She died on Thursday."

Giovanna stared out the window as we cruised down the street. Would she ask to return home now? I thought the question had been handled until she asked, "What about my grandfather?"

We had come to the stop sign at the end of the street, and I needed to concentrate on making my turn into traffic on the Loop. I gave her a pained look. "Your mother will do something for your grandfather later on." Would Isabella actually hold a memorial service? Would anyone come? Did Percy have any friends? When we were together, he had succeeded in alienating all of mine.

Thinking about Percy depressed me. I had not expected to feel anything but relief at his demise. I had certainly not expected to shed any tears. My brooding over feelings I might have had for Percy put me in exactly the right frame of mind for attending a funeral. I stole a glance at my granddaughter as I drove. She was reading *Gone with the Wind*. "How do you like that book?" I asked; she had covered quite a few pages since the last time I'd seen her with it.

"It's good. But Scarlett is mean to her sister, stealing her *beau* like that."

We had reached the parking lot of the funeral home and I pulled the rental car into a space. "You'll want to leave the book in the car, Giovanna. It's more respectful."

My stomach did a flip as Giovanna and I, hand in hand, entered the funeral home, where a small crowd had gathered. Somber organ music played softly in the background. I did not recognize a soul. What was I doing here? How in the world did I think I was going to scope out a suspect? Mark and Marie were right; this was a stupid idea.

I spotted Mrs. Landers and Tiffany standing beside the closed casket on which rested several framed photographs of Brittany Landers in various stages of her short life: a pink-cheeked baby, a pig-tailed toddler, a schoolgirl missing her two front teeth. The series continued with an overly made-up high-school glamour shot and a more recent photo of a young woman clad in a hospital uniform. I also noticed the photo of the three sisters I had seen the other night at the Landers home. And then there was a larger one taken at the Two Wells Rose Gardens, with Brittany and Tiffany standing next to a middle-aged woman who looked vaguely familiar. I led Giovanna toward the family. Maybe we should just pay our respects and leave.

"Mrs. Landers." I looked up from the photos and held out my hand. "Michelle DePalma. My brother and I stopped by your house the other night."

"Michelle." A flicker of recognition crossed her face as she clasped my hand. "Thank you for coming."

"Tiffany," I acknowledged the daughter as Mrs. Landers let go of my hand. "I'm so sorry for your loss." I turned to Giovanna, trying out the words, "This is Giovanna Rogers, my granddaughter."

"Hello, Jo-vanna." Mrs. Landers bent to address Giovanna at eye level. "Thank you for coming. And this is my oldest daughter, Sergeant Stephanie Landers."

The tall, unsmiling woman with bushy curls and military posture extended a stiff handshake. "Hello, Ma'am." I recognized her as the driver of the pick-up truck that had almost run over me the other night.

An awkward pause ensued. "We're very sorry about Brittany," I murmured, leading Giovanna away from the Landers women to make room for other guests with more business tying up the grieving family members. We were moving toward the door and freedom when the music stopped and a man in a dark suit commanded silence; the service was about to start. We had no choice but to slip into a couple of chairs near the back of the room.

"Excuse me." As the funeral director began his oratory, a couple squeezed by our aisle position to take vacant seats in our row.

I looked up as they passed. "Elaine! What are you doing here?" Accompanying my friend was a lanky, balding man. I recognized him from a photo my mother had taken of Elaine and him dressed to the nines for the theatre. Elaine's third husband.

"Michelle! Hi, Giovanna!" Elaine acknowledged my granddaughter, and then turned back to me, touching Jerry's arm the whole time. "This is Jerry Tillman, my ex. Remember I told you he'd be here today to defend your mother?"

A woman from the row forward turned around and shushed us. When she had returned her attention to the master of ceremonies, Elaine made a face at the back of her head. But she did lower her voice. "Jerry says to me, he says, coming to the funeral is a good way to see what kind of characters this Brittany Landers hung out with, and watch how they act. And maybe we'll find us some new suspects."

I smiled. Jerry and I must have read the same detective novels.

Jerry's bespectacled eyes swept the room. "Not a lot of people here, for someone so young."

"I've found that a lot of people didn't like her," I whispered wickedly.

The double doors opened to admit another late arrival. I recognized the young black man who had come to my door looking for Brittany; he was wearing what looked like the same baggy clothes, complete with headphones, but he had made an attempt to slick down his unruly curls. His eyes darted around the room but although there were still plenty of empty chairs, he leaned against the back wall. I nudged Elaine, motioning for her to direct Jerry's attention to the young man. When I had succeeded, I whispered, "That guy came over the other day, looking for Brittany. Didn't seem to know she was dead."

Jerry nodded. "Know his name?"

"Jamal Johnson. The police questioned him and said there wasn't enough evidence to prove he did anything. Left fingerprints at the scene, but he claimed he'd visited Brittany at work before the day of the murder." Scanning the room again, my eyes came to rest on the trio of Loving Care aides, like chocolate chips in the middle of a row of white mourners—Karen, Keisha, and Katrina. I wondered absently who was watching my mother, but then again, she *was* in the *hospital*, and when she'd first been admitted, she'd survived without anyone but hospital staff looking after her. Besides, Mark and Marie were headed over there this morning.

The minister finished his formal remarks, and then asked if anyone would like to come forward to share memories of Brittany Landers.

There was an uncomfortable silence; neither Brittany's mother nor sisters made any move toward the podium.

Then a well-dressed woman around my age rose and strode to the stage. Although her features were rather plain, she assumed the lectern with polish and grace. As she addressed the audience, I recognized my high school nemesis: Mary Lynn Hodges.

My head jerked toward Elaine. She made a face that showed as much surprise as mine.

Mary Lynn spoke about how Brittany Landers had involved herself in the church; she may have lost her way at times, but she had committed her life to Jesus Christ, accepted Him as her personal savior. Tempted to snicker, I looked straight ahead and kept my uncharitable thoughts about Brittany's thievery to myself. I could not keep from wondering how someone from Brittany's side of the tracks had grown so close to someone in the social elite like Mary Lynn Hodges.

"Mary Lynn Matthews, you're such a hypocrite!" cried a familiar throaty voice from the audience.

Elaine and I craned our necks and then looked at each other, mouthing in unison, "Psycho Sally!"

Flamboyant in an expensive red wool suit, teased hair, and too much make-up, Sally Jenkins pranced toward the stage. Throughout our school years, Elaine and I had been grateful for "Psycho Sally"—the nickname Mary Lynn had given the daughter of her father's oldest friend—because Sally took the focus of Mary Lynn's bullying off us. Sally shook her finger at Mary Lynn. "Why don't you tell the good people how Brittany Landers was getting ready to sue your ass?"

There was a hush over the crowd, and Mary Lynn paled. She fingered her collar as Sally continued, "Why don't you tell them how she worked for you and...?" One of the ushers from the funeral home took Sally's arm and escorted her out of the room. Music began playing, and Mary Lynn slipped off the stage.

Prompted by the organ, the congregation rose to sing "Amazing Grace." Giovanna mouthed the words like I used to do with hymns in church, hesitant to let my voice ring out, not trusting myself to stay on key.

The service ended and mourners poured out of the rows, some gathering around the casket, some chatting with family members. Both Sally and Mary Lynn were gone. I watched the scene from a distance, trying to identify unusual behavior. I felt like I had walked into a test for which I had not studied enough; if I had learned more about Brittany's life—her friends, her family, her enemies, her work history with Mary Lynn Hodges—maybe I would have been better prepared to analyze the interactions.

"Stacy's not here, is she?" I asked Elaine, as I remembered our brief conversation about Brittany at my mother's house. "Did you ask her if this was the same Brittany Landers she used to waitress with?"

"It is, but no, Stacy had to work today, so she couldn't come. They weren't that close anyway—in fact, I don't think Stacy even liked her," Elaine replied. "Want to ride with us to the cemetery?"

I had not thought that far ahead. Seeing my hesitation, Jerry chimed in, "Come on, Michelle. It'll give us a chance to compare notes."

"How about it, Giovanna?" I touched my granddaughter's hair. It felt soft and I marveled that Giovanna did not flinch or pull away.

Giovanna's answer was a bashful smile.

"Just a minute," I told Elaine. Out of the corner of my eye, I had observed the Jackson trio splitting off; Karen and Keisha were talking to another black woman whom I recognized as a part-time Loving Care employee—Virginia? I had seen her at my mother's house a couple of times. Katrina stood beside the casket, examining the photos of Brittany. I approached. "Hello, Katrina."

"Why hey, Michelle!" She had a toothy grin like her mother and sister, but her body was not quite as inflated yet. "And Jo-vanna! Hey there! Where's your mama?"

Giovanna had followed me like a puppy, rather than staying with Elaine and Jerry as I had expected. "Hello, Miss Katrina," Giovanna replied politely.

Puzzled, I looked from my granddaughter to Katrina. "How do you two know each other?"

Katrina shrugged. "I met Isabella and Jo-vanna at your mama's house. I thought they were friends of Brittany's."

I was so surprised to learn that my daughter-in-law knew Brittany, I forgot what I had planned to ask Katrina. Did Isabella know her friend Brittany was dead? Killed at my mother's house? Which she and Giovanna had apparently frequented before their supposed first visit to me? I looked at Giovanna. "You knew Brittany Landers?"

"Yes, Ma'am."

"She was a friend of your mother's?" I pressed.

"Yes, Ma'am. I guess."

"So, when you and your mother came over the other day, when you first met me, that wasn't the first time you'd been to my house?"

"No, Ma'am." Giovanna did not seem to understand my surprise.

"Had you met my mother before?"

"Yes, Ma'am."

"And Katrina?" I motioned toward Katrina, who had turned to talk to someone else. The crowd was thinning, and Elaine and Jerry waved for us to follow them. *Friends and enemies,* I thought. That's what I'd wanted to ask Katrina about. Maybe I would have another opportunity at the graveside service. And maybe Katrina would be able to tell me something about Brittany's employment with Mary Lynn Hodges. "Come on," I took Giovanna's hand, leading her toward Elaine and Jerry. "Does your mother know Brittany is dead?" Isabella may have been so consumed with Percy's situation, she had missed hearing about the death of her friend. Although I had told her a young woman had been killed in my mother's home, perhaps she did not realize the victim was Brittany.

"I don't think so, Ma'am. She never said." Giovanna slowed her pace. "What happened to Miss Brittany?"

More adult explanations. Was I ready for this? "We don't really know. Someone killed her. The police think my mother did."

"Your mother?" Giovanna stopped. "Why?"

"Come on, Elaine and Jerry are waiting." I gave her hand a tug, like the leash of a dog who had delayed his constitutional to sniff. "She was the only one in the house when it happened. That we know of."

Giovanna looked perplexed. "Is she in jail?"

"No, she's in the hospital. She hasn't been arrested." Giovanna's face relaxed when I added, "And she didn't do it." We had reached Elaine and Jerry at the exit. I sidled next to Jerry as we all walked outside together into the bright sunlight. "Any ideas about suspects yet?" Squinting, I reached into my purse for sunglasses. "And what do you think about that little outburst at the end?" I would have liked nothing better than for Mary Lynn to turn out to be the killer, and to see Keith slap handcuffs around her Cartier-adorned wrists.

Jerry took a cigarette from his pocket and lit it with a small gold-plated lighter. “I'll be checking the alibis for those two women for sure. And Mr. Music Box in the back of the room was an interesting character. My hunch says he's into drugs, and I bet I could convince a jury there’s a connection. Certainly an argument for reasonable doubt.” He inhaled, and then blew a cloud of smoke through his nostrils. Taking the cigarette out of his mouth for a moment, he continued, “The older sister has a chip on her shoulder. And the younger sister doesn't seem too torn up about the whole thing. I sense some jealousy, something not quite right.”

“I think Brittany and Tiffany were interested in the same boyfriend,” I supplied, although I had no reason to believe Tiffany’s grief was not real. The drug angle had potential, though. After all, Brittany’s mother smoked pot.

We piled into Elaine’s Dodge Durango, and I cringed when Elaine took the driver’s seat. “Fasten your seat belt,” I told Giovanna, as we situated ourselves in back, pushing aside a dry-cleaning bag to search for the belt tips. I gathered several empty cups and fast food wrappers and wadded them into an empty drugstore sack. “If we drive by a trash can, let me know.”

“Just leave it,” Elaine replied, meeting my eyes in the rear view mirror. “I’ll get the kids to clean out the car later.” When she started the engine, the stereo blasted some god-awful rap CD, suppressing any further conversation. Elaine quickly turned down the volume and switched to our local oldies station that was playing a pleasing Beatles tune. A musical ringtone sounded almost like it came from the radio; Elaine scrambled for her cell phone with one hand and with the other, steered the car out of the parking lot to join the funeral procession.

Jerry flicked his cigarette out the window and took his cell phone out of his pocket, dialed a number, and then placed it to his ear.

I glanced at Giovanna, wondering if she found it amusing that both front-seat occupants were engaged in separate outside conversations. Or maybe she was too young to remember the world being any other way. Lowering my voice so as not to disrupt the phone dialogues of my fellow passengers, I said to Giovanna, "Tell me about your mother and her friend Brittany Landers. How did they meet?"

Giovanna shrugged. "They worked together in Houston."

"You said your mother was a nurse at Memorial Hospital. Was Brittany a nurse, too?" I did not remember Brittany being that skilled.

"No, Ma'am, I don't think she was a nurse. She just worked at the hospital for a while. Then she came back home. Here."

"Giovanna." I studied my granddaughter's cherubic face. "When did you and your mother come to Two Wells?"

"Last summer," she replied. "When my grandfather got really sick."

"And you moved into his house?"

"Yes, Ma'am."

"Your mother got in touch with Brittany?"

"We went to see her when she was working at my great grandmother's house."

Her great grandmother. My mother. "Did Brittany know her employer was your great grandmother?"

"Yes, Ma'am. I think so."

Did everybody in town know about my secret son's wife and child? Was I the last to find out? How much had my mother known?

Elaine hung up her cell phone and looked at us via the rearview mirror. "Y'all know where we're going?"

"No. But follow the convoy," I replied. The traffic light turned red, but a uniformed policeman had stopped in the intersection, waving two cars ahead of Elaine through. We sailed through behind them.

"This is cool," Giovanna said, grinning, as we watched frustrated drivers stopped at their green light, waiting for our procession to file past.

"Whee... I feel like a cop!" Elaine cried with childish glee, steering her SUV through another red light, waved on by a policeman.

Our destination was the cemetery by the airport, the one with plenty of room left for future occupants. Elaine stopped in a non-parking place along one of the paved roads winding among the tombstones. I started to help Giovanna detach her seat belt, but she had already unfastened it. We piled out of the Dodge Durango and joined the small group of mourners gathered around an open grave. Neither Mary Lynn Hodges nor Sally Jenkins was among them.

I scanned the crowd for Katrina. She stood beside her sister, chatting with two young women I did not recognize. I excused myself quietly. Giovanna did not follow this time. She was engrossed in conversation with Jerry, who was demonstrating the features of his cell phone.

Snaking my way through the maze of mourners, I maneuvered to Katrina's side. "Katrina, can we talk a minute?"

She stepped back from the cluster. "What's up, Miss Michelle?"

My question now seemed a little stupid, and not nearly as urgent as I had implied. I plowed on anyway, "Keisha said you and Brittany were pretty good friends?"

"We got along."

"What was the deal with her and Mary Lynn Hodges?" Katrina's brow furrowed, and I clarified, "Mary Lynn Matthews. You know, the woman who got up and spoke about Brittany giving her life to Jesus?"

Katrina shrugged. "Never heard that before."

"She never talked about her time working for Mrs. Matthews?"

Katrina shook her head.

"Can you tell me who her enemies were?"

"Enemies?" Katrina's face darkened. "Brittany had issues with people from time to time. Some white girl named Stacy had it in for her. But no enemies."

I backed up. *Enemies* was a strong word. "Look around here. Think about the people who came to the funeral home. Anyone who didn't belong? Someone you were surprised to see?" *Besides me*, I thought.

Katrina pondered for a moment. “Did you see a black guy come in late, back at the funeral home? Baggy pants, headphones? Looked like a drug dealer?”

I nodded excitedly, remembering Jerry’s comments about him. “Yes?”

“Never seen *him* before. Don’t know what business he had with Brittany.”

As I searched the crowd to determine if our suspect had made it from the funeral home to the cemetery, I glimpsed Elaine rushing toward me, cell phone in hand, a somber look on her face. “Elaine, what is it?” I asked when she reached my side.

“Keith called,” she said breathlessly. “It’s your mom.”

Chapter Thirty-Six

Graveside service forgotten, we piled into the Dodge Durango. Elaine cranked the engine while the rest of us were fastening our seat belts. My hand shook, preventing the metal tip from connecting with the clasp. What had I been thinking, attending *Brittany's* funeral while my mother was dying? Giovanna reached over to help me with my seat belt.

Elaine maneuvered through parked cars along the narrow cemetery road, coming close to scraping paint off doors or knocking off mirrors, but managed to emerge onto the highway without a scratch. She dialed her cell phone as soon as she was on open road. In a moment, she disconnected, announcing, "Isabella doesn't answer. Should I keep Giovanna with me?"

"How did you get hold of Isabella?" I asked, ignoring Elaine's question.

"I didn't. But she's staying at Percy's."

"You have Percy's phone number memorized?" When we were in high school, Elaine had trouble memorizing anything: poems, formulas, and especially phone numbers.

"No, Silly, it's in my directory. What do you want me to do with Giovanna?" She turned around in her seat, momentarily ignoring the business of driving. "Giovanna, want to come to my house? Timmy'll be home from school soon."

Jerry grabbed the wheel as the SUV drifted into the next lane, earning a honk. "Pay attention to the road, Elaine."

Elaine made a face and flipped him off, no thanks at all for an action that may have saved our lives. Jerry turned sulkily back to his cell phone and began dialing. I suspected Elaine's driving had been a point of contention in their short-lived marriage.

I didn't think about my rental car, still parked at the funeral home, until after Elaine had dropped me at the hospital and I was in the elevator. But no need, Mark and Marie had my mother's Ford Fiesta. Besides, the funeral home was not more than a mile away; if I had to, I could walk from the hospital to retrieve my car.

I almost passed my mother's room; the armed guard was gone. I half expected to see Keith Matthews, because he had called Elaine to summon me. I backed up and entered to find Mark and Marie hovering at our mother's bedside, hands clasped, each with a free hand touching our mother. Karen lingered nearby, sniffling into a Kleenex, her eyes watering. I wondered how she had beaten me here, but then remembered I had not seen her at the cemetery with her daughters.

Marie broke away from her post to hug me, and then allowed me to displace her. "She stopped breathing for a couple minutes," she explained. "That's why we asked Keith Matthews to find you. She's breathing again, but it's really slowed down."

I reached for one of my mother's tiny, cold hands, as if my touch could restore her life.

Footsteps announced the entrance of two young women in street clothing. The younger one held a clipboard, and the older one slid on a pair of rubber gloves. Noticing our stares, she announced, "We're doing a study about bedsores. Can we take a look?"

"Excuse me?" I felt my jaw drop in disbelief.

"The hospital said it's okay," the older one continued, nudging us aside like pawns on a chessboard to invade my mother's space.

I refused to budge. "I think the hospital said it was okay if you got the family's permission. You don't have our permission."

"It will only take a minute."

"I said you don't have our permission. Now get out of here!"

The older one locked eyes with me for a moment, and then turned on her heel with a huff. The younger one jotted something on her clipboard as they left the room.

"I'm writing a complaint letter. This is outrageous!" Marie murmured.

Karen shook her head. "Mmm...mmm...hmm! What *will* they think of next?"

"I have to go out for a minute," Mark announced.

"Where...?" Marie started to ask.

"I'll be back," he said over his shoulder on his way out the door.

I shrugged. "Maybe he's going to complain to the hospital authorities about what just happened." Turning my attention back to my almost comatose mother, I murmured, "Sorry, Mom."

Marie had drawn closer, gently patting my mother's twig of a leg underneath the sheet. "How was the funeral, Michelle? Did you find what you were looking for?"

The parade of funeral attendees and potential suspects was a distant memory; my mother had again taken center stage. "Elaine was there with her ex-husband, Jerry. He's a criminal attorney and has offered to defend Mom, if it becomes necessary."

"I know. They stopped here on their way to the funeral home."

Elaine and Jerry had not mentioned that. "Jerry wasn't able to talk to Mom, was he? Did she even recognize him?"

"I don't think so. They were leaving when Mark and I arrived. Elaine introduced us, and told us they were going to the funeral."

"Was the guard still here then?"

"Why?"

I gestured toward the door. "He's gone now."

Marie seemed surprised, but not terribly concerned. "Maybe Keith Matthews released him when he stopped by." She sighed. "What a waste of taxpayer money!"

"It was never clear to me why they had the guard. To keep Mom in? Or the ne'er-do-wells out?" They could stop the people but not the pneumonia, I thought grimly.

"Where's Giovanna? Did you take her home?" Marie sounded like a mother asking me if I had put my toy away.

"Elaine has her. We couldn't reach Isabella."

Marie's eyebrows raised in silent disapproval of the woman who was rearing my granddaughter. Anxious to quell those unkind thoughts, I continued, "You guys don't know this yet, but Percy died last night. Isabella has a lot to deal with right now. She hasn't had a chance to tell Giovanna."

Some of the disapproval drained from Marie's face. "I'm sorry." She cocked her head. "Isabella was Percy's sole caretaker?"

"Apparently." Percy's grandparents were the only family of his I had ever met, and they were long gone. They had adored me until I got pregnant. Percy said the news would devastate them, so instead he told them we had broken up. Even after the baby was gone and life was supposedly back to normal, he maintained the ruse, saying his grandmother could never forgive me for the terrible way I had treated him. I could only imagine how he must have embellished the "break-up" story.

"Wow," Marie marveled, sounding like Mark. "Percy's gone. End of an era."

Someone else had recently used that term. Elaine? "Officially," I agreed. "But my Percy era ended a long time ago."

"Will you help Isabella with the arrangements?"

My head throbbed, and I pressed my fingers against my forehead to relieve the pressure. Funeral arrangements for Percy? Surely Isabella would know better than to ask me. "Highly unlikely."

"Sure? Aren't you a little sad?"

Before I could comment further, Mark entered, arms filled with yellow envelopes. He let them tumble onto the bedside table and without waiting for us to open our mouths, he announced, "A little unethical, I know, but I emptied the safe deposit box." Our mother's bank was just down the street from the hospital.

I finished his thought silently: because when Mom dies, the safe deposit box will be sealed, cutting us off from papers we might need before the will is settled. I shivered. How had we come to this point so quickly, waiting for our mother to die, when a few years ago we had assumed she would live another decade or two? "I don't want to look at that stuff now," I told Mark, shrinking from the pile of stock certificates, savings bonds, insurance policies, deeds, and who knew what else.

Mark touched my shoulder. "You don't have to." Leaning close to our mother, he asked, "How is she?" although it was plain we had the same information he did. Her body still struggled for shallow, irregular breaths, but her mind had escaped to somewhere far away.

Karen looked at her watch. "Y'all might as well go home and get some supper. I'll call if anything happens."

"What? We can't leave now!" Eating was the last thing on my mind.

Karen shook her head. "She could go on like this for hours, even days. You need to keep up your strength. It's what your mama would want."

The rumbling in my stomach warned me not to protest. I squeezed my mother's hand before letting go. "Hang on, Mom, we'll be back soon."

My rental car looked lonely in the empty funeral home parking lot, where Mark and Marie dropped me off and waited dutifully until my engine started. I put the car in *drive*, turned on the oldies station, and pulled onto the street to follow them home. I caught the last few notes of a Simon and Garfunkel song I had not heard in many years, and then the news came on. The announcer's smooth voice betrayed little trace of a southern accent as he read, "Another suspect in the Brittany Landers murder was questioned and released today. Brittany Landers, the caregiver who was found bludgeoned to death last Thursday in the home of her elderly employer, Lola Hanson, was buried this afternoon. Lola Hanson, who remains hospitalized and unresponsive, is still the primary suspect in this case." I shut off the radio, resentful of this public intrusion into our lives.

My body felt drained. My head throbbed. I reached into my purse for my vial of aspirin. I popped three into my mouth with only saliva to wash them down. Bad idea, as at least one of the tablets dissolved before it hit my throat, coating my tongue with a bitter powder.

I pulled into the driveway alongside my mother's Ford Fiesta as Marie and Mark got out; in the fading light, I noticed the front lawn had been mowed and neatly edged. Roberto had kept his promise.

My husband was snoring on the family room couch. I gave him a quick peck on the forehead and made a beeline for the kitchen in search of water to wash away the taste of the aspirin. Marie already had the refrigerator door open to take inventory of the vegetable bins. Mark flopped into my mother's favorite chair, propped his feet on the nearby ottoman, and reached for the remote control.

"Hey," Roberto murmured, squinting in my direction. "You call that a kiss?"

I set my water glass on the counter and returned to the couch. Roberto had moved aside so I could sit on the edge and embrace him. I kissed him tenderly. "That's better," he declared when we came up for air.

"Nice job on the front lawn," I told him.

"You didn't see the back."

"You mowed the back yard, too?"

"All that work, and no one even noticed." He maneuvered himself into a sitting position, rose, and taking my hand, led me toward the sliding door.

We stepped onto the concrete patio. The cool air felt moist against my face. A thick layer of clouds had moved in, dashing any hope of seeing the sunset. Such a change from the crisp, clear morning I had left in. The fickleness of the fall weather reminded me of the rapid change in my mother's condition.

I surveyed the back lawn, recognizing in the twilight that the weeds had indeed been mowed. "Nice," I assured Roberto, with a shiver. A sparkle at the edge of the patio caught my eye, and I bent to retrieve the object.

"Still weeds holding hands, but at least they're all the same height now," Roberto said. "Your mom needs some serious lawn care."

Did it matter any more? My mother would die soon, and we would sell the house—the Hanson family residence for over forty years—leaving the lawn problems for the new owner. I studied the object in my hand: a gold charm in the shape of a wolf that may have belonged on a bracelet.

"What's that?" Roberto peered over my shoulder to examine it. "I'm surprised it didn't get chewed up in the lawn mower. Yours?"

"No, I've never seen it before." I put the charm in my pocket. Something about it looked familiar.

"How was the funeral?" Roberto asked, slipping an arm around me.

"Got called away from the cemetery service when Mom stopped breathing." I looked into his kind eyes. "We almost lost her this afternoon."

He encircled me with his other arm, pulling me close to his chest. "I'm sorry." We both knew what it felt like to lose a parent, but this was the second one for me, and it seemed worse. "Then why did you come back here?"

I buried my face in his chest. *What a lousy daughter I was! Why hadn't I remained at my mother's bedside?* "Karen sent us away, told us to go get something to eat." I looked up. "Said it was what Mom would want. We'll go back right after dinner. Will you come with us?"

He stroked my hair. "Of course." He tilted my head gently, pointing my face toward his, and gave me a tender kiss.

"Thanks for being here," I told him, once our lips separated again.

He rubbed my arm. "You're freezing. Let's go back inside." As I slid open the glass door, he asked, "Where's the kid?"

"Giovanna?"

We reentered the family room, and Roberto latched the sliding door behind us. "Giovanna, yes. Did she go home with her mother?"

I shook my head. "My friend Elaine took her when I went to the hospital."

"Poor girl. She probably doesn't know what to make of all this shuffling around."

Not only was I a lousy daughter, I was a lousy grandmother, too.

"Is Giovanna coming back here tonight?" Roberto asked, interrupting my self-flagellation.

I eyed my husband, not sure how to read the expression on his face. Did he miss having Giovanna around, or was his question merely logistical? "I don't know. That depends on her mother. She's..."

"I'm making pita sandwiches," Marie announced from the kitchen, sparing me from telling Roberto about Isabella's connection with Percy. "How many do you want?"

"Just one for me," I replied. "Roberto?" He held up his index finger. "One for each of us. Thanks, Marie."

"Mark? Turn off the TV and come to the table. Your sandwich is ready."

Sighing, my brother obeyed his wife. He extinguished the glow of the television, to which no one was paying attention anyway, rose from the armchair, and lumbered toward the card table.

"Can I help, Marie?" I asked as my sister-in-law bustled around the kitchen.

"You could fill the water glasses," she replied. "Or if you want something else to drink, go ahead and pour that."

In a moment, the four of us were seated around the card table, silent except for the sound of munching and the occasional tinkle of ice against a glass. The phone rang.

Mark looked annoyed. We all knew there was no answering machine. I blotted my mouth, rose, and picked up the portable extension on the coffee table. "Hanson residence." I ran my tongue around my molars to dislodge the last bite of pita sandwich.

"Michelle, that you, Girl?" It was Karen. "Your mama ain't breathin' no more."

"What do you mean?" I asked stupidly.

"You and your brother better git on down here."

Chapter Thirty-Seven

I put down the phone without saying good-bye. Mark looked at me sharply, mouthed "Karen?" and I nodded. He pushed his chair away from the table and scrambled for his keys.

"Oh dear," said Marie. She had a pita sandwich in one hand, a glass of water in the other, and she was staring at her purse on the coffee table, as if unsure of which item to put down or pick up first.

Roberto rose, picking up his empty plate and Mark's. "I'll clean up. You don't want cockroaches overrunning this place." Gently, he pried the water glass from Marie's hand, freeing her from paralysis, like winding up a battery-operated toy that had run out of juice. He carried the items to the kitchen and set them on the counter beside the sink.

Jacket in hand, I walked over and gave him a kiss. "You're coming, too, aren't you?"

He helped me put on my jacket because my hands were trembling too much for me to slip them through the armholes. "Go with your brother. I'll be right behind you."

Our mother was gone by the time we arrived in her hospital room. Her body lay motionless in the bed, the labored breathing silenced. Like Brittany Landers when I first found her, my mother's skin had a blue-gray pallor but was not yet cold to the touch. Her eyelids were sealed shut, like shades pulled over a window for the night—or the season, or forever—and her mouth remained slightly ajar, as if death had come for her mid-breath. I could not help thinking that she had waited for us to leave, to spare us children from seeing her die.

My brother and I embraced, and I felt a hot tear slide down my cheek. "We're orphans," I murmured. It did not matter that we were in our forties; we were still orphans.

Karen, her dark face streaked with tears, hugged each of us. "I'm so sorry," she whispered. "I loved your mama."

A white coat entered the room. Doctor? Nurse? My eyes could not focus on the image well enough to interpret, and I was grateful when Mark went to talk to it, make it go away.

I turned back to my mother, a body without a spirit. What had been my last words to her, and hers to me? Had I ever told her I loved her? Had she known I had forgiven her for real and perceived injustices, just as I knew she had forgiven me for my many hurtful words and bratty behavior? I certainly had not told her good-bye. Gripping the bars of her bed, I realized I had not fully accepted the fact that she would not always be around. I had fantasized that her hospitalization was temporary, her memory problems were curable, and she would one day return home to live independently as she had always done, bossing me around, critiquing my choices, and offering unsolicited advice for improving my life.

I felt Marie's arms encircle me, and I let myself relax in them, loosening my hold on the bed bars. "She'll never get to see me make something of myself," I sobbed.

"That's not true. Your mother was proud of you. You and Mark both." Marie stroked my heaving shoulder.

"But I never solved the murder!" I sniffed. "I never cleared her name."

Marie shook her head. "Those were goals you set for yourself, Michelle, not her expectations of you. To tell the truth, I'm not sure she even understood that she *was* a murder suspect." She sighed. "And maybe it was better that way. There's nothing the police can do to her now."

"Michelle. My God!" My husband's voice interrupted our commiseration, like a new dance partner cutting in.

"Roberto!" Abandoning Marie, I flung myself into his arms.

He held me for a moment, and I reveled in his strong arms, my fortress against the evils of the world, as if I could stay there forever and never have to face the next phase of my life, as an orphan and a grandmother with no more excuses not to become an adult. “We were too late?” he murmured.

I blinked in the room’s bright light. “She waited for us to leave.” I caught a glimpse of Karen nodding at my speculation. “What was it like, Karen?” I asked her. “Did she ever wake up, cry out? Say anything?”

“No, Ma’am.” Karen shook her head. “She just sort of... expired. Took kind of a wheezing breath, then another short one, then nothing. I waited for her to take the next breath, but it never happened, so I called you folks.”

Still clinging to my husband, I peeked at the date on his watch. I gasped. “Is that right? Today is Dad’s birthday.”

“Payback,” Mark muttered. Our father had died somewhat unexpectedly the day before our mother’s birthday, which we had both agreed was a rotten thing to do, as if he actually had any control. Studying Mom, I wondered how much of a role coincidence had played.

With a deep breath, I willed the room back into focus. Mark, Marie, Karen, and even Roberto seemed dazed, immobile as in a game of “statues.” Although the dementia had been slowly stealing our mother away for many months, as long as her body remained occupied, hope had remained. Now that hope was gone.

I detected a presence outside the room, a slight commotion. “They’ll need to take her soon,” Karen murmured, breaking our spell of grief. As the hospital staff entered, we made our way out of our mother’s room for the last time.

The house had never seemed so empty. All her things remained as we had left them, suspended in time, but it was as if these inanimate objects sensed she would never need them again. I expected to hear her voice, to see her sitting in her chair or shuffling down the hall, asking me about my day and doling out platitudes on how to make life better.

I stared at the phone Mom would never again touch, almost afraid that using it and wiping away her fingerprints was akin to wiping away her memory. So many calls to make... Unable to bring myself to telephone the police to tell them their investigation into the murder of Brittany Landers was probably closed because of the death of their primary suspect, I decided to call Elaine, an indirect way of getting the message to Keith. And she also had Giovanna.

"Yeah?" The voice on the line resembled Elaine's, only less perky.

"Elaine?" I asked tentatively.

"She took the kids over to Dairy Queen." I could hear a sitcom blaring in the background. I had reached Stacy, Elaine's twenty-seven-year-old freeloading daughter.

"Hi Stacy. Could you give her a message then?"

"Huh?" A giggle told me she was paying more attention to the television than to me.

"A message for your mom," I repeated. "This is her friend Michelle."

"Call her on her cell." Stacy started to hang up.

"Wait! I don't have the number!"

With an exaggerated sigh, Stacy rattled off the number like an auctioneer and hung up before I could repeat it. Asking about her connection to Brittany Landers was out of the question.

Elaine answered her cell phone on the second ring. "Michelle, you're at home!" she said. "How is your mother?"

I was about to marvel that my friend must be psychic when I remembered her cell phone had caller I.D. And of course, if she had been psychic, she would not have had to ask how my mother was doing. "She's..." I gulped, barely able to say the words, each one grating on my parched throat like sandpaper, "She... she died."

"Michelle! I'm so sorry!"

"You'll...you'll tell Keith?"

"Of course. Anything else I can do?"

"Giovanna?"

"Don't worry; I'll keep her. She and Timmy have been playing video games." There was a pause; it sounded like Elaine had put her hand over the phone, muffling her comments to someone in the room, perhaps coordinating their fast-food order. "I still haven't been able to reach

Isabella. But I'll keep trying, and I'll let her know about your mom."

"No!" My protest came out a little too sharply. Isabella and Giovanna were *my* relatives, not Elaine's. "I mean, I'll tell her. I should be the one to tell her." I fingered the gold charm in my pocket.

"Okay." Elaine seemed unruffled by my tone. "Are you planning a service?"

"We haven't had much time to think about it, but probably Friday or Saturday."

"Let me know what I can do."

"Thanks, Elaine." As we hung up, I felt guilty for snapping at her, especially when she was being such a good friend.

With a glance at the clock, phone still in hand, I decided to place a call to my office to update them on the latest developments. Liza Morrison would be long gone by now, which was fine with me; I preferred to leave a message on her voice mail.

She answered on the first ring with an air of importance. "Liza Morrison."

Unable to believe my misfortune, I held the phone in silence like an obscene caller, waiting for the end of her greeting before leaving a message.

"Liza Morrison," she repeated.

"Uh…what are you doing there so late?" I cleared my throat to get better traction for my words. "This is Michelle DePalma."

"Hello Michelle. How's your mom?"

"My mother died this evening." The words hurt coming out, and a flood of tears pressed at the dam behind my eyes.

After a long pause, "Michelle, I'm so sorry." I heard paper shuffling. "When did this happen?"

"Tonight," I repeated.

"Hmm…well, we can give you three days off emergency leave, but I'm not sure how to show that since I've already marked you out on vacation. I don't think it's something we can tack on to the end of your vacation, because, frankly, the emergency would be over by then."

"Whatever," I muttered.

"Can I have the name and address of the funeral home? And when is the service?"

"We're thinking of having it either Friday or Saturday. We haven't contacted the funeral home yet."

"Well... let me know when it's been arranged."

"Why? Are you planning to come?"

"Well, you see, we're authorized to send flowers, you know, when it's the death of an immediate family member."

"Liza, don't bother. But we'll be using the Lonnie James funeral home on Front Street in Two Wells, Texas. I'm sure they can give you all the details if you call them tomorrow afternoon." I started to hang up.

"Wait! You can't expect me to look that up. If I'm going to approve this absence, I need you to call me back when you have all the information."

I would have thrown the receiver at the wall if Liza's body had been inside. "Liza, when are you scheduled for leadership training?" Before she could answer, I continued, "It's that class I developed last year. You were supposed to help with the train-the-trainer before John pulled you for a special project. I suggest you attend as soon as possible, and pay close attention to the section on 'sensitive issues.'"

"Michelle!"

"Good-bye Liza. Go home." I slammed the receiver into its cradle.

The others sat around the card table: Mark and Roberto pored over the contents of our mother's safe deposit box, and Marie was drafting a death announcement for Mom's Christmas card list. "While you're at it, can you start working on the obituary?" I asked her. "We can use a lot of the verbiage from your letter. I'll help when I get back."

Marie looked up. "Sure. Where are you going?"

"For a walk."

No one probed further, nor voiced an objection; either they were too numb to care, or they figured it was important to let me go, to grieve in my own way.

Without flinching, I passed through the entryway and let myself out the front door. I crossed the freshly mown lawn and headed up the street, perhaps in the tracks of my mother's final expedition.

When I set out, I had not known where I was going; perhaps I was walking to clear my head of the anger clouds that gathered whenever I had a conversation with Liza Morrison these days—petty anger that, if allowed to fester, would interfere with my ability to purely grieve the loss of my mother. But, independent of my head, my feet had been programmed to take me straight to Percy's grandparents' house.

Chapter Thirty-Eight

I had long forgotten the house number, but I recognized the car in the driveway—the brown Grand Prix Isabella had parked in front of our house the day she and Giovanna came into my life.

Moss had eaten away some of the mortar between the red bricks and the trim had been painted a lighter shade of blue within the last decade, but otherwise, Percy's grandparents' house fit the picture in my memory. The oak tree had grown so large that grass no longer survived in its shadow, which cast itself like an umbrella over almost the entire front lawn. In the flowerbeds next to the house, a low-maintenance holly had replaced Percy's grandmother's prize rose bushes.

I walked up the short flight of crumbling stone steps and rang the bell. Its melody resonated throughout the house. Isabella peered through the peephole and then opened the door.

With a weak smile she escorted me inside. The musty smell differed from the odor when Percy's grandparents had lived here; it was more like sickness than old age. A hospital-style bed dominated the living room, squeezing the other furnishings aside as if they were in storage. This must have been where she had cared for Percy.

Extricating a chair for me, Isabella threw me an apologetic look. Her green eyes were rimmed with red. "I just haven't got around to..."

"You've had a lot to deal with."

"Where's Giovanna?"

"She's with Elaine Nel...uh...Edwards." I gripped the upholstered back of the chair Isabella had offered me, leaning against it like an exercise prop. "My mother died today. That's what I came to tell you."

"Oh, Michelle!" She approached with open arms, pulling me into an embrace.

"It's been an awful week," I murmured, patting her sleeves.

"I knew this day would come," Isabella mused. "But I wasn't ready for it." She wasn't talking about my mother's death any more, I realized.

"When I came into town last Thursday, I had no idea..." I sank into the wing-style chair, and Isabella followed my lead by sitting in one nearby. There was a brief silence as I tried to fit my question into the natural flow of conversation. "Isabella, how well did you know my mother?" To her puzzled look I pressed, "I mean, you *had* met her before last Friday? When you came over and introduced yourself?"

Isabella bit her lip.

"That is, besides that time Percy told me about: when you visited my parents in 1991 to try to find me, to tell me about Jean-Paul's death and my new granddaughter." Isabella's bloodshot eyes shifted to her lap as I continued, "I'm talking about 2001, when you learned your friend Brittany Landers was working for the agency that provided home care for my mother."

In a voice choked with tears Isabella replied, "She wasn't a friend."

"Acquaintance, then," I conceded. "How did you and Brittany Landers meet?"

Isabella pushed a strand of hair off her face. "You know I used to be a nurse at Memorial Hospital in Houston. Brittany was in Houston for a summer, staying with relatives, working as a hospital assistant. I took her under my wing. She was from Two Wells, and that piqued my interest. But she didn't know your family, and I didn't think she paid much attention to my story about wanting to find you."

"Go on."

Isabella picked up an empty prescription cough medicine bottle from the end table beside her chair, and she spoke to it instead of looking at me. "That happened two years ago. Then last summer, when Percy got sick, I took a leave from my job and Giovanna and I came here to help him. When fall came, we couldn't go back to Houston, and I started home-schooling my daughter. I checked out the Loving Care Agency to see if they could help me with Percy part time. While I was in their office, Brittany Landers walked in."

"She remembered you?"

Isabella picked at the bottle's label. "And she said one of her clients was the woman I was looking for."

"You visited Brittany at my mother's house?"

Isabella's laugh came out like a snort. "She informed me her privileged position was worth something."

"What do you mean?"

Isabella ripped a strip of the prescription label from the bottle. "She charged me twenty bucks! I negotiated it down from a hundred."

"To see my mother?"

"To present me as someone your mother should know."

"You had the address. Why did you need Brittany?"

Isabella rolled the strip of label into a ball. "Percy told you: the last time I went to see your parents, it didn't go well."

"In 1991, when my father was still alive."

"Brittany thought," Isabella hesitated, stole a glance at my face, "your mother should pay to keep your secret from coming out."

"Blackmail?" My headache had returned with accompanying nausea. I flashed back to last summer: Brittany Landers lounging lazily on the family room couch, smug and defiant, ignoring my mother's needs, helping herself to the phone and whatever else she wanted; I'd written her off as a shining example of the "me" generation. *Mal élevée*, as they would say in France. But she had been harboring my darkest secret, snickering at me in silence and biding her time until she could reap the most benefit from that trump card.

"That girl was shameless. She applied for a credit card in your mother's name."

"A Visa?" I remembered an outraged call I'd made last summer to the credit card company, berating them for sending the card unsolicited to my mother.

"Visa. Maybe. She was taking things... Every time your mother would lie down for a nap, Brittany would dig around until she found something she wanted, then she'd hide it in her car or in the shrubbery so the aide on the next shift wouldn't catch her walking out with it." Isabella flicked pieces of label onto the worn carpet.

"Her sister returned a box of stuff yesterday. The family figured out my mother didn't 'give' it to Brittany after all." I watched Isabella scrape the bottle with her fingernails. "What did *you* do while Brittany was stealing from my mother?"

"You think I was in on it?" Her dark eyelashes were wet with fresh tears.

"You seem to know a lot about what she did."

"I only went there a few times; I didn't guess what she was up to right away."

"Once you did, what did you do? Confront her? Report it to the agency? Tell my mother?" I was not *trying* to make Isabella squirm; I just wanted to reconstruct her story so I could understand it, put myself in her place. But she did seem to be squirming, and like a curious child poking an insect with a stick, I pressed on—a technique I undoubtedly learned from my parents. "Tell me about the last time you saw Brittany Landers. Was it Thursday?"

Isabella set the bottle on the table. "I went to visit Lola. Once I thought I'd got through to her, but then the next time I saw her, she didn't remember who I was, or that she'd ever seen me before, and the aide who was watching her asked me to leave before I got her too upset. So I was ready to try again, start from scratch." She took a deep breath. "And I'd heard you were coming into town."

"Brittany was on duty?"

"Lola was asleep, and Brittany was 'shopping' for her next bonus."

"And by then, you knew Brittany was a thief."

"I had told her it was wrong, and that I'd report her if she took anything else."

"What was she taking on Thursday?"

Isabella shifted her attention from the stripped bottle to a tall brass candlestick holder, its sides heavily coated in layers of colored wax. "I don't remember." She picked up the candlestick holder.

"Then how do you know she was stealing?"

Picking at the hardened wax, Isabella whispered, "I told her to put it down."

"What?"

"She wouldn't."

"The brass pagoda?" The film in my mind played a scene in the entryway of my mother's house, with Brittany and Isabella struggling over my mother's cherished pagoda.

"I wrestled it away from her." Isabella's nails dug into the wax drippings, flicking them free from the tarnished brass surface.

"How?"

"She grabbed it away again, threatened to hit me with it."

"But she didn't." I bit my lip to keep myself from helping Isabella tell her story.

"I deflected her. Used a disarming technique I'd learned in a self-defense class I took in Houston about a year ago. I swear, it was reflex!" Isabella cradled the candleholder as if it were a kitten. "It must have been the angle she was lurching back at me, and the sharp edge..." She winced. "Her head hit the floor..."

"Why didn't you call for help?" The voice that came out of my mouth sounded like my mother's, the judgmental adult with sage advice guaranteed to work in a textbook case, but impractical in reality.

"All I could think about was getting out of there, away from her." Her fingers chipped at the wax on the candlestick holder.

"But she was down. She couldn't hurt you anymore. You're a nurse! You might have been able to save her."

Isabella shook her head, hair falling around her shoulders like a horse's mane, fuller than usual because of the humidity. Bushy? "I started to go out the front door, but then I saw a neighbor working in her yard, and I panicked. I had the brass thing in my hand. I dropped it in the flowerbed, then went inside again." She set the candlestick holder on the end table beside her.

Inside, past the crumpled, bleeding body of Brittany Landers, I thought, watching the scene in my mind like some X-rated film on a channel I'd mistakenly selected.

"I figured if I left through the back door, I was less likely to be noticed."

From my pants pocket I retrieved the gold charm Roberto and I had found in the back yard, and I held it toward Isabella. "Was that when you lost this?"

She plucked the charm from my hand, compared it with the bracelet on her wrist and discovered the empty spot. "You knew."

It was supposed to be my Detective Columbo moment, where I confronted the killer at the end of the movie with a carefully packaged explanation for every loose end and the fatal mistake that had unraveled the mystery. "I had suspicions. But I still don't understand. Why didn't you just call the paramedics and explain what happened?"

"I thought about that on the way home."

"You walked." No one had seen a car. Because Isabella had emerged from the back gate, and possibly cut across the next-door neighbor's yard, no one who might have seen her walking would have connected her with the Hanson house.

Her teeth chattered. "It was chilly, but I had my leather jacket and gloves on."

Gloves. Her fingerprints would not be found on the pagoda.

"I planned to call 9-1-1 when I got back to Percy's. I swear, I didn't think Brittany was dead, just knocked out. But when I got home, Percy was unconscious. Giovanna said he'd had a seizure, and we rushed him to the hospital. Brittany Landers slipped my mind."

"Slipped your mind? You left a human being bleeding and unconscious on the floor, and a confused elderly woman alone in the house without a caregiver? You're a nurse!"

"It was almost time for a shift change. That's why Brittany was in a hurry to grab what she could, before Karen arrived."

"You assumed Karen would take care of it? Clean up the mess?"

Isabella spread her hands to cover her eyes and ears. "I told you, I wasn't thinking straight."

"When did you know Brittany was dead?"

"Not until the next day. I was shocked when you told me she had died."

"They suspected my mother!"

"I didn't know. I mean, you didn't tell me she was a suspect, only that she couldn't remember anything that happened. And I was glad she hadn't seen me there."

"You were willing to let my mother take the blame for Brittany's murder?"

"I didn't think they'd ever put her in jail."

"You figured they'd close the case when she died or became too incapacitated to stand trial." I watched Isabella curl up and fold her arms around herself. "This whole ordeal no doubt hastened her death!"

"I'm sorry," she croaked.

"Sorry!"

Isabella sobbed harder.

"You can still make it right," I murmured. "Let's call the police right now and tell them what happened. It sounds almost like an accident, or at least self-defense. Maybe they'll consider the extenuating circumstances that kept you from reporting it right away."

"No! I can't!"

"What do you mean you can't?" Spotting a sleek portable phone on a table jammed against the wall, I rose and took a step toward it. "You'll let my mother go to her grave a suspected killer?"

"She's dead! I have a daughter to raise!" Isabella uncoiled and grabbed the brass candlestick holder she had been stripping of wax. She raised it over her shoulder like a club and eyed me with the fierceness of a wild beast.

"This is the message you want to send your daughter? Kill a person and then blame someone else for it? Someone weaker who's losing her memory?" I glanced at the newfound weapon in her hand and kept moving toward the phone. "Kill again if anyone threatens to expose you?"

Isabella lunged at me. "We have no one! Paul's parents are dead! Percy's dead!"

I ducked and took cover behind the wing chair. "Isabella!"

"My family…." She swung the candlestick holder at the space I had just vacated. "They were all massacred in the war." Sobs heaved in her chest as she rounded the wing chair.

"Isabella, put that thing down. I'm sorry about your family. The war in Bosnia? I didn't know." Still in my crouched position, I tried to back up. "This is insane! I'm not some Serbian thug who massacred your family. I'm your daughter's grandmother!" As Isabella raised the weapon to strike, I grabbed her ankle and tugged as hard as I could, knocking her off balance. She tumbled to the floor, losing her grip on the candlestick holder. I recovered it like a fumbled football.

"Michelle, I'm so sorry!" Sobs erupted from Isabella's chest.

I clutched the candlestick holder, looked around to ensure she would not convert another household item into a weapon. "You'll convince me of that when you turn yourself in."

"Giovanna will be all alone!"

"What about me? Isn't that why you got yourself into all this?"

"Percy said you have no interest in children."

Still flexing the candlestick holder like a barbell, I stood; Isabella stayed sprawled on the carpet. "Well, you know what? When we were together, Percy was an abusive, domineering son-of-a-bitch! Not fit to be a husband or a father. Maybe he changed; I hope so. Sounds like he was there for you and Giovanna, and I'm glad about that." My heart pounded, a delayed reaction to the assault. "I may have been naïve at seventeen, but I was smart enough to realize my son would be better off raised by someone else. I made the right decision, and I've never regretted it." Speaking those words washed away the seeds of guilt that had been germinating since Isabella and Giovanna showed up on my doorstep.

From the open front door, a masculine voice added, "Don't worry about Giovanna. We'll take care of her." Roberto, my protector. How had he found me? I chalked it up to his uncanny ability to figure out what I wanted even before I did.

Roberto moved from the doorway to my side. I hugged him. "Are you sure?" I whispered. Was I? Was I finally ready?

He slid his arm around my waist. "I don't see any other solution at this point."

"Yes, Isabella, if you have to go away, we'll take care of Giovanna," I echoed. "I'll make sure she's enrolled in school at the right level and that she has as normal a childhood as possible."

Isabella's eyes panned our faces as she got to her feet. "Thank you."

"So you'll turn yourself in," Roberto confirmed. "Let's go to the police."

I set down the weapon, just a candlestick holder again.

At the police station, we were asked to wait; it seemed no one was quite ready to take a murder confession. "Are you the attorney?" the dispatcher asked me.

"Attorney?" The picture of Giovanna's mother behind bars, the school kids taunting my granddaughter, made my stomach turn flips. "Uh, no. Is there a phone I can use?"

Elaine answered on the first ring.

"Hi, Girlfriend. Is Jerry still there?"

"I'm talking!" Elaine screamed to someone in the room. "Timmy and Giovanna won't let him leave. He's teaching them card tricks."

I felt my face brighten at the sound of my granddaughter's name. "I'm at the police station. We have a job for Jerry after all, if he's still willing."

"What...?"

Elaine listened as I recounted the whole story. I had never known her to stay quiet for so long. "Michelle, I'm so sorry! What can I do?"

"Right now, send Jerry to the police station. Maybe he can work his magic, make this into a case of self-defense." I took a deep breath. "And then later, I need you to bring Giovanna to the house. Please let me be the one to tell her, but perhaps you can prepare her somehow."

"You got it. And Jerry's on his way."

"Thank you so much. You're a good friend, Elaine." I hung up and returned to Roberto and Isabella. "Elaine's ex-husband Jerry is a defense attorney, and she brought him to town to help my mother. Lola doesn't need him any more, but now he might be able to help Isabella."

"You would do that for me?"

"For Giovanna." Isabella's face fell. Even after what she had done, even if I was not yet ready to forgive her, it was hard to hurt her, to shut her out of my life. "And yes, for you, too."

"Thank you," Isabella said again.

Right or wrong, I had pegged the mother of my grandchild as a basically good person who had made a tragic mistake and then painted herself into a corner. I would make an effort to forgive her. We may never have the comfortable mother-in-law/daughter-in-law relationship that I had with Roberto's mother, but we would always be bound together because of Giovanna.

I patted Roberto's knee. "You're still okay with this?" He replied by slipping an arm around my shoulders. "No turning back now."

Made in the USA
Columbia, SC
14 December 2017